Staring at the Ceiling

By Steven Crane

For Jennifer & David.

With immeasurable love for
29205, 2416, 1993 and Mondays.

With eternal gratitude to Carie,
without whom this could not have happened.

"A creature in its prime doing harm... is known as going against the Way. That which goes against the Way, will come to an early end." – Lao Tzu

1

Graduations are supposed to be fun, and if he were capable of thinking about it properly, Andy Maxwell had plenty to celebrate. But as his parents backed out of the short gravel driveway and left him standing in the front yard of his home on Cornwall Street, Andy couldn't help but think he was probably the least satisfied person he knew.

"Are they gone?" Jeff asked.

"Yeah. Just now. And look."

Andy dug a fist into the pocket of his green corduroy pants. What emerged was thick and equally green. He took the stack of bills and began to peel off twenties and fifties.

"Holy shit!" said Jeff. He'd only ever seen that much cash on the other side of a television screen, and it usually meant that something illegal had either just happened, or was about to. "That must be..."

"One thousand, six hundred and seventy four dollars." Andy cut his roommate off before pausing to light the cigarette he'd been dying to smoke ever since his parents showed up at their house this morning. "But it doesn't even matter. Every dime of this is already spent, and I still owe more. This little windfall is nice and all, but it ain't enough to keep me from having to move back home."

"You'll figure something out," Jeff reassured. He wanted both of them to believe it, but his optimism was growing thinner and less justified with each passing week of his roommate's unemployment.

4

"Figure what out?" Andy countered. "What the hell I'm doing? What I'm *supposed* to do?"

Jeff knew better than to light his friend's short fuse. Andy hardly ever needed an excuse to go off.

"I mean, look around." he continued, his voice rising right along with his indignant arms. "What's the point? There's assholes driving truck bombs under the World Trade Center... and our own government is burning armed zealots to death in Waco. What are *any* of us doing here?"

There was no answer to that question. And attempting to defuse Andy's cynicism was something Jeff had learned the futility of long ago. The best he could do was to offer a practical redirection.

"Well, right now, what we're doing is taking you to the bank, so you can put that shit away, before something stupid happens."

"Can't," Andy said. "Bank's closed on Saturday."

"So then, what?"

"Get in," Andy ordered, turning back toward his car. "I've got a better idea."

"You're just gonna give all this shit away? For free? I oughta kick your ass on principle alone," Jeff said as they began to unload a phenomenal alcoholic arsenal from the back of Andy's brand new forest green SUV. The graduation present he'd received from his parents a few weeks ago was lavish by any realistic standard – a fact that was at least partially lost on its young, unaccomplished owner. None of his friends drove anything even remotely as nice or new.

"Yeah, well technically, everyone who sent me graduation money is giving this stuff away. Besides, if this works out, it'll be worth every penny."

"Whatever, man. But, do you really want to celebrate your graduation in jail?"

"For what? I'm not sure anything about this is going to be illegal. Don't think of it as a crime; think of it as redecorating—sort of an urban beautification project. Anyway, quit worrying about it and help me ice all this shit down."

Jeff went to the back of the house in search of two large coolers. Andy settled into an over-stuffed brown armchair and puffed on a cigarette.

"But, why shoes? What's the big deal about shoes?" Jeff asked, returning through the kitchen.

"Nothing really. It's random," Andy replied. "Shoes are universal, you know? Just one of a million things nobody thinks about—until they see them in a place or way they don't belong. It's when things pop up that aren't supposed to be there, that people get all freaked out and start asking a bunch of questions."

"So this is a political thing, then?"

"Hell no! Fuck politics, man. It's just shoes. If it weren't shoes, it'd be something else, but this time it's shoes. It's whatever you want it to be. It's universal, like I said."

And you think people are just going to give you the shoes straight off their feet?"

"Are you kidding me? Half the people we know would sell their girlfriends for a night of free beer. Don't worry, they'll come; and there will be shoes. But not if we don't get off our asses and get the word out. Oh yeah, and we need a band, too. We can't have a party without a band."

"For free? Are they crazy?" Ellen said, confused.

"Yeah, it's all free. Well, almost free anyway," Traci answered across the bar at The Green Room. Ellen had been tending bar there for over a year – the last five months, full-time, ever since her parents' finances took an unscripted plunge. Given the choice, she'd have gladly continued school. But when her college fund ran dry halfway through her undergraduate studies, she pragmatically folded her tent and moved on to the next best option.

"What do you mean, almost?" Ellen pressed, tugging and rolling a strand of her shoulder-length brown hair impulsively around her index finger. The twirling was a nervous habit she developed as a child, which had lay dormant for many years, but seemed to be making a resurgence as of late.

"Get this. They want shoes. Don't ask me why, but that's what they said. Everybody who brings them a pair of old shoes drinks for free."

"Sweet Jesus, I can't wait to see this one," Ellen said as she snubbed a Marlboro in the ashtray. "I gotta get back to work Trace, but do me a favor…get over there a little early and make sure nobody fucks up my stuff. And tell Jeff to close my door too. With all the freaks we know, just about anything could happen."

Five hours, and not enough money in tips later, Ellen fell behind the wheel of her piece-of-crap two-tone brown '82 Chevrolet Chevette, which she lovingly referred to as 'Chet', partly for its phonetic similarity with 'shit' when said just the right way. She took a deep breath and lit a Marlboro Red for the four block commute back home. As she made the last left onto Cornwall Street, her suspicions were confirmed. The first and most disturbing thing she saw was the gaudy bright yellow school bus parked outside their equally hideous brown house.

Oh, God. It's Graham, and he's probably brought the whole fuckin' cavalry, she thought, as she looked for a safe place to put Chet down for the night.

Graham Lafley was only twenty-three years old, but he'd already lived through more than most folks twice his age. His mother had succumbed to cancer when he was twelve. And then, just eighteen months ago, the hand of fate punched Graham square in the face again. On a routine business trip from Atlanta to London, his father was among 108 passengers lost on a plane that inexplicably fell out of the sky and into the Atlantic. It was one of those things that people who tout the relative safety of air travel say 'almost never happens.' Except apparently, sometimes they do.

Through no desire or doing of his own, Graham had become instantly independent—no parents, no siblings, no real family. On one hand, he had no support, but on the other, he had no responsibility. And, due to a substantial inheritance, he'd also become relatively wealthy.

Not long before leaving Bradford, Graham had acquired an old, decommissioned short bus that had previously served the "special" kids of Preston County's public schools. It was a highly impractical vehicle, but Graham had little use for practicality.

There was plenty of amusement, but no real surprise, the first time Graham came rolling back through Bradford behind the wheel of the rolling freak show. He'd kept the first two rows of benches and added seat belts. But he gutted the rest, outfitting it with a killer stereo, bean bag chairs, a small refrigerator, and a fold down futon bed. For more than a month, he'd used it as a literal mobile home, driving wherever the wind and whim took him. But once he put a double-wide trailer down on 30 acres of land outside of Asheville, the bus resumed its station as a full-on party-wagon. It might not have come exactly full circle, but on plenty of occasions the bus was still charged with transporting "challenged" youths. After all, the Cornwall Street kids we're "special" in their own way, although most of their damage was self-inflicted.

#

As Ellen approached, the wail of angst-driven guitars poured from their under-insulated four bedroom dive. The dilapidated rental house was more than eighty years old, and the sonic battle was one the walls could never win.

A small group was huddled together on the front porch, engulfing a hideous, smoke-stained, orange couch which had once belonged to Jeff's grandmother. The group acknowledged her, making no attempt to conceal the joint being passed between them. Ellen wasn't bothered, but she was instantly glad she'd taken the small handful of ephedrine tablets after Traci's preemptive visit to The Green Room. It was going to be a long night, and a little speed would go a long way.

A blast of sound and smoke greeted her as she entered the house. Not five feet from the front door, the bassist of a local rock group was feverishly pounding on his long fretted friend, oblivious to her arrival. A drum kit lay where once there was another couch. A thin man with no shirt and a greyish-white crew cut was beating a drum kit like a rented mule.

Taking it all in stride, Ellen closed the door and began to wade through the sea of people. Her plan was to check her bedroom first, just in case it was on fire or someone was riding in small circles around her bed on a Harley-Davidson. Jeff and Traci intercepted her before she even got close.

"Wow, not bad," Ellen shouted. "Who are all these people?"

"Andy can be a dick; but at least he's a loyal dick who knows how to throw a party."

"So, where *is* our happy little graduate?"

"He's over there, with Graham," Jeff said, without looking at her or Andy.

The boys were sitting on top of a metal desk in the far corner of the room, sharing a joint and looking at each other like lost brothers reunited after a too-long absence.

"El! Jesus, it's about time!" Andy said, handing her the contraband.

"Actually I'm early, you stoner. This is great, but we're not going to be talking to cops tonight are we?"

"Probably not," he replied, shrugging.

"Why, Miss Ellen, so nice to see you again," Graham drawled with intentionally exaggerated formality, extending his hand to hers.

"Hey Graham, how's it going? Did you get bored out there in the big weird world and have to come home to us again?"

"Something like that. It is good to be back, though," he said flashing a grin and sliding into the crowd.

They all knew the drill. Graham would stay away for months at a time, and then pop up unexpectedly, and with great fanfare.

Ellen parked herself next to Andy on top of the desk. They both took a long drink and exchanged the joint several times, before sharing words.

"So, how was work?" he asked, as if the answer would ever change. Surrounded by scores of their degenerate friends—and plenty of strangers—with a live band wailing in the background, the question took on an almost comedic casualness; the kind of stock inquisition an old married couple had been trading for years.

"Same old shit," she said. "You know how it is. People got problems, people go drinking, people get drunk. They forget the problems they came in with or trade 'em in for new ones. As long as they keep tipping, fuck 'em. It's all good."

"Alright then," Andy said. "You wanna see something crazy?" he asked as he rose and began walking away, knowing she'd be right behind him.

5

The smallest of the four bedrooms at Cornwall separated Andy's room in the back of the house from Ellen's, and served two primary functions. On one hand, it contained most of the home's electronic equipment, sort of a poor man's multimedia palace. Being the most central, discreet, and comfortably furnished room in the house, The Den's other purpose followed naturally enough. It also became the home's de facto epicenter of debauchery.

Posters celebrating heavyweights like Hendrix and Kubrick and Dali adorned the walls. The incandescent bulbs overhead worked just fine, but were usually left off in favor of the black-light lamp in one corner. Opposite this sat a mini refrigerator, the contents of which were restricted to beverages of the alcoholic nature. The room's single window was covered by a large black tapestry adorned with smiling psychedelic moon and sun faces.

As Jeff and Graham made their way through the house, bellows of laughter guided them straight toward The Den.

"You're full of shit!"

"No, no, no. I'm serious as hell, man."

The accuser was still a mystery, but the defense came from none other than Eddie French. The exchange itself was of no real help to Jeff and Graham, as much of what Eddie said was far-fetched and unbelievable. Sometimes it was intentional—a devious ruse to keep people guessing. But just as often, his delusions seemed disturbingly genuine.

"I'm not shittin' you man, it's real," he persisted.

"What's real, Eddie?" Graham asked through the smoke and noise.

"Holy shit! Graham?" Eddie said, trying—but failing—to stand and greet his old friend. Graham thrust a hand toward Eddie, who settled back on the couch and shook it.

"Been too long, man," said Eddie. "Hey, you still got the Magic Bus?"

"Hell yes. She's right outside. Now what kind of bullshit are you feeding these people?"

"Wow, that's just what we need. We could pack that fucker up and leave tonight!" Eddie burst out, forgetting he had been asked a question.

"What the hell are you talking about, Eddie?" Jeff asked, trying to expedite matters.

Eddie looked up through a veil of short curly black locks, pushed the silver-framed glasses up the bridge of his nose, and rose to the occasion with a devilish grin and a single word.

"Stull."

"Jesus, you're still on about Stull, Eddie?" Graham insisted, as if the point needed no further explanation. His tone was more condescending than he intended, but only because Graham had watched this scene play out more than once before and he already knew the ending.

"What's Stull?" asked a girl with short blond hair and wide, interested eyes.

Graham and Eddie examined each other briefly, trying to decide who would field the question. Eddie was a master at creating awkward situations, whipping everyone within earshot into a minor frenzy of interest, and then leaving someone else to defuse the bomb. The first couple of times you experienced this trick, it was pretty funny. But soon enough, it began to wear a little thin. Graham had been down that rabbit hole often enough to find it annoying as hell.

"Stull," Graham began, keeping careful watch on the young girl's face to see how the story played, "is this ridiculous little bullshit town in the middle of Nowhere, Kansas. Eddie's got this warped idea that it's a bit of a magical place."

"No. For real. It's true," Eddie blurted out. For once, he couldn't resist the urge to finish what he'd started. "You see, there are these things called trans-dimensional gates—or portals really—between this world and an alternate reality. It's all based on forces of the natural world... you know, electromagnetic fields, the moon, stuff like that. Anyway, there are supposed to be seven of these gates on the planet, one at the exact geographic center point of each of Earth's continents. Stull, Kansas is the exact center of North America, and therefore has a portal."

"You know that's just the continental U.S., right?" Jeff corrected him. "The epicenter of North America is actually in a field somewhere in Rugby, South Dakota. "I looked that shit up after the last time you tried to sell this adventure, Eddie."

The group sat through the bonus geography lesson in silence, as Eddie's pale cheeks began to fill with the hot red embarrassment.

"Whatever, fucker. It's Stull. The portal's in Stull." Eddie insisted. Clearly, to him at least, the roughly 350 miles between the two destinations was inconsequential.

"So you're suggesting that we just load up the bus and drive thousands of miles to some desolate, bullshit Mid-Western ghost town in search of an alternate dimension?" Graham asked. He was pleased with exactly how ridiculous the words sounded as they rolled out of his mouth.

"I've got an alternate reality for you, Eddie," Jeff joked as he went to The Den's closet. He paused dramatically before opening it and bringing forth the three foot, double-chambered hookah bong the residents of Cornwall Street reserved only for special occasions. Tonight was already special, but diffusing an Eddie French adventure in midstream was also reason enough to break out the heavy artillery.

"So, whatcha got for me this time?" asked Ellen as they neared the back of the house.

"I think you might like this one. Sit there on the bed and close your eyes."

She finished pulling her long brown hair into a tight bun high atop her head, sat down, and waited to be amazed. Andy went to the corner of the bedroom and grabbed a large black trash bag. Ellen's eyes were still closed as the shoes began spilling around her feet.

"I've always thought you were crazy, Andy – and don't get me wrong; I love that. But this is weird, even for you."

"Thanks. I try."

He emptied only one of the five large black bags, and made sure she took note of the others he'd stockpiled along the wall.

Andy lowered himself onto the overstuffed ottoman across from her and began to massage his kneecaps. He'd been born with a muscular defect that left his lower extremities severely under-developed, and with legs that resembled those of a chicken—matchstick-thin calves struggling to support comparatively massive thighs. After a childhood that had featured more surgeries than birthdays, and thanks to modern medicine, he could walk, albeit with a noticeable limp. Two decades of uneven force and pressure on his legs, coupled with chronic arthritis, regularly left his knees and back throbbing after only brief periods of exertion.

"How many are there?" she asked, rifling through the assorted footwear with genuine interest.

"At last count, we had thirty seven pairs."

"You know my next question."

"What would a twenty-two-year-old straight man want with one-tenth of Imelda Marcos' closet?"

"Do you think she misses these?" Ellen asked, holding up a fabulous pair of neon pink Reebok high tops.

"There's no accounting for style," he said, fetching two cigarettes from the carved rosewood box on his desk. "You want one?"

"Sure. Now what's with the shoe fetish?"

Andy only half heard the question, distracted by both a cloud of intoxicants and the strategic plans swirling in his head. He often struggled to maintain a single, linear path of thought, getting lost in tangents until something recaptured his focus.

On this particular occasion, that something was a burgundy leather wingtip colliding with his chest at modest speed. Ellen sat studying him from across the room. In her left hand, was the other wingtip; in her right, the slow-burning Dunhill.

"You were saying?" she prompted.

"Not yet. We need Jeff and Graham. Oh yeah, and Eddie too. I only want to go through this once. I'll go round up the boys; you go get beers. Meet me back here in five minutes."

Five minutes passed quickly, and so did the next thirty or so it actually took to round up the necessary personnel for the mission Andy had in mind. This wasn't going to be their first late night expedition, but it was the strangest to date.

An odd pattern had formed not long after they'd moved into the house on Cornwall Street. Like moths to a light, their friends and associates would flock there, drawn by the glow of readily-available debauchery. All three of its residents were sociable people, but Andy had more of an agenda. He preferred to think of hosting as having home-field advantage, which came with the luxury of calling the shots. For him, it was all about control – Andy's truest addiction.

In the beginning, he got enough of a fix just by being in his own predictable environment. Sometimes he'd exert himself more, wrangling control of the music or the distribution of party favors. Slowly but surely though, like all addictions, his need to control began to escalate. And at a certain point, Andy began to ponder where the boundaries of that control might lie, and how far he could push them.

And that's when the "missions" began. They were almost always simple outings for which the spontaneity of the event was reward enough – fun for the sake of fun; which is not to say there weren't rare occasions on which the group would return with something of value.

By virtue of these expeditions, Cornwall Street had become home to a small assortment of treasures. They'd acquired a parking meter, from which the kingly sum of $41.75 had been rescued. A few random road and building signs haphazardly decorated the house. And then there was the picnic table, which was unique in that none of the Cornwall residents had been involved in its procurement. To his great surprise, Jeff had discovered the table, placed neatly in a shaded corner of the home's small back garden, one Saturday morning. In the months since, several of their friends would claim involvement, but none of the residents would ever be sure exactly who was responsible.

Many of their previous adventures were spontaneous, lacking focus or even purpose. Tonight was different. Tonight, Andy had a plan.

The five of them settled in an arc, not quite encircling the bounty of black plastic trash bags. In the process of rounding up the gang, Andy had noticed the house was now almost completely empty. It seemed just about everyone who could walk or stumble away from the house had already done so.

Each of them held a can of Milwaukee's Best beer, though Graham and Ellen hadn't opened theirs. Like locusts, the party-goers had come and decimated the generous supply of free booze. Andy had managed to stash a 12-pack of the Beast in Andy's closet, just in case the well ran dry. The beer was nasty and warm, but no one complained about free alcohol, and never at 2:00 on a Sunday morning.

Eddie rubbed his glasses with the sleeve of his dirty t-shirt and said with a delirious grin, "So what's with the pow-wow, Andy?"

"It's time to have a little fun, Eddie. We're going out tonight."

With this, Andy began to relieve the bags of their cargo. In total, forty-one pairs of shoes tumbled to the floor between them. A remarkable crop they were. Among the very normal white Nike tennis shoes, sandals, and multi-colored Converse All-Stars they would expect to see, there were some real prize-winners. One pair of ten-hole Doc Martens (one blue, one red); several pairs of heels, each varying widely in height, color, and seriousness; a lovely pair of sequined ballet slippers; a pair of U.S. Marine issue combat boots, which according to a reliable source, had actually been worn in the Desert Storm invasion; and many other oddities lie before them. Andy had been hoping to find a pair of bunny slippers among the haul for maximum comedic effect. He would instead have to settle for a pair of purple and green high-top canvas sneakers which bore a rather ominous rendering of The Incredible Hulk down each side.

The group sat silent, contemplating. Maybe they were fucked up and confused. Maybe it was just late. But for the most part, they decided that when confronted with a man who, for no good reason presents you with forty-one pairs of shoes, it was perhaps wise to allow him to speak first.

After a short, dramatic pause, Andy cleared his throat and reached again for the rosewood box. He pulled from it a single Dunhill, lit it, and passed the box to Graham on his left.

"Anybody want a smoke?" he offered. The box made its way around the arc, and each of them took a cigarette, except Ellen, who had a lit Marlboro of her own. Even Eddie, who smoked about as often as an electric train, bellied up for a piece of the action.

"What we have here, is about eighty shoes, gentlemen."

It was commonly understood, and not altogether unappreciated by her, that Ellen was in fact not considered a female by either of her roommates. Plenty of guys they knew found her attractive, and she effortlessly played the role of sister, or mother, in their little family; but she was widely accepted as 'one of the boys,' at least as far as Andy and Jeff were concerned.

"I think it's time we made something," Andy continued, "or at least confused the hell out of a bunch of people." he teased, before finally cutting to the chase.

"I want to build a shoe tree," he declared, as if it made perfect sense.

"A what?" Graham asked, now looking up from the desktop upon which he'd just finished rolling another joint.

"A shoe tree," he repeated. "I want to see what these forty-one pairs of shoes look like hanging from a tree in the middle of this crappy little town."

"But why?" Eddie needed to know.

"Because I want to watch people try to figure out why somebody would put them there. Besides, I think it'll look cool."

"Hey, these are mine!" Jeff had been rummaging through the haul and sorting the shoes into like piles.

He held aloft a pair of dirty, old black Vans and said again, "These are fucking mine! I let Paul borrow these about a month ago and haven't seen them since. That son-of-a-bitch traded me my own shoes back for a whole night of free drinks. Bastard!" he added for good measure and reclaimed his pilfered footwear.

Jeff quit ranting long enough to take the joint as it reached him. He pulled deeply, letting the smoke fill his lungs and brain. Andy seized the moment of silence to elaborate.

"I've got the perfect tree picked out, too. You know where the Gryphon theater is; right next to that big-ass Baptist church?"

They all nodded, trying to picture the target, or perhaps what it might look like when they'd finished with it.

"That sucker's got hundreds of branches, and it's tall as fuck. It's perfect." Andy had no idea even what type of tree it was, he just knew it looked right.

"So now wait a minute," Eddie shot out, with glazed eyes. "My little road trip to Stull is 'crazy as fuck,' but running around and throwing 80 shoes in a tree in front of a Baptist church in the middle of the night is perfectly sane?"

"Next door," Andy insisted

"Fuck your neighbors, man! This is crazy!" Eddie shouted.

"The tree is *next door* to the church, Eddie, not in front of it."

"Like it matters, Andy. There's still gonna be a helluva lot of wigged out Baptists wandering around Decatur Street tomorrow."

"Very good," Andy beamed; sure that Eddie was beginning to see the point. He had grabbed a legal pad off the desk and sketched a crude map. He placed it in the middle of the floor and began to explain.

"There's this wall here, between the theater and the church, surrounding the cemetery. If two of us stand here, on the far side of the..."

"Wait. So now we're in a cemetery?" Ellen said, a bit uneasy.

"No," Andy corrected, becoming frustrated at the lack of focus amongst his cohorts. "No one's *in* the cemetery. But the wall will help shield us from view if anyone is around."

Andy kept moving, referring again to his sketch. "We'll need two throwers, two more on the street as lookouts, and one on the far side of the tree catching the errant shoes."

"Not bad," Graham commended, snubbing the burnt roach in the ashtray. "Sounds like you've been watching reruns of *The A-Team* again."

"Well, they do keep threatening to cut our cable off, so, I'm getting it while I can."

Andy began re-bagging the ammunition. There were now exactly forty pairs of shoes. He liked the round number even better. They briefly discussed the map, each deciding where they were to be stationed. Ellen and Eddie would be lookouts. Andy and Jeff would be sending the shoes skyward, and Graham would sweep behind them, retrieving the misses.

24

The shoes were placed ten pairs to a bag, two bags apiece for Andy and Jeff. He figured it would take maybe fifteen minutes to get all forty pairs securely in the tree, but being a shoe tree virgin, the estimate was rough at best.

"And what about the police?" Ellen wondered.

"What about them?"

"Well, let's suppose, there we are, just hanging out in front of Bradford Baptist at three o'clock on a Sunday morning, and the cops wander by. What then?"

"Tell them you couldn't wait six more hours to talk with God," Graham joked.

"Cops are easy," Andy broke in. "It's all about psychology."

"Go on, doctor," Ellen said, waiting to be reassured.

"Well, for starters, why does anybody become a cop in the first place? Because they have a desperate need to serve and protect? Bullshit! It's all about power. They want power. They need it. They lust it in fact. They're control freaks."

"You would know," Jeff said wryly.

"Or, they're crooked; thieving bastards, hiding in plain sight." His point was tangential, but valid nonetheless.

"What they want is your respect," Andy continued. "But they'll settle for fear. It doesn't matter as long as they keep control. Most people will tell you they *respect* police officers, but what they really mean is they *fear* them. Whether it's the fear of an expensive ticket, or of jail, or of getting the shit beat out of you, it doesn't matter. Everyone's got something to be afraid of when the blue lights start flashing."

25

"And your point is?" Ellen asked, now seeking closure.

"The point is," Jeff interrupted, "if a cop wants to talk to you, you talk to him. But you only tell him what he wants to hear, something that reinforces his perception of control. They want you to know they have the unquestioned authority to bust your ass, or even your skull, but really they'd prefer not to have to fuck with you in the first place."

"Here's all you need to know," Andy concluded. "As long as you can convince a cop that his time would be better spent dealing with real threats to society rather than wasting it harassing a productive citizen like yourself, you're fine."

"Is that why you never get busted even though you've been pulled over about a thousand times?"

"Well, yeah. That and the handicap placard. The police don't generally mess with the disabled - 'cause we're *harmless*," Andy said with a sarcastic smirk.

"Fine, you and your handicap placard can drive then," Ellen agreed.

Andy finished packing and snubbed his cigarette in the ashtray before rising.

"At least your parents got their money's worth sending you to school."

"Why is that, Graham?"

"You're pretty good at getting people to do things they don't want or need to do. Maybe you *should* be in advertising."

9

Sundays on Cornwall Street were slow, simple and recuperative. Most of their elderly black neighbors rose with the morning sun, donned their finest clothes, and enjoyed hearty home-cooked breakfasts before heading out in time to make the early service at church. Andy and Ellen hardly ever awoke before Bradford's various congregations had concluded their recessional hymns and began turning their thoughts towards post-worship lunches.

Jeff had a different arrangement. He worked every single Sunday, holding a position that required him to rise early, in the service of employers who had little or no sympathy for the ill after-effects of ambitious Saturday evenings.

Although it was often a struggle to rise and shine, Jeff could not be happier. He was one of the lucky few who actually got paid to do what he loved. And what Jeffery Aaron loved to do was sing. He was a vocal powerhouse. From Motown to metal, he could do it all. A country boy from the rural sticks a hundred miles outside of Bradford, he'd come to the *big city* school to study vocal performance. And he'd come armed for the challenge, with a boatload of confidence and plenty of actual raw talent.

By his third year in school, he'd done his share of local theatre, including several performances at the Gryphon Theatre—the same venue to which he had so recently helped donate a quite impressive collection of footwear.

Jeff honed his chops at school and on stage, but that's not where he earned his money. On Sunday mornings and in the early evenings a couple times a week, he distanced himself from the debauchery of Cornwall Street with the three-mile journey to his gig in the House of God.

One of his drama teachers was a parishioner at St. Timothy's Episcopal Cathedral, and when word came down of the need for an Assistant Choral Director, he'd enthusiastically approached Jeff with the opportunity.

The pay was as good or better than most of the part-time, dead-end gigs his friends held down, and aside from Sunday mornings, the schedule was perfectly accommodating for a late-rising night owl like Jeff. Plus, he'd get paid to showcase and develop his true passion and his most marketable skill. It was a position that suited him well in many ways, but one he nearly turned down.

Jeff had gone to church all his young life, attending Methodist services with his mother, where the youth choir had been responsible for sparking the flame he still carried for singing. But his few years in Bradford, and particularly his time on Cornwall Street, had affected his perspective. He'd fallen out of practice of attending church regularly. The fire within him had cooled to a tepid stream, which still flowed, but with noticeably less force. It wasn't intentional, but during those first years of living completely away from home, rising early on Sundays gradually fell behind sleeping off hangovers on the priority list. And as much as he'd come to love his new group of school friends, there seemed to be few among them to whom the idea of church, or even God, was appealing.

The prospect of plugging back into a church—especially if it meant getting paid—was intriguing to Jeff, and on several levels desirous. But the offer at St. Timothy's did not come without the burdens of conflict and guilt. Jeff was aware, sometimes painfully so, that much of what happened on Cornwall Street was morally questionable at best.

Jeff struggled. He talked a lot with himself, a little with God, and not all to his roommates or other friends, about the challenges and the consequences choosing such a job might bring. After much deliberation, Jeff accepted the position at St. Timothy's. He worked hard in the beginning, until it became much easier through constant practice, to convince himself he could handle driving straight down the line that separated two such duplicitous paths. And most of the time, if you didn't inspect too closely – which nobody but he himself did – he appeared to be pulling it off.

Over time, it became less a question of whether he could live with a foot planted in each of the contradictory camps, and more an exercise in trying to glide back and forth, with as little friction as possible, across a boundary that was steadily fading away. His belief in God, and his intention with St. Timothy's, were both genuine. And there *was* a dividend of joy that came back to him as a result of his return to church. But if he was being honest, he knew he had revised the balance of his investment in both sides.

A year later, Jeff was more or less running the show at St. Timothy's—the de facto leader of a choir of 50 souls, most of who were old enough to be his parents. That kind of responsibility, and the regular morning hours it required, weren't the kind of thing you could hide for very long from roommates who were paying even a little bit of attention. What was at first a shocking revelation to Andy and Ellen had ceased to be anything abnormal at all by now. Ellen could not honestly have cared less. And Andy, even though he was challenged philosophically by Jeff's faith, came to accept as a matter of fact that one of his roommates worked at a bar and the other at a church. The only distinction he drew most of the time was that he'd far prefer Ellen be the one that brought her work home with her.

Like so many Sundays before, the sound of the local college station blasting at full volume from his clock radio was his wake up call. On this morning, it was instantly obvious his half night's nap had not been enough. It may have even been counterproductive. His eyes stung from a lack of sleep as he fought to keep them open.

Jeff inhaled deeply, only to be reminded of the strenuous workout his lungs had received the night before. His chest burned, and the pounding in his head was becoming more pronounced. A hot shower and two cups of coffee would have saved his life right then, but he was already running late and would have to do without either.

He approached the mirror with great modesty, hoping like hell he looked much better than he felt. He found a green rubber band on the dresser and pulled his shoulder-length brown hair into a neat ponytail. Jeff turned to face himself and was relieved. His blue eyes were tell-tale bloodshot, but the facade would suffice.

He stepped into the kitchen and grabbed a cold Coke from the fridge. He popped the can open and closed the refrigerator door, but not before noticing an unopened twelve pack of Budweiser on the bottom shelf. It was the last thing he really wanted to see right then, but he lingered a moment. He was almost sure it hadn't been there the last time he'd looked in the fridge, a mere four hours ago.

Jeff pondered the mystery beer only long enough to locate the omnipresent bottle of ibuprofen above the kitchen sink. He shook three tablets from the bottle, chased them with ice-cold caffeine, and invited the healing to begin.

Not fifteen seconds later, his face was rudely introduced to the hardwood floor of the home's front room. Something awkward had found its way under Jeff's feet and had caused his balance to fail. Caught completely off guard, Jeff met the floor with a tremendous crash. The full can of Coke flew a remarkable distance across the room. It collided with a bookshelf across the room in an explosion of thick brown carbonated foam.

The incident had happened in a flash, and had made an awful racket. Graham, who had been snoring steadily on the couch in the front room, shot upright.

Jeff slowly picked himself up, regained his bearings, and turned his attention to the cause of his accident. There on the floor, no worse off for having been crushed by his foot was a pair of black stiletto high heels, slit down the sides and strung together by a common white tennis shoe lace. The phantom of vague recollection cruised through Jeff's head, and he cursed loudly.

"God fuckin' dammit!" he blasphemed, kicking the shoes into the wall.

"Wha...?" Graham groaned through a thick mental fog.

"I'm late for church," Jeff huffed, slamming the door in frustration.

Graham mumbled, recovered the thin itchy blanket from the disgusting floor at the foot of the couch and rolled back over. He was asleep again before Jeff turned over the engine of his black Toyota pickup truck and sped away.

The house remained still for several more hours until the shrill cry of the phone pierced the tranquility. Andy rolled out from a mountain of pillows and blankets and, with eyes closed, made a valiant attempt to silence the screaming beast. He also managed to upset a half-full can of Milwaukee's Best into an overflowing ashtray. The mere stench of his spontaneous creation was sufficient to cause Andy to rise with haste.

"Hello?" He said, with equal confusion and irritation.

"Andrew Maxwell, please," came the too-pleasant response. The woman sounded young and very awake.

"Speaking," Andy said, trying to focus.

"Mr. Maxwell, my name is Brenda from Creative Credit Services. How are you today?"

"I'm tired," he offered honestly. "How are you?"

"Um, fine." The woman hesitated, surprised by the non-standard answer to her very standard question. "Listen, I was calling in reference to your VISA account, Mr. Maxwell."

His attention was fractious at best. Still shaking the sleep from his brain, he scanned the cluttered bedside table. He found a pack of Winstons, now slightly dampened with a smattering of The Beast. He rescued it from the small pool of spilt beer and considered lighting one up as he sat up in bed but decided against it.

"Sir," she continued, now finding her place again in the script, "we show that your account has become dangerously delinquent, and we were wondering if a recent payment had been made?"

"*Dangerously* delinquent?" Andy repeated, amused by the ominous adverb.

"Umm, yes sir." Brenda was again caught off guard by his reply. "The account is overdue, and nearing its limit." she clarified. "Has a payment been made?"

"Well, let's see," Andy said, with quite a bit of mock seriousness. "Yes ma'am," he lied. "That went out just this past Thursday. I paid the minimum balance due."

"One fifty-seven forty-three?" Brenda asked.

"Um, right," Andy agreed, as he would have to any figure she offered.

Yes ma'am indeed, 'the check was in the mail.' Andy had been anticipating his modest graduation windfall. His grand accumulation of seventeen hundred dollars was mostly spent. The fine folks at Creative Credit would get their due; just like everybody else though, they'd have to wait their turn.

"I guess it hasn't gotten there yet," Andy suggested as innocently as possible.

At this point, what else was there for Brenda to say? She was a mere customer service rep. She didn't have—and probably didn't want—any real 'power'. "Well, we'll give it a couple of more days to get here then. Sorry to have bothered you, Mr. Maxwell."

"No problem, Brenda," Andy offered with a hint of snark. "You have a lovely day."

As he returned the phone to its cradle, and once again eyed the dampened pack of Winstons, Andy considered what it must be like to have Brenda's job. He imagined spending most of the day, day after day after day, being lied to by people who couldn't—or wouldn't—pay what they owed. He didn't have a job at all at the moment, but he knew he'd rather be in that boat, than rowing in endless, meaningless circles like Brenda.

#

The sound of water rushing through the plumbing came through the wall that connected Andy's bedroom to the home's central bathroom. Intrigued and now fully awake, he rolled from the bed. Pulling on a white cotton t-shirt and a pair of black jeans, he went in search of conversation. He'd expected to see Graham rambling through the house, but was met with a far more charming sight.

There stood Ellen in front of the open refrigerator, intently slurping orange juice straight from the carton. She looked up in mid-swallow to see Andy watching her and smirking.

"Sorry. There's no clean glasses, and I had to get this taste out of my mouth."

"I know. I feel like a beer."

"You cannot be serious," Ellen said with disgust.

"No. I mean I feel as if I *were* a beer, a very warm, very flat beer," Andy clarified.

Ellen was a frightful mess. Her hair, though long and straight, seemed confused as it sprawled in various directions. A small stream of juice flowed down her cheek and splashed onto the collar of her pink and white terrycloth bathrobe as she gulped. Her robe hung open to reveal a long white nightshirt, upon which was printed in large black letters, "I LOVE ROCK 'N ROLL." Thick black socks protected her feet from the film of filth which had accumulated on the kitchen floor over the course of last night.

"Damn, you're sexy first thing in the morning," Andy mocked.

"Fuck you," she played along.

"Hey! The bus is gone! Where the hell's Graham?" Andy asked.

"Don't know. But he'll be back. You know he'll be back."

"Oh, I know," Andy admitted. "But he's always running off to somewhere else. I just wish he'd stick around a little longer."

"Why, so we can take him for granted like everyone else we see every day? The reason you value him so much is because he's *not* around," Ellen suggested.

She was right, on both accounts. And Andy *did* value him, immensely, and for reasons she and most others didn't even realize.

Graham and Andy, at least in Andy's eyes, were kindred spirits; brethren united by a common experience—suffering. In his myopic view, Andy had come to believe he'd endured the kinds of hardship that few of his contemporaries could understand, let alone rival. In fact, until he'd met Graham, Andy wasn't sure there was anyone else he knew who'd really suffered much hardship at all.

Graham conversely had managed to maintain a far more cheerful outlook, powering through his tribulations in a way Andy truly admired but couldn't bring himself to emulate.

Each time Graham came back, there was a sense of elation for Andy. And every time he left, it was like a light going out, leaving his world a little dimmer until their next reunion.

"Fuck it," Andy lamented, finally lighting the Winston he'd brought with him from the bedside table. "What do you say to breakfast? My treat. You don't have to shower, but you can't wear that to Coleman's."

35

"Coleman's? Hell yeah!" Ellen cheered, already headed for a change of clothes, as Andy searched for his shoes.

Ellen piloted Chet out of their neighborhood and to the top of the hill on Paxton Avenue. The car crested over the apex bringing a new, troubling horizon into view – a sea of flashing blue lights. About a quarter mile down the hill on their left, a disturbing number of emergency response vehicles were assembled. They approached the intersection of Paxton and Juniper Streets and rolled to a stop, joining a growing line of cars going nowhere fast. Traffic was backed up for several blocks with each car slowing to a near halt as it pulled alongside The Cactus Club.

"Damn," said Andy. "That's gonna be a problem. Detour around that shit."

Ellen maintained her slow roll down the hill, but began looking for clearance to do exactly as her roommate had suggested. "Don't you want to see what's happening down there?"

"Yeah, but to be honest," Andy replied "I'd rather go see what our shoe tree looks like. Besides, by the look of all those police cars, whatever it is – it'll still be there after we've eaten."

"And so will your shoes," she said, executing a u-turn in the middle of Paxton Avenue. "We can go down Firth and take back roads. That way we can stop by the store. We need smokes."

On face value, there was nothing special about The Cactus Club. Every college town in America has its share of unremarkable two-bit nightclubs, and Bradford was no exception. Like most of the twenty or so bars within a five mile radius, The Cactus Club was a shithole; but to the residents of Cornwall Street, it was *their* shithole. It was the closest belly-up to their house, which certainly factored into the frequency of their visits. But something about it made it feel different – like theirs, a clubhouse filled mostly with friends. Unlike The Green Room, the Cactus was primarily a music venue. Nearly nightly, someone was onstage making some kind of glorious racket. A few big acts would play there occasionally, but for the most part, The Cactus Club was a proving ground for the throngs of local bands tightening their chops or just blowing off some steam in a live setting. And since almost everyone they knew was either in a band, lived with someone in a band, or dated someone in a band, the Cactus Club organically became a second home to them.

They knew plenty of people who worked there and Andy started making a mental list of folks he needed to call—after breakfast, of course—to get the inside scoop on what the hell had happened. If it hadn't been for the party they themselves had hosted the night before, they and many of their friends would probably already know firsthand.

Even with a bit of church release traffic folded into the mix, the journey to Coleman's Diner was straight and short. They'd managed to make it in a mere ten minutes, but that was still plenty long enough for their modest desire for grease and carbs to become a desperate craving.

Ellen eased the Chevette into one of the few remaining spots along the diner's east side. A small sigh escaped her tired lips as she killed the engine.

"So what do you think went down at the Cactus?" Andy asked, as they waited for a police cruiser to cross the parking lot in front of them.

"I'm sure I don't know." Ellen admitted, closing the car door and already moving toward the heavenly smell of bacon.

Coleman's Diner was a glorious contradiction – at once a redneck eyesore and a genuine historical landmark. The walls were plastered with 1950's style advertisements for everything from Coca-Cola to Coleman's own brand of pancake mix, which was still available for purchase at the counter on the way out. A chronological visual history of Bradford, in the form of aerial black and white photographs – now tinged an uneven shade of sepia by decades of cigarette smoke – hung neatly on the wood-paneled wall at the back of the diner.

The air inside Coleman's was cool and processed and offered a welcome change from the hellish humidity of a Bradford summer. Ellen kept her dark sunglasses hung loosely over her eyes as they took a booth near the back, where the diner still allowed patrons to smoke. Before they'd even sat down, she had a lit Marlboro dangling from her lips.

"You want one?" she said, offering the open pack across the pleasantly cool faux marble table top.

"Hell no! How can you do that?"

"Do what?"

"Smoke so early in the morning."

"First of all, there's about 45 seconds left in this *morning*. And second, I believe it's called addiction."

"I can't smoke a cigarette until after I've eaten something," Andy said, as if this made him somehow superior.

"Shit, sometimes I wake up just to smoke a cigarette and then go back to sleep."

"That's nasty."

"Like *you* never smoke in bed."

"Only after sex," said Andy, with exaggerated suaveness.

"Now who's being gross?" she said, turning to acknowledge their waitress, a 40-ish looking woman with voluminous hair. She had arrived midway through their juvenile exchange and was pretending to be patient.

For them, ordering breakfast at Coleman's had become so practiced, it was nearly a reflex. Years of on-site research, in various states of sobriety, had culminated in their discovery of the perfect culinary experience. The Coleman's Breakfast Sampler Sandwich was delicious, but deadly. Piled high, between two signature square-cut pancakes, were three farm-fresh eggs, multiple strips of grease-laden bacon or sausage, and enough cheese to choke a Frenchman. The true thrill-seekers, those in the express lane to heart failure, could even top it off with a little butter or sour cream.

"So, who was on the phone this morning?" Ellen asked, through a cloud of smoke.

"Brenda, from Creative Credit. She was calling to let me know that my account has become dangerously delinquent."

"Dangerous?" Ellen pondered. "To whom? In what way?"
Andy laughed, enjoying the affirmation of his own earlier confusion.

"I'm not sure. Maybe if I don't pay up, they'll send the Credit Mafia over to the house to break my thumbs."

"She called on a Sunday morning? What a shitty job that is!"

"I know. But on the upside, she gets paid to sit on her ass all day and harass people she'll never even meet, about a bunch of money that nobody's ever going to see or touch. All the while, she's probably working from home, throwing back screwdrivers, and watching daytime TV."

"Well, when you put it that way... where do I sign up?"

They both smiled and sat upright to greet the waitress as she arrived with their food.

Heaven had no pleasure, and hell hath no fury like the Coleman's Breakfast Sampler. It seethed with fat, cholesterol, and every other fabulous tasting wonderfood which will just fucking kill you. It was pure plated hedonism, and it required the briefest moment of solemn reflection before digging in.

Ellen was busy cutting in to the culinary monster, checking to see if the egg yolks were cooked solid or runny. Andy felt strong, and mostly without thinking, reached for one of the four small pitchers of Coleman's syrup to his left. Seconds later, a river of pure blueberry flavored sugar flowed over the already volatile creation.

"Damn. You're going to die," Ellen said, almost gagging.

"Yeah. And so are you."

"No, I mean you're gonna die right *now* if you eat that."

"What? It's blueberry, I needed something from the fruit group."

"Nice balance."

"Take a left. Here, take a left. We're almost there," Andy demanded, so excited he seemed to almost be vibrating.

"Chill, dude. I know where the fuck I'm going. I was here too – like eight hours ago."

Chet rounded the last corner onto Providence Road as Andy squirmed in his seat trying to gain a more perfect line of sight. She angled toward the Post Office. It was closed on Sunday and its big empty parking lot offered the perfect vantage point on their target just across the street.

Depending on one's perspective, their arrival was timed either perfectly or horribly. Ellen watched with great interest as the parishioners of Bradford Baptist filed out of the sanctuary, many of them milling casually in the courtyard. Andy hadn't even noticed the people yet. He was transfixed by the spectacle next door. The car had barely stopped before he was out in parking lot, heading toward the street about as fast as Andy ever really moved.

"Oh, that's fucking beautiful!" he raved, as if he was viewing a master work by Matisse or Rembrandt. He wasn't.

Andy stood on the curb, still bounding with noticeable energy, and stared at the massive live oak tree in front of the Gryphon Theater. If not for the DO NOT WALK sign holding him at bay, Ellen would never had caught up to him.

"You're not going over there," she instructed, now standing next to him.

"The fuck I'm NOT. Look at it!"

"But, look at all those PEOPLE!"

She had to know he wouldn't be denied. The lights at the intersection switched, and he was off, moving across the street. "I know. That's the best part!"

Ellen kept a step behind, until Andy had stopped on the curb right in front of the Gryphon Theater. She'd been so busy chasing her roommate she hadn't really even seen it yet. Then she looked up.

It was absurd, and insane – but also, as Andy had correctly stated, oddly beautiful. Hanging from those branches, bathed in the full, glorious light of day, were a ridiculous number of shoes. Too many to count; although with their necks craned to the sky it looked like that's exactly what the two of them were doing.

Andy scoured the scene, reveling like some deranged pyromaniac standing next to the hook and ladder truck watching a vacant building burn. His eyes trailed from the highest branches, all the way to the ground. There, he noticed at least two pairs of shoes lying harmlessly on the ground. His first instinct was to run to them and hurl them upward to live with their brethren, but he fought that.

"It's pretty fucking cool, Andy," Ellen admitted, still looking skyward. They were both smiling.

"This is ridiculous." said the bent old lady behind them. She was dressed in her Sunday finest, and propped on the arm of her husband. Andy and Ellen stopped as the octogenarians trudged past.

"Stupid kids." the old man added to his wife's critique.

"Damn," said Andy. "That's awful judgmental for folks who just spent the last hour gettin' 'churched up'."

"Screw 'em. I think it's awesome. See? You're creative. When you want to, you can do some pretty cool shit."

"Thanks."

Her praise conflicted him. Of course he wanted it, but it made him feel weird. This had been easy and foolish. The serious business of life was proving more difficult to conquer.

"I can't believe I fuckin' forgot the camera." he said, now deflecting.

"You can come back later and shoot it, but now, we should go home." said Ellen.

14

Ellen's Chevette settled into the dirt and gravel driveway and came to rest behind Andy's dark green SUV. A small sidewalk divided the driveway into two defined parking spaces, four if you included the fact that they shared the driveway with their neighbors, the Murphys.

She sprang from the car and made a bee-line for the front door. Although delicious, the Coleman's Breakfast Sampler had a nasty reputation for repaying its consumer fairly quickly with bouts of severe abdominal distress. Andy felt solid enough for the moment. He lingered, closing Chet's door, and meandering towards his own vehicle. He leaned on the SUV's front quarter panel which had warmed well in the early afternoon heat. Reaching into the breast pocket of his shirt, he grabbed his crumpled pack of Winston Lights and began fumbling to retrieve one.

Andy sat soaking in the shade of a giant oak tree, until his peace was fractured by the sound of a heavy screen door crashing against its frame. His eyes shot open and filled with the sight his neighbor, Quenton Murphy, loping down the steps to his front yard.

A black man in his early 60s, with mostly-salt-and-some-pepper hair and thin wire spectacles, Quenton was an ideal neighbor. He'd been married to the same lovely woman, the former Miss Lula Franklin, for 39 years. In that time, they'd had four children; three boys and a girl. Those children had grown up well, right there in that house on Cornwall Street, and had all moved on. In fact, Quenton and Lula had lived on Cornwall Street for over twenty five years, and in all probability, were going to die there too. The Murphys had had their share of neighbors in that time – some good, some anonymous, but probably none as raucous as now. Andy somehow suspected Quenton didn't really mind, and was probably even a little amused at his current situation.

Quenton and Andy had become unlikely associates, exchanging occasional pleasantries in the driveway or across the sad chain link fence that separated their back yards. Quenton was nearly three times older, and probably worked that much harder too. Even though he was 'retired', Mr. Murphy worked the earth religiously, maintaining his small yard and garden. Maybe it was at Lula's urging, or maybe it just gave him something to do, but he was out there sweating almost daily. The young renters next door had no such attachment to the land they occupied, and it showed.

"Hey Murphy," called Andy, as he bounced off his SUV. He tossed the butt of his cigarette, but did so with enough care so as not to traverse the imaginary line which divided their properties.

It was an odd reference, calling a man that much your senior by his last name only. But Quenton wasn't the least offended. He preferred the cordial sort of syntax his surname offered, especially as it ran off of the young white tongues of his neighbors. And certainly he preferred it to the relentlessly over-sweet cadence of Lula, as she called "Quent-ton Dear..," which was more often than not followed by "could you..."

"How are you this beautiful Sunday?" he asked Andy, through thin puffs of a Salem menthol.

"I suppose I'm fine. And yourself?"

"Well, it was either come out here in this damned humidity, and wax down the Caddy," he started "or wait for the wife to come home from church, and start preachin' about how I should be out here waxing the Caddy instead of sippin' on a beer. This way I can do both, and there's no naggin'."

Sure enough, Quenton's wrinkled left hand bore a six-pack carrier of Budweiser longnecks, two of which remained. Murphy bent down to place the carrier on the ground, opened both bottles with surprising speed, and stood back up. He may have been in his sixties, and a little wiry, but Quenton was what they called "old man strong." You'd never guess it by looking at him, but years of working with heavy tools – first as an aircraft mechanic in the Army, and then later in machine shops and factories – had strengthened and thickened his dark, aged hands. Andy had learned the first time he'd accepted a vice-grip like handshake from his neighbor, there was more to Quenton Murphy than met the eye.

"Drink up, son," Quenton said, offering a cold beer to Andy, with a wistful smile. "What's a little more on top of the damage it looks like y'all already did last night?"

Andy suspected somewhere inside of Quenton Murphy there still lived a younger man who'd quite like to sit and share a cold beer, or even a little weed, with his neighbors every now and then.

"You know what?" said Andy, after downing a mouthful of cold lager. "I sure have enjoyed the hell outta living here."

"Have?" replied Quenton, noticing the tense. "You sound like you got plans Maxwell. Where you going?"

"Well, that's just it, Murphy, I don't having a clue where I'm goin'. But I get the feeling I might be close to done here. I finished school, which is why I came to Bradford in the first place. And I managed to avoid finding a future ex-wife here, so it's probably time to start thinking about what's next."

"Sounds like the ambition bug's gone and crawled up your ass, son. But that's aw-right. That's what it's all about. A young man's gotta go out there, look around, and see what the world's got for him. Ain't nuthin' wrong with that."

"Yeah, but that shit's scary," Andy admitted in a way he wouldn't have to his contemporaries.

"Good. It's supposed to be. Nuthin' worth havin' should be easy. And a man who ain't afraid of nuthin' is either naïve, or stupid."

"I guess. So what about you then?"

"What *about* me, Andy?" asked Quenton, with greater focus on his big grey Cadillac than on his neighbor, as he cracked the seal on the car wax.

"You know? Is this everything the world had with your name on it?"

Andy had meant no offense, and probably didn't even realize the condescension in his question – inferring that a 60-year-old man had maximized his lot in life to be living next to a shit-hole house filled with ignorant twenty-somethings who were just 'passing through on the way to something better'.

"In a lot of ways, Maxwell, I got everything I need right here, and nuthin' to complain about. But on the other hand, Hell no! If this was all there was for me, God would have already come down here and taken me up there with Him by now."

"No, I mean, are you happy with the way it's all come down for you?"

Quenton emerged from the driver's side door. He'd rolled down the windows and turned on the stereo. A pleasant sort of smile spread across his face as the James Brown cassette tape in his deck switched sides and broke into the jubilant opening of '*Super Bad - Part 1.*'

"See, you gotta relax. You're a young dude. You got the rest of your life to be worried about the rest of your life," Quenton suggested, through a blast of minty smoke.

"But that's kind of my whole point. I don't know that I feel very young at all anymore. I mean, I look around, and all I see are people my age, and even lots younger, who are famous actors and rock stars, and I can't help but wonder when *whatever* is supposed to happen to me, is gonna happen to me." A wave of anxiety built within Andy as he spoke.

"So, that's it? You want to be a rock & roll star, Andy?"

"No, not really. I mean, I've tried that. It didn't pan out for me. But yes, I do want to be something, you know? Someone."

"Shit! Do I know? Lemme tell you sumthin', Maxwell. When I was about your age, the one thing that I wanted most in the whole world was to be this dude right here." Quenton threw his thumb over his shoulder at the tape deck, as the Godfather of Soul belted out *'I'm real Super Bad. Ain't nobody good enough to take the things I have.'*

Andy knew better than to argue with The Gospel According to J.B. and silently threw back another long swig of Budweiser.

"You really wanted to be James Brown?"

"Heck yeah!" said Quenton, through another blast of menthol. Sweat cursed his dark brow as he began to make small wax circles on the Caddy's massive hood. "Used to dress like him, too. I even put that relaxer crap on my hair one summer and tried to grow the man's do. To this day, I'd love to know what his hair was made of. I looked at myself in the mirror, hoping to see the Godfather, but you know what? It was still me. Ain't no point in spending your life trying to live somebody else's. You start doin' that shit, and before you know it, all that stuff out there, the stuff with your name on it, you miss it. And you only get one shot."

"I know all of that. Besides, I don't really want to be somebody else. I want to be me—but with more money and less troubles. It's just frustrating not to know what the hell I'm doing with my life."

"At least you're thinking about it, Maxwell. Plenty of people your age are too busy chasing the bottom of a bottle, or getting wasted on junk, to figure out that one day they're gonna have to grow up and actually live life."

Simple wisdom wrapped in a massive dose of irony. Andy leaned against his car and wondered if Murphy knew just how close he'd come to nailing Andy as most of those horrible things he'd described. In that moment, he was paralyzed. He knew there were only two things he could do. He could try to change the subject, acting as if his neighbor's assessment was inapplicable to him, or he could run. His mind raced in small circles, searching for a friendlier topic and found nothing.

Then, as if in answer to a prayer Andy hadn't even made, Jeff's black pickup truck came grumbling up the hot asphalt hill. An angel of mercy, straight from his gig in the House of God, Jeff had come to rescue him from Quenton's unintentional inquisition.

"Ah. Speaking of rock stars, here he comes now," said Andy, pointing at the approaching truck. "Now see, Jeff could do it. He could actually make the big time. But, who knows what he really wants either? He's a mystery. It wouldn't surprise me if he packed up his shit and moved to New York tomorrow. Or, he could just as likely stay here forever. Could go either way."

As was often the case, Quenton listened patiently and with amusement to Andy's anxious ramblings.

"It could," Quenton agreed, smiling. "But either way, he'll be *happy*."

"Why is that?"

"'Cause he ain't wasting time or energy fightin' the future. You know, it's all gonna work out the way *He* wants it to, right?"

"He who?" Andy asked, pointing back to the Caddy's dash. "The Godfather?"

Quenton laughed up another billow of smoke, but quickly refocused. "That's funny. But don't play, son. The Godfather is the real deal, for sure. But Father God is the Truth."

"So, how come you're skippin' church to wax the Caddy, then?"

51

"Oh, me and God, we have an understanding. Sometimes I go to his house to talk, and sometimes we hang out in other places. He don't mind. He's always around – ain't hard to find Him, so long as you're lookin'."

15

Still clad in his choir robes of blazing white with royal purple trim, Jeff was a sight to behold. He started across the short front yard to the house, dark sunglasses hiding the portion of his face not obstructed by the mane of hair that flew in the breeze. Andy couldn't decide if Jeff more closely resembled Jesus or a young Ozzy Osbourne. It wasn't until they met at the foot of the porch that he noticed the small brown paper bag in Jeff's left hand.

"So, how was church?"

"Excellent, but pipe organs are loud as hell when you're hung over. I couldn't sing for shit though. It's a good thing I didn't have any solos today."

"Next time you have solos, let me know. I wanna go."

"Bullshit! You've been talking smack about goin' to church with me for the past nine months, but you never quite make it. I don't want to hear it anymore."

"No. I will. I mean, I would. I really would. It's just that the thing happens so damn early. I think I might be better at talking to God a little later in the day."

"Now God has to work on your schedule too? You don't ask for much, do you?"

"Forget it. What's in the bag?" Andy asked as they reached the top of the steps.

"In a minute," Jeff deferred. "Gotta find Ellen first."

The awful stench of spilled beer and wet ashes assaulted them as they stepped inside the house. The front room alone was littered with at least two dozen 16-ounce blue plastic cups.

"Well, so much for hoping that you guys would have all this shit picked up by the time I got home."

"No sir. We had to go to Coleman's for the Sampler this morning," said Andy, lighting a Winston and hoping to ignite a little jealousy as well. "Besides, that didn't seem like it would be fair to you."

"Well, aren't you considerate? Now where the hell is Ellen?"

In the time it had taken Andy to share a leisurely drink with their neighbor, Ellen had gone at least part of the way towards greeting the new day. As Jeff had reached the living room, she stepped into the hallway, freshly showered but wrapped in the same pink and white terrycloth robe she'd donned just a few hours before.

"Check it out, Ellen," Jeff offered.

She walked straight to her bedroom, as if neither of them had even been standing there.

"I'm getting dressed first," she reprimanded.

Jeff took the delay as an opportunity to slip out of his choral robes and return them to his bedroom. This left Andy standing alone at the exact center of their home, silently surveying the damage around him. It was remarkable and widespread. Suddenly the air inside the house seemed warmer and more humid to him—nearly unbearable.

The notion surprised him, but after Quenton had primed the pump, Andy found himself craving a second beer. The phantom 12-pack in the fridge was unopened and certainly fair game. He grabbed three bottles from the box and let the refrigerator close on its own behind him.

54

Andy rounded the corner out of the kitchen and headed for the Den. He took the chair directly opposite the television and waited. A moment later, Ellen entered and lay herself down on the couch next to Andy's chair. Jeff was only a few steps behind, still clutching the brown paper bag. He leaned against the closet door, sweeping a curtain of hair away from his blue-green eyes.

Andy tossed one of the unopened Budweisers at him and held aloft the third bottle, offering it to Ellen.

"Hell no!" she replied with conviction, as Andy placed the unclaimed freight back on the table between them. In order to open his beer, Jeff was forced to release his death-grip on the bag, and Andy strained to get a closer look at what was hiding inside.

Settling in, Jeff reached into the sack and produced a half-full bottle of 100-proof Smirnoff vodka.

"Double Hell no!" exclaimed Ellen, much more emphatically than her last refusal.

"Bravo! Where'd you score the Sunday booze?" applauded Andy.

"It's not liquor," said Jeff, in a noticeably hushed tone.

His roommates opted for silence, knowing Jeff would fill in the blanks anyway.

"Seriously?" Jeff muttered, as his patience expired. "Am I the only one who remembers last night?"

Andy and Ellen exchanged puzzled glances.

"Apparently," Andy replied. "I got no bells ringing."

Ellen sat silently on the couch confirming that she too was in the dark.

"Last night? When we got back? You don't remember? It was the three of us, and Graham sitting on the.... Hey! Where's Graham?"

"Disappeared again. Early this morning sometime I guess," said Ellen.

"No. He was there on the couch when I left for church. He woke up and talked to me."

"Well, he's not there now, so I don't know what to tell you," said Andy.

"Well that's fuckin' great," Jeff said sarcastically. "Graham's gone, and you two idiots don't even remember talking about THIS." He was shaking the small, half-full glass bottle furiously as he spoke.

"It's all good, man," Andy replied. "Relax. Just start over. It's sounds interesting."

"YOU started it, you dick!" Jeff said, pointing at Andy. "Remember? When we got back from your little shoe tree adventure? We were talking about doing bad shit. Somebody brought up the question of Hell. And YOU started asking people what was the most surefire way to end up there."

"It DOES sound like something you'd say," Ellen agreed.

"You can't even remember what you said last night?"

"I'm probably not gonna remember saying any of THIS later today," Andy admitted. "Stuff comes in, stuff goes out. Whatever." His nonchalance wasn't soothing Jeff's growing agitation.

"Seriously?!" Jeff ranted. "You brought it up last night. And after we tossed the idea around a bit, Graham came up with... this!"

"So, what's THIS?" Ellen asked.

"Like I said. It ain't liquor. You honestly don't remember Graham talking shit about using Holy Water for bong fuel?"

"Wow," Ellen said, matter-of-factly. "That would do it."

"Jesus!" said Andy. "That's fucked up."

"Hey! This was *your* idea," countered Jeff.

"I thought you said it was Graham's idea," Ellen suggested.

"No. He brought it up, but Maxwell here dared me to do it," explained Jeff, now getting defensive.

"I don't remember that at all," said Andy, quite innocently.

"Really? How exactly is it that you can say something like 'Hey, you're going to a church tomorrow. See if you can get us some Holy Water, and then not remember?"

"I dunno. People say a lot of crazy shit around here. If we did everything somebody suggested, we'd all be in jail or dead."

"Or in Hell, apparently," Ellen added.

"Sorry, man," Andy apologized. "I don't remember saying that. And if I did, I definitely didn't think you would actually do it. That's just crazy. Sometimes I talk, just to be talking. Plus, I was pretty wasted last night, so I could have said anything."

"What? Like 'let's throw eighty shoes in a tree'?" Ellen asked, laughing.

"Shut up. THAT was a good idea last night, and it still is. You saw how awesome that shit looked." Andy had said it to Ellen, but was hoping to use it as a segue for sharing his grand accomplishment with Jeff.

His roommate was having none of it. "So, let me see if I have this right..." Jeff said. "One asshole has a dumb idea, and then another asshole dares me to do it. Then, like an asshole, I do it. The next morning, Asshole # 1 takes off, and Asshole # 2 can't even remember his own name... which is 'ASSHOLE'!, by the way! Does that about cover it?"

"Wow!" declared Ellen. "I see you're getting good use out of that *Webster's Cursing Dictionary* I got you for Christmas."

"Have you got to the B's yet?" Andy said.

"Bastard and bitch!" Jeff added for good measure, pointing to each of them respectively.

"Very good," said Ellen, knowing it was time to quit. "So, that's really Holy Water then?"

"Yeah. Or as holy as it gets these days."

"What does that mean?"

"Well, it's actually only tap water, or in this case spring water. They've got tons of the stuff in big jugs in a storage room. The priest blesses it a closet-full at a time. This morning they left a nearly empty jug sitting out on the counter. Honestly, I wouldn't have even noticed it, and would have never thought of taking it, if you and Graham hadn't planted the seed in my head. In the end, I guess I figured no one was gonna miss a half a pint of water. There wouldn't have been enough left to use, so they probably would have tossed it and started with a new one for the next service. I've seen it happen."

"So, see? It's not like you really stole it after all. That should make you feel better." Andy clearly wanted a little absolution too. As much as he enjoyed pushing the boundaries of 'acceptable behavior,' there were still some lines Andy was hesitant to cross.

"So, what do you want to do?" Jeff asked. The three of them sat there, each like Robert Johnson at the crossroads, wrestling with the notion of consummating a deal with the Devil.

"Well, I want to get high," said Andy. "But I'm sure as Hell not smoking through Holy Water."

"But you don't even believe in God, so what do you care?" Jeff argued.

"Just because I don't believe, doesn't mean I can't still be afraid. Who knows? I could be wrong. But there's no sense in poking a bear with a stick, just to see if it will maul you."

#

Andy, like both of his roommates, had grown up in the Christian church, learning about a loving God and his son, Jesus. Those ideas had been comfortable enough for him, until a few years earlier, when suddenly they weren't.

The defining moment so far of Andy's young life had come during the autumn of his fifteenth year. His brother, Tristan, was only eleven at the time. Their difference in age wasn't enough to keep them from being close. More than brothers, they were genuine friends. But four years is a wide berth and brought with it some natural separations – different schools, different schedules, different friends. In younger years they were always with one another. But as they grew, Andy drifted toward new interests, often leaving his brother behind to play with kids his own age.

On a Friday afternoon in the early fall of 1987, Andy left Tristan alone, as he'd done plenty of times before. It was only for a few hours, until their parents came home. When a neighbor boy, Brock, who was one year older than Tristan, invited Tristan to hang at his house, the younger Maxwell gladly accepted. Brock's parents also worked, leaving him unattended for large stretches of time in a house Tristan always thought of as much more fun, with better toys and fewer rules than his own. When Tristan got there, Brock was more excited than usual, quickly ushering Tristan downstairs to the basement where many of the best 'toys' were kept. In addition to the pool table and a few real arcade style video games, Brock's father also had a safe roughly the size of a pay phone booth. Tristan had never given it any real thought on his previous visits to the house. On that day, Brock's excitement was the product of pure parental negligence. Young, inquisitive, unsupervised Brock had discovered that the safe his father had failed to secure contained four hunting rifles and two handguns. Brock led Tristan to the safe and pulled open the door, revealing its all-too-alluring bounty.

Both boys stood wide-eyed, perusing the small cache of weapons. Brock, with absolutely no malice of forethought grabbed one of the handguns and wheeled toward Tristan, brandishing a Hi-Point 9mm pistol. He thrust the gun in Tristan's direction several times, making explosive 'pow' sounds with each extension. It was easy enough to imagine, an innocent, ignorant pre-teen boy pretending to be any one of the countless armed heroes or villains he'd seen in the movies. Tristan laughed, albeit nervously, as he stepped to move away from the gun's barrel. Brock followed him, stabbing at the air between them twice more. The gun exploded with a noise and violence neither of them could ever have imagined. The discharge forced the weapon from Brock's too-small hand, leaving him stunned. Tristan was rendered speechless too, for an altogether different reason. From less than six feet away, a 9mm slug entered his tiny torso, ripping flesh and decimating bone before it exploded out his back.

With his friend lying on the cold concrete basement floor bleeding profusely, Brock froze. His parents had lectured him often on safety in general, and even specifically about the dangers of the guns they owned, but now, when it really mattered, it was all a blur. Several minutes went by as Brock attempted to comfort his still conscious friend or somehow correct the damage he'd done, but clearly he lacked the faculties to manage the situation. Eventually he called 911. Eventually the paramedics came. But it was too late. Tristan Maxwell, age 11, died in the back of an ambulance, the victim of an accident so random and senseless and sudden it defied comprehension. As a result, 15-year-old Andy Maxwell's relationship with God perished abruptly but definitively too.

#

"So," started Ellen, disregarding the idea of the Holy Water wholesale, "put that shit away then. Let's just desecrate our bodies in the normal, not-go-straight-to-Hell way."

"Yeah, just one problem," Jeff pointed out. "My stash is cashed."

"I got it!" Andy shot out, bounding down the hall. "It's the least I can do."

"It usually is," Jeff replied under his breath. He placed the vodka bottle back in the bag, relieved but partly disgruntled that his sin of theft was committed for naught.

"He really can be such a bastard sometimes," Jeff said to Ellen, with Andy well out of earshot.

"Yeah, it's true. But how often are you bored?"

Not two minutes later, Andy returned. Jeff was cleaning the screen in the bowl of his favorite pipe, a little purple piece of PVC about 5 inches tall. It was emblazoned with a shiny iridescent sticker – the kind a child might get from school or the doctor – which said 'Super Star'.

"Damn! This was a quarter yesterday afternoon." Andy was staring forlornly at the shabby quantity of marijuana. "We're gonna have to go see Pete again."

Each of them took turns filling the chamber, and then their lungs, with smoke as the pipe made its way around the circle.

"I do wonder, though…" Ellen pondered, "if it would have tasted any different, or felt any better."

"I don't know, El, but I can't imagine it'd be worth it to find out," Andy offered. "Besides, I'm feeling pretty disconnected right now anyway." Warm inebriation washed over him, bringing with it a sense of calm. It didn't last long.

"So, what are you gonna do about a job, Andy?"

Whoa. Where had that come from? As quickly as he could begin his escape, reality drew tight its leash and proceeded once again to prod him sternly in the direction of responsibility.

"Damn. You sure know how to kill a buzz," Andy said sadly.

"Sorry, but we gotta talk about this sooner or later."

"I know. And I feel bad about it. It's getting down to the wire. Now that I've graduated, I can't really squeeze much more out of my parents under the pretense of looking for a job. If something doesn't happen real soon, I'm probably headed back to their basement."

"I thought you had a couple of prospects," Ellen pressed.

"Yeah, one of them fell through. But I actually have an interview with a real ad agency tomorrow."

It had been a sore subject at the house for weeks. Andy had come to the painful realization that where he was and where he was supposed to be might be two very different places. Bradford was great. In fact, Andy had grown quite fond of its small metropolitan charm. But opportunity, at least the kind he was looking for, was not in abundant supply. Most of the jobs in town were either with the government or the university. Neither option really applied or particularly appealed to him. If he was determined to do something of "real value," he was staring down the cold barrel of forced geographic relocation--or so he had decided.

"Yeah, it's either that, or I figure out a way to come into a helluva lot of money, real quick," said Andy, thinking aloud of ways to stay in Bradford a little longer.

"Legally or illegally?" Ellen wanted to know.

"Well... TV and movies have taught me that crime is fun, glamorous, and very lucrative. But I can't really see it as a career path."

"Yeah. Take it easy, sister. Shoe Boy here doesn't need those kinds of ideas running through his brain," Jeff kidded.

"Although, I think I have figured out the way that people do make a lot of money, legally that is," Andy submitted. The cloud of cannabis smoke he'd just inhaled was now driving his train of thought.

"Shit. And you've been holdin' out on us? Give it up, Einstein."

"No, seriously, check it out. People are stupid, right?"

It was an antagonistic premise upon which to build a sales pitch for sure, but intriguing nonetheless.

"Right," agreed Ellen. "But what does that have to do with making lots of money?"

"Everything. People are stupid – and lazy," Andy resumed. "This world is full of lazy bastards just waiting around in line to buy up the next thing that comes along that's supposed to make their lives a little easier."

"Hence the remote control?" Ellen offered.

"Perfect example – the lazy man's best fucking friend."

"So what are you saying?" Jeff asked.

"I'm saying, the best way to make money in this world is to create something that doesn't already exist. Then all you have to do is to convince a bunch of people, people who've been doing just fine without your help so far, that they couldn't possibly go on living another single day without whatever it is that you've invented."

"Really?" Jeff mocked through a billow of smoke. "Whatever happened to 'woe to he who willfully innovates', Mr. Zen Master?"

After severing his relationship with the God of his childhood, Andy had taken a break from religion altogether. In his junior year, he'd come up one class short of a full load, and had decided to try Comparative Religion, as much or more for its favorable schedule than for any real interest in the subject. To his surprise, he'd found some semblance of logic in the Eastern philosophies, particularly the *Tao Te Ching*. His interpretations ranged from broad and liberal to completely misguided, but they were almost always good for a laugh.

"Oh, I've got that covered." Andy beamed.

"Yeah? Lay it on me."

"In fact, I'm glad you asked," lied Andy, whose mind was now racing to catch up with his mouth.

"Okay. So, 'woe to he who willfully innovates', right? Woe is described by Lao Tzu as *the burden brought on man by his preoccupation with his own worldly possessions*. So, therefore, the man who willfully innovates is destined to incur excess woe, or more specifically, lots of worldly possessions."

"I don't get it," Ellen admitted.

"And the beauty of it is," Andy continued, ignoring her, not out of rudeness, but to keep his train of thought, "it doesn't even matter what you create, as long as it's new. Bad books, bad movies, bad records, they all make millions of dollars. You could invent a better mousetrap, or toothbrush, or crack pipe for that matter. It doesn't really matter. *Somebody* out there is gonna lay down the cash to buy into it."

"Hey wait. That might work," Andy pondered, interrupting himself. "What if we created a self-lighting crack pipe? Well not a crack pipe, cause crack sucks, but a pipe anyway? It would have a lighter built into the side, right over the bowl."

"Not bad," commended Ellen. "You'd never have to look for a lighter again."

"That sort of thing could save you weeks over the course of a lifetime," Jeff agreed.

"And you'd have a free hand, so you could smoke while you wrote, or ate, or did your homework. And it would sure make driving while smoking a lot easier."

"Well thanks for making the world a safer place for all the children," congratulated Ellen.

"Fine then, what would you invent?" Andy asked, his skull still tingling.

"Actually, I was thinking about this just the other day, at work," she said, to his surprise. "Every day, these miserable bastards come in there and throw back half their pay in beer and liquor."

"Which happens to pay your check," Andy added.

"I know. Not the point." she shut him down. "Check this out. Think about the water company. They've got pipes that run all under this city, gunning water to every home in Bradford, right? For a small monthly fee, of course."

"Yeah" they both agreed, seeing her conclusion approaching from a mile away.

"So, apply that technology to getting wasted, and what do you get? You take a brewery, run pipes to every home in the neighborhood, and offer people the luxury of continuous beer, mainlined straight into the comfort of their own homes. At a small nominal monthly fee to subscribers, of course, and Voila!"

"Damn. That might be even better than cable television," Jeff applauded.

"No. That's not possible," Andy replied curtly. "But it is damned good thinkin' El. Woe unto you."

"Thanks. But wait, there's more." she gleamed. "What does the water or cable company do if you forget to pay them? They cut you off until you cough up the dough."

"So, you give people credit, at crazy-high rates of course, on an endless supply of beer - delivered directly to a population of obese, underemployed bastards strapped to La-Z-y Boys. Almost overnight, they'd become used to that shit – dependent on it, like an alcoholic welfare state. Wow. Congratulations, Ellen," Andy said, genuinely impressed. "You just figured out how to take over the whole fucking planet!"

"Except that some people don't drink," Ellen noted.

"Sure they don't," Andy laughed, dismissing the statement as patently false.

"You know what I'd like to see?" asked Jeff.

"No," Ellen said obviously.

"I'd like to see somebody make a movie that was real. And not like a documentary, or anything like that. Just a movie where things happen completely realistically."

"That happens all the time. And they're typically very boring," Andy argued. "People don't want to see real shit happen. People go to the movies for the same reason they do drugs – to escape reality; 'cause they see reality every day. We need fantasy to keep us sane."

"No, I agree. That's not what I'm saying. Like, I was watching this Rambo kind of movie the other day. You know, the ones where one guy, with ungodly luck and a big fat grudge, takes on seven hundred heavily-armed bad guys, and wipes 'em all out. That's not fucking reality."

"True. So what are you suggesting?"

"I want to make a movie that lasts about thirty seconds, 'cause that's all it would really take. It'd be called *Bad Guys with Good Aim*. Quick character intros, you know, one guy's good, the other guy's bad. Pretty straightforward. Both of them have guns, but realistically, the Bad Guy just knows how to handle his a little better, cause sometimes, that's the truth. So he whips out the firepower, and cold-cocks Mr. Nice Guy right between the eyes, dead just like that, with no set-up. Now that kind of shit happens every day too."

"What a happy little story that is," cautioned Ellen, shifting to look at Andy, who had no intention of entering a discussion on the topic.

"It's kind of short though, don't you think?" she asked, attempting to move Jeff along.

"No. That's the whole point. I mean we could have the Bad Guy steal the dead Good Guy's unfaithful girlfriend if you like. Boom! Now you've got a love interest. We could stretch it into a full two minutes probably."

"Much better" quipped Ellen. "A little somethin' for the ladies."

"Wouldn't it be great if it were all that easy though? One big idea, and bang, you're filthy fucking rich. No way. The only way to make any money in this world is to bust your ass or your back, or your brain, or whatever it is God gave you that's worth a damn," Jeff lamented.

"Or you could inherit it," added Andy.

"Or you could marry it," suggested Ellen.

"Fuck. You actually *are* a *girl*, aren't you?" teased Jeff. "I hate it when you do that."

"Man, this place is wasted. It would be a lot easier just to move," she said, finally finished procrastinating.

16

For most people, and in most circumstances, taking drugs results in a net loss of productivity. But with Andy, house cleaning was a notable exception. With a head full of narcotics, he somehow acquired tunnel vision and a sense of hyper focus. Jeff and Ellen had learned that as long as the task was straightforward, singular, and in his best interest, all they really had to do was load him up, hit the start button and stay out of the way.

With two overstuffed black trash bags at arm's length, Andy walked faster than normal towards the front porch. To his surprise, the door swung inward with no apparent help. It stopped only after it had assaulted the wall behind it, where a neat hole the size and shape of the door's handle had been forced into the Sheetrock.

Standing there in the open frame, nearly blocking his exit was Cricket Lowe. Instantly, Andy became aware of just how bad he must have looked, and smelled, just then.

"H-Hey, Cricket." he stuttered. "What's up?"

Andy slid past her and dropped the bags in the trash can beside the porch.

"Nothing," she said, entering the house without waiting for him. Her tone was a little cold, but Andy was used to it.

To Andy, Cricket was gorgeous, in a very basic way. She wore no makeup and never really styled her hair, which fell in the smallest of curls near her shoulder blades and hung loosely in her eyes when she wore it down. Her long, thin frame had a lovely curve, but she often wrapped it in flowing ankle-length skirts which hid her a little too well for Andy's taste. She wore leather sandals or went barefoot most of the time, and Andy thought even her toes were cute.

Like so many other local young ladies, Cricket enjoyed Jeff's company. But unlike most of them, she had also proven to be quite handy at acquiring illicit substances. Many a dry and sober night had been remedied at her hand, and so Cricket was always welcome on Cornwall Street. She didn't come calling often, but when she did, it was always for Jeff.

Cricket made her way towards the center of the house. Andy watched her go; the large brown suede bag on her shoulder bouncing subtly off her hip with every other stride. He sighed and turned his attention back to the task at hand.

"Hey, sweetie. How are you?" Cricket purred, addressing Jeff as she swept a blonde lock from her face.

"It's all good," he said turning away from the pile of debris at his feet. "But where the hell were you last night?"

"Nobody told me. But it looks like you had a helluva time."

"Yeah. It was pretty good. Sorry. You're probably the only freak in Bradford that didn't walk through our door last night."

"Not true. The fucking Cactus was packed," she replied.

Ellen's head swung right around. "You were there? What the fuck happened to that place? Hey Andy, get in here!"

"It's on the front page of this morning's paper," Cricket said, as Andy walked into the Den.

"About the shoes?" he asked.

"Shoes? What shoes?" Cricket said, equally confused.

"Fuck your shoes, Andy. Tell us about the Cactus," Jeff urged, turning the floor back over to Cricket.

"Holy shit! You were there?" said Andy, now getting up to speed.

"Shut up and let her tell it."

"The place was packed. You could hardly move. We went to see Cold Gin. You know? The KISS cover band?" Cricket began.

"Shit! We missed that."

"Sorry," Andy offered sarcastically, as if their party was a poor substitute for an evening with four art school drop-outs who'd taken to dressing up like the world's premiere geriatric glam-band.

"Anyway," she continued, "it was way late, and I was pretty messed up, but..." Each of them had now lit up and settled in for story time.

"We're sitting in the back, you know, by the pinball machine. It's me and Pete, and four or five others. I can't remember. So, the band breaks into *Flaming Youth*, and we head straight for the front."

"So, what happened?" Andy asked, mostly just wanting to say something.

"You really don't have *any* patience at all do you?" said Cricket.

"No."

"So, there we are, rockin' out, and then out of nowhere, BAM!" She punctuated the point with enough gusto to startle her audience.

"Apparently, Cold Gin thought it would be a good idea to set off fuckin' flash pots inside the Cactus. You know, to give it that real KISS feeling?"

71

Jeff couldn't believe her. "They let 'em bring in flash pots?"

"Who knows? But it happened," Cricket explained. "So, anyway. The band is set up in front of that big window by the street, you know."

"Oh, shit," Andy didn't have to try very hard at all to imagine the resulting carnage.

"They get near the end, and… BOOM! The fucking pots go off, right underneath that big ass window. It might have been the loudest thing I've ever heard. The window couldn't take it. The whole fucking thing blew up and shot out onto Paxton Street. A couple of people got cut up pretty bad."

"That explains the police convention down there this morning," said Ellen.

"So, what else did the paper say?" Jeff asked, now engrossed.

Cricket had stalled, and was eyeing the unopened Budweiser on the table.

Andy grabbed the beer. "You want one?"

"Sure. Thanks," she said, and reached out to receive the cold fresh bottle. He was hyper aware of his hand touching hers, and a small bolt of electricity ran through him as his pinky finger swept lightly across the back of her hand as he withdrew.

Cricket uncapped the bottle and started again. "The blast was loud. I mean like shotgun loud. In fact, that's exactly what it sounded like. And you know how small the Cactus is. Well, I guess that's what everybody else thought it sounded like too. And when the window bought it, all hell broke loose.

"You guys remember when that guy got shot, down at Riley's Pub?" she asked. They all nodded their heads, recalling the botched robbery which had left one man dead, and a whole bar full of people emotionally scarred for life.

"Well, the Cactus is too small to handle any of that kind of bullshit. One person thinks they hear a gunshot and starts freakin' out; suddenly, you've got a riot on your hands."

"What did the band do?" Ellen asked.

"What *could* they do? They'd fucked up. But it was too late. Every drunk in the place made a beeline for the doors at the same time. The whole place was probably empty in three minutes flat. We stuck around 'til the cops came, and I never saw the band come out. There was no fire, just the explosion from the flash pots. I guess they knew there was no other danger, and they stayed inside, hiding. They were probably too embarrassed to face the crowd in the parking lot."

"Jesus Christ," Andy said, at a loss for anything else.

"Exactly. Jesus fuckin' Christ man," Cricket agreed, now reaching into her oversized hip bag and retrieving the Sunday edition of the Bradford Exchange.

"And here's the really crazy part. Listen to this. Jessica Hammond, 21, of Willow Creek has been missing since the incident occurred early Sunday morning. Authorities have not ruled out the possibility of foul play in her disappearance," Cricket quoted.

"Who's Jessica Hammond?" Andy asked.

"Like I know," Cricket scolded. "She's just some random chick who went to see a Cold Gin show, like everybody else we know who wasn't here last night. Except, she wound up slipping off the face of the planet. Coulda just as easily been me or you."

"Nah-uh," said Andy, "Not me. I was hanging out with the shoes."

"What's all this bullshit about shoes?"

"You can read about that in *tomorrow*'s paper," he said to Cricket, quite pleased with himself. He turned to Jeff, still eager to regale him with the tale of their triumph. "Dude, you gotta come see it. We went earlier and it…"

Ellen cut him off again. "She's not just some random girl to her parents or her boyfriend, or *somebody*."

"That would be nice," replied Cricket, just under her breath.

"What?" asked Jeff.

"Nothing. Never mind," she said, making eye contact with him. "Hey. Can I talk to you for a minute?" she asked, already on her way toward his room.

The two of them rose, leaving Andy and Ellen to exchange puzzled glances. Andy leaned back on the couch and began to mentally lick his wounds after yet another unfruitful go-round with the enchanting Cricket Lowe.

"What the hell is wrong with her?" Andy asked through a cloud of smoke.

"What? Just because the girl won't sleep with you, she's a psycho or something?"

"I was just trying to tell Jeff… You know, never mind. Fuck you."

"Can't. I'm crazy too, remember?" It was her final taunt as she reached for the broom she'd carried into the Den. A second later she was gone too.

Andy sulked in silence, but only for a moment. Knowing he had no audience, he grabbed another trash bag and headed back to the battle.

A few minutes later, Jeff and Cricket emerged from his bedroom. Jeff had changed shirts and was carrying a black backpack on his shoulder.

"Looking good, man," Jeff said of the much cleaner room.

"Where are you going?" Andy asked, his tone almost parental.

"To Overton. Cricket's in a jam and needs a ride back to her folks' house."

Cricket was waiting in the other room, leaning against the couch which had reclaimed its spot from the drum kit.

"When are you coming back?" Andy wanted to know.

"Tomorrow. Early probably. If that's okay with you, Dad."

"Fine, don't worry about your Mother and me," Andy played along, putting his arm around Ellen. "We'll get along fine without ya. You just go then."

"Oh grow up," Ellen finally said. "I swear you two are lovers or something."

Sometimes it was hard for her to understand the strange relationship the two boys shared. For sure they were friends – oftentimes the best of; brothers even. But like brothers, they fought constantly; incapable of being too near or too far apart from one another for very long. Mostly they battled with words, but they weren't above occasional fisticuffs

75

either. Ellen loved them both, like brothers, too, but sometimes found it exhausting jumping in or out of the middle.

"By the way," Jeff turned to Andy, "good luck on your interview tomorrow. Maybe you won't have to move," he said, wanting to believe it. "Later." And out the door they went.

Almost as quickly as they'd closed it, Andy reopened the front door and chased after them.

"Hey, Cricket!" he called from the porch.

"Yeah?"

"Are you holding? We're kinda slim after last night."

"Nope. Sorry." There was a tenderness in her tone that was alien to him and he thought it was the sweetest sounding rejection he'd ever heard.

"That's cool. See you later." He wished for a longer exchange between them, but she was already walking away.

Andy lingered for a moment on the porch. He watched with fascination as Cricket strode through the tiny patch of too-tall grass in their front yard towards Jeff's waiting truck. Her long blue and white tie-dyed skirt bobbed and nipped at her ankles as she walked. The tight cotton tank top she wore became almost obscenely white in the bright sunlight. Jeff was already behind the wheel, the door ajar, and Andy watched him fool with the radio knobs for a second before turning away. He heard the truck's doors close behind him as he walked back into the house.

17

Ellen was sweeping the front room as he made his return, a lit Marlboro hanging from her lips. The house would pass for clean, mostly because they just felt like quitting. Andy grabbed the other full bag of trash from the central room, and headed once more for the door.

"Leave it open," Ellen implored. "It smells like ass in here."

Again the wall was rudely introduced to the swinging door.

"What are you doing today?" she asked.

"Not a God-damned thing," he answered, with extreme pleasure.

"Yeah, me neither. I was thinking of having a few drinks and then trying to figure out what to do with that damned table."

"Still?" Andy asked, as if the matter had been pending for years. He was leisurely thumbing through the Sunday Exchange which Cricket had so kindly donated to the house. He often bought one himself, but today she'd saved him the trouble and money. And as a bonus, he noticed the cheap rag paper still carried a hint of the strange herbal scent she wore.

"Yeah, well, I've been busy," Ellen replied, through the wall. She'd gone back to her bedroom and left Andy alone with the paper.

He sat busily dividing the sections of the gigantic Sunday edition into two neat piles. There were only certain ones in which he was interested, and he liked to separate the wheat from the chafe before reading a single word.

His selections were always the same. Always the front page, the classifieds, and the comics - in that order. Looking for a job, which had become a full time position itself lately, was awfully depressing, and it helped to chase the defeat with some foolishness. And finally, the sports page. This he considered the dessert of the exercise, the cherry on top.

Satisfied with his stacks, he left them and walked lazily to Ellen's door. Poking his head inside, he found her cleaning piles of "stuff" off of a makeshift wooden table.

Among the things he loved most about her was the diversity of her interests. Ellen had a ton of hobbies, and she excelled at most of them. But she lacked motivation and follow-through. Ellen painted, played the violin, viola and piano quite well, and had recently begun trying her hand at woodworking. Eventually she'd hoped to combine her passions, learning to sculpt masterful musical instruments.

Her first project was considerably less ambitious. It was a simple table, qualifying as such by having five uniform legs and a relatively flat surface. It was ugly, and kind of wobbly, but not too bad as a first shot at carpentry. The two-foot-by-six-foot surface had become increasingly cluttered with random items, and had all but disappeared along the far wall of her room.

"What are you going to do to it?" asked Andy, leaning against the cheap wood paneling that covered the walls of her room.

"Don't know. But it needs something. I might just paint the thing."

"That's boring."

"I agree. Help me take this bitch out back."

They each grabbed an end of the table and began working it out of her room, into the tiny hallway through the kitchen. Stopping at the back door, Ellen propped her end up on one knee and reached behind herself to get the door. Andy could lift reasonably heavy stuff, but had learned the hard way that his bad balance made him unfit to carry furniture while walking backwards.

"Damn it's nice out here," she said, inhaling the fresh air.

"A helluva lot nicer than in there."

"No doubt. Hey, go turn on your stereo, will you?"

"Groovy tunes comin' up!" He climbed the stairs and took an immediate left, past their other bathroom and into his bedroom, which overlooked the back yard.

Sunday afternoon hangover? Manual labor outside in the warm pre-summer Bradford sun? The conditions begged for Led Zeppelin, and there was no better place to start than *Houses of the Holy*. Andy grinned wide, happily watching Ellen ponder the table. The din of *The Song Remains the Same* began to wash over the yard as he went to grab his stacks of paper and rejoin her.

18

Jeff's black pickup rolled out of the gas station and hung a right. Down the entrance ramp they went, merging onto Interstate 26. Traffic was light and moving fast. Overton was just over a hundred miles from Bradford, about an hour and a half away by Jeff's math.

But time was irrelevant. Things had turned out well for him. Cricket had offered him fifty bucks to drive a hundred miles; well, two hundred counting the return. But getting paid to cruise the open highway with a pretty girl and good tunes was a helluva lot better than cleaning the house, at any price.

Jeff rolled down his window, and lit a cigarette as Cricket bent forward to retrieve her brown bag from the floorboard. Mick Jagger was still belting *Heartbreaker* through the truck's four speakers, but not so loudly that she couldn't hear his question.

"You don't waste any time do you?"

"Sorry, I didn't know you weren't ready," she cooed.

She had gone to her satchel, retrieved a plastic sandwich bag and began unrolling it in her lap. The pungent stink of the neon-green grass made its way to Jeff's nose. She reached into the suede sack, and brought out a book of extra-wide rolling papers. Harvesting the last two leaves, she tossed the empty package out the window.

"I thought you told Andy you didn't have shit."

"I did. But don't take it personally, it's all just part of the game," she said with a smirk.

"Why is there always a game? I'd give anything for a normal girl who's just straight-up."

"You think you would. But if you *had* a straight-up girl, she'd probably bore you to death. Men require intrigue."

"Whatever," he said, knowing she was right.

"So you don't mind then? We don't have to smoke it now. I just wanted to roll one. I like to roll joints. I find it relaxing."

For the next couple of minutes, Jeff drove on in silence, half-watching her slender fingers work the large buds into more manageable shake. Spreading the pieces evenly, she folded the paper and began to roll it atop an empty Girl Scout cookie box she'd found behind the seat.

She held the perfectly round joint aloft for his approval. "Ta Dah! Anytime you're ready, big boy."

"Very nice."

The roadside sign ahead told them that Overton was now about eighty-five miles away.

"Fire it up!" With a devious grin, he reached down and located a pair of silver framed sunglasses. The radio was absent for a moment as Jeff flipped sides of the compilation tape they had been listening to.

Seconds later, the first galloping bass notes of Swervedriver's *Deep Seat* began to fill the truck's small cab, as Cricket set fire to the joint.

Sweet, stout smoke came forth as Jeff activated the truck's cruise control. Set at a modest 72 mph, they'd still make some pretty good time into Overton.

She passed him the burning stick and Jeff lifted the smoke to his lips and pulled hard. It burnt his lungs and throat, but left a very nice taste. He held his breath as long as he could, and exhaled, passing it back to Cricket.

A warm fuzz filled Jeff's brain, accentuating his joy in hearing one of his favorite pieces of music on the planet.

"Do you know this one?" he asked her, smiling.

"No," Cricket admitted. She liked music, but didn't quite love it the way many in their circle seemed to. She'd been at plenty of gatherings that devolved into the boys waxing over how 'great' or 'amazing' or 'life-changing' a particular song or album was. She got the sense he was headed to that place now, and was actually a little surprised when he didn't.

"That's some pretty stiff shit, Cricket."

"Yeah. Cold Gin is cheesy, but the real hardcore freaks come crawlin' out of the woodwork when they play, and they're always holdin'."

"That's a fucked-up story about the Cactus."

"Yeah. After a while though, you get tired of crazy shit like that happening to you."

"Nothing like that has ever happened to me," he said, gratefully.

"Careful what you wish for," she cautioned.

Cricket was a weird one. Jeff knew she was eccentric, and had learned that with Cricket Lowe in the mix, just about anything could happen. Even so, he could never have foreseen what was about to go down.

Jeff was busy adjusting the level of his window, and immersing himself in the sonic tidal wave emanating from the truck's shitty speakers. He didn't even notice Cricket fumbling through her bag again. But when she withdrew her svelte hand and he saw it was now clutching a silver pistol with a pearl colored grip, he snapped to attention. Jeff was

82

forced into an incredulous double-take, which ultimately paid off. Upon further review, he recognized the pistol for the toy cap gun it was. It was one of those Lone Ranger six-shooters, with the rolls of red caps you loaded on the side. Every boy, and apparently some girls, their age had probably had one at one time or another growing up, but it'd been years since Jeff had seen one.

"What the fuck is that for?" Jeff asked.

"It's not for anything, it's a toy. It's for fun," she said, smirking.

"Guns aren't *for fun,* Cricket. They're serious."

"Not this one," she smiled and pointed it straight at him. "Jesus, take it easy. You sound just like tight-ass Andy."

"No, I don't," Jeff answered. "Besides, he's not *always* wrong, you know."

"Really? So why are you always bustin' his balls about everything?"

"Somebody's got to. I mean, he's a mess, but I still love the guy. He's like family. But he's his own worst enemy. If he was half as motivated as he was smart, none of us would be sweatin' his future right now."

"Why do you care?" she asked, spinning the toy gun around her slender index finger. "The future takes care of itself."

"That may be true. But people have to take care of each other – even our idiot brothers." Jeff had been glad for the break this little unplanned road trip had provided, and the reminder of the mounting tension back home was unwelcome. He tried desperately to think of another topic, but all he could come up with was: "Stop pointing that shit at me!"

As he finished his thought, she playfully pulled the trigger. The gun produced an audible click, but nothing else as the plastic hammer fell. Still, on instinct alone, Jeff fidgeted nervously behind the wheel.

"Geez, lighten up," she repeated and buried the barrel an inch deep in her mouth, clicking off another round of nothing. He was beginning to remember his passenger's penchant for crazy drama. But now, like a kid who'd instantly regretted his decision to brave the baddest roller coaster in the park, it was too late. He was strapped in and the car was already clicking up the first big hill.

She put her hand gently on his knee and squeezed lightly. "This isn't real, you know?" He smiled uneasily at her, not knowing how else to respond.

#

A blood-red Ford Taurus cruised in the right lane ahead of them as they crested a long, gradual hill on I-26. Jeff hit the blinker and changed lanes, looking to pass the slower traffic.

"You've got no sense of humor," she criticized.

Cricket rolled her window all the way down, as Jeff's truck pulled alongside the Taurus. Holding the toy gun tightly in both hands, she popped up and leaned out of the window, just as the two vehicles drew even.

"BANG!" she howled, clicking the gun wildly and repeatedly at the unsuspecting driver, her long blond hair flapping insanely in the highway-speed wind. "You're dead, motherfucker!"

Jeff never saw it coming.

"Jesus, Cricket!" he screamed, grabbing a handful of her white cotton top and reeling her back into the cab. "What the fuck is wrong with you?"

The Taurus slammed on its brakes and let the truck fly by. Cricket doubled over with laughter.

Jeff checked the rear view mirror to find the Taurus had filed in behind them, continuing to follow at a safer distance. The truck's cruise control had disengaged when he'd braked to collect her, and Jeff now eased down on the accelerator, resuming a practical speed. He looked over to find her curiously studying him. Cricket smiled just wide enough to reveal the two rows of perfect teeth that hid behind her thin lips.

"You have to admit, that was pretty fucking funny."

"I couldn't tell you. I didn't see a thing."

She laughed again. "Trust me, it was funny. You shoulda seen his face. I can't believe he hasn't pulled over to check his pants yet."

He checked his mirror again. Nothing. Jeff threw his head to the left just in time to see the dark red sedan crossing through his blind spot and drawing even again.

"Holy shit! What's he doing?" Jeff blurted.

"Probably coming up to give us the bird."

Compared to what Jeff actually saw, their victim's middle finger would have been completely welcomed, or even comforting. The driver of the Taurus, a rotund man with thick glasses, held aloft a simple notebook. Scrawled quite legibly, in characters four inches high, was the license number of Jeff's truck.

"He's got my tag number!" said Jeff, not exactly sure what that meant.

"So what?" said Cricket, still unworried.

"Fuck!" cried Jeff as the Taurus stayed parallel.

"What?"

"Look!" he said, pointing to their new friend.

The man was now holding the most powerful non-lethal weapon known to man. Clutched in his liver-spotted hand was a cellular phone.

"Fuck!" Jeff repeated. "He just called the cops!"

The smile disappeared from Cricket's face. "Are you sure?" she asked softly.

"Pretty fucking sure."

"What should we do?" Cricket asked, now showing concern for the first time.

"Well, for starters, you could put the fucking gun away," Jeff suggested.

Without so much as a whisper, the toy found its way back inside the brown suede bag at her feet.

"Don't worry," she said, attempting to tender the situation. "He probably just wanted to scare us."

"Mission, fucking, accomplished! I *so* don't need this bullshit."

"Just keep driving."

Cruise control, much like his sense of comfort, had gone straight out the window as Jeff eased the truck down the highway at five miles an hour below the posted speed limit.

Seventy-one miles outside of Overton, the situation officially went from bad to worse. As they cleared the top of the next ridge, with the Taurus still very much in tow, they passed the first police car. The cruiser was backed neatly into the brush on the side of the road, but its front end and ominous rack of blue lights was perfectly visible from their vantage point.

The truck eased past, well within the speed limit. The Taurus, now at least a hundred feet back, also passed the cop, at which point the cruiser casually entered the highway. The wave of fear that washed over Jeff at that moment was unlike anything he'd ever experienced.

Looking almost exclusively in the rear view mirror now, Jeff watched the cruiser steadily advance on them. His brain discarded the possibility of coincidence, and ran straight into controlled panic.

"Turn that shit off!" demanded Jeff, uncharacteristically ruffled. He was suddenly failing to appreciate the mammoth, churning, swirling guitars he had been enamored with just moments ago.

Cricket sat beside him, barely breathing at all. "Why hasn't he pulled us over?" she wanted to know.

"Careful what you ask for," Jeff threw back at her, as it all began to fall apart. The three-car caravan was now running at forty-five miles an hour along the slope of the approaching curve.

There, hidden in the shadows of the overpass, was Cruiser # 2. Jeff's speed was fine, but his anxiety meter blasted into the red zone as Cruiser #2 pulled in behind them and joined the party.

"We're fucked," Jeff said. "We can't even ditch the weed, Cricket. We're going to fuckin' jail."

"Oh shit, the weed. I forgot," she said, snapping to and reaching once more for the bag at her feet.

"Take out the gun," Jeff said, now with an eerie calm. "Take it out, and open the cap chamber so they can see it's a toy. Lay it right on the dash."

Cricket did as she was told, emerging from the bag with the gun in one hand and the dope in the other. She flipped up the side panel and set the toy pistol down between two tape cases on the dash.

"We can't hide that, Cricket," Jeff was sure. "We're fucked."

"You just keep driving till they cut on the blues. And roll the windows down to air this bitch out," she said, starting to gather her long skirt up from the bottom.

"You're gonna put it in your panties?" asked Jeff, not having a better idea, but not liking that one much either. "What if they frisk us?"

"I don't wear underwear," she said plainly. "And if they frisk me where this is going, we'll sue the whole fucking state."

Just then, the rear view mirror erupted in a sea of flashing blue light.

"Fuck," Jeff said again. "Do it then! And make it quick, cause this is it."

"Don't watch me!" she demanded.

"Just do it!" he snapped, very aware of what he *wasn't* watching.

She winced slightly as her body accepted the contraband.

The truck slowed. Jeff waited only until Cricket had opened her eyes and let back down her skirt to start pulling over. He'd been fumbling to light a cigarette, in an attempt to masque any lingering smell from the weed. They exchanged nervous smiles as the vehicle left the road and came to rest on the shoulder.

Jeff had barely shifted into park before the vehicle was engulfed. From out of thin air, the first two cruisers were joined by a third, then a fourth. A brown four-door with no official markings approached from the side and came to a halt a few feet from Cricket's door.

"Goddamn," said Jeff, in utter disbelief. "Whoever's robbing banks and liquor stores around here, has it fuckin' made right now."

A nervous laugh escaped the tightly pursed lips of his passenger. "What now?"

"Whatever they want. Sit still. Don't say shit until someone asks you a question. Answer it honestly and then shut up again."

The irony of it all was not the least bit lost on him. Roughly twelve hours ago, he and Andy had been advising their Shoe Tree conspirators on the finer points of interacting with law enforcement. Their theories, which was all they really were in truth, were about to be tested by fire. Most of the time Jeff Aaron had confidence in spades, but now, with Johnny Law bearing down on them, he was sweating bullets and praying hard.

The engine was off but the keys still hung from the ignition. They both sat transfixed as two officers approached in cinema slow motion. Both held their service revolvers drawn high, and very visible.

Jeff clutched the hard plastic steering wheel, mindful to keep his hands in plain view. Cricket's arms lay palms up in her lap, uncrossed – the least threatening position she could think to assume. The officers' eternal approach culminated with the sickening thud of a steel revolver butt crashing against the driver's side door.

"Hands up!" the officer shouted at the open window. The doors' seals were broken and both passengers were snatched from the cab by their own armed escorts.

The blinding whirlwind of justice crashed down upon them as everything blurred into strobes of blue light and noise. Jeff could hear a plethora of garbled questions being hurled at both he and Cricket. Police radios buzzed and the sound of a hundred passing cars filled his ears to capacity.

The two young threats to public safety stood side by side, clutching the truck's tailgate. Cricket's slender fingers held tightly to the sun-warmed metal. Facing the truck, they watched helplessly as two new officers entered the vehicle and began to search it. Instantly, the cap gun which still lay chamber-open on the dash was recovered and brought to an officer who stood somewhere behind them.

In the odd silence at the center of this shit storm, Jeff found himself wondering how all of this commotion and drama must have looked to the passersby; business men, couples, whole families en route to someplace more friendly. Somewhere on that highway, carloads of children bombarded their weary and suddenly uncomfortable parents with volleys of questions, and stared wildly at the coolest thing they'd ever seen in real, three-dimensional life. The smallest of smiles crossed his lips, but it didn't stay long.

The crisp sweep of the officer's hard shoe against Jeff's ankle was enough to break up that daydream. His legs spread wider, leaving him prone to his captor's intentions. Cricket fared no better, as a taller, thinner arm of the law executed the same maneuver on her.

"Ow!" she said, possibly attempting to elicit some sympathy or even an apology from her oppressor; neither came of course.

The frisking began at Jeff's midsection. The officer's ham-fists moved around Jeff's waistband in vain. His pockets were invaded, their contents

90

emptied onto the lowered tailgate of the truck. One black wallet, one pink plastic cigarette lighter, a loose dollar bill and forty one cents in change, and three ibuprofen tablets, and that was it. No bullets, no drugs, no knives, no nothing. In fact, nothing more dangerous than expired headache medicine was found, which as far as he knew was not illegal. So far, so good.

Cricket, on the other hand, had no pockets. Her white tank top hugged her form tightly, and plainly concealed nothing more than what God Himself had seen fit to give her. Her attending officer ran his hands slow and firm against her curvaceous hips. His fingertips made their way around her middle and checked the waistband of her flowing skirt.

Jeff watched intently from the corner of his eye. He knew he was clean, but he caught himself actively praying that Cricket's secret remained safe. The thin cop bent on the roadside and patted her bare ankles. She recoiled slightly at the touch of his coarse skin against hers. Reaching upward, he ran those long fingers up the backs and outsides of her legs.

"Hey!" she snapped, not very innocently at all, as his dry, calloused hands neared the curve of her buttocks. The officer stopped short.

Jeff's attention was divided equally by Cricket's frisking and the two officers who had begun sifting through his backpack. The bag lay unzipped in the truck's bed as a gigantic black cop took inventory of its contents. Cricket's canvas shoulder bag also lay in the bed alongside the other objects in question.

A snickering laugh that seemed so out of place pierced the tension. It had come from the huge black cop, but was deceptively high in pitch. His enormous hands emerged from Jeff's pack and a little wave of laughter flew around the scene. Held aloft for God, and every passenger on I-26 to see, was a pair of white cotton boxer shorts, lavishly decorated with pink and red valentine hearts. Any previous benchmark Jeff may have had for embarrassment was instantly destroyed.

"Those are really cute," Cricket teased quietly.

"Shut up!" came simultaneous demands from Jeff and an officer behind them.

"Mr. Aaron. Ms. Lowe. Sit your asses down." The voice was new, but authoritative.

The newest cop, a full sheriff, directed them to sit on the tailgate, which they did, sheepishly waiting to be addressed.

"What the fuck is your problem?" the sheriff needed to know.

Recognizing a rhetorical question was a valuable skill, and both of them possessed it. Each deferred a response and awaited the next inquiry. Jeff scanned the officers' badges and registered they were being spoken to by a man named Slocum.

"I've run both your I.D.s." said the sheriff, tossing Jeff his wallet and handing Cricket hers. "Not even a speeding ticket. So why do I have twelve men out here?"

"Because..," started Jeff, apparently losing the ability to disregard rhetoric.

"Because," Slocum interrupted, "somebody thought *this* shit might be funny."

Clearly, the *shit* Slocum was referring to was the cap gun he now held clutched in his meaty fist.

"What you also failed to realize was, that your friend back there in the Taurus, is also *my* friend – off-duty Deputy Sheriff McVee, to be exact."

Jeff looked at Cricket as if to say *you stupid bitch*.

"And really, you're pretty damned lucky," Slocum pointed out, slipping the dark sunglasses from his face for maximum effect. "If that had been me that you'd pointed a gun at, fake or otherwise, I'd have shot you both dead on the spot, and filled out the paperwork over coffee and doughnuts on Monday fucking morning."

A pregnant pause followed as the sheriff studied their young faces for a response. He wasn't kidding either. He was merely explaining, without much exaggeration at all, how close they'd come to being dead, for no good reason at all.

"I should haul both your asses in for reckless endangerment. But with no priors for either of you, and nothing on you – it's probably not even worth the time. Besides, I think you've both probably crapped your pants enough from all the attention this little stunt has gotten you."

Cricket and Jeff sat silent and expressionless on the back of the truck.

"Lessons learned?" Slocum asked.

"Yes, sir," they offered in unison, in major disbelief of their apparent turn in fortune. They both fought the urge to smile or look at one another. Yes sir, wide-eyed obedience was the way to finish this one.

Slocum turned away and barked at the officers still milling around the busted scene. "Pack it up boys. We're done."

He turned and offered a final suggestion. "Get in your car, Mr. Aaron, and drive away; the further the better. And if we ever see either of you again, you can rest assured that meeting won't have a happy ending."

"Oh yeah, and one more thing," Slocum added. Both of them turned on a dime from either side of the vehicle to hear his parting sentiment. "Happy Birthday, Priscilla."

The words made no sense at all to Jeff. He'd known Cricket for over a year, and in that time, the topic of her actual first name had somehow never come up.

"*Priscilla?*" Jeff mouthed over the top of the cab, trying not to laugh or even smile in the presence of the police.

"Yeah. So, what? Shut the fuck up," she sneered, opening the door.

"Priscilla," he said once more to himself as he gathered the emptied contents of his pack from the back of the truck and placed them back inside.

By the time Jeff had fallen back behind the wheel, Slocum and his boys had merged into traffic, and left them on the roadside alone. In that moment, neither of them knew quite what to say.

"It's your birthday?' Jeff settled on.

"Yeah. That's part of the reason I needed to get home. You know, there's some things you just need to do at home."

"So, what do you want for your birthday?" He asked, turning the truck's engine.

Cricket reached across him and turned the key back, pulling it out of the ignition before he could engage the gears. The motion was swift and catlike. Her left hand landed mid-way up his thigh as her right hand withdrew with the keys.

"Kiss me," she said. It was almost a question.

Jeff faltered and pretended not to have heard her. "What?" he faked.

"That was the most exciting experience I've ever had fully clothed, and I want you to kiss me." Her voice was rock steady and dominant, further fueling his hesitance.

Cricket saw the look in Jeff's eyes, and she understood. It wasn't often that your best-looking friend of the opposite sex asks you flat out to plant one on her, and he was dazed.

Cricket slid closer to him and watched his blue eyes close as she drew near. They met with a friendly, confused passion, each no doubt recalling multiple instances when such a thing could have happened but never did. It was a short-lived union. Cricket withdrew her mouth and formed a lovely wide smile, before Jeff really even had a chance to enjoy the exchange.

"Thank you," she whispered.

"Um, sure," he answered, a bit pink in the cheeks. "Happy Birthday, Cricket."

"It's Priscilla, remember? But if you ever tell a single living soul, I'll rip your nuts off and feed them to you," she threatened, still smiling.

"About your name, or about that kiss?"

"Yes," she clarified with a giggle as she tossed him the keys. "Now take me home."

The rest of their trip was downright boring by comparison. The jumbled ramblings of a local classic rock radio station, and Cricket's sparse directional commands provided most of the commentary. Thirty minutes after they'd slipped Slocum's noose, Jeff's truck pulled into the Lowe family driveway and came to rest behind her father's silver Mercedes-Benz. The house was large and set safely in a posh suburb of Overton.

Including their unexpected visit with the sheriff and his boys, the trip had taken a little over 2 hours. In time and distance, they weren't worlds away from Cornwall Street. But everything seemed foreign and unbalanced to Jeff.

Somewhere along the way, and without him even having noticed, Cricket managed to rescue the luckiest plastic bag on the planet. The engine idled and they shared another silence before she turned to go.

"You'll be alright tonight then?"

"Yeah, fine. I'm gonna crash with Vince out in Jasper. It's been a while since I've been out this way. It's not far, and I could use a break from the usual scenery."

"That's cool," she said, flipping the wad of rolled up plastic into his lap.

"No thanks. I think I just quit."

"Whatever," she replied, dismissing the possibility of his statement. "But I don't want it either after all that. Why don't you give it to Andy? But if you tell him a single thing about where that's been I'll..."

"Feed me my own testicles?" Jeff guessed.

"Worse."

Gathering her bag, she turned once more to face her friend.

"I love you, Jeff," she said, with a ting of sweet sadness. It was the most serious thing he'd ever heard her say. His distraction granted her enough of a pause to plant another light peck on his lips and slip out the door.

Jeff sat behind the wheel of his truck, trying to understand the past few hours. He was tired and confused, but he was also not in jail, and he decided that was a pretty good place to be. He watched her bound up the drive. The canvas shoulder bag bumped and bounced lightly off her hip with each step, and it made him smile.

"I'll be back tomorrow morning. See you then," he called through the open window.

Cricket was most of the way up the drive. She was still within earshot, but continued without acknowledging him. Jeff ran his sweaty hands through his hair, eased the truck into reverse and drove away.

19

The front door of the house on Cornwall Street flew open, again crashing wildly into the wall behind it. Even when Andy was simply being careless, that wall still suffered. But when he was angry or frustrated, it really took a beating.

Andy's tirades had grown more frequent in the wake of his recent job search, and he sadistically preferred to share them with an audience. His entrance this morning was plenty loud but also premature. Jeff was not yet back from Overton, and Ellen was still fast asleep.

This would not do. Anger of this magnitude deserved to be witnessed, he thought. Several items suddenly found themselves dangerously in his path. A steady stream of pillows, books, a chair, and even the cordless phone from atop the central room's table took flight and crashed to the hardwood floor on his way to the kitchen.

Sadly, Ellen knew the score even before she opened her bedroom door and made her way towards the ruckus.

Andy's suit coat lay crumpled at her feet as she entered the living room. Following the sound of crashing cabinet doors and clinking ice cubes, Ellen turned the corner to the kitchen. The freezer door was open, obscuring his upper body from her view, but she could tell he was still wearing a tie. She approached with caution.

A second glance revealed the brown paper bag clutched in his right hand; vodka for sure. Apparently the interview had not gone well.

"Andy?" she said softly, as the freezer door swung away from her and bumped shut.

"What?" he asked, not looking at her. He'd meant to snarl, but found himself lacking the energy.

Andy's eyes were large and wounded; deeper and shinier than normal by a lot. He was either remarkably sober, or about to break down and cry. His thick dark hair, which was often held at bay by a dollop of styling gel, now towered disheveled over his furrowed brow as if he'd been repeatedly running his angry hands through it.

She watched in silence as her roommate poured three fingers of vodka into a tall glass and then searched the refrigerator for a mixer.

"Breakfast?" he asked, lifting the bottle at her.

"No thanks. Do you wanna talk?"

"What the fuck is there to talk about? It's over. I failed, and it's over. I'm outta here."

"Damn, Andy. That's pretty dramatic, even for you. It's not that bad."

"No, it *is*. I might as well call my parents right now and tell them to get the fucking basement ready for me."

She watched as he tried to swallow his failure along with the alcohol. Ellen could tell there were tears hiding just behind the surface, but he was determined not to set them free.

Her roommates may have considered her one of the boys, but Ellen's maternal instincts were strong; and they'd gotten an earnest workout from living with these two. She drew nearer and wrapped her strong arms around him, pressing a gentle kiss against his freshly shaven cheek.

"I'm really sorry. I still love you though."

She held him and waited, treading lightly and feeling out the pause in his tirade. She knew he was hurt; his mind racing a mile a minute in an attempt to process this latest failure.

"I love you too, El." He'd said it a thousand times before, in various states of sobriety or merriment, but never had he meant it quite as he did then and there in that nasty kitchen.

"Enough mush," Ellen said, releasing her embrace and heading straight for the Den. "Come in here and talk to me."

She was already cuddled up on the couch by the time he joined her. Taking his customary position across the table, Andy eased into the overstuffed rocker and dug for his cigarettes. Breaking his own rule, he lit a pre-meal smoke before extending the pack to Ellen.

"Cancer?"

"Please," she said, not even realizing he'd transferred enough of his anxiety to jump-start her subtly tugging and twirling her hair.

#

Andy grabbed the remote control and summoned forth the warm, consoling glow of television. It didn't take him long to find what he was looking for. Talk shows, goddammit—that was the answer. Any unemployed person worth their salt knew that.

Talk shows had one major redeeming quality as far as Andy was concerned. They were entertaining, for sure, but that was just gravy. The real meat of the matter was in the power of rationalization. It was simple. Anyone willing to go on national television—whether to solve a major crisis, win back an estranged lover, or just to argue pointlessly with someone they hated – had to be far more pathetic than the audiences that couldn't wait to cheer or mock them. Yes sir, daytime talk shows offered those who watched them one gigantic comforting truth – *my life might suck, but at least I'm not this asshole on TV*. Yep. *It could always be worse* he'd thought on many occasions, and now it was worth repeating. 'I am unemployed and worthless, but I *could* be bitching about being unemployed and worthless on national television.'

The *Mack Riley Show* was Andy's favorite by a mile. Nasty, irreverent, and juvenile, it also created just the background Andy needed to recount the details of his brutal morning. Trying harder than normal to relax, Andy forced himself to breathe and to take smaller sips of his disappearing cocktail. "I never saw it coming, El."

20

A hundred miles away, things weren't going any better. Jeff had told Cricket he wanted to pick her up as early as possible the next morning, so he could get back to Bradford. Cricket had never been terribly connected to the concept of time, and Jeff assumed that no matter when he pulled up to the Lowes' house, she'd probably be ready to leave within five minutes.

The late morning air was cooler than normal, and pleasant. There were no clouds in the sky and the sun shone bright enough to hurt his eyes. Donning dark sunglasses, he pulled the truck along the sharp curve of road which led back to Cricket's parents' place. A dull ache rose in his stomach as Jeff approached a four-way stop. Directly across the intersection, a Blooming County sheriff's car came rolling to a stop. While he couldn't think of a single illegal thing he had done since waking up, Jeff found himself still a bit gun shy from yesterday's adventure. Then he remembered the small sack of marijuana Cricket had left with him, and the minor discomfort began to escalate.

Jeff looked both ways, twice, and appeared to be waiting for the cop to pull through, even though he clearly had the right of way. He pressed the accelerator and rolled past the officer, who took no real notice of him as he went by.

A quarter mile down the road, Jeff turned left onto Crescent Circle. Cricket's parents' house was the ninth down on the right, as she'd reminded him last night. Simple enough instructions, except for one thing; as soon as Jeff hung the left turn onto Crescent, what he saw made him immediately loose count. The gathering was small, at least in comparison to yesterday, but no less conspicuous. A few houses down the circle, on the right, stood two more police cars, but they were not alone. The obnoxious orange and white top of a county hospital ambulance loomed over the blue bulbs of the cruisers. Jeff somehow knew that continuing to count houses would be unnecessary. The low rumbling in his stomach was now a thorough stabbing bordering on nausea.

He inched toward the house until he neared the perimeter of response vehicles, then pulled to the curb and cut the engine. It was almost noon on a Monday, and while most of their neighbors' homes lay quiet and empty, the Lowes' driveway was filled with cars and activity. Mrs. Lowe's grey Mercedes sat next to her husband's red Audi A8, both exactly as they were when Jeff had dropped Cricket off the night before.

Jeff had never met either one of her parents, but he'd heard Cricket bitch often enough about them to make it unnecessary. He didn't have the right to assume they were bad people or bad parents, but according to Cricket, there was no shortage of screaming, fighting, and drama in the Lowe home.

Everyone yelled at everyone else. Cricket's mom and dad both yelled at her, until she left, and then they kept yelling at each other. Jeff felt bad for her. He tried to empathize with her situation, but he had no context for what it must be like to live in a family where no one seemed to like anyone else. He was one of the few people he knew whose birth parents were still happily married.

Jeff moved closer, walking along the driver's side of the ambulance until nearly colliding with a young EMS technician who was rounding the front of the vehicle with more speed than focus.

"'Scuse me," said the tech, too casually.

"Sorry." Jeff was still trying to gauge the situation. He noticed the tech was not much older than him.

"What happened in there?" asked Jeff, expecting no answer.

"Just doing our jobs."

Jeff couldn't decide if he was being cavalier or intentionally vague. In either case, the tech's nonchalance suggested to Jeff he could probably ask another question without being shooed away.

"Some sort of accident?" Jeff quizzed as the young EMT began to climb into the driver's seat.

"No. I'm pretty sure not," the tech said, with certainty. It was already more information than a more seasoned or sensitive colleague would have offered, but he didn't stop there.

He grabbed the door frame by the bottom of the opened window and pulled it to, now sitting a foot taller than Jeff stood.

"It's a shame, too," the tech added for no reason. "Beautiful young girl like that, no older than us, just gone."

Jeff was thankful not to have been looking the tech in the eyes as he spoke the words. He was standing so close he could feel the ambulance's hefty engine roar to life. Seconds later, the tech punched it into drive and drove away. None of his lights were flashing.

Realizing he was now standing conspicuously alone in front of what could be a crime scene — one to which he could in some twisted way be connected if the right people asked the right questions — Jeff turned and shuffled back to his truck. He slumped low behind the wheel, almost hiding beneath the dashboard. He needed to believe that the officers from the two empty cruisers in the Lowes' driveway had never seen him. More specifically, he needed to believe that the chance of him answering any questions about whatever the fuck happened in that house was absolutely zero. He raised his head like a prairie dog over the dash, and watched the still, empty street before him. Sad, angry tears welled up in his eyes, but he managed to drop the truck into gear and pull away before losing his composure. Jeff felt certain the tech had given him all the information he needed to know she would not be rejoining him.

#

Ninety miles of open road was the best and worst thing Jeff could have hoped for. No co-pilot; no traffic; just caffeine, nicotine, music, and time. Whether he wanted it or not, he had at least an hour of soul-crushing solitude in front of him. Try as he might to vanquish them, thoughts of Cricket invaded his weary head, as the tears kept coming.

He wasn't even sure why he was crying. They hadn't been super close, but that didn't matter. He was sad, of course—death is death. But more than anything he was mad—furious really. Mad at her for doing it, and madder still for involving him. Mad at himself for not seeing it, or being able to stop it. There was a time he thought, not that long ago, when he'd been clearer, more focused; when something like this might not have gotten past him. What had happened? He found his anger drifting toward Andy, but that seemed misplaced—at least in part. Those frustrations were specific, and recent. No, if he was being honest, Jeff's own choices had put him on this road.

He filled his lungs to capacity and unleashed a series of primal screams into the rushing wind as he floored the accelerator.

21

"So, I'm sitting in this guy's office, right?" Andy started again. "And I figure, no big deal right? I've met this guy before; it's cool, no pressure. We talked for about ten minutes, about nothing really, which only made me feel more comfortable, 'cause I can talk about nothing *forever*, you know?"

"Oh, I know," she said.

"So we're talking, right? And from out of nowhere, he says he needs me to meet with another guy. Well not just another guy; the vice president of the place. 'No problem.' I told him, I'd love to meet him. Well, that's where the fucking bottom fell out," said Andy, pausing for a deep breath and another long sip of breakfast.

"So, what happened?" Ellen asked, for what seemed the eleventh time already.

"He totally kicked my ass. I fucked it up big time," the volume of Andy's voice grew louder along with his frustration. "I walked in there ready to tell this guy all about market shares and gross rating points, and every reason why I'm smart enough and creative enough to sell every flavor of shit they've got. And then he screws me!"

"He starts asking me all these personal questions. Apparently he was more interested in my marital status and long range economic plans than in seeing any of my work."

"He asked if you were married? I didn't think they were even allowed to do that."

"Yeah. I don't know. But I had no idea what to tell him or what he wanted to hear, so I told him that you and I we're engaged."

"You what!?"

"I know. How stupid is that?"

"Pretty fuckin' stupid," she agreed. "And honestly, it's a little sweet, but as proposals go, it kinda sucks."

"Ha!" he allowed himself a small smile. "Don't get me wrong, El. I think you'd make a great wife, but we both know that would end with one of us being dead, right?"

"I know," she teased. "And people would really miss you, so let's not."

They both laughed as Andy crushed the last of his Winston in the crystal ashtray between them.

"How was I supposed to know?"

"What? That they were gonna want to know something about the person they would be working with?"

"Yeah. But it got worse from there. That one question threw me off so hard, I stuttered and staggered through the whole rest of the interview. To be honest, I don't even remember what else I told them."

"But just because you got tongue-tied and a little flustered, you think that's enough to keep them from hiring you?"

"Oh, you didn't see it, El. I looked like a blithering idiot. Nobody wants a guy who can't even tell you if he's married to write ads with million dollar price tags on them. You need better communication skills than that, I'm afraid."

"Big deal," she insisted. "So you didn't get this one. That means your life is over? Just go out and find another place to work. It's not like you have to leave town, Andy."

"That's what nobody understands. For as long as I can remember, I've only wanted to do one thing–write. My whole life, people have told me it's the one thing I should be doing. And I happen to agree with them. Except now, when it really counts, I can't get anyone to *pay* me to do it for a living. I came here to get my degree so I could get a job doing what I want to do, and if I can't find that job here in Bradford, than yes, I have to leave." He was near the bottom of his screwdriver and feeling pretty ready for another round.

"But there's got to be somebody else in town you can write for."

"You don't get it. I don't want to work for just anybody. Work isn't fun enough to do for just anyone, especially creative work. I need a place that makes me get excited about *getting* to go to work, not *having* to go. Otherwise, what's the fucking point? This was probably the one place in this whole shitty little town that was even close to that for me."

"You love this shitty little town, and you know it." she said, now running low on advice and empathy. "So, what are you going to do?"

"Well, right now, I'm gonna pour myself another drink, watch the rest of Mack Riley, and wait for Jeff to get back from kissing Cricket's sweet ass."

Ellen wasn't sure there was anything left for her to say as he turned towards the television set and readjusted the volume.

#

"And so, after he left and took your son, things got worse?" asked Mack to the middle-aged woman who was obviously wearing a wig. Talk about rhetorical questions. Of course it had gotten worse, or she wouldn't be crying her eyes out on television.

"A lot worse," she blubbered. "I started drinking; well drinking more. And it really didn't help anything. I know that now."

"She must have been doing it wrong," Andy said, rising to pursue the second course of his liquid brunch. "You want one?"

"Not yet. Too early for me." Ellen replied.

"So, what's this one about?" he asked as another ad rolled.

"As far I can tell, it's a bunch of folks bitching about how good their lives used to be and how terrible they are now. Sound familiar?"

"Welcome back," Mack Riley said. "Today, we're joined by some real heroes; people living true nightmares; clutching desperately to the very edge of sanity, and somehow finding the will to go on." The hyperbole was ridiculous and masterful.

"Wow. That's a bit dramatic, even for him," said Andy after downing a mouthful of Orange Juice Plus.

"I don't know. Some of these people are really fucked up. There's this one lady who…, wait, yeah her, listen."

"Eight months?" Mack asked the young woman.

"Yes sir," she told the smug British host who was more than twice her age.

"You really stayed in your house for eight whole months?"

"Yes."

"Why?"

"It all got to be way too much for me." Small tears began to break from her eyelids as she spoke. "Last year was the worst year of my whole life. It started when my brother was killed in a factory accident. I quit working, going to school or spending time with my boyfriend. He couldn't understand why I couldn't just 'get over it', and he got pissed. He started cheating on me. Then he left me. Then, a drunk son-of-a-bitch without any insurance totalled my car, giving me back problems which the doctor said might never go away. Oh, and my dog Mickey died of cancer." She was really turning it on now, as the tears streamed down her fully flushed cheeks.

"No fucking way," blurted Ellen, now getting sucked in. "No way all that shit happens to one person in a year. No wonder she locked herself in the house. I would have, too."

"I just kept thinking it couldn't possibly get any worse. If I just stayed in the house and didn't answer the phone or the door, nothing else could get to me. I got more and more paranoid and withdrawn. I just lost faith in people in general."

"People can be very cruel." Mack comforted his guest, milking her angst for every last rating point it was worth. "I'm amazed you were even able to be with us today." The empty congratulations came complete with the box of tissues which never seemed to be too far away.

"Ding! Ding! Oh yeah, we've got a winner!" Andy shouted. "This bitch is *way* more fucked up than I am."

"I don't know, Andy. I think I heard her say she had a job," Ellen teased.

"It got to the point where I couldn't even get up in the morning. Then I hit what I call rock bottom, and I had to get help." Oh yeah, she was playing it just the way the network boys loved it – pathetic, but with a glimmer of hope.

"Tell us what happened," Riley said.

"I didn't even know how bad it had gotten. Then, one day, I realized I was sitting around the house all day, drinking boxed wine and eating ginger snaps. I gained 62 pounds. I even stopped bathing for a while." She left a beautifully pregnant pause that couldn't have been scripted any better, for the studio audience to paint their own picture.

"I looked at myself in the mirror and all I saw was this disgusting, fat, drunk shell of a woman who couldn't even think of a reason not to drive off the nearest bridge."

"Cause you didn't have a car after that fucker wrecked it!" Andy said, as he burst into laughter.

"You heartless bastard," Ellen accused. "Like you'd be turning cartwheels if all that shit happened to you."

"No. But it didn't happen to me. I just can't get a job."

"Correction. You *won't* get a job," Even before she'd finished the sentence, she knew it was a mistake.

"Fuck you, Ellen!" he said, with real venom. "What do you know? You dropped out to be a fucking bartender."

"Not really." Ellen said, now seriously offended. "More like I went out and found a way to keep living after my parents' money ran out. There's something *you* don't know shit about. You know what? Fuck you, too! It's hard to feel sorry for someone who's so good at feeling sorry for theirself."

And there it was; the ugly truth. They'd all gotten pretty good at lobbing hand grenades of good-natured bullshit at each other, but they usually knew where to draw the line. Ellen had loaded up a barrel full of real, honest-to-God truth, and shot him right in the face with it.

"That's what you think of me? Just because I can't relegate myself to working some bullshit, go nowhere job that means nothing to me? I *do* want more than that, and you should too. You're so smart and talented, and you're rotting away just like I would if I stayed here. Bradford sucks like that. Fuck Bradford."

Ellen stared at him, conflicted. She knew he was only being so mean because he was wounded. But she also knew deep down he might be right about her, and that hurt even worse. Still, telling Andy how she saw it wasn't exactly the cruelest thing she could have done.

Quiet invaded the Den as both of them sucked hard on cigarettes. Neither of them looked at the other as they waited for the tension to thin. They weren't waiting long when the unmistakable sound of the front door crashing into that poor wall broke the silence.

"Good. They're back," Andy said sulking, as if Jeff was going to waltz in and start throwing solace at him.

#

Somewhere between Overton and Bradford, the blood in Jeff's body had managed to quit flowing to his face, which was now pale and drawn. The beads of sweat dripping from his brow didn't help either. As if on auto-pilot, Jeff headed for the Den.

"Jesus!" said Ellen as he broke the threshold.

"Man, you look like french-fried shit," Andy added.

"Didn't get any sleep last night?" Ellen asked with thinly-veiled innuendo, as she moved her bare legs off the couch to make room for him. He declined and remained standing.

Jeff looked weak and dazed. "I think I might be sick."

112

"Well don't give it to me. I've had a bad enough day already," said Andy, attempting to segue back to his own suffering.

"Trust me." said Jeff. "I know all about bad days."

"Aw, poor you," Andy whined, eager to start another fire. "You had to miss cleaning the house so you could go out of town with Her Majesty."

"Not now, man," The last thing Jeff wanted right then was to argue with him.

"You're just pissed because she still won't give you any," Andy said with jealousy so obvious he may as well have been neon green.

"Fuck you, Andy!" Jeff yelled. He was going to quit there, but the juvenile smirk on his roommate's face was just enough to drive him over the edge. "Cricket's dead, you self-absorbed son-of-a-bitch!"

He didn't even wait long enough to watch it register on their faces before burying his own in his hands and beginning to cry. He'd only managed a few quiet sobs when Ellen stepped in. She rose to comfort him, but not before shooting serious eye-daggers at her other roommate. She was used to being the buffer between them when it got this way; but right then she mostly just wanted them to stop fighting.

"I ... uh... What? I.... I'm sorry, man," Andy mumbled. "What the fuck?"

"I don't know," Jeff said quietly, with his head still down, staring at the floor. "She just gave up. She did the one thing you can never do. She gave up. And worst of all, she had me drive 200 miles, just so she could shove that shit in her parents' faces. I didn't see it, but she knew yesterday when she came over here, she was never coming back."

"Oh my God." Andy said. "I'm sorry." Every bit of his righteous indignation disappeared in an instant.

113

Jeff was withdrawn, but not so much so that the rare apology from Andy Maxwell failed to register. He looked at his roommate with swollen, surprised eyes and said nothing. He had no interest in sharing the few details he knew from this morning, and he sure as hell wasn't up for telling them about their adventure on the side of I-26 just yet. For the moment, there was nothing left to say.

"Alright, we've definitely hit our quota for bullshit today," Ellen announced. "You boys need a reset button."

"Jeff", she said quietly, wrapping her arm around his shoulder and pulling him close. "if I promise you're gonna like it, are you up for a little field trip?" she asked.

"I don't know." Jeff said. "Anywhere is probably better than here right now. But I gotta take a shower, or at least change clothes," he said, rising to move toward his room at the front of the house.

"That sounds good," Andy agreed, splitting off to the house's back half to slip out of the rest of his suit.

Ellen stood alone in the small, square bit of hallway which separated the Den from her bedroom on one side and the home's main bathroom on the other. From there, she could hear each of her roommates rumbling in their respective corners. It wasn't always easy living between them – literally and figuratively – but it was a place she felt comfortable; secure even. More than anything, it felt like home, like a place worth protecting and holding together. And she did. In fact, she excelled at keeping the peace, even if her methods were sometimes a bit unorthodox.

Closing her bedroom door, she pulled off her grungy t-shirt and replaced it with a racy luminescent silver rayon disco top with three-quarter length sleeves and ambitious lapels. Next to her black denim jeans, the flashy silver seemed to explode. Satisfied with the

114

transformation, she was only slightly bothered that she had yet to bathe for the day.

She walked toward the front of the house with the confidence of a girl who knew she was the prettiest thing in the room. Jeff sat forlorn on the ratty couch. She approached with care, placing herself gently on the armrest beside him and slipping an arm around his shoulder. He twitched by reflex at her touch, but then fell into her, laying a mop of long brown hair across her lap.

"Do you want to talk about it?" she asked, stroking the locks away from his face.

"I don't know," he said. "It's not like we were even close friends."

"I get the feeling she didn't have too many of those," Ellen suggested, not sure whether the thought should have made him feel better or worse.

"But she knew I would take her there, no questions asked."

"Oh Jeff, you had no idea. You couldn't have known."

"I know that. And I know I'm not responsible for her choices either. But it still fuckin' sucks."

"You want to stay home?" she asked.

"No. I think I'd like to be distracted."

"Perfect. I can do that," she assured him, lifting his head and kissing it, before popping off the couch. Only then did he notice her attire.

"Geez. It's a little early for clubbing, don't you think?"

"Depends," she said with a grin.

"What about Andy?" Jeff asked. "What's he all pissed about?"

"Bombed his interview."

"Shit. That sucks... for all of us,"

"And now this with Cricket. That's probably not going to help either." Ellen was considering whether the plan in her head was really the best idea.

"Why?" Jeff asked. "He knew her even less. He just wanted her, but more like an object than a person. For him, it's probably like losing his favorite poster or something. I think he just liked looking at her."

"OK. I'm ready," Andy said from the kitchen, breaking their tension.

"Wow!" He marveled as he entered the front room and saw her, "That's pretty hot, El." Placing a fresh pack of Winstons in the breast pocket of his blue short-sleeved shirt, part of him wished he had not changed after all. "All of a sudden, I feel under-dressed."

"You'll be fine where we're going."

Ellen donned a pair of dark shades and made for the door. The boys filed in behind her, completely at the mercy of her plan.

#

Quenton Murphy stood at the base of the wide common driveway, retrieving the empty trashcans from the curb.

"Morning, Murphy," said Jeff.

"Afternoon," he corrected, exhaling a blast of menthol smoke. "You look nice today, Ellen."

116

"Thanks," she replied. Normally, a girl Ellen's age would be put off, repulsed even, to elicit a compliment from such an older man; but this felt good. In fact, now that she thought about it, in the last five minutes, she'd been complimented on her appearance by three very different men. She had no reason whatsoever to suspect any of their motives and it made her wonder if she might want to spend an extra few minutes in her closet every now and then.

"Where you off to all slicked up?" their neighbor asked with a wide smile.

"We don't know," Jeff said, opening the Chevette's passenger side door and climbing into the back seat.

"She won't tell us," Andy added as he folded back the seat and jumped in shotgun.

"Sounds like fun."

"You have no idea," Ellen said with a wicked grin.

Quenton stood there smoking and smiling as they backed out of the short driveway and headed down Cornwall's gradual southern slope.

"So, what's the big mystery, El?" Andy asked.

She gave them nothing— not a word or even a glance. The boys took the hint and remained silent as Ellen guided the car left onto Peters Street. Four blocks down on the right, she pulled to the curb and cut the engine.

"Excuse me?" Jeff asked from the back seat. "You got all jazzed up to come to Dave and Jimmy's?"

She was already out of the car, closing the door and lighting a Marlboro on the side of the road.

"Chill," she demanded, "it's just a pit stop." Ellen had a plan, and it wasn't up for discussion. She was already halfway up the yard.

22

People came to see Oklahoma Dave and Jimmy the Fish for one reason, and pretty much one reason only. They were drug dealers. Most visitors arrived under the pretense of random social calls. They didn't stay long, and they rarely left empty-handed.

Bradford was like most places, in that if you looked for something long enough, you were probably going to find it. And Dave and Jimmy made it pretty easy, especially if you were a 'friend'. But when you're in the business of dealing drugs, it can be hard to tell friends from the people who just want something you have. The residents of the house on Cornwall Street were semi-regulars in Jimmy and Dave's circle, even if the truth stopped somewhere short of real friendship.

Andy shrugged at Jeff in confusion as they started up the lawn. Ellen was already knocking on the front door. Its two rectangular windows were masked by an American flag. As Andy and Jeff hit the porch, the door swung open. Jimmy stood there, shirtless, adjusting his squinting, red eyes to the aggressive sun outside.

"Right on," he said, opening the door wider. It was early afternoon, but the house was midnight dark. Every window was covered with something—drapes, blankets, flags, whatever—as long as it looked cool and kept out the curious.

"Nice top," Jimmy said to Ellen, his tone just short of lecherous.

"Thanks," she answered, now beginning to question the extra attention her choice of wardrobe was creating.

Jimmy liked her. That is to say, he *wanted* her. Unfortunately for him, he couldn't have been further from her type. She was brighter by light years than the stable of tragically attractive *ladies* he seemed to wake up next to.

"Dave's around here someplace," Jimmy said speaking to all of them, but addressing her. As they followed him into the house, the front door closed, sealing out the only sunlight in the room. The blare of an acoustic guitar being strummed with more confidence than proficiency came from the back of the house. The four of them rounded the corner, nearly tripping over Dave, who sat in the open doorway, eyes closed, still plucking away. A thick stream of smoke rolled over and through the brim of his straw hat. It smelled a thousand times better than Marlboro country and was decidedly narcotic.

"Hey kids," Dave greeted. "Long time no see." It was something he said with great regularity, even though he saw most people either quite often, or not at all. He reached up to shake Jeff's hand. Informal greetings made their way around the impromptu circle in the dark hallway. Dave rose to his feet and began to move back through the house. Jeff and Andy fell quickly in line. Jimmy tapped Ellen lightly on the shoulder and ushered her in the other direction.

"What are you guys looking for today?"

"Just the usual," she replied.

"Cool. But, come check this out," he offered, casually taking her arm.

#

The boys stopped briefly in the kitchen as Dave perused the refrigerator. Jeff and Andy stood waiting and contemplated the many glass aquariums that were scattered throughout the house. The particular box that caught their attention was home to several small salt water eels.

"When did you get these?" Andy asked.

"They're not mine," Dave said. "I think Jimmy put them in last week."

"I know," Andy clarified. "I meant *you* in the general sense."

120

"I know, too. I just like to go on record as often as possible that all of these fuckers aren't mine."

Pulling a cold six-pack from the fridge, Dave walked into the front room and began fumbling with remote controls. He tossed a beer to each of his guests and turned again to address the machines. The house may have been a dump, but business had obviously been good. A selection of top of the line audio and video equipment sat neatly arranged in their front room. The collection easily put Cornwall's to shame, but the comparison was hardly fair.

#

"Have a seat," Jimmy pulled the chair out from beneath his small wooden desk for Ellen.

He reached over her shoulder and opened the desk drawer, pulling out a small box. Jimmy put it on the desk right in front of her and reached into the pocket of his trousers. A small plastic key chain landed on the desk with a slight jingle. A one-inch tall plastic Godzilla figurine on one end was connected to small, oddly shaped key on the other. She smiled nervously, instinctively pulling a strand of long brown hair from behind her ear and beginning to twist.

"Open it," he said, now also smiling. He'd walked across the room and was pulling on a white cotton t-shirt as she lifted the metal lid and then sat back.

"Is that what I think it is?" Ellen asked, the lock of hair wrapping ever tighter around here finger.

Jimmy laughed a little bit, reveling in the innocence of someone who couldn't positively identify cocaine.

"Depends on what you think it is."

121

"Very funny," she said, still studying the small glass vial that lay inside the box. "I know it's coke, Jimmy. It's just not something I see every day."

"Huh. I don't remember what that's like," he said honestly. "Do you have any smokes?"

She gave him a Marlboro and held up her lighter. Taking her hand in both of his, Jimmy bowed towards the flame.

"I'm a bartender in a shitty college town, Jimmy," she said. "I can't afford coke. And besides, even if I could, I don't think I'd ever really be into it."

"I don't recall asking if you wanted to buy any," he clarified. He reached over her shoulder again to grab the box, and then around her, to snag the first CD case he could find. He placed it ceremoniously in front of them, unscrewed the vial and spilled a small pile of white powder atop Black Sabbath's *We Sold Our Souls for Rock & Roll.*

"Do you have a dollar?" he asked.

"Wow, that's pretty cheap coke," she joked.

"No. For a straw, dummy." He took a small red rubber band off the desktop and snapped it at her.

She reached into her pocket and pulled out a crisp ten. "You got change?"

The Fish unsheathed a razor blade and began chopping the small crystals into an even finer powder. Picking up the rubber band, Ellen wrapped it around the rolled up Hamilton a few times until it held tight. She placed the straw on the desk and sat all the way back in her chair, not sure what she should do next.

"Nicely done. I don't believe you've never done this before."

"I always figured I never would, unless it was like some perfect situation."

"What? Like if you were trapped on a desert island with Hunter Thompson or something?"

"Who's that?" Ellen asked, in all seriousness.

"Never mind," he replied. The Fish bent low across the desk and inhaled the fattest of the six lines of white he'd drawn on the CD cover. He was amused to think there were a few things he could actually teach her. Whether or not those things were in her best interest never crossed his mind.

Jimmy raised his head from the desk and sniffed heavily to make sure he'd wasted nothing. Ellen gave him a look of strange curiosity as he handed her the straw.

# # #

"Did you hear what went down at The Cactus?" Andy asked Dave casually, as the bong drifted from their host's lips to Jeff's waiting hands. Before Dave could even answer, Andy was marching on. "Cold Gin nearly blew the fucker up the other night."

"Yeah, and on top of that..." Jeff added "there are cops crawling all over the place, asking questions about some girl that disappeared."

"Oh yeah," said Dave. "I think I saw her picture in the paper. It's too bad, she was cute."

"And there's a twenty-five thousand dollar reward out for whoever finds her," said Andy.

"You mean for whoever finds who killed her," Dave corrected.

"Why do you say that?" Andy asked.

"I don't know. People go missing all the time. But Barbie-pretty coeds without so many problems? What's someone like that running away from? When people like her go missing, it's usually 'cause somebody took 'em."

Jeff found Dave's assessment callous and disturbing. Thoughts of Cricket invaded his head, and he almost called out his host. But he knew that conversation was more trouble than it was worth, and he reconsidered.

"Or maybe she pissed off the wrong people or owed somebody a lot of money," Andy suggested.

"Shit. If that's all it takes to get whacked, how come you're still around?" joked Dave.

Jeff only half heard it. His mind was busy replaying Dave's words. It occurred to him that, aside from Jimmy and Dave themselves, there weren't all that many people in a town this size to whom it might be life-threatening to owe that kind of money. It was unsettling to Jeff to consider that if Dave was right, Jessica Hammond might have spent her last moments on Earth at the mercy of someone not too different from Dave himself. And Jeff was also smart enough to realize that Jimmy and Dave probably knew everybody else around Bradford that was even just a little bit like them.

Jeff tried to chalk all of this paranoia up to a combination of good drugs and a very bad day. But his brain was intent on drilling the rabbit hole ever deeper. He found himself contemplating his own recent choices. Sure, he dabbled in a little debauchery in the free time between his responsibilities – they all did. But these guys were in a different league altogether. It wasn't as if he was afraid, but suddenly all those 'slippery slope' cautions from his parents and mentors about the dangers of drugs seem to ring in his head. He wondered how far up, or down, the slope he and his roommates were from these guys; and more importantly, whether or not that distance was shrinking.

As he sat there, trying his best to enjoy their superb weed, Jeff was ninety-nine percent sure that Dave and Jimmy had nothing to do with the mysterious disappearance of Jessica Hammond. But the other one percent was driving the bus right now, and asking plenty of questions along the way; one of which was: *Where the hell is Ellen?*

#

"I don't know," Ellen hesitated as Jimmy held the rolled-up bill out to her. A big easy smile had settled across his face.

"What's a good reason not to?" Jimmy asked, skipping right over devil's advocate and playing the part of Lucifer himself, as he lowered his head to a second, smaller line of powder.

"I don't know," she repeated. "It seems like there's a big difference between something that grows out of the ground naturally, that really just chills you out, and something some asshole cuts with baby laxative in his basement that eats all of your money and makes you super paranoid."

"Wow. You make it sound so bad," Jimmy said as he wiped the white residue from the stubble under his nose.

"OK, so maybe I am a little scared."

"Do you really think I would do something to hurt you?" Jimmy asked, taking her hand in his.

She recognized the line as something cheesy, slimeball bastards said to secure trust they didn't deserve; but for some reason, she could sense he meant her no real harm.

A million thoughts raced through her brain. The week had been long, draining, and full of drama, but she wasn't sure it was enough to justify climbing another rung on the drug ladder. Then she remembered why they had come to Peters Street in the first place, and where they were going when they left.

She laid her burning cigarette in the ashtray and gathered the hair away from her face. Taking the straw in her right hand she clamped shut one nostril, lowered her head to the tray, and inhaled much harder than necessary.

"Whoa!" It was improbable she would be feeling the rush yet, but her brain didn't know any better.

The line she'd inhaled was pretty fat, and at least a quarter of it still lay on the plastic CD cover. Jimmy picked up a razor blade and began chopping at what was left.

"Clean your plate, girl," he grinned with sly satisfaction.

"Just a second." She squirmed a little in the chair, unsure of her choice, but now in midstream. "It tastes terrible."

"You kinda get used to it."

"Fuck it," she said, puffing again on her Marlboro. "If you're gonna do something, do it. Right?" She bent again to the tray and deposited the bill squarely in her other nostril. The powder shot up her nose as she swept the tray.

"Bravo," he offered, lying down on the double bed, and smiling as he locked his hands behind his head.

Ellen rocked back and forth in the wooden chair. Nervous energy pulsed through her body. Lightning storms clicked in her head. Under normal circumstances, her brain was a machine of extreme logic, used to examining and resolving one thought before moving on to the next. But now, a thousand people and places cruised through her head, each demanding a sliver of her attention. As she struggled to catch any one of them, Ellen had a moment of clarity. She recalled Andy's description of exactly the same feeling — confusion, and a longing to be able to concentrate on a single thing. She remembered him saying it was the way he felt most of the time. *No, that's not right.* she thought. He said it was the way he felt when he was *sober*, which was considerably less than most of the time. She wondered what it must be like to approach drugs as a way of escaping the very feeling she found herself engulfed in now. The idea of living like that was a sad thought, but like all her others just then, it stayed for only a moment before being replaced by another.

"Goddamn, you look good in that top," Jimmy said.

"What?" she asked, once again aware of his presence, and that he was now approaching her.

"I said, you look hot today. I mean, hotter than usual," he elaborated, now standing directly in front of her.

"Jesus. I wish people would stop saying that. I think I liked it better when nobody noticed me."

"That's bullshit," Jimmy said. "Everybody wants to be noticed. I notice you all the time. It's just you look *extra* hot today."

Before Ellen could fully process the situation, Jimmy dropped to one knee and came to rest between her slightly open legs. Bracing his forearm along the top of her thigh, he extended a hand, until it met with the back of her neck. He advanced, his large, glassy pupils disappearing as he closed his eyes and kissed her full on. Her heart pounded with a

127

mixture of narcotics and surprise, and any sort of normal response failed her.

His lips were strangely soft and warm, much gentler than she imagined he might be. Jimmy's mouth trailed slowly from the base of her neck, finding her chin and then circling her mouth. He placed a light kiss on her nose before moving back toward her mouth. The sheer confusion of the moment had left Ellen's mouth slightly agape, and Jimmy accepted the unintended invitation.

The touch of Jimmy's thin tongue brought her focus back with alarming speed. No sooner had the wet intruder crept between Ellen's teeth, than Jimmy went reeling backward onto the floor from the force of her thrusting arms. Before his ass even hit the carpet, she was standing and gathering her smokes and lighter from the desk beside the bed.

"Sorry," Jimmy said, sincerely. Ellen looked down at him as he leaned on one elbow, making no attempt to rise.

"Don't get me wrong," she said. "That was interesting, but that's never gonna happen again. Thanks for the high…I think. We gotta go."

She made her way through the kitchen, passing the various fish and reptiles in their glass houses as she went. Approaching the front room, she heard laughter and could already smell the dope smoke before she took the last corner.

"Where ya been, Ellie?" Andy asked.

"Talking to Jimmy. Let's go," she demanded.

"What's your rush?" Dave asked, reaching once more for the bong. "Take a toke for the road."

"I think not," she said, repeating her command: "Let's go."

Ellen wasn't adamant all that often, and the boys knew it was best to take her seriously when she was. Rising to leave, both Andy and Jeff gave Dave a quick handshake and thanked him for the buzz. Ellen was already out the door.

"Hey, Maxwell," Jimmy called out from the porch as they left, "I saw the paper today. You might want to pick one up." He laughed, closing the door and returning to the darkness inside.

Sweeping her hair from her face, she swung Chet's door open and got in. Before she could reach across and grab the passenger side handle, Jeff pulled the other door open and folded the seat forward for Andy.

"I got shotgun," he explained, smiling and waiting for his friend to climb in.

"What's with you?" Andy asked from behind her as she made an awkward U-turn in the middle of the street.

"Nothin'," she said, with too much energy. "We just got shit to do."

23

Doubling back on their original route, the Chevette rolled along Morton Avenue. They were now running parallel to Morton Park, which was busier than normal on a Monday afternoon. The basketball courts teemed with activity in the sticky summer heat. Jeff tracked a golden retriever as its owner launched a pink Frisbee. Even at their modest speed, it was hard to hear with the wind coming through the open front windows.

"What the fuck is she talking about?" Andy asked Jeff.

"No idea. I wasn't listening."

"Never mind. I was talking to myself about something that had nothing to do with either one of you, which makes no difference anymore, because I can't even remember it, and nobody was listening anyway," Ellen blurted in one hurried breath.

"Whoa!" Jeff said. "Slow it down. You alright there, partner?"

She was trying to light a Marlboro, as small beads of sweat began to form between her hairline and the top of her sunglasses.

"I'm fine, but it's hot as a bitch out here today, and this goddamned lighter won't work and all I really want is a cigarette. Is that too much to ask?" She reeled, tossing the spent lighter on the dashboard.

"Easy," said Andy, offering a flame over Ellen's right shoulder. "We need to get you somewhere with air-conditioning and cold beer."

"Don't worry," she replied. "We're almost there."

Hold on, not much farther now, she kept telling herself. *Talk less, and slower. Sweat less and thank the Lord for sunglasses.*

The boys had already started craning their necks from side to side, casing the passing neighborhood streets for clues to their final destination. As Chet crawled over the pavement and slowed to turn onto the access road, cheers went up all around her.

"No way!" Andy crowed from behind, like a 4-year old whose mom had just pulled the minivan into the local McDonald's. "Tell me you're serious!?"

"Oh, I think she's for real, man"

"I think I love you," Andy told her.

"I know," she said. "You both do."

24

The Chevette made one final right turn and pulled into the large, newly-paved parking lot of Wonderland. It was mid-afternoon on a Monday, just shy of Happy Hour, and already the lot was surprisingly full. Bradford was a pretty small town, so when new establishments opened their doors to the public, it usually didn't take long for folks to notice— especially new strip clubs.

"You're 100% serious, right?" Andy asked.

"You had to know we'd get here sooner or later," she replied, taking an extra second to revel in the excitement of her passengers before killing the engine and collecting her smokes from the dash. "You boys have been busy lately. Graduation. Road trips. Job interviews. You know, all that heavy, grown-up shit. Figured it was time to blow off some steam."

As far as her roommates were concerned, among Ellen's most endearing qualities was her ability to appreciate adult entertainment. Different from most of the girls they knew, and certainly unlike any of their ex-girlfriends, Ellen was perfectly willing to visit these establishments. It's not like she'd ever go alone, but on some level she actually enjoyed watching the dancers—and watching her male friends take in the scene, too. She was also remarkably hard to offend or embarrass, more so than either of her companions.

"Shit! Wait a minute!" said Andy. "I've got zero cash."

"Handled." Ellen dismissed the objection, pointing at one of the grand neon signs protruding from the building's brushed metal façade.

Bright tubes of noble gas bent and flashed before them, heralding an unbeatable collection of marketing phrases: "Live Nude Girls", "Beer & Liquor", and the three little letters that made even the most grandiose fantasies seem possible: "ATM."

"Right on!" shouted Andy.

"Right on is right!" she repeated, opening the door.

Heavy techno dance beats seeped out into the parking lot as they approached. Ellen made it to the door first, pulling it open and ushering them into a blast of cold, smoky loudness. The whole place glowed with an eerie pale blue hue that seemed unbalanced.

"Damn, it's like X-rated *Tron* in here." Andy said, amazed and amused.

Jeff turned and grasped his roommate's shoulder. Leaning in close, he shouted, "And loud as shit, too."

"What?"

"Never mind." Jeff said, smiling as he turned and walked deeper into the club. Standing in a room full of semi-beautiful, semi-clothed women, the various frustrations he had brought in with him seemed to tangibly dissipate. The lights were low, the music was loud, and T-bone steaks were only $4.95. What was there to be mad about?

"Where's Ellen?" Andy shouted over the speaker right in front of them. Jeff pointed to the bar where their friend was collecting three cocktail glasses.

"Goddamn. She is the best."

"Amen, brother. Amen," Jeff agreed.

The crowd was surprisingly large for a Monday afternoon, but they found a table and set up shop. Less than a minute later, just as Ellen rejoined, a slender brunette girl made her way to the stage right above them. According to the cheesy strip club MC, her name was Tiger and this was Stage Two.

The tall, shapely dancer eased her back into the brass pole and performed a bend so deep it stretched her skin-tight animal print bodysuit to its limits.

"Damn." Jeff muttered.

"Down, boy," Ellen said.

Black fishnet wound its way three quarters of the way up Tiger's long legs. Her equally dark hair was absurdly over-permed. Her deep brown eyes had been trained to scan the floor continuously, to make "meaningful" eye contact with customers while constantly watching out for the next big spender.

Several younger men, college students for sure, approached Kelly on Stage One. A well-executed spin on the brass pole drew wide eyes and exuberant whoops from the soon-to-be-contributors to her "college fund."

"You know what?" Jeff said. "Tiger here isn't really doin' it for me. I think I'm gonna piss and then check out the rest of the scenery. Everyone good?"

"Yep," Ellen said, without looking at him. She was still spiraling a bit and was going to have to adopt a sit-and-sip strategy for as long as it took to steady the ship.

Song two faded from the sound system, and Tiger and Kelly basked in a quick moment of mediocre applause. The last number was a bit sleepy, and the tipping had suffered. Surely something raucous was coming down the pike next, but the selection delighted Andy to no end.

After a few seconds of dead air, the chunky, monolithic opening riff of *Sin's A Good Man's Brother* blared forth from the speakers. It was an old Grand Funk Railroad tune, but Wonderland appropriately opted for the more recent heavy-as-hell remake by dope rock lords Monster Magnet.

"No fuckin' way!" Andy extended his hand to Ellen, looking for a high-five that never came.

"Screw the dancers. I might have to go tip the fuckin' DJ!" he said.

Fuzz-encrusted guitars gave way to Dave Wyndorf's sadistic howl, and there was no question; it was wake-up time. With renewed energy, Tiger shot across the stage, almost running at the brass pole across from her, in five inch heels, no less.

She leaped high, catching the pole near the top and began a series of mind-boggling twists, leg flares, flips and turns.

Ellen sat mesmerized, impressed by the display of coordination and grace. Her mouth agape, she managed to push out the words "Wow. That fucking rocked!"

They were already standing when Tiger's whirlwind came to rest on the stage floor. They both jammed their hands in their pockets, fishing for cash with which to reward the ambitious young girl.

#

Jeff stood at the bar, waiting for fresh cocktails. The service was slow, but he was content to hang back and take in the scenery. As the bartender placed three glasses in front of him, a playful voice crossed his ear.

"You must be thirsty," joked an elfish girl with fine golden hair that reached just past her small breasts.

A neat row of alcoholic beverages separated Jeff from his new acquaintance: a screwdriver for Andy; a Bloody Mary for him; and a rum and cola for Ellen.

"Hi. My name is Swan," she said. "It's a little early in the day to be drinking like that isn't it?"

"Yeah, well..." Jeff hesitated as he completed a not-so-subtle visual inspection of the waifish blond. Of all the times to be speechless.

"Hanging out in a room full of naked strangers is like voting," he recovered, hoping she hadn't heard the joke before.

"How's that?" Swan asked.

"You should never do either one sober."

"You're cute...and funny." She tilted her head and flashed a smile, signaling she was interested in continuing a conversation with him. "What's your name?"

"I'm Jeff, and these are for my little party over there." He pointed at Andy and Ellen.

"Nice to meet you." It was something she said all the time, but hardly ever meant. In fact, she couldn't remember the last person she was genuinely glad to meet, but she was sure it wasn't at work.

As quickly as that, Jeff and Swan had reached the veritable strip club crossroads; that place where polite conversation gives way to contract negotiation. Jeff's options were clear – either choose to "spend time" with the lady or politely wish her a good day. He took the plunge and accepted Swan's offer of a little company, and the meter started running.

"How long have you been dancing here?" he asked.

"A couple of months."

"What did you do before that?"

"Nothing. I came to Bradford from North Carolina to study Sociology. Just started in the fall."

"How old are you?" Jeff said without thinking. He knew it was something you never asked a lady, or a stripper. It had no chance of being answered honestly and every chance of being considered offensive.

"Nineteen," she said, clearly not bothered. "Well, I will be in July, anyway."

"So, what would you do if you could do anything in the whole world?"

"Including stripping?" Swan asked for clarification.

"Sure."

"Probably stripping," she said, but Jeff couldn't tell if she was serious.

Tiger's set was coming to an end, and Swan knew this was always the best time to make moves and close sales.

Her hand landed on his shoulder. She winked a green eye at him as her fingers sifted through his hair. "Do you want a dance now?"

"Sure. But come meet my friends first."

Jeff was taking liberties with Swan's time. She had made a specific, legitimate offer – "do you want this, or not?"— and he was pushing his luck by asking for at least another song's worth of her time. Swan didn't really care, though. As she followed Jeff away from the bar, she noticed that aside from his friends and the frat boys, the rest of the crowd was a homely collection of middle-aged, balding business men. She'd heard enough of their stories to know that no matter who Jeff was taking her to meet, it was probably an upgrade from her other options.

"So, you brought a lady with you."

Jeff wasn't sure if it was a question or statement. "Actually, she brought us," he laughed. "I hope that's okay."

"Oh, it's all good. We love seeing ladies in here. It breaks up the testosterone. And honestly, they're usually a lot more fun than you guys."

Jeff was a step in front of her, but stopped abruptly before they reached the table. Swan almost ran into him but managed to avoid spilling even a single drop of her gin and tonic.

After paying for cocktails and tipping the bartender, Jeff had set aside two more twenty dollar bills from his modest bankroll. He leaned in close to make sure Swan could hear his proposal over the din of the loudspeakers. She smiled and gladly accepted the cash.

"Your moves are awesome," Andy told Tiger. She smiled just enough to veil how dreadfully weary she was of these meaningless, post-shift interactions.

"I enjoyed the hell out of that," Ellen added. She still felt her pulse racing a little, but at least everything was starting to make sense again.

"Boys and girls," Jeff announced, "this is Swan."

Tiger silently curled her lip and rolled her eyes at Swan as they performed the changing of the guard. She was set free to seek her fortunes elsewhere, while Swan was being welcomed into the fold.

"Hi. I'm Ellen," she said, taking the drink from Jeff. Swan gave her a polite, cautious smile.

"I'm An...", but before he could even get the second syllable across his lips, the speakers destroyed his introduction with the announcement of the next set. Andy conceded defeat to the sound system, sat back down, and took a long gulp of orange-juice-plus.

A new rhythm began to dominate the club–faster, less rock and more techno than the previous offering. Swan began to sway in response to the new frenetic beat. She had punched the clock and was ready to work.

Swan passed seductively by the boys, allowing them ample time to take her in visually. Her wardrobe–a white tight-cut vest and very short, sheer white shorts–paid proud homage to her stage name. Her vest, which zipped down the front, was fastened about half-way up, suggesting, but not revealing, her modest cleavage.

Ellen felt a sudden rush of heat flow through her, as it became obvious she was the target locked in Swan's radar. She was sure her face was escalating through various shades of red as she came to realize the score. Jeff had set her up, but she was going to fight hard to not give him the satisfaction of publicly embarrassing her. *What the hell*, she figured. It had already been an interesting day full of "firsts" for her. She decided to roll with the punches and worry about payback later.

Swan extended her arms full over her head with majestic effect and, with one elegant step sideways, stood directly in front of the girl who would be playing the part of her new "best friend," at least for the next three minutes or so.

Typically, Swan avoided looking male customers in the eyes as she performed. There were really only a few stock expressions she ever found staring back – lost drunkenness, demented lust, or smug objectification. None were the least bit appealing and like most of the girls who'd spent more than a day in this game, she had perfected the art of looking "through" people.

What Swan saw in Ellen was different. Her eyes, wide pupils aside, conveyed a mixture of amusement, intrigue, and general willingness. She was good to go.

The song's intro accelerated into a fever of swirly, processed guitars that provided the perfect back track to Swan's silky gyrations. Her long blond locks obscured her face from the boys on either side. Now only inches from Ellen, their combined tresses formed a sort of intimate two-toned enclosure that gave Swan the "privacy" to formally introduce herself. By instinct, she found the back of Ellen's chair with her hands. Pausing for a second, she drew near and locked gazes with her blushing dance partner.

"Is this cool with you?" Swan asked, sweet and gentle.

"Sure. Why not?" Ellen was never one to let embarrassment get in the way of having a little fun.

"Okay then. Relax. I'm not gonna hurt you."

Swan nudged her victim's knees together, and slid herself down onto Ellen's lap. Ellen resisted the urge to laugh out loud, but it was hard. Swan couldn't have weighed more than 100 pounds, and Ellen couldn't imagine a scenario where the dancer's "warning" was even plausible.

Jeff and Andy sat there, looking like a pair of ridiculous smoking bookends to the action happening between them.

Swan straddled Ellen's waist, moving in perfect rhythm to the music and tossing her hair in exaggerated fashion. Jeff was watching, but he was also aware their table had now become a focal point. In fact, the most interesting thing in the whole place was happening about two feet to his left. The small group of college guys, who moments ago were patronizing Kelly, now leered at the cute chick getting a lap dance from the thin little blond number they'd previously ignored.

"Lean back," Swan instructed. "Enjoy this for a minute. It's going to be fun. The boys will be disappointed if I don't get just a little bit naughty."

Ellen felt her shoulders and legs relax–as much as was possible with 98 pounds of slightly sweaty stripper flesh on top of her. Swan leaned all the way back. Keeping her legs wrapped around Ellen's waist, she reclined almost perpendicular to her dance partner's torso. She reached up slowly, finding the zipper on her tight white vest and began to slide it down. The boys unabashedly leered at the spectacle.

In one swift move, Swan unwrapped her legs, and bolted straight upright, landing softly back in Ellen's lap. To Ellen's surprise and everyone else's delight, Swan's vest had stayed behind on the floor.

Swan was now topless and standing upright. She bent over, close to Ellen's face and planted a light kiss on Ellen's cheek, playfully close to the corner of her open mouth.

She popped up again, now not touching Ellen at all for the first time since the dance began. Ellen used the break to adjust in her chair and take a deep breath. The baby bluish neon lights masked the flush of red that enveloped her face, but she still made a conscious effort to avoid eye contact with either of her roommates.

#

Swan pranced seductively around for a few seconds, allowing the boys a more unobstructed view of her assets.

Jeff had selected her, but Swan was Andy's type to a tee, from the top of her blond head, to the tips of her stiletto-strapped toes. In fact, Jeff would have probably thought of her as 'plain' or 'boring', if he passed her on the street or in the grocery store at random. He preferred women with a more 'exotic' look – dark skin, dark hair, with bonus points for sporting an accent that might suggest she was something other than the typical American girl next door.

Andy knew this, and even through the haze of chemicals and current distractions, the gesture wasn't lost on him. He and Jeff could both easily pick each others fantasy girl out of a line up—especially at a strip club, where such a thing was precisely possible.

Both of them should have been investing every ounce of their energy to committing the spellbinding visuals before them to memory. But looking up, Andy found Jeff looking straight back at him, a devious smile, almost a smirk, on his face. He shot a casual salute at Andy. Perhaps the strangest peace offering in history had just been tendered, in the form of a beautiful blond dancer named Swan. It was Andy who had been the biggest asshole of the day, and clearly it was Jeff who had suffered the most. In that moment, and in spite of all the junk swirling around in his head, Andy was convicted with almost total clarity.

The gesture revealed an awareness and kindness in Jeff that Andy knew he himself did not possess, and maybe never would. The unlikeliest of teaching tools—a silly, seedy lesbian lap dance—had crystalized for Andy that Jeff was somehow a better human being than he. Through the sting of shame, he raised his near-empty screwdriver and offered a silent, solemn toast to his friend.

The music wound down, and Swan wrapped up her performance. Ellen was long over any embarrassment, and the event had actually helped her emerge from the depths of her haze. As the last notes of the song trailed off, a hearty round of applause rode through the club. Two other girls had been on stage at the time, but the decent-sized crowd in attendance that afternoon was lauding Swan's exhibition almost exclusively.

Ellen sat relaxed in her chair, puffing on a Marlboro Red. Swan zipped her vest, smiled, and gave a quick cheesy bow, as if to punctuate her performance. Another round of applause from the three roommates followed, and even though Jeff had already paid for Swan's services in advance, Andy and Ellen were both waiting with additional tips to show their appreciation for her efforts.

"Thanks," she said, inviting each of them to place the bills in the white lace garter that sat midway up her left thigh.

"Join us for a drink," Andy offered.

Jeff smiled at his roommate, knowing it was impossible for Andy to let a girl so closely built to his ideal specifications just walk away.

"I don't know." she said, clearly ambivalent. "You seem like pretty nice guys."

It was the first time she'd acknowledged him since joining their little group. She was friendly, and less guarded after spending three minutes of quality time with Ellen, but she was also still on the clock.

"Ha! You don't have to live with these bastards," Ellen said.

"Yeah..." Swan said, now even less engaged. Their transaction having been completed, it was amazing the speed and ease with which Swan shifted gears. She had enjoyed her time with this party, and she didn't really want to be rude, but the subtext was clear. Swan had places to go and dollars to make. It was time for her to move on in search of the next green pasture.

Jeff and Ellen were on the same wavelength; also ready to go. Andy was a little less clear of purpose. It's not that he would have lobbied to stay longer, it just hadn't occurred to him yet to leave.

Swan stood and straightened herself. "Thanks for the good time," she said, waiting, as the rest of them gathered their belongings.

"Our pleasure. Thank *you*," Andy said, with an over-eagerness that loudly broadcast his attraction to her.

Swan stepped to Ellen and hugged her more robustly than she expected. Adding a little sugar to the fire she'd built, Swan gave her a quick kiss, full on the lips. "Bye, baby. Take care of these boys."

Again Ellen was red-faced and without words.

The boys didn't fair nearly as well. Swan gave Jeff a half-hug and small peck on the cheek, and then moved quickly to Andy, who got the same treatment. Although, ever the professional, Swan was keen to capitalize on opportunities whenever they presented themselves. "Come back and see me sometime," she whispered in his ear, and walked away.

"Damn," said Andy. "She's good at her job."

"Speaking of jobs," Jeff replied. "Don't you still have to find one?"

And there it was—the ultimate buzz-kill. As the three roommates walked out of the air-conditioned, fluorescent blue fantasy into the unrelenting afternoon heat, reality had reared its ugly head once again.

"Fuck." Andy sighed. "Why not? Tweaking my resume is definitely one way to kill a hangover and a hard-on. Let's go."

The three roommates piled back into the Chevette, each inching back toward sobriety at their own pace. None of them would admit to being "addicts" in the traditional sense of the word, but withdrawal was a physiological reality. The roller coaster went up; the roller coaster came down.

Ellen became quiet and introspective. Jeff, who had slight manic-depressive tendencies, often became near-narcoleptic on the backside of a binge. It was not uncommon for him to fall into deep slumber without warning, particularly in the absence of loud noise or direct conversation. The drive home from Wonderland took only about 15 minutes, but Jeff was already passed out before Chet even reached the highway.

Andy was the wild card. His response to withdrawal–irritability–was always the same, but the object and severity of his attacks were far less predictable.

Jeff snored lightly in the back seat, while Ellen played the part of distant chauffeur. Andy stared blankly out the passenger side window. It wasn't until the Chevette was firmly planted in the middle of Bradford's modest rush hour traffic that they were reminded of the time of day. Ellen let out a barely audible sigh as she attempted to change lanes.

Andy processed the traffic on a whole other level. For him, it was an instant reminder that–whether here in Bradford, or somewhere else–the elusive job he had yet to capture was also going to *capture* him. Without fail, he'd become just one more of *these people*–driving to and from work in long, uninspired lines of drudgery. His already-half-empty glass drained just a touch more.

Ellen had little interest in creeping along the interstate in prolonged silence, especially with Sleepy & Grumpy in tow. She maintained the right lane, deciding to get off at the next exit and wind their way through the less crowded surface streets.

"Where you headed?" Andy asked.

"No worries, my friend. I got this," Ellen suggested, fully expecting a follow-up question. Telling Andy not to worry was like telling most people not to breathe—it just didn't work that way. She was pleasantly surprised to find him not in the mood to argue.

"Can we get some food? I'm starving."

"My thoughts, exactly," she replied. Andy figured Ellen must have had something specific in mind as he watched several options get passed by.

He would have thought she was going to at least involve him in the decision-making process. But he supposed she was still enjoying calling all the shots. And so far, he had very little to complain about.

"Hell, yes!" Andy exclaimed, as the car pulled into a small lot in desperate need of repaving. "You're batting a fucking thousand today, El."

Andy's exuberance was sufficient to wake Jeff, who rubbed his eyes and enacted a dramatic yawn-stretch that made him look like a deranged 180-pound kitten rising from slumber.

"You ready to eat, Sleeping Beauty?"

In front of them was another of Bradford's culinary treasures, Phat Phil's Fine Eats – home to some of the best authentic Southern comfort food in their city, or anywhere else. A couple of doors down was the Cubby Corner convenience store they frequented, mostly for beer and cigarettes. And right next to that, on the corner where Paxton Avenue intersected the next block at Juniper Street, sat the Cactus Club. Even from a couple of blocks away, the bright yellow police tape was still screaming around the club's perimeter.

"Hey, I gotta get some smokes," said Jeff, starting toward the Cubby.

"I'll come with you," Andy replied. "And Jimmy said we should get a paper today."

"Y'all go for it," said Ellen. "I'm gonna grab a table."

"Cool. See you in a minute."

"You had like a whole pack of smokes when we left Wonderland," Jeff pointed out to Andy as the two walked side-by-side up the uneven sidewalk that paralleled Paxton Avenue. "You hoarding?"

"Nah. I just wanted to take a quick look at the Cactus since we're right here," Andy admitted.

"That shit's closed down, man. Roped off in police tape. What else is there to see?"

"I don't know. But I want to look at it," Andy repeated, with no better explanation at the ready. "You do your thing. I'll be back in a second, and we'll go get some eats."

"Whatever, dude." Jeff had no real interest in Andy's extra intel mission. "I might not wait for you."

Andy kept walking, now a bit faster, as Jeff veered off into the Cubby. He knew his roommate wasn't kidding.

A cowbell strapped to the crossbar of the heavy glass door announced Ellen's entrance to Phat Phil's Fine Eats. The smell of garden fresh collard and mustard greens simmering hung heavy in the air. Mixed with the scents of fried chicken and baked fruit pies, the greens became part of a grand olfactory symphony that blurred the line between pleasant and intoxicating.

Phat Phil's was one of the smallest restaurants in Bradford, offering only a handful of tables. Depending on the day and time, you might have the whole place to yourself. On other occasions, you might encounter a line out the door and a lengthy wait for a seat.

Today the place was almost empty, except for a woman in her early 40s and her pre-teen son sitting across from one another at the table nearest the door. Their drinks were gone and a plate of partially-eaten pie swimming in melted vanilla ice cream sat between them. Ellen looked for the table furthest away to spare them from the unsavory clouds of smoke and obscene language that would inevitably follow her roommates into the restaurant.

Serendipity made the decision all the easier. In the opposite corner of the small room, she saw the unmistakable orb of Graham's balding head. He was staring out the window from his booth along the back wall. She approached him from the side, making it all the way to the table without drawing his attention. It was only when she slid in beside him that his gaze broke from the window.

"Howdy, stranger!"

"Hey, Ellie!" he replied, too surprised to address her with his usual formality.

By the look of the near-empty plate and half-full ashtray on the table, Graham had been there for a while.

"Where are the brothers?" he asked, pushing the plate across the table to clear the space in front of her.

"They're getting smokes at the Cubby. Should be right back."

"Good. I'd hate to miss 'em."

"Likewise, I'm sure," Ellen agreed. She was about to ask him where the bus was when she was interrupted.

"Hey, shu-gah."

It made Ellen smile every time she heard it. Ms. Philomena Mascoll – Phat Phil herself – was standing tableside. At nearly 250 pounds, and with a disposition as sunny as her parents' native St. Croix, Philomena was a jolly mountain of a woman. She'd grown up working in the Caribbean-themed restaurant her parents had owned for years, even though she never really loved the foods of her family's ancestral land.

Phil had lived her entire life in the Deep South and much preferred its culinary traditions. Her parents had retired a few years back, leaving her to assume control of their Blue Sky Cantina. She kept the Caribbean thing going for a short while – essentially out of respect for the years of sweat he parents had poured into the place. But it was clear to all of them it was not something she loved. With their blessing, Philomena closed the Blue Sky, and immediately set about transforming the once-airy, beach-tinged café into a genuine, down home Southern kitchen much more in line with her own personal palate.

In the two years Phat Phil's Fine Eats had been open, its popularity and profitability easily eclipsed that of the Blue Sky Cantina. It was a low enough bar to clear, though. Hung-over college kids are going to prefer homemade mac and cheese and biscuits smothered in country gravy over jerk-seasoned mahi mahi every day of the week.

"Hey, Phil," Ellen replied, scooting to the edge of the booth and standing halfway up to give her a one-armed semi-hug, before flopping down again. "How you been?"

"Ooh, slow as honey, baby," Phil said with a mix of flair and exasperation, neither of which were fake. "Dem crazy boys blew up da Cactus. And dat girl went missin'. Lotsa cops this week. Not lotsa customers. What choo want?"

"I'm gonna wait on the boys for food. But can I get a sweet tea?"

"Shure ting, baby," Phil said, with a giant toothy smile. "For real sweet, or just kinda sweet?"

"Make my teeth hurt. It's been one of those kinda days."

"Ain't every day one of them kinda days with you kids?" Phil teased, rolling her big eyes.

Philomena was thirty – not *too* much older than Ellen, or any of the other college-aged "kids" who frequented her eatery. But Phil was most definitely a grown-ass woman. She'd worked hard, for a long time, and had carved out a respectable place for herself. She called them "kids" partly in jest, but compared to her experience and accomplishments, that's exactly what they were.

"Pretty much," admitted Ellen, proud and guilty. "I'd tell you where we've been today, but you wouldn't believe me."

"Oh, I doan wanna know. But dat's what young is for. You have your fun, girl. Just don't be gettin' no one hurt."

Ellen knew enough about Philomena to have great respect for her, and for the years of hard work she'd put into running her own business. Most people who came into the restaurant probably saw Philomena as just a fat black lady frying chicken and serving lemonade. But Ellen saw

151

an impressive woman who'd found happiness in something she'd busted her ass to create. They had little in common and never saw each other outside of the restaurant, but Ellen thought of her as a friend just the same.

"Speakin' a them boys; where dey at?" Phil asked.

"They're up the street. Should be here any minute."

28

Andy walked the two short blocks up Paxton Avenue to the corner of Juniper Street. The shabby gravel driveway which served as a parking lot for the Cactus Club was occupied by three vehicles. A red Chevy Blazer, which he knew belonged to their friend, Echo Thompson, a jack of all trades for the Cactus Club, was parked right by the exit doors nearest the street. Further down the building, a few lengths away, were a white panel van and a police cruiser. A slight summer breeze was slapping the slackened line of bright yellow police tape against the building's brick façade. As Andy approached, the reason for the panel van became evident. The large plank of plywood that had been nailed to the rectangular window frame was now sitting on the ground against the outside wall of the establishment.

Andy stopped and studied the two men as they worked to place a large, pristine sheet of glass into the void. Andy guessed it would soon be darkly tinted, like its predecessor, but at the moment, it was perfectly transparent. From his vantage point, Andy could see clear through, past the stage and halfway down the long narrow galley to the bar along the club's left side wall. He watched them seal the new glass into the frame with great interest until a new character entered from stage right.

Like some Vaudevillian actor trapped in a surreal performance piece, Peter "Echo" Thompson strode drearily into the scene, dragging a broom across the floor that lay concealed below the bottom of the window frame.

Andy watched Echo swing the broom in small arcs for a few seconds before he was noticed. Looking up from the floor, Thompson ran a sleeve across his sweaty brow and stood staring at Andy. Normally, he would have stopped and talked with him. But now they were separated by about twelve feet, and a thick plate of sound-killing glass. Peter let the broom come to rest against his shoulder, freeing his hands to give Andy a quick wave. He followed with a simple shrug, palms to the sky, as if to say: *"Shit happens, man. Whadda ya gonna do, right?"*

Echo's appearance made Andy laugh, but also think. He couldn't imagine himself on the other side of that glass, in Echo's shoes. He'd worked his share of shit-jobs before, but at the age of twenty-two, still a handful of years younger than Echo, he felt like he was done with that, or at least desperately wanted to be. The prospect of being nearly thirty and pushing a broom around a shithole nightclub was terrifying to Andy; soul-crushing, really. Why on Earth would anyone settle for a job so meaningless? And yet, by all accounts, Echo was content. Maybe the ability to joyfully do unglamorous work was something you grew out of – or into. Andy didn't get it.

On the tails of his guilt from Jeff's offering of Swan at the Wonderland, this was the second time in the span of an hour Andy had been shown a glaring flaw in his own character. *Damn,* he thought, *selfish AND lazy; every girl and parent's dream.* Most of the time he failed to receive these transmissions, or simply ignored them. But for some reason, that frequency was wide open today.

"Move along!" The command came from the uniformed officer who was rounding the corner at the front of the Cactus Club. The cop's bark broke Andy's trance. He imagined he probably looked kind of stupid, standing pointlessly in front of a club that was not only closed and damaged, but also currently an active crime scene.

Andy gave a quick smile and a salute to Echo and obliged the cop's request. Head down, hands in his pockets, he turned and started back toward Phat Phil's, just in time to see Jeff walking toward the eatery.

Andy arrived a few seconds later, meeting the departing mother and son on their way out. The door opened inward, and even though it required him to awkwardly push past them first, Andy attempted to make the chivalrous move and hold it for her. The brass cowbell clanged again.

"Thank you," said the woman, appreciating the spirit of the gesture, if not its execution.

154

"Of course," replied Andy. He made an actual distinction between 'of course', which he used when responding to a kindness he was proud or willing to give, and the less-friendly 'you're welcome', which to him more often than not denoted some sort of obligation.

The restaurant was now deserted, save for his two roommates and their surprise guest. He too perked up instantly at the sight of Graham sitting next to Ellen.

Philomena and Andy were both approaching the table but from different paths. He carried a folded newspaper; she a tray with two tall beverages.

"Hey, Phil!"

"Hey shu-gah. Whatchoo drinking?"

"Oh, man. Can I get an Arnold Palmer?" He'd been thinking about the heavenly combo of sweet tea and lemonade since the first second Ellen pulled into the lot.

"Sure, baby. Be right back."

Andy waited for Jeff to scoot toward the wall and then sat with a heavy thud. He reached down and began to rub his under-developed calf muscles which were throbbing after even such a short walk to and from the Cactus Club.

"Hello, my friend!" Graham welcomed him, reaching across the table to shake Andy's hand.

"Mr. Lafley," Andy accepted. "Good to see you, sir."

Graham withdrew and turned to the small tin box on the table. He popped open the lid and quite publicly displayed a shuffled assortment of expensive clove cigarettes and neatly rolled joints.

"Want one?" he offered, speaking to all of them at once.

"I don't like cloves, but..." said Jeff.

"I love the smell of them," Ellen suggested, "but they give me a fuck of a headache."

Andy declined too, with a simple wave of his hand.

"Do you mind if I light one?" Graham asked.

None of them did. They'd all probably light up soon enough too, but Ellen in particular was glad the mother and her son had left, so she didn't have to feel guilty about smoking them out of the smallish place.

They contemplated the menu, each trying to have their food orders ready before Phil returned with Andy's drink.

"Can we get food to go?" Andy asked.

The option hadn't occurred to either of his roommates, but neither had an objection.

"You got somewhere to be?" Graham wondered.

"Naw. I just want to get home. I've got job search stuff to do."

Seeing his chance to offload the newspaper he'd been holding, Jeff handed it to Andy. "Here. This might help."

"Oh yeah," Graham enthused. "How's that goin'?"

"Nowhere, and fast."

"That's not the worst way to live, you know."

Of all the people they knew, Graham would be the trusted authority on that matter. Andy would have loved to live with the lightness Graham seemed to exhibit, but the frame of mind that required eluded him.

"Speaking of going places..." Ellen interjected. "Where are you headed? And where's the bus?"

"Bus is down by the park. It's hard to find a place to put that big ol' bitch. I just left it down there and walked."

The park to which Graham alluded was over a mile away. The mere thought of trudging that far in the afternoon heat made Andy's legs hurt even worse.

"I gotta go back up north, and get closure on some shit," Graham said. There was a heaviness in his voice they were unaccustomed to hearing. None of them asked for clarification, but he obliged anyway.

"I was living on this piece of land up in Appalachia. It was beautiful; base of a mountain, running stream, blue skies, the whole package. This guy I met had like a hundred acres or more up there. Way more than he knew what to do with. We hit it off. I asked him about buying a piece of it from him. He said he liked the idea and that I could even put a trailer down there by the stream – you know, set up a real place."

"Sounds pretty good," said Jeff, a country boy himself who understood the appeal of off-grid life on some smaller level.

"It was. Until a few weeks later when the fuckin' DEA came swoopin' down in helicopters like bats outta hell."

"What!?" Andy blurted.

"No shit, man. Turns out, this dude was using most of his hundred acres to grow high-grade weed. And apparently, The Man can come and just take all that shit away from you."

"But you said you bought some of it," Ellen asked.

"Nope. I was *gonna* buy it. He never got around to any paperwork to make it official. I guess in the end, it's better there's no paper trail between me and him, but they still got my trailer. I'm out about 10,000 bucks, but at least I'm not him – that dude got *years* of jail time."

"Fuck." It was all Andy could think of to say. It was like everything else in Graham's life. Crazy, dramatic, tragic. But somehow, he still managed to find the silver lining.

With perfect timing, Philomena came lumbering back to the table with Andy's sweet and sour concoction in tow. She pulled a small white towel from the pocket of her huge apron and wiped the sweat from her dark round face.

"What's for suppa?" she asked.

"Ladies first," Andy replied, as more of a stalling tactic than a courtesy.

"We're gonna get it to go, Phil," started Ellen. "Can I have a veggie plate, with collards, mac & cheese, and black eyed peas?"

"Shore thing, baby. Biscuit or cornbread?"

"Cornbread."

"And you, shu-gah?" Phil said turning to Jeff.

"Mmm. Country-fried steak and gravy, please. With green beans and cornbread." Jeff requested, with great anticipation.

"You ready?" Phil asked Andy.

"Yep. A veggie plate sounds good," he said, following Ellen's lead.

"I'll have mac & cheese, mashed potatoes, fried okra, and a biscuit."

"Ain't no veggies on that plate, shu-gah," Phil corrected, prompting all three of his friends to laugh at his 'healthy' selection.

"Whatever." Andy defended. "That's what I want."

"Okay, y'all. Suppa to go. Be ready in a minute." Phil was still chuckling as she made her way back to the kitchen.

They settled in to wait, puffing away and starting to fill the small restaurant with smoke.

"So, what'd you learn about the Cactus?" Jeff asked Andy.

"Nothin', man. Nothin' we didn't already know. Like I said, I just wanted to look at it. I was only there for a second before some asshole cop told me to leave. Echo was in there cleaning shit up. I figure we'll talk to him sooner or later and get the real scoop anyway."

He placed his burning cigarette in the ashtray at the center of the table and turned his attention to the newspaper in his lap. The Monday edition of the Bradford Exchange was meager by comparison to the pulpy behemoth Cricket had brought them yesterday.

Jeff moved on without him. "So, check it out. These are up on the wall at the Cubby and probably all over town, by now, too." He pulled out a white piece of paper and laid it on the table for all of them to see.

Staring back at them was a young girl with light shoulder length hair and a cute, although slightly uneven smile. "Missing" read the huge banner above here photo. Below it, in letters not quite as large: "Jessica Hammond." The flyer went on to share that she was 20 years old, 5' 3" tall, approximately 105 pounds, with blue eyes and sandy blond hair.

"Damn," said Graham.

"She looks so young," Ellen noticed.

"It might be an older picture of her, but the best one they had for the posters." Graham suggested.

At the bottom of the flyer, in letters bigger than Jessica's name, it read: "Reward: $25,000", and finally a 1-800 number.

"Well, there you go, Andy" Jeff suggested. "With that kind of money, you could go a lot longer without getting a job."

Andy wasn't listening. He was busy leafing through the thin sections of paper.

"My guess is..." Graham said, "finding a random missing girl is probably pretty close to a full-time job." He hadn't meant it as a joke, but Jeff laughed all the same.

"It's amazing that someone can just disappear into thin air like that, with no trace, and without somebody seeing *something*," said Ellen. She seemed to be internalizing the situation on a completely different level than her male companions.

"Oh, somebody knows something," Graham said. "Somebody knows *everything*."

"That's true," Jeff agreed. "It makes you wonder. I mean, she's been gone for more than 48 hours now, which is kind of when they say most runaways show up."

"Her family, or whoever, came up with twenty-five grand pretty quick, too." Andy suggested. "I'm not sure my family could do that."

"Or want to, "Jeff teased.

"Fuck you."

"Both of you shut up," urged Ellen. "That girl is gone, and you guys are getting off on trying to figure out what happened to her."

Perhaps the new attachment of a face to the name of the missing girl had made it that much more real for her. She was done listening to their theories about her fate.

Ellen was rescued from further conjecture by the sight of Philomena approaching their table with two white plastic bags full of delicious home cooking. To everyone's surprise, Andy offered to pay for the entire meal— even Graham's.

"Why are you in such a good mood all of a sudden?" Ellen wanted to know.

"Well, your little field trip was pretty awesome," he said. "But I just found the cherry on top."

Andy held aloft a folded page of newsprint for all of them to see, flashing the biggest shit-eating grin any of them had ever seen plastered on his face. A full quarter-page in the Lifestyle section of *The Bradford Exchange* was devoted to a photo that would have been intriguing to the average reader simply for its oddity. All of them knew instantly what it was. A pair of dark, strappy high-heels connected by a white tennis shoe lace hung from the branches of an oak tree. A closer inspection would

161

reveal several other pairs behind it in the blurred background. Andy sat there, basking smugly in the tiny little spotlight for a moment while they looked. His small audience, each of them co-conspirators, were almost as enthused as he. Almost.

"No fucking way," Jeff said.

"Yes, fucking way," Andy replied. "And listen." He'd turned the page back toward himself and was now reciting the small caption under the photo. "'About thirty pairs of shoes were discovered hanging from a tree in front of Bradford's Gryphon Theatre early Sunday. The theatre's owners confirmed that the origin of the shoes is a mystery.'"

He laid the paper on the table and sat back, now somehow smiling even wider.

"They shorted you about ten pairs," Ellen noticed.

"I don't even care," Andy said, beaming.

"Nice," said Jeff. "You got exactly what you wanted, eh?"

"I totally did." The satisfaction in his voice and face were palpable. For whatever failures he may have endured recently, this one was going squarely in the win column. He'd started with a blank canvas, added a little flair and created something that had gotten noticed. He imagined the feeling he'd have one day seeing his words in magazines or on billboards would be more or less exactly like this. He felt somehow vindicated, or maybe just happy. Either way, it felt good.

"Well done, Maestro," Graham congratulated. "So, what's next?"

And there it was. The brutal reality of fleeting fame, summed up in one statement. No matter what one accomplishes, you're only ever as good as your next act.

"Next, he has to figure out how to get paid for all that creativity," said Jeff.

"You really do know how to piss on a parade, don't you?" said Andy, still plenty pleased with himself.

They collected their belongings and thanked Phil in advance for what they already knew would be a fabulous feast. Retreating to the Chevette, Ellen offered to give Graham a lift back the Bus, but he declined, preferring to put another mile on his shoes.

29

For most of the two-plus years they had shared the house on Cornwall Street, Andy had shown little or no interest in the mail that was delivered to their home six days a week. Ellen and Jeff took the lead when it came to keeping the lights, water, and cable TV running, and he'd learned he could depend on them to just tell him how much he owed for his share. Over the past month, though, checking the mail had become another minor obsession of his. Lately, he'd been watching the rusty letter box like a hawk.

In the five weeks that preceded his graduation, Andy had sent out nearly 100 copies of his anemic resume to a host of prospective employers around Bradford and beyond. "Beyond" was a fairly relative term, though, as Andy was really only considering two options. He'd been both narrow in his focus and short-sighted about saving any real money to help launch his post-graduate independence. So, either he would secure a position with one of the few advertising agencies in Bradford, or he'd resign in defeat to the basement of his parents' house in suburban Atlanta and cast his net in the much deeper job market of the nearest "big" city. And that was it, as far as he could see.

He knew plenty of people who'd planned to move to *real* big cities, and a few who'd even gotten real offers for jobs already. But he wasn't quite up for independence on that level yet.

Andy Maxwell was a 22-year-old man-child who loved the concept of comfort—physically and mentally; and who became nearly paralyzed in its absence. And the worst part for him was that he wasn't even sure when or how that had happened.

In Bradford, he'd found a level of comfort he'd never known before. In the beginning, he loved that it was a place where no one knew him. The chance to reinvent himself was something he'd been desperate for after graduating high school with most of the same people he'd known since first grade.

Now, the prospect of leaving all that behind for another completely new experience was something in which Andy was not even remotely interested. Everything about Bradford was simple. Andy and his friends had mastered the art of having as much fun as they wanted, legal or otherwise, without suffering any real consequences. Of course, some of them went to school, too. And they worked an assortment of unimpressive, unchallenging jobs that paid enough to keep the party going. But that was it really. Simple.

Andy knew that he *could* go on living like that forever, and that some people did. He could stay in that small pond forever, paying only the price of his own disappointment, and possibly that of his parents, for making the easy choice. Or, he could brave paths unknown; paths fraught with opportunities to succeed, and fail, gloriously. He figured his road lay somewhere in between, but for now, he was lost.

30

Jeff gave way to Ellen, ushering her through the front door and proceeding straight to his bedroom, eager to unburden himself of shoes and empty his pockets before rejoining his roommates for what he assumed would be a quiet wind-down from an eventful day.

"Holy shit!" Andy gasped from his perch atop the living room's well-worn couch. Its upholstery had originally been something in the crème spectrum, but two years of heavy smoking and semi-regular staining had left it a grotesque, dingy grey.

Ellen was in the kitchen fetching cold drinks from the refrigerator as Jeff came back. They each stood there, like patient bookends about five feet on either side of Andy, waiting for the follow-up.

"You plan on sharing?" Jeff asked.

Ellen plopped herself down on the nasty couch next to Andy and took a long, recuperative drink.

"Holy shit," Andy repeated, this time more sedate, but no less dumbfounded. "I think I have an interview."

"What? Wow!" Ellen said, with an unintended level of shock. "That's awesome."

Jeff came to rest on Andy's other side. "Cool, man. What's the gig?"

"I don't know exactly," Andy said, once again scanning the brief letter. "It's some company called Firebrand Marketing. The name doesn't ring a bell. When I sent out resumes, I grabbed the Red Book – this giant directory of all the local advertising agencies – and sent letters to almost every shop in town. There are really only about three decent agencies in the whole lot, but I sent shit to like 40 places."

"Sweet. So, what's it say?" Jeff asked.

"Dear Mr. Maxwell," Andy began. "Thank you for your interest in Firebrand Marketing. We currently have an opportunity available for a candidate with your qualifications and would like to speak with you to discuss the position. Please contact me at your earliest convenience, and we can set up a time to meet. We look forward to hearing from you. Sincerely, Gina Lavell, Human Resources Coordinator."

"That's it," Andy said, plainly. The letter was four sentences – not any longer than most of the form rejection letters he'd been steadily receiving over the last couple of weeks; four little sentences, carrying with them a mountain of hope and possibility.

He'd had exactly two interviews so far, and both had been train wrecks. The first, before he'd even graduated, had been with a "marketing" company that had posted a flyer on a job board outside one of his Journalism classes. Andy arrived at his "interview" to find himself one of 51 people who had shown up to what the company was calling an "orientation" for new marketers. Confused, Andy sat quietly amongst the ranks of the unemployed, willing to go along for at least a short ride. He noticed a striking number of his fellow applicants were not exactly dressed for success. In the charcoal grey suit and red power tie his parents had bought him as a graduation present, he felt grossly overdone.

The only other person in the room wearing a coat or a tie was a slick looking young man in his late twenties. As the lights dimmed, the man strode to the front of the room and began giving a presentation entitled "the opportunity of a lifetime." Less than a minute later, it was clear to Andy that he had wandered into a heavy-handed sales pitch aimed at recruiting new 'associates' into a 'multi-level marketing organization'. All you had to do was pay $500 for the *privilege* of becoming an 'associate', and you were instantly qualified to start selling the general public 'an array of state-of-the-art, next generation solutions in water filtration and purification'. But wait, there was more. Of course you made modest

167

commissions on your own sales, but that was just the beginning. The 'real big money' came from recruiting your friends, family, and whomever else into the organization as your 'team', on whose sales you also made commissions.

If he hadn't chosen a non-aisle seat near the front of the room, Andy would have bolted before the lights even came back on. As it was, he sat there fuming for five more minutes while the wonder-kid in blue pinstripes regaled the audience with 'success stories' of the many associates of the company who had "become millionaires, often times by working only part-time, and completely on their own schedules." As the lights came up, the facilitator made a manipulative appeal to his captive audience, admitting that he knew "this opportunity wasn't for everyone – only the most bold, confident and truly successful among you." He closed with the suggestion they take a quick break, perhaps to use the facilities or get a drink of water, and that all those who were "seriously interested in serious money" should remain to begin their training immediately. Pissed at having wasted a good chunk of a sunny afternoon on this bullshit, Andy left immediately. Although, by the time he'd returned home, he found himself wishing he'd waited five minutes in the hall and then stuck his head back in the room, just to get a look at all of the suckers who had either bit on the pyramid scheme or who simply had nowhere better to be that day.

This sham aside, the only other serious opportunity at employment Andy had encountered was that morning's debacle with the marriage question. But now, he felt a spring of renewed possibility and purpose. Invigorated and still clutching the single piece of paper in his hand, he rose from the couch and headed straight for his room.

"Where you going?" Jeff called.

"Gotta go put this up, check my portfolio again, and see if anything needs to be ironed," Andy said, as if some phantom 'responsibility' switch had been tripped in his brain.

"Hey! What about your food?" Ellen shouted. He'd already disappeared through the kitchen and around the corner.

"Fuck it," Jeff said. "That boy's gonna do whatever he wants to. I'm not waiting on him. Let's eat."

31

Andy couldn't remember the last time he'd used the small white alarm clock on his bedside table. For years, he'd custom-tailored the schedule of his classes, and most of the other things in his life, to eliminate early risings.

This morning was different, though. Andy had gone to bed early, but not before anguishing over his wardrobe and his portfolio of writing samples. His single suit – the same one he'd trotted out for his last disastrous meeting – was ready to go, but this time featuring a more subtle silver and purple patterned tie. His portfolio, a black, faux-leather case containing the paltry sum of his writing experience to-date, was equally meager.

The suit hung neatly from a thin border of molding outlining his closet. The portfolio sat on the stuffed chair across the room. Both lay in wait as the little white box sprang to life, screaming shrill beeps less than a foot from Andy's head.

Most mornings, that sound would have been met with animosity, violence or profanity – possibly all three. But this morning, Andy was clear of purpose, and uncharacteristically enthused from the get-go. He'd slept well, and rose without any stalling and grumbling. He felt a foreign energy pulse through his body, like a small electric current bringing his brain and extremities to life. It was 8:30 in the morning, and to his great surprise, Andy Maxwell was not only awake, but happy and excited to be alive.

His first instinct was to check the bedside table, in search of the single tri-folded piece of white paper. It was, of course, exactly where he'd left it. Andy unfurled it and pored over the short correspondence once more. In his haste, he had quite possibly jumped the gun. Upon re-reading the letter, it occurred to him their only request was that he contact them to schedule an interview. Perhaps laying out his suit and prepping his book had been presumptuous. But Andy had already built a head of steam in the few short moments he'd been awake. He decided he'd simply move forward. It was just after 8:30. By the time he peed, got himself a cup of tea, read a bit of the newspaper, and watched a few minutes of SportsCenter, surely it would be 9:00. Andy was determined that the first thing Ms. Gina Lavell was going to do today at Firebrand Marketing was hear his voice.

He was close. He'd scanned the morning headlines, and was sitting upright in the living room's blue recliner, staring impatiently at the muted TV as last night's baseball highlights and scores filtered across ESPN. He stared at the clock above the TV, watching as the second hand inched around the circle; four more minutes.

Given the butterflies churning in his stomach, Andy had no intention of eating until after he'd concluded his business with Firebrand Marketing. But the pack of Winston Lights on the makeshift coffee table called to him.

Andy lit a cigarette and let the smoke fill his lungs. The white-grey cloud he released mingled with the rays of early morning sun crashing through the windows. In the two years he'd lived there, he would have thought he'd smoked in every inch of the house at just about every time of day imaginable. But this combination of smoke and light was new and interesting. He stopped fixating on the clock, sending more streams of smoke into the bright column of light.

"Oh shit!" Andy muttered to himself, in a hushed tone, as he glanced back up at the clock. 9:01 AM. He hastily crushed the Winston and reached once again for the piece of paper.

32

Andy sat on the edge of the couch, stiff and hunched like a cathedral gargoyle, clutching the phone to his ear. The line rang. Like so many others he'd made in recent weeks, he assumed this call was bound for voicemail purgatory. Instead, to his surprise, a tinny and not-so-chipper female voice burst into Andy's ear.

"Good morning, Firebrand Marketing."

Andy froze. Introducing yourself was a simple enough thing to do, but somehow, the sound of a real human had flummoxed him.

"Hello?" the voice offered.

Say something, you stupid son-of-a-bitch! countered the equally-annoyed voice inside his own head. That voice was *never* at a loss for words.

"Hi. Yes. Hello." Andy, finally muttered, now feverishly scanning the short letter clutched in his left hand for the name of the woman he was supposed to be asking for.

"Good morning," the voice repeated. "How may I help you?"

"Good morning, ma'am," Andy responded, fumbling for focus. "May I speak with Ms. Gina Lavell, please?" He'd only spoken two sentences, but the level of hyper-politeness he'd achieved was immediately horrifying to him.

God. This is the EASY part, and you're even fucking THIS up! he thought as he waited for the voice to speak again.

"And who may I ask is calling?" the voice inquired.

"Yes, ma'am" Andy started again with the same politeness, and making a mental note to stop doing that. "My name is Andy Maxwell. She sent me a letter, asking me to call her about a writing position available there."

Too much detail? She doesn't care why you're calling. She just wants to know which button to press so she can transfer you and then go back to doing whatever you interrupted, and forget you even exist.

"One minute, Mr. Maxwell. Let me see if she's in."

Ah, Andy loved that one. He'd heard it a hundred times in the last few weeks, making unsolicited cold calls. The receptionist *has* to answer the phone. For everyone else, all bets are off. Most of the people he was trying to call were busy; Creative Directors, or other agency brass, had far more important things to do than talk to graduating students begging for jobs. Andy figured once again he was destined for voice mail. Once again, he was wrong.

"This is Gina."

He was surprised, not only to have gotten directly to her, but even more so by the tone of her voice. It was alarmingly high-pitched and carried an accent he couldn't place.

"Umm, good morning. Ms. Lavell?" Andy half-stated and half-asked.

"Yep. This is Gina," she replied.

"Hi. My name is Andy Maxwell. I received a letter the other day asking me to call you about a writing position available with your company."

"Okay," he thought to himself. *"That whole thought came out fine and might even have passed for professional."*

"Why, yes, Mr. Maxwell," answered Gina with a touch of enthusiasm that made her already-impossibly-high voice rise even further. The sounds of shuffling papers and typing were audible through the phone, as if she were trying to find some record or context for him as she spoke. "We are looking for a good writer. Is that you?"

"Yes, ma'am. It might be," he responded, as if by reflex, and as if there would be any other answer to a question like that. "I would love to come by and talk with you guys, and show some samples of my work."

Andy had shifted into the next highest gear, and was entering sales mode. He could feel his pulse quickening as he attempted to present himself as interested, but without the sense of over-eagerness that smacked of desperation.

And then, as if solely to counteract and disrupt that balance, the door behind Andy opened with a sharp, sickly creak. It startled him, wrecking his train of thought. Jeff lingered for a moment in the doorway. He stood, blurry-eyed on the threshold, gazing in confusion at the spectacle of Andy, awake and seemingly productive at ten after nine in the morning. Andy immediately put a raised index finger to his lips, silently beckoning his roommate to "shut the fuck up!", and then waved his arm furiously, attempting to usher him out of the room. Jeff wandered through the living room on his way to the bathroom, shuffling past Andy without ever saying a word.

"Well..." Gina began again, her shrill pitch demanding Andy's attention. "That'd be great..."

Andy's spirits rose in concert with Gina's voice, at the prospect of another interview.

"But..."

Dammit! Why was there always a 'but'? Andy wondered.

"You're gonna need to meet with Mr. Forrester, our VP of Marketing. He's our creative guy. But he's leaving this afternoon for two weeks of travel. Let me check his…"

"I can come this morning!" Andy blurted, now fully crossing the line into desperate territory, and without even considering whether it was feasible for either of them.

"Hmm. Can you hold for one minute?" Gina asked, taken aback by the suggestion, but apparently willing to consider it.

"Of course."

"K. Be right back."

Andy wasn't sure what had just happened. He'd either shown some degree of tenacity and determination, albeit still out of desperation, or he'd chosen to make his first impression that of a self-righteous, ego-maniacal newbie grad who assumed that the schedules of corporate vice presidents were flexible enough to accommodate his particular needs and wants.

"Shit," he said softly, into the dead air coming from the phone.

"What?" Jeff had finished his business, and was sitting bare-chested on the arm of the couch across the room.

"I'm on hold – about a job – shut up!" Andy said tersely, intent on making his point before Gina came back on the line. Jeff was content to slump into the couch, puff on his cigarette and watch the show in silence.

"Mr. Maxwell?" Gina returned.

"Yes. I'm here."

"Mr. Forrester is leaving at noon for the airport. Can you be here at 10?"

"Uh, sure." Andy stammered. It was almost 9:15 already.

"Do you know where our office is?" Gina chirped

"I've got the address from the letter, but can you give me directions?" Andy asked. He was starting to power-load anxiety in earnest as the clock's second hand continued its relentless sweep.

"Sure. We're down in the warehouse district on Century Street, by the riverfront. The complex is called Rayner Industrial Park. We're around back, off the road. It's suite 140."

"I know where that is," Andy replied. "It's not too far from here. I should be able to make it by 10."

Luckily for him, it was the truth. The riverfront was less than five miles from their house, and the warehouse district was an area to which he was no stranger. Actually, he'd been there quite often, but never to visit a company.

The district was home to a variety of businesses, but his context for the area was completely different. It also featured several vacant spaces which the landlord, in lieu of other more desirable suitors, was happy enough to rent to various local bands as practice spaces. There were, however, conditions. These bands were not allowed to 'interfere with or cause undue hardship upon' the operation of their business neighbors. All this really meant was that they couldn't make a shitload of crazy noise or pack the parking lot with droves of intoxicated misfits – at least during normal business hours during normal business hours.

Sure. Andy, like all of his friends, had been to the warehouse district – probably a hundred times. But he'd hardly ever been there in the daylight. To think he was headed there for a job interview kind of fucked with his head a little bit. But, as the clock on the wall reiterated, there was no time for that now.

"Ok, Mr. Maxwell. We'll see you shortly."

"Yes ma'am. Thank you, ma'am," said Andy, to no reply. Gina was already on to the next thing in her day.

"Oh shit!" Andy burst, louder and in the general direction of Jeff. He was moving now, racing back toward his room, with no time to waste on conversation.

"What? What happened?" Jeff wanted to know, following him.

"I have an interview. In… 42 minutes." Andy said, pulling at his plaid pajama pants and white t-shirt. He was a bit frantic but happy, feeling the small smile forming on his face even through the shroud of anxiety.

"That's awesome, dude," Jeff encouraged.

"Yeah. Awesome. Except I have 41 minutes to shave, shit, shower, dress, and drive over to the riverfront."

"Go, man! Go! I'm outta your way!" Jeff cheered, retreating back to the kitchen to start making a pot of coffee.

33

It wasn't even 9:30 yet, but Andy could already tell today was going to be a scorcher. He'd read somewhere that cold showers invigorated the body and mind, brought greater mental focus, and had a way of steeling one's nerves against adversity. It was brutal self-flagellation at first, but proved a solid strategy in the end.

As he stepped from the ultra-narrow shower stall, naked and dripping, he could feel his body's temperature trying to regulate to the warm, heavy air around him. He wrapped a large, ripped pink towel around his waist and traveled the four feet from the bathroom to his bedroom in two quick hops. Before the door even closed behind him, he was naked again. 9:36 a.m.

The matter of his wardrobe required no thought at all. It wouldn't have taken him long to put something together anyway, but he was proud of his choice to iron and prep his ensemble last night.

As he began to assemble the various layers—underwear and undershirt, pants and shirt, tie and belt, and finally shoes and jacket— Andy's body temperature rose incrementally. Four minutes ago, he'd been standing naked in a cascade of cold, cleansing water. And now, as he pulled the cheap suit jacket on and turned to face himself in the mirror, he could feel and see tiny beads of sweat forming below his hair line. He bent down, picked up the moist pink towel, and mopped his brow with it before tossing it over the back of the chair to dry. Andy checked his reflection. After fiddling with the placement of the knot in his tie, he decided he was presentable enough. 9:43 a.m.

He gathered his portfolio case and threw open the bedroom door. Thanks in large part to adrenaline and hope, he felt miles better than usual. He was ready.

"Want some coffee to go?" Jeff asked, as Andy buzzed through the kitchen.

"Nope. I'm already jittery from excitement. And coffee gives me the shits. But, thanks."

"Okay, then." Jeff said, moving past the unpleasant thought. "Well, good luck!" The door closed behind Andy, his friend's well wishes widening his smile as he stepped off the porch.

He tossed the portfolio case across the center console of his SUV and into the passenger seat. He sat behind the wheel and draped his suit coat carefully over the top of the case. The vehicle's engine roared to life, along with its dashboard lights and too-loud stereo. A raucous blast of musical rage, courtesy of Soundgarden, punched him right in the face. With veins already full of natural adrenaline, it was the last thing he needed just then. Whether by serendipity or sheer luck, the tape in the deck was a double-sided, dichotomous mix—mayhem on one side, mellow on the other. Andy pushed the flip button with haste and was instantly rewarded. The first few bars of Jimmy Page's Celtic-tinged acoustic masterpiece *Bron-Y-Aur* came forth to soothe the savage beast. 9:48 a.m.

Twelve minutes to drive four miles, park, and walk into the offices of Firebrand Marketing. He actually had a shot at being on time. Andy yanked the vehicle into reverse, backed out of the driveway, and aimed up Cornwall's steep hill toward the riverfront.

Traffic was light, and his luck with green lights was adding to Andy's overall feeling that everything might just work out. This was exactly the kind of last-minute adventure—the kind he himself did not orchestrate—that would normally throw him into a spiral of nervous panic. But he'd started to learn it wasn't so much the situations themselves that made him suffer, as the anticipation. Once the ball started rolling, and he had to react in real time to things, he usually did quite well. It was when he had time to think, analyze, and over-analyze a situation that dread fear and paralysis took hold.

Bolts of sunlight bombarded his windshield as Andy approached the turn-in to Raynor Industrial Park. As he guided his vehicle into an alleyway between two distressed red brick industrial buildings, he noticed a sign atop one of the buildings announcing the name of the complex. He'd been here dozens of times but never noticed it. He wouldn't have been able to tell you before today what the place was actually called. They'd always just referred to them as The Warehouses. 9:54 am.

He continued down the narrow, brick-lined canyon, emerging on the other side into a small blacktop parking lot. At nearly 10 in the morning on a weekday, there were a surprising number of cars already here. The sign directly ahead ushered him to the left. A hundred yards down, back in the original direction he'd traveled on the street side of the complex, he located Suite 140.

As he approached, his instincts drew him toward the white, green and blue signs that designated handicapped parking. For years now, he'd been conditioned to look for them. The several surgeries he'd had to his legs justified his ownership of the placard that legally qualified him to park there, but he chose instead an empty regular spot across the aisle. The difference in distance was negligible, but his real motivation was not wanting anyone at Firebrand Marketing to see him pulling up and parking in a handicapped spot, and then more-or-less walking "normally" into the building. He figured that was the kind of first impression that could earn him more asshole points than his resume could overcome. 9:56 am.

Andy shifted the SUV into park and leaned backwards until his head came to a full stop against the cushioned grey cloth of the head rest. He breathed deeply and deliberately. He closed his eyes for a moment, and breathed again – slowly, deeply, deliberately. No radio. No engine noise. Just the last gasps of the air-conditioned coolness escaping from the vents and dissipating into the warming summer air. He could feel a slight tightness in the middle of his chest as the silent car cabin let his beating heart take center stage. He lifted the cover of the SUV's armrest console. There inside, amongst a smattering of pocket change and receipts, he found what he sought—an ever-present plastic box of peppermint Tic

Tacs. Popping the top, he spilled two small oblong mints into his palm and took them. He'd read somewhere that peppermint was a natural digestive calmative. He didn't know if it was true, but between fresher breath and the placebo assurance of gastrointestinal serenity, he didn't really care. 9:59 am.

34

At precisely 10:00 am, as if by some grand design, Andrew Maxwell walked up the four small concrete steps that led to Suite 140 of Raynor Industrial Park.

It wasn't until he'd reached the precipice of the establishment that he started to notice a few non-traditional details. For starters, the front door was not glass, or even wood, but a sturdy, unattractive metal. There was a simple placard affixed to the brick wall, affirming that this was in fact Suite 140, but no corporate name or other descriptors. He registered these facts, but was focused more on setting foot in the lobby before the minute hand made one more lap around the clock. As he opened the heavy metal exterior door, it was clear this was no typical office environment.

Andy was surprised, first by the strange weight of the door, but also to find himself standing in a small glass room not much bigger than a phone booth. Behind him, the metal door closed with enough emphasis to create a sudden sense of claustrophobia. To his left, there was a floor-to-ceiling brick wall. The walls in front and to his right were glass, and included another door. Andy reached for its handle. A quick tug revealed the glass door was locked, presumably with a magnetized security seal. Only then did he notice the intercom box attached to the wall to the right of the door frame. It had a small circular red button and a plaque underneath it which read, "Ring For Service, Please."

Confused by the odd entryway and awash in fresh anxiety, Andy pushed the button not once, but twice in quick succession. Instantly, a voice came through the intercom.

"May I help you?"

The voice was female, and soft but robotic. Andy couldn't be sure to what degree this effect was caused by the intercom itself or the strange echo that seemed to result from its broadcast into the small glass booth.

"Hi. Andy Maxwell, here to see Mr. Forrester." Andy managed to push out the response.

"Ah." came the monotonous reply. It was followed by a buzzing sound and a loud click from the door frame, signaling that the magnetic field had been broken. "Come in." This last bit seemed a bit more human, if not actually cordial.

Andy pushed the glass door forward far harder than necessary and nearly fell into the lobby. It would have made for an awkward first impression if there had been anyone watching. There wasn't.

He composed himself—standing up straight, slowing his breathing, and smoothing his cheap purple tie. A young girl with shockingly shiny jet black hair sat behind a massive reception desk to Andy's right. She had paid him enough mind to buzz him through the security door but was otherwise ignoring him from behind the pages of the paperback she was apparently being paid to read. Andy was grateful for the momentary snub. He took a deep breath and approached the desk.

"Andy Maxwell. Here to see…"

"Yes. I know," the receptionist said curtly. The intercom in the glass booth had accentuated her disaffected monotone, but not by much.

"Mr. Forrester is busy. I'll ring Ms. Lavell for you," she droned, still averting her gaze.

"Thanks," Andy replied, having loudly received the message from the World's Least Friendly Receptionist.

He watched her for a few seconds more as she used the phone to announce his arrival. Her death-black hair, alabaster skin, and the exaggerated mascara around her freakishly green eyes gave her the appearance of a bizarre gothic china doll. She was attractive in a scary,

183

plastic sort of way, but completely unapproachable. Besides, Andy had other goals today. He turned and stepped away from the desk, satisfied to occupy another portion of the lobby while he waited.

Less than a minute later, a woman of disarming height and appearance rounded the corner. She was close to six feet tall, even without the bonus of three-inch heels. Andy attempted to survey her discretely, but it was impossible. Pink, textured tights encased her prolonged legs before disappearing beneath a plain black skirt. Even her haircut was intriguing. It was close cropped, nearly razor shaven at the back with increasing volume as it came forward over the crown of her head. It also had more colors—a full gradient of reds, browns and blonde—than he could comprehend in one quick viewing. Andy thought it looked cool. He finished scanning upward just in time to make eye contact as she reached him.

"Hey, Andy. I'm Gina. We spoke on the phone this morning," she said, extending her long arm to shake his hand.

Andy grasped her cool, ring-less hand. "Hi. Nice to meet you."

"Thank you, Sera." Gina said to the receptionist, who was no longer ignoring them.

"Sure, Gina. My pleasure," replied the now-not-at-all robotic young girl behind the desk. It was as if someone had pushed a button on the back of her cold ceramic neck, instantly transforming her into a polite, engaging human.

"Yes, thank you." Andy repeated, before turning his attention back to Gina.

"Thanks for coming in so quickly," Gina offered. The tone of her voice was not quite as high as he recalled from their phone conversation, but it was still unique and trill enough to demand his undivided attention.

"No problem. I'm just glad I could catch Mr. Forrester before he headed out of town."

"Absolutely," Gina agreed. "Come this way."

She made a half turn back toward the corner wall from which she had emerged and led Andy down a narrow hallway that ran behind the foyer. The interior passageway was flooded in artificial fluorescent light. If there were any windows in the building, he couldn't see them. The floors were cold polished concrete, and all of the walls were either stark white or the same natural brick as the building's exterior. *Not exactly warm and welcoming,* Andy thought.

Andy's under-developed legs struggled to keep pace with Gina as she cruised down the tight hallway. She took a sharp left and disappeared from his view for a second. Andy rounded the corner and found Gina stopped at the entrance of a conference room. He saw her standing there, but his gaze was transfixed by something altogether different.

Directly behind her, twenty feet in the distance, stood a floor-to-ceiling vault door—the kind you would expect to see at a bank or in some Hollywood heist film. Andy studied it in awe for several seconds as he continued to advance toward Gina and the open conference room door.

"Pretty cool looking, huh?" Gina said, with measured nonchalance that was almost ironic.

"Uh, yeah," It was all Andy could muster as he considered the behemoth mystery.

Gina ushered him into the conference room, which also had no exterior windows. It did however have a glass wall that provided a perfect view of the giant vault down the hallway.

"Have a seat. Can I get you something to drink? Coffee? Water?"

185

"Water would be great. Thank you," Andy replied, clearing his throat. He chose a seat along the long side of the table, near but not at the corner, from which the safe was still visible.

"Sure. I'll be right back."

Andy fought the urge to blurt out a question about what they kept in the safe. He knew better, though. That would have been rude, and he was hoping to get context for that, and the other interesting things he'd seen this morning too, during his chat with Mr. Forrester.

Andy sat calmly in the conference room, silently practicing the presentation of his portfolio. The few interviews he'd had up to this point hadn't exactly polished him, but they had at least made him aware of some pitfalls to avoid. He glanced once again at the vault door down the hall, wondering to himself not only what was inside, but also what it would be like to spin the five-spoked wheel handle, open that massive door, and step inside it.

Another wave of anxiety washed over him as he started second-guessing the seat he'd chosen. Originally, he *wanted* to be staring at that vault, but now it was proving to be a major distraction. He looked up at the clock that hung above the door. 10:08 am. He wondered if he had time to change his position at the table. But before he could act on the impulse, it was too late.

35

"Good morning, Mr. Maxwell."

Andy, who'd been looking down at his portfolio case, heard the gruff masculine voice before he saw the body it belonged to. He raised his head and instinctively stood up at the notion of someone entering the room.

Evan Forrester was a tank-like slab of a man. Roughly the same height as Andy, he appeared to be nearly twice as wide. He wasn't fat, just solid and oddly square. A high-and-tight box of mostly grey hair sat atop his head, and from the base of his nearly non-existent neck to his mountainous shoulders and on down, there was almost no taper to his frame.

Andy would normally have tried to break the ice with a half-joke, or casual statement, like asking to be called 'Andy', instead of 'Mr. Maxwell'. But he was taken aback by Forrester's stature and assertive entrance and opted instead to extend his hand in silence.

Evan came the rest of the way to him, stopping at the corner of the table. He clasped Andy's young, unhardened hand in his, which appeared to Andy to be about the size of a glazed Virginia ham. Andy looked him straight in the eye. Even though Forrester wore a smile in the middle of his square, grizzled face, Andy could tell he was a take-charge kind of guy who was going to do most of the talking here.

"Good to meet you son. Have a seat," said Forrester. Andy happily obliged. Only once seated did he notice that Gina had also entered the room, and had closed the conference door behind her.

"I'm a busy guy, Maxwell. Too busy, in fact, which, hopefully is why you're here," Evan started in. Andy guessed, although it took no real expert deduction, that Mr. Forrester was ex-military. The chiseled physique, no-nonsense demeanor, and apparent habit of referring to people by their last names were all fairly decent indicators.

As he sat, Andy glanced back in Gina's direction, as if seeking some sort of reassurance. Her eyes shone bright from behind her square-framed glasses, and she gave him the slightest of smiles before turning her attention back to Evan in a subtle, but direct manner that suggested he do the same.

"You're a writer."

Andy couldn't tell by the tone of Forrester's voice, or his delivery of the line, whether this was a statement, a rhetorical question, or an inquisition that required his reply.

"Yes, sir," Andy replied simply, assuming the answer would satisfy any scenario.

"And you've done technical writing?" Forrester asked.

Andy had learned, the hard way, the dangers of answering questions in too great of detail, or worse, getting sidetracked and answering a question you weren't even asked. He was determined to play this one cooler and more direct.

In any real sense, the truthful answer to Forrester's question was 'no'. But like most other recent graduates, Andy's resume was an exercise in creative presentation and spin. What he lacked in real experience—which was substantial—Andy tried to compensate for with clever, vague packaging. In reality, he'd been responsible for creating an embarrassingly basic, ugly newsletter for a company owned by friends of his family, since he was a senior in high school. On paper, this translated into his being a "Communications Liaison" and a "Marketing Consultant." And as for "technical writing?" Sure. Those 200 pages of sales scripting and maintenance catalogs he'd edited for the same small company qualified him, right?

"I have." Andy replied, with an intentional vagueness he hoped would buy him a follow-up question that he could attack more squarely.

Forrester continued to pace the conference room floor, maintaining a constant momentum.

"So then, let me get to the point, Maxwell," Evan stated bluntly. "You're a writer. And I need one, like yesterday. I had a guy, a real smart guy—a reserve in the Marines—doing this job for about a year. He just went active duty, so now I gotta replace him."

Andy was about to break in and ask a question, but Forrester kept rolling.

"You caught me at a good time...and a bad time. I need someone fast. Someone good. We have a lot to do around here, but I'm going to be traveling for most of the rest of the month. In fact, I'm leaving for the airport in about ten minutes. I'd hate to wait a couple more weeks to hire someone."

"Okay," Andy stated, sure that Forrester was going to continue.

"So here's, the deal," Evan continued, checking the large silver chronograph on his wrist, even though there was a clock on the wall right in front of him.

"We're what you'd call a specialized marketing company. We deal exclusively in firearms. We create highly-detailed technical manuals for a variety of automatic and semi-automatic weapons. Hand guns, shotguns, hunting and assault rifles—you name it. If it shoots, we can teach you how to assemble it, disassemble it, fire it, clean it, and care for it."

Andy could feel the blood draining out of his face as a wave of cold despair built in his skull, and washed straight through his chest to his legs and feet.

189

'Fuck'. The single word was loud and clear inside his head. He was pretty sure he hadn't said it out loud...at least he hoped not.

Forrester kept talking.

"We do some catalog stuff, too, and the occasional ad or booth for local and regional gun shows. But mostly, I need someone who can crank out a ton of mechanical documentation on the latest line of weapons from our manufacturing partners."

"That's what's in the safe," Andy said, this time very much aloud, but to no one in particular. The non-descript building, the heavy metal front door and the glass booth, the giant safe. It all made pretty simple sense when you pulled the curtain back. But Andy couldn't have imagined a more disappointing or disheartening grand reveal. He was staring again at his portfolio case, realizing now that there was little or no chance it was even going to get opened today.

"Very good," Evan responded, in a matter-of-fact way that suggested he wasn't giving Andy much credit for connecting the dots. "There's about a million dollars worth of firearms locked up in there. We get to hold onto them for 'hands-on reference' while we document them, and then most of them we send back when we're done. Some of them—the really cool ones—I buy to add to my personal collection. Of course, there's no ammo in the building, but we can take just about anything we want over to the range and well, you know, blow off some steam."

There was a gleam in Forrester's eye and a much wider, almost maniacal grin on his face as he reveled at the notion of endless gun play. Andy tried hard to have no reaction at all.

"Okay," Andy repeated, searching for other words and failing.

"I know. It's kind of cool to think about," Forrester assumed for Andy. "In fact, if you love guns, or even like 'em, this could be a bit of a dream job."

Forrester was clearly talking to himself at this point and hadn't noticed Andy's lack of shared enthusiasm. He had a schedule to keep, and he was simply moving forward.

"Alright. This is a little rude, but I gotta get moving," Forrester announced. He extended his massive hand again to Andy, who stood and accepted it.

"You got some thoughts in your head, son. I can see that. And I'd like to hear 'em, but I'm gonna miss my flight. Miss Lavell here has shared your info with me, and she has all the details of the job, so you can ask her anything you'd like. Here's my card. Why don't you talk to Gina, and call me on Monday, and we can work out getting you started."

"Okay." It was all Andy seemed capable of saying at this point, as the Forrester Express kept rolling along.

Evan handed Andy a business card and swiftly walked out of the room. 10:12 am.

The whirlwind had come and gone in less than five minutes, during which Andy had managed to speak only seven words. He sat back down, a bit dazed and very confused. Had he just been offered a job? He looked up at Gina, who sat across the table, fingers interlocked, smiling at him.

"So... that was Mr. Forrester," Gina said, with a semi-apologetic but amused smile.

"Can I get that glass of water, please?" Andy answered quietly.

36

In Andy's absence that morning, the house on Cornwall Street was noticeably more serene. Ellen emerged from her bedroom freshly showered, but still sporting a blue and white striped towel piled high like a beehive atop her wet head. Entering the living room, she found Jeff sitting alone on the couch, reading a paperback. Steam from a coffee cup and smoke from a quarter-burnt Winston wafted over the makeshift table before him.

"Hey."

Jeff lingered in his book long enough to finish his current sentence and then looked up. He swept his long hair behind his ears and smiled, offering a slight wave in lieu of any words.

"Damn, it's quiet in here. When is Andy coming back?"

Jeff cleared his throat and took a long sip.

"Who knows? I guess the longer his interview takes, the better, right?"

"Yeah, I guess. He was really excited when he left here. So, I guess we'll see. Fingers crossed," Ellen said, redundantly acting out the expression for good measure.

"I know. I hope he finds what he's looking for."

"Me too. Actually, I just hope he finds some happiness," Ellen said, taking a cigarette from the open pack lying on the table and continuing to the kitchen in search of coffee.

"I think it's one and the same," suggested Jeff. "I think he's so pent up because he thinks he's gonna find some perfect situation that will magically make him happy."

"Isn't that what most people are looking for?" Ellen said, realizing she'd probably count herself amongst *most people*.

"Yeah. But that's the problem. Happiness doesn't work from the outside in. That's called 'pleasure', and people confuse the two all the time. Real happiness comes from the inside, and shines out."

"That's pretty deep, dude. Simple, but deep. I believe all that, but I guess it's a hard idea to sell to most people. Andy's sure not buying it."

"Yeah. Probably not. But it'd make his life a whole lot easier if he did," Jeff suggested. "You can struggle against the truth all you want, but there's nothing on that road except frustration and misery."

"Damn. I don't know if we should talk like this more, or less often." Ellen replied. "I feel better and worse about myself at the same time."

"Oh, you're fine. You..."

The ring of the phone seemed even louder in the unusual mid-morning calm. Sitting in the home's center exaggerated the sense of volume, as rings could be heard coming from four different phones at once.

"I got it." Ellen sprung from her chair and walked toward the kitchen.

Jeff, whose quiet morning session of reading seemed to be over, lifted himself from the couch and headed back toward the front porch to enjoy the rest of his smoke and his second cup of coffee.

Jeff ambled onto the porch, leaving the door open behind him. The slight breeze flowing across the porch provided a pleasant alternative to the staler, warmer air inside. The tail end of a bright blue garbage truck rolled through the intersection of the downhill block at Victory Street.

A young brown-haired girl jogged up the hill behind a golden retriever. As she passed the house, Jeff offered a friendly half-wave, which the girl never saw. He continued to watch her trudge up the hill, turning his head to the right, until something out of place registered in his peripheral vision.

Taped to the rusted letter box on the home's front wall was a small white envelope. Jeff exhaled a puff of smoke and stepped toward the box. In blue ink, in handwriting he did not recognize, was the simple word, "Friends."

Jeff pulled the envelope off of the letter box and was about to open it when Andy's green SUV came into sight. Jeff watched the vehicle as it barreled down the hill in obvious disregard for the posted speed limit of 25 mph. Jeff leaned against the peeling white bannister and waited with anticipation to hear his roommate's report.

37

Raucous music blared from the vehicle's open windows, as Andy swung the SUV hard left and pulled into the loose gravel driveway. Jeff was conflicted. He was intrigued by the mysterious envelope he was holding, but couldn't compel himself to turn his attention away from his roommate's arrival.

Andy killed the engine and flung the driver's side door open. As he climbed out and pushed the door closed, Jeff noticed immediately the stark contrast between Andy's present appearance and how he looked as he left less than an hour ago. The suit coat was absent. Once neatly pressed and tucked, Andy's bright white oxford shirt now hung loose and disheveled. He was still wearing the tie, but it too was loosened, and hung sloppily a few inches from the top of his unbuttoned collar. Even Andy's dark hair was in disarray, standing straight up off his head as if he'd been running his hands through it in anger. This was not the look of a man who'd just achieved a great success.

Jeff knew Andy like a book – a book wrought with few recurring themes and teeming with foul, caustic language. He knew it was unnecessary to ask for the details of his morning because Andy was the type of person who was going to tell you whether you wanted to hear it or not. Jeff remained quiet, leaning against the bannister with his coffee and cigarette as Andy approached. From closer range, Jeff could see there was a powder keg lurking below the surface, and a look in Andy's eyes that almost begged for someone, anyone, to light the fuse so he could go off. Jeff was determined not to be that person.

Jeff tried hard to not make eye contact lest he be baited to speak. He also found himself fighting the urge to giggle. Clearly Andy was agitated, and to do so would have been just plain rude. Jeff knew this dance, and more or less how it was going to play out. Jeff pulled hard on the cigarette, intent on extending the silence even if only for a few seconds more.

Gauging his roommate's body language and demeanor as he landed on the porch, Andy seemed to realize Jeff had no interest in sparking his impending explosion. Without a word, Andy set his path toward the front door. Before he got there, Ellen emerged through the open frame and joined them on the porch. She was still carrying the handset of the cordless phone.

"Hey! Andy! How'd it go?" Ellen asked with excitement, oblivious to the black cloud around him.

Jeff's head turned and lowered, and he closed his eyes as if preparing to shield himself from the shrapnel he knew was coming.

"It was fucking GUNS!" Andy blurted, uttering a response neither of them could have possibly anticipated or understood. "Fucking guns!"

Ellen was shocked by the volume and venom of his reply. She took a step to her left and cleared a path for him. He kept moving and entered the house. Ellen shot a confused look at Jeff, and mouthed the word "fuck" with exasperation. Jeff simply shrugged. The pin was already out of the grenade.

They followed him into the house, first Ellen, and then Jeff, who was still holding the small white stationery envelope in his hand as he closed the door.

In the span of mere seconds, Andy had managed to hurl his portfolio case onto the nearest chair and was already in the kitchen. Ellen and Jeff entered the living room and sat together on the nasty beige couch, leaving the recliner vacant for Andy upon his return. They waited patiently through the clinking of ice cubes and the shaking of the orange juice carton, neither of them daring to chastise Andy for making a pre-lunch screwdriver. Watching him go through the motions of making a drink; finding a cigarette, a lighter, and an ashtray; and coming back to address his audience was like sitting through the previews before the feature presentation at a movie theater. There was still a tangible funk surrounding him when he returned, but Jeff was hoping that at least a little fuel had burned off before Andy opened up.

Andy took a long, aggressive drink from the glass of pale yellow poison. He lit a Winston, tossed the lighter onto the side table next to the recliner, and dove in head first.

"So, I bust my ass to get ready in like no time," Andy started, with a full head of steam. "I drive out to the Warehouses, and there's a bunch of shit over there you can't even imagine. I pull up, and this place is like fucking Ft. Knox or something—all locked down, with double security doors and cameras and shit. Totally crazy. I get in there, and this jacked up old Army dude starts telling me about the million-plus dollars worth of fucking guns he's got locked up in a giant bank vault down the hall. And that's the job. He wants me to write a bunch of tech manuals about automatic and semi-automatic weapons. That's the whole fucking job – all guns, all the fucking time!"

Andy had worked himself into a lather, flailing his arms and spewing bits of alcoholic spittle as he ranted.

"And the worst part is he made it pretty much sound like the job was already mine for the taking."

"How is that the worst part?" Ellen wondered aloud. "Doesn't that solve your problem?"

She knew better, or at least she should have. She knew all about Tristan, about the past he wasn't about to let go of—both of his roommates did. But in the same way that Andy couldn't change who he was, or how he reacted to certain stimuli, neither could Ellen.

Ellen was a "fixer." She was patient, and liked talking to people about their problems, with the intention of actually resolving them. Unfortunately, Andy was every bit her equal – and opposite. For every solution, he was able and willing to find another problem.

Andy reveled in the art of argument and had remarkable stamina for it, as long as someone was willing to play the foil and keep pressing him. He was always going to have the last word, and the worst thing you could do was to keep asking him questions.

Jeff had figured this out long ago, and it was a game he had grown tired of playing. Eventually, he'd begun avoiding these kinds of conversations altogether. But this one was larger, with implications that affected them all.

Andy's failure to solve this particular problem would mean the dissolution of their little family home and a 33% increase in Jeff's own rent, at least until they could find someone to replace Andy. This reality was motivation enough for them to at least have a conversation about it. So Jeff and Ellen settled in and waited for the next episode of *The World According to Andrew Maxwell* to begin.

"Fuck no," Andy countered. "It doesn't solve my problem. It's a cruel joke."

"I know exactly what I want to do, and I've been trying for weeks now to get someone to take me seriously—to give me a shot. I know I can write. I have good ideas, and know how to work with other people to make shit happen."

"Like throwing 80 shoes in a tree?" Jeff asked.

"Exactly!" Andy defended. "That *was* a good idea. That shit got put in the newspaper. It got noticed. Talked about. People are *still* talking about that."

Suddenly, Jeff and Ellen were fighting a losing battle not to laugh at the detour Andy's explosion had taken.

"Screw you, though" he blasted, determined to finish his point. "You know that's not what I'm talking about. All I want to do—the only thing I know *how* to do—is write. It's all I'm good at. But so far, the only lead I've got is the fuckin' gun palace."

"So, there's no way you'd even consider..." Ellen persisted.

"Are you fucking serious?" Andy blurted. "You know I fucking hate guns. They only have one function: to kill a living thing. So no, I don't think I could spend my whole day waxing on about all the virtues of probably the most evil thing ever invented."

"But don't people in advertising have to sell shit they don't believe in all the time?" Jeff asked.

"Yes," Andy admitted. "They do. But there's a sliding scale. I know cigarettes and alcohol are bad for you. But I could write about those all day long. I could find some moral loopholes to justify peddling those brands of death. They help certain economies. They're non-violent choices that more often result in harm to the purchaser than others. Hell, it'd be hypocritical of me to blast those things. Even politics I might be able to stomach. But guns? I can't do it. I just can't do it."

He stopped ranting long enough to take another long sip of his screwdriver. Andy stared for a moment at his shiny black leather wingtip shoes. He consciously tried to slow his breathing and suddenly found himself with nothing left to say. Ellen and Jeff sat likewise silent on the couch across from him, neither sure exactly what would or should happen next.

Ellen's gaze turned to the blue plastic clock that hung above the door frame leading into their kitchen. Its sweeping second hand served as a reminder that she had somewhere to be. She promised Traci she would meet her at the restaurant in 30 minutes, and she still needed to dry her hair and finish getting ready.

Her primary job, bartending at The Green Room, was typically a happy-hour-to-close shift. It almost always paid for her portion of the rent and basic living expenses, but she also had a pretty solid backup plan to help pay for incidentals and "extracurricular activities."

She had plenty of experience in the restaurant business, doing everything from hostessing and waiting tables, to tending bar, prepping kitchens and working as a sous chef. Her former roommate, Traci, was now the daytime manager of Bradford's gaudiest Mexican cantina, El Lagarto Guapo – *The Handsome Lizard*.

From time to time, when any of the many slackers who staffed the kitchen or bar called in 'sick', Traci would call Ellen and see if she wanted to pad her pockets by picking up a bonus shift. For Traci, it was easier than having to constantly fire mostly reliable people and hire unknowns who weren't probably going to be any more reliable. For Ellen, it was easy, non-committal work. In the short view, it was a win-win.

"Andy," she said gently. "I don't want to walk away from this, but I gotta go help Traci through the lunch rush at the Lizard. Can we talk more later?"

Jeff had turned his attention to the stationary card he'd found taped to their mailbox. He'd opened the envelope and had been reading the short note inside during the awkward silence that followed Andy's tirade.

"Yeah," replied Andy, dejected in general, but not by her. "Whatever. I don't know what else there is to talk about. It's cool. Go do your thing."

"Hold up," Jeff suggested. Ellen had risen and was already walking toward her bedroom. "There's something else."

Jeff held aloft the small white note card. "This was on our mailbox this morning."

"What is it?" Andy mumbled through an ice cube.

200

"Dear Neighbors," Jeff began. "Quenton and I would love if you could join us for dinner on Thursday. 6 PM. Bring nothing but yourselves. Signed, Lula Murphy."

"What the hell?" Andy replied.

"Okay. That's weird," Ellen added, now walking back into the room.

"I know." Andy joked. "Who the hell is named Lula?"

"No, dumbass. The whole thing. We've been here for like two years, and I don't think I've said 100 words to either one of them in that time."

"Really?" said Jeff. "I talk to Quenton, all the time."

"Me too. I drank a beer in the driveway with him just the other day. But I don't think I've ever even met Mrs. Murphy."

"Looks like you're gonna get your chance," said Ellen.

"Wait. Did that say Thursday?" Andy asked. "*Today* is Thursday."

"Uh, yeah," replied Jeff. "So, what do you wanna do?"

"Fuck it," said Ellen. "I say let's go. I mean, I gotta do the lunch thing with Traci, but I'll be back by 5, and I don't have to be at the Green Room until 8:30. I'm in, if you guys really want to go."

"Really?" asked Andy.

"Sure," Jeff agreed. "First of all, I bet whatever Lula Murphy is cooking tonight is way better than any of us were going to eat otherwise. And second, none of us has anything better to do, so bailing would just be rude."

He was right on both accounts. And so it was settled. At six o'clock, the three of them would join their elderly black neighbors for an evening of conversation and cuisine far more sophisticated than they experienced on most Thursdays.

"Well shit!" Ellen exclaimed. "Now I'm gonna be fuckin' late."

"Nobody's gonna care how your hair looks at the Lizard. Traci's gonna make you wear a net or a cap anyway," Andy teased. Both boys laughed at her expense as she slipped on her shoes and worked a brush through her still-damp hair.

"As for you and I..." Andy continued, now pointing to Jeff, as he walked towards the Den. "We better get busy."

"Busy with what?"

"We've only got a handful of hours until we have to be sober as church mice. Better top off the tanks."

38

With Ellen gone, Jeff and Andy migrated to their own rooms at the far ends of the home, but only for a moment.

The two shots of vodka Andy had wolfed down were beginning to bring a sense of calm. He took a few deep breaths and finished changing from his interview clothes into a pair of athletic shorts and a cleanish t-shirt. He didn't need to dress to impress for his next appointment.

Reclaiming his near empty glass as he swept through the living room, Andy took a left into the narrow hallway that led to the Den. There, he found Jeff already waiting for him. A telltale rosewood box lay on the table between them.

"I was going to ask you if you wanted one, but it looks like you found your way onto the train all by yourself," said Andy, eyeing the freshly poured screwdriver that sat in front of Jeff.

"Sometimes you *do* have good ideas," Jeff joked. "And here's *my* good idea... Grab the Hydra."

"That *is* a good idea," Andy replied.

Jeff was testing the airflow on the Hydra, pulling deeply on one of its four hoses until small bubbles appeared in the bulbous yellow chamber. All systems were go.

Andy scanned the surface of the coffee table. Locating the remote control peeking out from an old issue of *NME* magazine, he clicked the TV set to life. He didn't care what was on, or even that the volume was presently muted. In fact, when it wasn't being used as a video game monitor, the small color set was often on but silent.

Either the Den's small TV or the other slightly larger set in the home's living room was almost always on. Edward R. Murrow was right –

television was indeed the new opium of the masses. It might not have been clinically diagnosed as an "addiction," but Andy definitely had a psychological relationship with, if not an actual dependence upon, the very idea of television.

He'd been self-conditioned—first as a latch-key kid, and now as a less-than-ambitious quasi-adult—to turn to television as a source of comfort. It was an ever-present companion, like a good friend, a frequent entertainer that often bolstered his self-esteem and only occasionally told him things that made him angry or uncomfortable.

It was 12:30 in the afternoon, which meant another dose of *The Mack Riley Show* was gracing the airwaves. Even with the sound off, Mack made it easy enough to follow along. The title of the episode was always superimposed, in can't-miss white letters along the bottom of the screen. Today's episode was entitled, "I Was Better Off in Prison."

Andy watched the silent screen with strange delight as Jeff packed the Hydra's bowl and finally announced "we're ready."

They each grabbed one of the Hydra's tentacles, placing the rubber-tipped ends to their pursed lips. Jeff lit the huge bowl, and they both began to inhale. A normal, one-person bong could be fogged and dispersed in the span of a single breath. The Hydra required a bit more effort. The first breath of the partakers was almost always dedicated to filling the large chamber with smoke. Once it had reached capacity, it was wise to pull back from the hoses, cap them with a thumb, and take a few deep clean breaths before proceeding.

"One. Two. Three," Jeff counted. In lock-step, the synchronized smokers dove back toward the hoses, filling their lungs with the ice-cooled, super-potent smoke. It was nearly impossible to manage an entire lungful from the Hydra without coughing, and they both did their best to hold their breath for a moment before gasping out thick billows of smoke. Before they'd even exhaled, the chemicals had begun buzzing their brains, firing certain synapses and inhibiting others.

Andy gave his attention back to the TV. He had been half-watching the silent drama brewing on the television set, as members of Mack Riley's panel shared their angst. He reached for the remote again, and notched the volume up. A scrawny white dude with a shaved head and several neck tattoos was blabbering in an exaggerated ghetto accent about how bad his life was now that he was 'free.'

"Serious, man. At least in the joint I had food, clothes, a roof, some TV. I'm outside now. Ain't no jobs. Ain't no money. I gotta hustle a new place to sleep all the time. For what? I'm sp'osed to go outta my way to stay clean and to try, when there ain't nuthin' in it for me? Might as well knock over another store, and go back inside. I know it in there. It's easy. Don't cost nuthin', ya know?"

"Damn," Andy said, his head pulsing pleasantly now. "That's fucked up."

"What?" Jeff asked, not really paying attention to Andy or the TV.

"This guy. He'd rather go back to prison than try to get a job and live straight."

"Yeah. I don't really recommend that for you."

"Ha. Funny," said Andy. "But think about that for a minute. For that dude, his standard of living was better *in* prison than outside it. At least that's what he thinks, which I guess makes it true for him. He had someone giving him everything he needs, and now, his 'freedom' is actually like a burden because it comes with the cost of having to be responsible for himself. He'd prefer to have no responsibility, even if it means giving up all his rights. It's totally crazy, but there's a weird sort of logic to that."

"So, that's what you'd prefer?" Jeff asked, now engaged.

"Not *that* exactly. But think about it. Think about how we live. Shitty little house; shitty little jobs. We pay a few hundred bucks a month in rent and piss the rest away on having fun. Some people might look at that and say, "Screw it. Why does it *ever* have to get any better than that? I have everything I need. I could do better for myself, and I probably should, but that would mean I would have to try. So, why bother?"

So, now you're living in a prison?" Jeff concluded, connecting the dots his roommate had plotted.

"Aren't we all? I mean, we can all be content to stay where we are, where we know what's gonna happen and what's probably not—where we know our limits. The only other alternative is to doing something harder—try harder, do more, put yourself out there and risk getting hurt trying to learn something or do something new. That's what we're all living in."

"I could stay here and just keep doing this—do what's easy. I'd have to get another bullshit job to pay the rent. But the world—my parents, professors, my gut, and even the bullshit commercials on daytime TV— everything tells me I'm supposed to do more than that. I just don't know if I want to."

"Wow," Jeff said, through a billow of grey-white cigarette smoke "You really spend a lot of time thinking about shit like that, don't you?"

"Sometimes, shit like that is *all* I can think about. It drives me crazy. Makes my brain hurt."

"So, if that's 'not enough' as you say, what do you *really* want?"

"I just want to be happy," Andy blurted. The answer came fast and defensively, like a reflex.

"See, that's the problem right there," Jeff diagnosed immediately. "Happiness isn't something you can *get*. It's something you have to *give* yourself. It comes from being content with what you have and with who you are as a person."

Normally, that kind of response would get an argument from Andy, or would at least shut him down. Maybe it was the creeping calm of the weed that had started to filter through his brain. Or maybe his roommate had struck a chord. But for some reason, Andy was at least willing to hear more.

"I've read enough of that *Tao Te Ching* book you're always talking about to know that even the central idea of Buddhism is that 'the root of all suffering is desire'. If you're always *wanting* to be happy, you're always *going* to be miserable. If you just *decide* to be happy, there's a much better chance you actually will be."

"Can I be honest with you?" Jeff continued, now looking him square in the eye.

Andy was instantly uncomfortable. He recognized the sincerity in his friend's tone, but he also knew that nobody asks that question and then follows it up with anything nice.

"Sure," Andy said, almost out of defeat.

"You *are* living in a prison," Jeff stated. It wasn't what Andy expected.

"And it is mostly one of your own making – although, the like rest of us, you've had some help in building it."

"You've had bad shit happen to you, I know. We all have. But in a lot of other ways, you've had it pretty easy. Your parents put you through school and didn't ask that much of you in return. You just graduated from college with almost no real debt. Most people don't get that. I didn't get that. Ellen sure as shit ain't getting' that."

"What's worse…" Jeff continued, "is you've got all the talent you need, and more, to do exactly what you want to do. I've seen your work. I've seen you do your thing, and you're *good* at what you do. You just can't get out of your own way."

"I think you're afraid to step up and do what you gotta do on your own because you've never *had* to. Your parents were doing what they thought they should be doing, making it easy for you to succeed. But maybe they made things too easy. Now, you're up against having to do it alone, and you're scared. You're locked in a prison of self-doubt, scared to death of disappointing people, including yourself. And *that's* the worst prison of all, man."

Even if Andy had wanted to argue, there was no logical response to surgically-accurate assessment Jeff was doling out.

"Your biggest problem is that you honestly give a shit about what people think about you."

"Damn." Andy finally broke in, taking issue with that last critique. "*Everybody* cares what other people think, Jeff."

"No. They don't," Jeff corrected, not missing a beat. He sensed this might be the one opportunity he was going to get to say some of the things he'd been keeping inside for a while now, and he wasn't going to let it go.

"Most people *notice* what other people think about them and maybe even make adjustments based on that. But there's a world of difference between that and actually *caring* what they think – especially to the point that you live your entire life trying to please other people. 'Cause guess what? That's fucking impossible. And it's pointless to even try. No matter how smart you are, or how good you are at whatever you do, there's always going to be somebody out there who's just dying to tell you you're not good enough. No matter what. Chasing happiness through other peoples' approval is a fool's game. There's no way to win."

By the time Jeff finished his mini-lecture, Andy had subconsciously curled himself into the corner of the couch—defensiveness personified.

"So you just don't give a fuck what anyone thinks?" Andy asked.

"I didn't say that. I care what some people think. Like you. I care what you think, believe it or not. But I don't get my self-esteem or confidence from it. For the most part, I live my life, and do the things I want to do, the things that make me happy. I try not to hurt other people. If that's not good enough for people, then it's not good enough for *them*. Fuck 'em. But the best part is, I'm not responsible to *them* for anything. I don't owe anybody their happiness. And neither do you."

"Think about it, Andy. I do a lot of 'weird' shit people could easily make fun of. And maybe they do, who knows? I do theater. I sing and dance, for God's sake. And speaking of God, I work at a friggin' church. You think people think that stuff is *cool*?"

"I think a lot of people think it's cool the way *you* do it," Andy had to admit.

Jeff was taken aback by the odd endorsement.

"And it's cool that you think that," Jeff acknowledged in return. "But that's the point. The *way I do it* is with total joy for myself. And if what I do makes other people happy – that's a bonus. But if it doesn't, that's on them."

"Even the church part?"

"Especially the church part."

"I thought you just did that as a job, as another way to make money singing."

"No. I really do like church," Jeff said. "And believe it or not, I *love* God," he added emphatically.

"How can you say that?" Andy asked unexpectedly. Jeff had been playing offense the whole time, and the shift caught him off guard.

"Why?" Jeff projected back on him, "Because He lets bad shit happen, and how can I love Him for that?"

"No," Andy said plainly. "Because you're just as much of a degenerate as me—sometimes worse. But you go to church and *love God*, so it's all good? How does that work?"

A look of blank shock rolled across Jeff's face. For once, Andy hadn't even been looking for a fight. In all honesty, the shot he'd landed was much more of a random, blind deflection than some carefully planned body blow. But Jeff had felt the sting of the hypocrisy his roommate's assertion implied, and he was compelled to counter-punch.

"I thank God every day for the gifts He's given me," Jeff defended. "I may not wear that love on my sleeve like some people, and I certainly don't put it in other peoples' faces, like the friggin' zealots that give God a bad name in the first place."

Andy remained quiet.

"It's not something I need to talk about. I know how I feel about God and what that relationship is for me personally. I also know that most of the people we hang out with don't have that same experience, so I just don't talk about it."

"But isn't it more complicated than that?"

"What do you mean?"

"I don't know," Andy started, not really knowing where he was going. "Isn't it hard trying to live in both camps like that?"

"It used to be," Jeff admitted. "Until I realized that all of it makes me happy."

"So, as long as you're happy, that's all that matters?" Andy continued.

"Wouldn't you agree?"

"Absolutely," Andy said. "But I'm not trying to please God at the same time. Wouldn't He expect more from you?"

"You know what?" Jeff said, now glassy-eyed and miffed. "Why don't you just shut the fuck up?" He scoffed and lit a cigarette, looking to dismiss his friend's pointed assertion. Maybe if he was clearer of mind, he would have had a better answer. But at the moment, Jeff had nothing.

"How did we even get here?" Andy asked.

"Now, *that's* a question for God," Jeff joked. "The question for you is, 'why don't you stop talkin' shit and hit that again?'"

Already sufficiently damaged, Jeff offered one more solo pull from the Hydra to Andy, who was all too willing to oblige.

Alcohol, marijuana, failure, and self-help sermons can all be strong depressants. But at the moment, Andy's brain was marinating in a warm bath of euphoria. In truth, the extra helping was probably too much for him. A few short minutes later, they were both giddy and lethargic, nearly incapacitated at the hands of the Hydra.

They'd stopped talking, opting instead to let the nonsensical rambling of the television mesh with the humming in their heads. Without words, they both acknowledged the session was complete, their mission accomplished.

Andy couldn't remember telling his legs it was time to move, but suddenly they were. He was almost to the kitchen before it occurred to him he was up and walking toward the back of the house. From somewhere deep in his subconscious, his brain was sending signals to his extremities, demanding they cooperate in making sleep the next order of business.

The final toke of weed was clearly overkill, and Andy was profoundly intoxicated – just past the point of comfort. Making it to his bedroom by muscle memory alone, he eyed the sweet sanctuary of the bed across the room. But before he could get there, his equilibrium failed. His legs ceased to support his weight, and he stumbled forward. Halfway there, with a head full of static, liquor sloshing in an otherwise empty belly, and lungs burning in his tight chest, his knees buckled. He went down hard.

The last thought that crossed Andy's challenged mind as he slipped into the semi-consciousness of sleep was a simple, perhaps unintentional prayer: "God, help me."

Five hours had passed since Ellen left them unsupervised. Upon her return, she found both of her roommates' cars parked exactly as they had been, suggesting neither Andy nor Jeff had left while she was gone. The front door was unlocked, as it always seemed to be.

She was used to returning to an occupied and lively home. In fact, she was rarely ever in their house by herself. As she came through the door, she expected to be greeted by smoke or noise of some sort. Instead, she found herself standing in the front room, surrounded by absolute silence and still.

The door to Jeff's bedroom was closed. Being so near to the front entry way, it was a high-traffic zone, and Jeff correctly assumed keeping the door closed was the best way to protect not only his privacy while he was home, but also his belongings while he was not.

Ellen became hyper-aware of the shabby, loosened floorboards which creaked with her every step. As she reached the kitchen, the groaning of the hardwoods was replaced by a grosser, more depressing combination of sounds. That floor was covered by a sad layer of buckled and cracked linoleum which might have originally been something close to white in color. With each step down, the floor seemed to release some quantity of air trapped between the linoleum and the sub flooring. And with each step up, came the faint but grotesque ripping sound made as one's shoe soles broke the grip of the sticky film that seemed ever-present on that room's floor.

She placed the cardboard box she'd been carrying on the kitchen counter, and continued to the back of the house. Turning towards Andy's room, she expected to find his door closed, too. But it wasn't. From a distance of fifteen feet, Ellen peered through the open doorway upon a site she could not immediately process. There, on the bedroom floor, Andy lay face down and slightly fetal. He was still in the white undershirt and black socks which he wore to his interview—but now with a pair of dark blue athletic shorts. The rest of his suit lay strewn across the stuffed tan easy chair in the corner.

Seeing someone passed out, in their own house or someone else's, was nothing new to any of them, but this made her uneasy. As she came closer, now standing right next to his body, she heard the unmistakable sound of muffled breathing——a half snore. A gear in her brain shifted, moving her instantly from a sense of concern straight to severe agitation.

Only seconds ago, she would have knelt beside him and carefully checked on his condition. But now she now had a much less gentle technique in mind for waking him. Placing the kitchen-sticky sole of her shoe against his shoulder, she kick-pushed him onto his back.

"Wake up, princess!" she said, with no kindness.

"Huh?" Andy raised his hands to cover his still closed eyes.

"Get up," she repeated. "It's after five already. We have to be next door by six."

"Fuck," Andy groaned.

"Fuck is right," she continued "That's what I was saying as I walked in here after working an extra shift to find you passed out when we're supposed to be going to the Murphys' house for dinner. And where the fuck is Tweedle Dee?"

"I dunno," Andy said, struggling to shake off the webs of his afternoon nap. He was tired and still incoherent, but not so much so that he couldn't see she was pissed. "He's probably sleeping, too."

"Whatever. Get up, and get dressed. Be ready and happy about it by 5:45." she said curtly, and walked out the door.

Andy sat on the floor, listening as she retraced her steps back toward the front of the house. He heard a door being opened indelicately, and then her agitated voice again. He could hear Ellen loud and clear, but not Jeff, presumably because he had also just been awoken.

"Whatever..." she repeated, now loud enough to be heard throughout the entire house. "...he doesn't know his ass from his elbow lately, but you should know better." Clearly she was mad at both of them, but for different reasons. "Get up!"

One door slammed, and then several seconds later, another. If Jeff wanted to take a shower before heading over to the Murhpys, he was going to be second in line behind her.

Andy craned his neck to glance at the red digital readout on his bedside clock. 5:11 p.m. For the second time in eight hours, he would have to scramble to make himself presentable. He'd already completed the same drill earlier that morning, and knowing his evening appointment was far more casual, he felt less stressed than he normally would in a time-sensitive situation.

In fact, he felt tangibly less stressed in general. He rose to his feet, surprised at the looseness in his shoulders and back – surprised that he actually felt 'good'.

Over the course of the day, the heat had seemed to stack like layers, adding weight and a sense of burden to the air inside their home. The smallness of the back bathroom and its lack of any ventilation only compounded the problem. With the door closed, the heat and humidity conspired to create a thick, choking atmosphere, like being sealed in an eight square-foot Tupperware container.

Once again, Andy opted for the wakening punch of a colder shower. The sting of the cool water on his sweat-covered skin was brutal for the first few seconds. But as he began to adjust, the feeling turned from agony to near ecstasy. The heat rose through him, pouring out from the

215

top of his head, like a demon being forced from his body. He lingered, basking in the total refreshment of the cold cascade. He could have stayed there for much longer, but he was well aware of the time constraints Ellen had placed on him. He turned the water off and reached for the same ripped pink towel he'd used earlier that day.

5:30 p.m. He was right on schedule. A few short minutes later and he would be dressed and ready. He slipped on a pair of khaki pants – the kind he only wore when he used to work at the front desk of the nearby Howard Johnson's hotel, or whenever his parents would come to visit and want to take him to a 'nice' dinner somewhere. To these, he added a lightweight, short sleeve button down in green, white and yellow plaid. He wrestled with whether or not to wear a belt, which he hated. Ultimately he acquiesced in the name of making a decent impression. Slipping on a pair of brown topsiders, he decided he was as presentable as he was going to get.

Turning into the kitchen, he saw Ellen standing in the middle of the living room, brushing out her hair as she looked out the window. He said nothing to her at first, opting instead to take her in visually. Ellen was a jeans and t-shirt kind of girl. But there she stood, looking very unlike herself, in a greyish-blue, knee length skirt and a simple black top that was sheer and stylish. Black hose wrapped her suddenly-shapely-looking legs. Andy desperately wanted to crack a joke about someone letting a girl into their house, but based on the last interaction he'd just had with that *girl*, he thought better of it.

Instead, he wisely went with "Wow. You look awesome."

"Thanks," Her tone was neither angry nor friendly, and Andy was unsure how to proceed.

"Sorry about earlier," he said. He wasn't even sure what he was apologizing for, but he figured it was the best thing to say next.

"Yeah, me too. I guess there's a little tension around here lately, and I had a shitty time at The Lizard today. I didn't even want to go, but I did it anyway. Then I got home and you guys looked like you'd had quite the party without me. Kinda rubbed me the wrong way."

"Sorry," Andy repeated. "You know, that's one of the things I love most about you."

"What's that?" Jeff asked, now emerging from his room, also clean and wearing some of his better clothes. "When she plays sexy dress up?"

It was exactly the kind of barb Andy had resisted throwing out a moment ago, and completely counter to the sentiment he had planned to share.

"What?" she asked Andy, ignoring Jeff's adolescence.

"I love that you are willing to do things you don't *want* to do to help other people. I kind of suck at that."

There was actually a long list of things she legitimately loved about him too. But his apology and the unprovoked kindness that followed it caught her by such surprise, she blanked.

"You don't suck..." she started.

"Oh no, I do," Andy interrupted. "For the most part, I don't really do anything I don't want to do. I've been able to get away with that for a long time, but it's probably not a very practical way to live long-term."

Ellen was confused. Apparently she'd missed more than just a random round of bong hits while at The Lizard. She shifted her gaze to Jeff, who sort of gave her a 'We'll talk later' look...

"We gotta go," Jeff said. "We're gonna be late."

"Oh shit!" said Ellen, walking back toward the kitchen. "I almost forgot the pie."

"Pie!?" Andy said, with surprising enthusiasm. He loved pie.

"Yes," Ellen stated. "Pie. You can't just show up to someone's house empty-fuckin'-handed when they invite you for dinner. So, after my shitty afternoon at The Lizard, I stopped at In Your Face and got a pie."

"What'd you get?" Andy asked, with the bouncy excitement of a third grader.

"Mocha banana crème,"

"Damn. Not apple?"

"It's not about you," said Ellen, starting to get pissed again. "First of all, when your lazy ass is the one that spends the time and money to go get the pie, you can pick apple. But just so you know, apple is boring. Everyone knows banana crème is the most socially interesting of all pies."

Not everyone knew that; not even everyone in Ellen's house – or anyone other than her for that matter. They both looked at her as if she was speaking a foreign language, and laughed hard.

"Fuck you both," she snapped. "And secondly, you pricks both owe me eight dollars. Now say thank you, and let's go."

"Thanks, mom!" they cheered in unison, still laughing, and heading for the door.

41

It was all of 75 feet from their front porch to that of their neighbors next door. Chivalry, and perhaps trepidation, guided Jeff and Andy to fall in behind Ellen as she led the boys on the short walk. Where their broken-down driveway met the even-more-cracked sidewalk, she took a right and headed up the hill, carrying that pie like some sacred artifact. Ellen reached the door first and waited a few seconds for her straggling roommates to join her. In that moment, she had a horrible realization.

"Oh shit," she whispered, wheeling around to face her friends. Jeff failed to anticipate her move, and crashed into Ellen with enough force to buckle the pie box slightly between their midsections.

"What?" Andy asked, at full volume.

"Did either of you guys tell them we were coming?"

As stares went around the small circle, it became evident none of them had bothered to RSVP. There they stood, dressed and shiny, in near 100 degree heat, on their neighbors' porch, with a pie, quite possibly about to find themselves unexpected and unwelcome.

"What now?" Andy asked, now adopting a hushed tone and taking a step backwards. "Should we bolt?"

"Fuck that," Jeff said. "I'm hungry. Just ring the bell. They invited…"

"Yeah," interrupted Ellen, "they invited, but we never accepted, so they probably think we're total …"

Just then, the door opened behind her.

"…assholes," Ellen finished, still facing away from the house. Andy's face plumed red with embarrassment for her. Jeff bore a passable shit-eating grin.

"Well, goodness! Hello, y'all," said a voice none of them had ever heard. "Quenton, they're here!"

Miss Lula Murphy, all five-foot, one-inch of her, stood straight upright in the open doorway. The dark skin of her face first concealed and then revealed a set of large, impossibly white teeth, as she grinned at them. They stood still on the porch, smiling back at her. An inelegant rustling approached from behind Lula as Quenton made his way to the door.

Lula wore a navy blue Sunday dress with small white flowers scattered across it. In the present light, it was difficult to distinguish the deep blue fabric from the darkness of her skin. Her hair, which was shockingly black for a woman in her mid-sixties, further accentuated the effect. Quenton filed in behind her. At six-foot three-inches, he towered over her. Her shortness aside, Lula appeared solid and confident—the kind of woman you'd think twice about messing with.

"Hey, y'all," said Quenton, his hands firmly on both of Lula's shoulders.

"Mr. Murphy," Andy acknowledged, extending his hand. "Mrs. Murphy," he added politely, as Quenton received him.

"Hi," Ellen said, a bit tentatively to both of them at once.

"Hello, sir," Jeff offered, following Andy's lead and shaking Quenton's hand. "Ma'am," he added, with a simple nod that carried the perfect amount of Southern white boy charm.

"Y'all come up off this porch, and git inside," Lula insisted. "It's hot out here."

Their hosts backed into the house, with Quenton holding the glass door until each of them had entered. The first thing Andy noticed was the air conditioning and the sense of physical relief it brought. A/C was a

220

luxury they had to leave their own home to enjoy. The second stimulus—the heavenly smell of home cooking wafting through the small house—was equally pleasant.

They stood for a moment in the cramped entry way, a narrow portico that forced one to go either left to the living room, or right towards the dining room.

"This is my lovely wife, Lula," Quenton offered, presenting her at arm's length like the prize she was to him.

"Andy Maxwell, ma'am. Pleased to meet you," Andy said, deciding to take the lead. They'd all seen Lula before in passing, but none of them had ever spoken to her. He reached out, expecting to politely shake her dainty hand. Instead, the strength of her handshake caught him by surprise.

"And these are my friends... Ellen Norris and Jeff Aaron."

"Hello," Jeff said, still smiling.

"Hi." Her acknowledgment of Jeff was warm enough, but really she was focused on Ellen, who was becoming increasingly self-conscious about the large white box she was still clutching.

"We brought you a pie," Ellen said, with a touch of nervous energy.

"Aww. Ain't you sweet?" Lula pined. "Now, you know you didn't need to do that."

Those were her words. What Ellen knew she meant was *I sure am glad your momma raised you right enough to know you needed to do that.*

"Yes, ma'am," Ellen said smiling, as she relinquished the box to Lula with some relief.

"Quenton, take these boys on into the living room. Me and Miss Ellen will be in the kitchen." Lula directed. As Mrs. Murphy walked away, Ellen looked at the three men. Quenton gave her a friendly smile. Her roommates were both trying hard not to laugh, and she threw daggers at them with her eyes as she turned to follow Lula.

The men moved in the opposite direction, retreating to the living room where Jeff and Andy continued to take in their unfamiliar surroundings.

Seen from the street, the exteriors of their two homes were similar enough to be unnoticeable, but the interiors weren't even from the same universe.

Lula, with some help from Quenton presumably, kept an immaculate home. The living room's light, cloth-covered furniture sat atop dark, rich hardwood floors polished to a glossy shine. A tall curio cabinet fashioned from thick glass and wood of nearly the same finish stood in the corner. It was filled with pieces of antique china and an ancient looking rag doll.

Quenton moved with the pace and unevenness one would expect from a man his age, methodically making his way to a light blue, high-backed chair. Lowering himself into the seat, he placed his feet upon the matching ottoman and ushered the boys to take a seat on the couch across from him.

"Welcome to our home," Quenton offered, outstretching his arms and flashing a toothy grin. Behind him was a small fireplace, which seemed too shallow to function safely. The mantle over the hearth held a few neatly framed family pictures, and above that hung a large needlepoint primer proclaiming the Scripture, "As for me and my house, we will serve the Lord. – Joshua 24:15."

Seeing Quenton there seemed an odd juxtaposition to Andy. This was the same man he had just recently watched skip church to wax his Cadillac while enjoying a beer and cigarettes.

"Y'all want something to drink?" Quenton asked. "Mrs. Murphy makes the best sweet tea you ever tasted." He paused, his hands folded in his lap, flashing that wide grin as part of a deeper, knowing expression that said, *'Y'all know I got some beers up in this place, but this ain't one of those nights.'*

"I'm fine. Thank you, though," Jeff declined.

"I'm good, too," Andy lied with a thirsty throat. "I'll wait until dinner, which smells amazing by the way."

The aroma of southern home cooking engulfed the small home, and the sounds of plates, silverware, and glasses being set upon the dining room table rang out from across the hall. The men could hear scattered bits of small talk being exchanged by the two ladies. Most of it seemed to be directional on the part of Lula as they worked to bring the steaming dishes of food to the table.

Jeff twitched with nervous, conflicted energy. He'd been raised to know he should be helping Ellen and Lula. On the other hand, he felt compelled to honor Quenton's request for company, even though it was really just a sad, transparent excuse to stay out of the way until the work was done. Neither Andy nor Quenton seemed to be sharing his struggle.

"Quenton, dear..." came the sweet call from across the hallway, "Bring the boys. Supper's ready."

The boys hopped up much more quickly than their host and were several steps ahead of him as they made their way to the dining room.

"What can we do to help?" Andy asked as he reached the table, knowing the ladies had already done everything.

"Y'all have a seat, and get what you want to drink," Lula chirped, setting down a big basket of golden brown yeast rolls. Two pitchers, one full of iced tea and the other with lemonade, sat near the center of the large oval table that took up most of the dining room. Distributed around it was a bounty of serving plates and bowls, loaded with meat loaf, mashed potatoes, macaroni and cheese, turnip greens, and spiced apples. The plates were fine china, the silverware might have even been real silver, and the glasses were actually glass.

Andy was watching Jeff, who was watching Quenton for a cue on how to proceed. Quenton had gravitated toward one head of the table and stood behind his still tucked-in chair. The boys assumed correctly that the chair at the other end of the table, the 'I'll get it' seat, nearest the entry to the kitchen, was reserved for Lula. They stood together on one of the oval's long sides, leaving Ellen alone opposite them. Quenton stood with studious patience until Lula had finished placing the last dish on the table. Only after she had taken her seat did he begin to pull back his own chair. The boys followed suit, waiting for Ellen to seat herself before they did the same.

Eager to break the silence and also to compliment their hosts on the spread before them, Andy began, "Thank you, Ms. Murphy, this loo…"

"Just a minute, son," she corrected. "We thank the Lord first in this house. Let's pray." Lula folded her wrinkled hands together and bowed her head.

"Heavenly Father," Quenton began; his voice gravelly but confident; "thank you for this home, and for these friends who have come to it to share in the fellowship of this bounty which You have provided. May this food nourish our bodies, as Your Word nourishes our souls. Keep us safe as we travel the path You would lead us on, and give us the wisdom to always seek and welcome Your company in this journey we call life. In Your Son's holy name, we pray… Amen."

"Amen," they all concurred.

Andy found himself again surprised by his old neighbor. The prayer was an eloquent and stark contrast to the jive-infused smack talk they traded in the driveway or over the shoddy fence between their back yards.

Even before he had stepped away from God, Andy had always felt uncomfortable in the presence of those who prayed openly. To be fair, most of those times he encountered them as street preacher types who were combatively praying for the lost souls of the heathen masses. Still, even in less threatening situations, the practice still elicited strong feelings of discomfort in him.

But this felt different. Quenton's words were simple, humble, full of grace and thankfulness, and more noticeably to Andy, devoid of any judgment. They were miles more heartfelt than the near-meaningless dinner blessing rhymes of his childhood. He found himself wondering if the words had been practiced or simply delivered. He was still contemplating as the warmth of the bread basket being passed to him by Jeff registered against his forearm.

"Thank you again, Mrs. Murphy..." Andy said, turning to face her as he completed his compliment.

"Oh, y'all are more than welcome," she answered. "But it's Quenton you should be thanking. It was his idea to have y'all over."

"Thank you, sir," Ellen offered. "This is so nice of you both."

"Yes, thank you," Jeff echoed, as the serving dishes circled the table and plates began to fill.

"The pleasure is ours," Quenton beamed. "It's overdue. Y'all been right next door a couple years now, and I get the feeling Mr. Maxwell over there has an eye on movin' on sometime soon. Seemed like the right thing to do."

Andy felt self-conscious all of a sudden, as if an unwanted spotlight had been shone upon him. A quick scan around the table confirmed his suspicion that they were all looking his way.

"How's that going by the way? The whole job search?" Quenton asked pointedly. Andy hadn't expected the topic to follow him to this supposedly neutral arena.

So be it, he thought. The questions about his future had become persistent, to the point of nagging. Perhaps dealing with them publicly would bring a sense of closure, or at least a fresh point of view, to a topic he'd grown tired of avoiding. In any case, hashing it out in their elderly neighbors' home all but guaranteed the exchange would be a civil conversation as opposed to a fight.

"It depends on your perspective, I suppose," Andy stated cautiously.

"Everything does," Quenton countered, now passing the bread basket to Ellen.

Andy dished a healthy scoop of Lula's macaroni and cheese casserole onto his plate, and watched the steam rise as he took a sip of sweet tea. "I do have an option or two," he started. "I guess I just don't really like any of them all that much."

"What do you mean?" Lula asked. She and Quenton were both focused on him, while Ellen and Jeff acted as if he weren't even there. They'd already heard this story, and knowing a better deal when they saw it, they began destroying the ample plates of food they'd built.

Andy wasn't sure where he should start. Not knowing how much to assume either of them cared to know about his situation, he rewound to close to the beginning and pushed play.

"So, I just graduated, and I've been looking for a job where I can put my degree to some practical use."

226

"What's your degree, and what do you want to do?" asked Lula.

Jeff and Ellen kept their eyes on their plates, intent to shovel Lula's delicious home cooking into their mouths while Andy covered this well-beaten path for a new audience.

"Advertising, ma'am. I want to be a writer."

"Oh, that sounds exciting," she replied, with genuine interest. "Good for you. I would never be able to do something creative like that."

"I'm guessing it's not as glamorous as it sounds," Andy admitted, mostly hoping he was wrong. "Besides, writing's not that hard or impressive. It's just putting words together. All the answers are in the dictionary."

"Careful, son," Quenton said, with a seriousness that surprised all three of his young guests. "It's one thing to be humble, but you best never be glib about the talents God gave you. He gives everybody some kinda gift; something that makes you like nobody else. Some people know exactly what theirs is. Other people, they search their whole lives trying figure out what it is they got from Him."

There was a tension in Quenton's voice. It wasn't quite anger, but at least a frustration that suggested he might be one of those 'other people'.

"If you know what you love to do, and you happen to be good at it, you best be countin' yourself as blessed, 'cause that's rare in this world."

Andy had only meant his comment as a joke, but Quenton wasn't playing; and his point wasn't lost on Andy either. "Yes sir," Andy answered, feeling like he'd just been admonished by an older, blacker, slightly kinder version of his own father.

"He's right, dear," agreed Lula. Her voice was much softer and sweet, but just as firm. "What you think is easy, someone else might find impossible. Don't lose sight of the value of that."

"Besides," Lula continued, now showing her own quick wit. "You're right about one thing. There *is* a book out there with all the answers in it, but it's not a dictionary."

Andy took to staring at his own plate, feeling the weight of their well-meaning criticism.

"Now, continue," she said with a smile.

"So, I know *what* I want to do..." Andy moved on. "It's the *where* and *how* I just don't have figured out. I've had a couple of interviews, but those were total failures. And then just this morning, I think I got offered the worst job in the history of the world."

"Oh, I seriously doubt that," Quenton said, still not back to the friendly tone to which his young neighbor was accustomed. Clearly, the Murphy home had a lower tolerance for hyperbole than he enjoyed next door.

"You ever dig a hole for a latrine, Andy?" Quenton asked. He, and everyone else, already knew the answer. "Or work 15 hours a day on the railroad in the hot-ass Alabama sun?" Quenton was a good, kind man and a friendly neighbor. But what he didn't have was much patience for a spoiled-soft, white boy college graduate who wasn't *happy enough* with his *all of his options*. He'd grown up in a different time; a time when you only had *one* option – find a way, doing whatever you had to do, to make enough money to take care your family. *Happiness* was a luxury you worried about after you had taken care of business.

The point was sufficiently made—so much so that Andy knew well enough to skip past the part about his back-up plan being a return to his already-too-helpful parents. This safety net, which had become a very real option for so many of Andy's age, was obviously not standard issue for the members of the Murphys' generation.

"Quenton," Lula reprimanded her husband, "there's no need to..."

"It's fine, ma'am." Andy admitted. "He's right. About all of it." He kept his gaze locked on Mr. Murphy. It was partly out of respect, but at least as much about not having to see the looks on the faces of his roommates, who had to be loving every second of the verbal beatdown he was taking.

"Here's all I'm sayin'," Quenton continued, finally softening his tone. "I've had a lot, probably more than my share, of what you might call the 'worst jobs in the world'. I didn't like them, but I did 'em, and was glad for them. Every one of them was part of the road that led me to where I am today, and I wouldn't change that; not for nuthin'. There ain't a lot of fun or happiness in doing crappy jobs, but there's a sense of pride and self-worth in it you can't get from skippin' over all the hard stuff."

There was nothing for Andy to argue there.

"I'll just say one last thing, then I'll hush, so you and me can both eat this fine meal that's getting' cold on us." He took a sip of lemonade, and pointed his long dark index finger across the table at Lula.

"I met this here lady when I was about your age. Didn't have no money, no prospects, no future and no faith. I was goin' nowhere. Didn't even know where I wanted to go. All's I knew was I wanted her to go with me. She said she wanted that too, but she couldn't go through life livin' with a faithless man. She told me if things were gonna work, I was gonna have to trust her, and trust God. I told her I would try—and I don't even know if that was the truth at the time. In the beginning, I did a lot of fakin' it, cuz I just wanted to be with her. Over time though, I don't know. Maybe she wore me down. Maybe some of it actually sank in. Who knows? But I remember feelin' as lost as you. Thinkin' there wasn't no happiness comin' my way. But she never stopped encouragin' me. Used to read me

229

Scriptures all the time. Most of it went right over my head, or straight through my ears. Every now and then one would hit me the right way, and make me feel a little better. But there was one that hit hard and stuck."

Quenton's eyes got big, and his voice raised just a touch, as he reached the crescendo of his sermon to Andy. Taking his hands from the table, he slipped his palm into the back pocket of his dress pants. It re-emerged clutching a two-tone brown leather money clip.

"Turns out, this is everything I ever needed to know about working and being happy." He placed the wallet on the table, and slid it over to Andy. As Quenton removed his dark bony hand, Andy could clearly see the letters and numbers stamped onto the hardened, leather-covered hinge of the clip. *Proverbs 16:3*

"Turn it over," Quenton said.

Andy sat looking at the well-worn clip for what seemed an eternity. Again, he dared not look at Jeff sitting next to him, or across the table to Ellen. Hesitantly, he reached out and ran a finger along the stitched edge of the leather. Proceeding with as much caution as he would have given to handling a poisonous snake, Andy grasped the leather rectangle in his hand and flipped it over. More words were stamped in the surface on the facing side.

Commit your work to the Lord, and your plans will succeed.

Andy wasn't predisposed to believe in divine intervention, and he certainly wouldn't have raced to admit it in this instance, but it was pretty hard for him to deny the surreal relevance of what Quenton had produced.

"Now," Quenton began again, slower and much more like the guy Andy was used to seeing puffing menthols on the front porch, "let me see that."

As Andy handed back the money clip, a wave of flush warmth flowed through him. He was embarrassed; embarrassed to be emasculated by an older, wiser man; embarrassed to be laid bare in front of his friends; and certainly embarrassed by the ugly truths Quenton had exposed about his attitude, work ethic and myopic world view.

Quenton grasped the money clip in his work-worn hands, and freed the small stack of bills it contained. Stuffing the cash into the breast pocket of his dress shirt, Quenton turned the money clip over a few times, as if contemplating it, and then outstretched his arm to Andy.

"Here. This belongs to you now. I already learned what it was supposed to teach me."

"I can't take your..."

"You can, and you should," responded Lula, who'd been silently watching her husband educate their young neighbor. Her eyes were wide and soft, with a welling of pride.

"Took Quenton more years than he or I'd probably like to admit for him to embrace that lesson—to learn that it didn't matter what he did, as long as he found joy in it and did his best. God rewards that, and good always comes from it. Same is true for helping people. So you let him help you, and you listen; cuz when you listen, you can understand, and when you understand, everything gets different."

Andy took the clip from Quenton and thanked both he and Lula, for the gift and the wisdom that went with it. His roommates had cleaned their plates while school was in session. Ellen was sitting quietly, with her arms folded on the table, looking across at Andy. There was a smile on her face he couldn't quite read. It wasn't judgmental or mocking, more like pleased amazement. Jeff had used the distraction of Quenton's sermon to reload his plate, and was halfway through his second helping. Andy didn't even have to look at him to know he was probably smiling, too.

"I don't want *everything* to be different," Andy said, quietly. "I just want to make the right choice, and not feel like I have to choose between bad options because I need the money."

"So, what would you do if money was no object?" Ellen asked. They were the first words Andy could remember her speaking since they sat down.

"I'd probably stay around here," Andy said without much thought or delay. "But that's probably the easy way. I guess I don't know. What I do know is I would take my time and not rush into anything, just to be *doing something*. I'd look around and find the place I'm really supposed to be. I think that's what I was supposed to be doing for the past four years. But I was too busy having a good time to think ahead. This place has been great for me—best time of my life. But I wasted a lot of opportunities. If I had a little more time, I'd probably think differently about it."

"We've all said that before in this life," Quenton remarked. "Just about everybody would take a second chance at somethin' if they could git it. Good luck with that, though. Most of the time, He's trying to move us forward, even if it's not what we want."

"That's enough of the heavy talk, Quenton," Lula admonished. "I tell you what we *do* want right now… some of that pie Miss Ellen brought. C'mon girl. Let's go get it."

They laughed and Ellen rose to follow Lula back into the kitchen. Andy looked at his plate, and realized that he'd done a lot of talking and not nearly enough eating. In the commotion that followed, as the plates and dishes from dinner were swept from the table, he hastily jammed forkfuls of meatloaf and mac and cheese into his mouth.

For a while, the two sets of neighbors sat at the Murphy's big oval table leisurely enjoying cheap coffee and Ellen's over-priced, highly-decadent banana crème pie. Ellen and Jeff each shared various details of their lives and how they ultimately found themselves in Bradford. Andy, by contrast, was largely silent. He would chime in occasionally with the answer to a question or a half-hearted laugh at a good joke. But mostly, he spent dessert quietly, almost sullenly, contemplating his earlier exchange with Quenton. The money clip sat there on the table next to his plate, staring him in the face. As if repelled by some unseen force, he couldn't quite bring himself to remove it from the table and take ownership of it by putting it in his pocket.

Two cups of coffee and a one and a half slices of pie later, Ellen noticed the clock. She'd pulled the extra lunch shift at The Lizard today, but she still had her regular night job waiting for her at the Green Room, too. She was due there in about half an hour, and still had to change into something she'd be less bothered about drenching in bar swill and cigarette smoke.

"Ma'am," she spoke politely, turning to Lula. "I have to work tonight, so I need to get ready to go. Can I help you clear the table, or with the dishes?"

"Absolutely not," answered Lula with a smile. "Cookin's my job in this house. Clearin' is manly work."

Jeff and Andy looked up from their pie in time to see the same amused grin beginning to emerge on Quenton's face.

"Sorry, boys," Quenton lied. "Shoulda gave you a heads-up on that. This one's on us." He rose from the table and began to gather the dessert plates and forks nearest him. The younger men were still seated, but quickly realized their host wasn't kidding about the division of labor.

"You go on home, Miss Ellen, and git to work. I'll send these boys home when I'm done with them," Quenton said.

Ellen smiled back as she rose and placed her napkin next to her plate. Andy and Jeff were grateful that at least she couldn't—or more

233

accurately wouldn't—mock them openly in front of their hosts. But they were certain they'd get an earful of smack from her later.

"Ok. If you're sure," Ellen said, now milking it just for the sake of it. "Boys, I'll see you later. Are you coming to the Room tonight?"

"Nope," Andy said without pause. "Doc's having people over. We'll be there, probably late. Meet us there."

Lula took a step backwards from her chair and created a pathway. As Ellen moved past her, Lula opened her arms wide, inviting her young neighbor in for an unexpected hug. Ellen was surprised by the gesture, but she went with it, offering Lula a quick embrace as she reiterated her gratitude for their hospitality.

"The pleasure is all ours. Hopefully we'll keep seein' you 'round for a while."

"That'd be nice, ma'am."

She thanked Quenton from across the table and made her way to the front door. A second later, she was gone.

Looking at the used dishes and glasses on the table before him, Andy took a deep breath. He grabbed the money clip, stuffed it in the back pocket of his pants opposite his current wallet, and started clearing the mess.

42

Lula Murphy sat at the head of her table like a contented statue, hands folded in her lap as she smiled and looked into the distance through the windows across the room. Andy stacked plates and gathered the used forks, trying not to stare at her. Her motionlessness and silence was oddly disturbing. He assumed she was deriving some degree of joy from sitting back and watching her husband and his two young charges clear the mountain of dishes she'd dirtied in her service to them.

Jeff shadowed Quenton in the kitchen, rinsing serving bowls and platters and handing them to his host who arranged them with precise expertise in the dishwasher. Along with the air conditioning, this appliance was another modern convenience Jeff was grateful to see his neighbors possessed.

A minute or so of cleaning went by with little more than minor instructional exchanges between the two men. But as soon as Quenton was confident his assistant knew the drill, he resumed his teacher's pulpit, this time directed at for Jeff.

"You know," Quenton said with a small chuckle, "that boy in there has a lot to learn."

Jeff misread the trajectory and confidently agreed, "You don't have to tell me."

"Oh, but I do," Quenton said, now flashing the grin of a master reveling in the folly of too-sure student.

"We ALL have plenty to learn. Y'all might be graduating, but real school ain't never over."

Jeff knew there was more coming. He handed another platter to Quenton, straightening his posture and fixing his attention on his elder neighbor.

"See, you might think you got it all figured out; got yerself right and all that. But I see something else…"

Quenton's tone was the same he'd used when taking Andy to task earlier. What at the time was amusing to Jeff now caused an unfamiliar tension to course through him. He couldn't remember the last time someone spoke to him that way—not even his own parents. And it wasn't like it was one of his asshole friends giving him shit, which was easy enough to shut down. This was different. Whatever Murhpy had to say, Jeff was gonna hear, whether he wanted to or not.

"I see you in them choir robes every week. You look the part when you come and go. But what about the rest of it?" Quenton saw conflict in his young neighbor's eyes, but not confusion. He could tell Jeff was following along just fine.

"That wallet was talkin' to Andy in there. That's what HE needed to hear," Quenton continued. "God's got something different for you."

The old man stood tall, maybe to stretch his aching back, or perhaps to further focus Jeff's attention on him. He wiped his hands with a damp dishtowel and extended a bony black finger. Jeff followed the line it drew. Amongst a jumble of pictures and reminders affixed to the stark white refrigerator he found Quenton's target. Another needlework primer, this one no larger than a Post-It Note, hung from a magnetized metal hook.

'Revelation 3:15-16'

"Do you know that one?" Quenton asked, apparently willing to give Jeff the benefit of the doubt.

"No sir," Jeff replied, now even more uncomfortable, "not by heart."

"That's okay," Quenton reassured him. "I'm sure you got a Bible over there, right?"

"Yes sir."

It was the truth. It hardly saw the light of day any more, but the very copy of the King James Version he had received at his childhood Confirmation was sitting on a shelf in his room next door.

"Good," Quenton said. "You read it on your own then. But I'll tell you this much…"

Jeff assumed the next words he'd hear would be the beginning, or a summation of the Message. It wasn't.

"That one I gave Andy. That was mine," Quenton pointed back at the small primer on the fridge. "This one here—it's Lula's." He paused for just a second, and then continued.

"See, that lady in there—she's the best woman I know."

Jeff could feel Quenton's pride swell as he lauded his wife, but the old man wasn't done complimenting her just yet.

"But better than that? She's also the best Servant of God I've ever seen. And do you know why?"

"No sir?"

"'Cause, you might not know it just to look at her, but she's got a *fire* in her for God that burns like nuthin' I ever seen. Ain't a lukewarm bone in her body. Puts me to shame nearly every day."

"Yes sir," Jeff agreed, at a loss for any other response.

"Anyway," Quenton relaxed, turning his attention back to the dishes, "You read it. I think you'll see."

"Yes sir," Jeff repeated, handing the last platter to Quenton just as Andy entered the kitchen with a stack of dessert plates.

"Hmm," Quenton said, with surprise. "More plates. Ain't a lick a room left in the dishwasher."

The boys looked at each other with a shared fear that his next directive was going to be that they finish the remainder by hand.

"Tell you what. You boys have probably had enough for one evening. I'll finish these up once y'all go, while Miss Lula's gettin' into her night clothes."

A great relief swept over them both as they accepted their release. Jeff wiped his hands on the dishcloth and offered a dry hand to Quenton, who shook it earnestly. Andy responded in kind as they backed out of the kitchen.

Lula was still seated at the dining room table, but rose as they prepared to leave.

"Thank you again," Andy offered.

"Not at all," Quenton replied. "Thank y'all for comin', and for listenin'. Y'all be safe, and have a good night now."

43

As soon as they stepped foot on the sidewalk, Jeff was putting flame to a Winston. He turned back to offer one to Andy, and couldn't help but be amused by the sight of Quenton on his front porch, a billow of smoke emerging from his own menthol stick. As punctuation to the surreal visit, Quenton held aloft the cold beer in his other hand, as if offering a toast to cap the evening. Apparently things were back to whatever *normal* was.

"So," Jeff said, as they walked the short distance down the hill toward their house. "You've been talking shit about going to church with me for a while now. How'd you enjoy that?"

"Very funny. Screw you."

44

"What time do you want to head to Doc's?"

The two of them pushed through the front door, jostling shoulder-to-shoulder like adolescent brothers battling for supremacy.

"I don't care," Jeff said. "But I'm guessing we'll be there a while, so what's the rush?"

"Fine by me. I'm definitely getting out of these, though." Andy was already headed toward his room, unbuttoning his shirt as he walked and talked.

The idea of changing might not have even occurred to Jeff. But since Andy was already in transition, and he had nowhere else to be, he did the same.

Andy quickly traded his dinner costume for a pair of worn jeans and a black Sun Studios t-shirt. Adding ratty sneakers to complete the ensemble, he felt much more like himself again. He picked the dress pants up off the floor and reached for a hanger. He had no immediate plans to wear them again.

Grasping the pants near the waistband, he was reminded of his wallet in one of the back pockets. And then also of the gift he'd received. He pulled out both leather squares and tossed them together onto the desk. Andy stood and considering the pair of money holders. He knew he would need to take one of them, and he found himself rationalizing a choice between them—until he chose not to. He stuffed his old wallet into the pocket of his jeans and left the money clip alone on his desk.

"So, Ellen's gonna meet us over there later?" Jeff asked.

"Who knows? Guess it depends on what time she finishes."

"Do you wanna walk to Doc's?"

"No," Andy stated, as if he ever really wanted to *just walk* anywhere. "I need a pack of smokes. I'll drive us up to the Cubby and we'll hit Doc's on the way back."

Doc's house was literally three blocks from their own—a relatively easy walk. But the distance was irrelevant to Andy. "We'll drive over there, and then we'll have a car if we need it. If we get too fucked up, we can always leave it and walk home."

"Sure," said Jeff, "Whatever." He was pretty sure that wasn't gonna happen either.

45

Andy guided the SUV into the small parking lot of the convenience store. He'd taken the longer route down the hill along Paxton Avenue, mostly because he wanted to see if the Cactus Club was still encased in bright yellow police tape. It was.

"You coming, or what?" Jeff asked, already out of the car.

"Yeah. Let's go."

"You buy smokes, I'll get beer."

"That works. But get something good," Andy clarified. "I'm not drinking PBR tonight."

"Beer snob." Get one pack of Winston Reds and one pack of Lights. Oh yeah, and a lighter. I lost mine."

"Anything else?"

"No, that's good."

Two minutes later, they reconvened at the register. Jeff was carrying a twelve pack and two 40-ounce bottles of Crazy Horse malt liquor.

"Damn," Andy howled. "What kind of shit are you planning to get into tonight?"

"I dunno. It's Doc's house, so you *never* know. Just seemed like the right thing to do."

"Maybe for you. I can't drink the Horse anymore. It makes me angry."

"Ha! *Everything* makes you angry. What's the difference?"

"Whatever. Just get 'em."

Andy handed Jeff a ten to cover the smokes, and moved down the counter. He was perusing the multitude of winning lottery tickets taped to the wall above the register when his eye gravitated toward a payout of a completely different nature. There, plastered over some of those same lottery tickets was a new take on an increasingly familiar face.

A stark white flyer, printed in full color bore the beautiful, smiling face of a young girl. Her dirty blond hair was different—shorter—and her dimples were more pronounced in this new photo, but it was unmistakably the visage of Jessica Hammond. The word "MISSING" was pasted in huge black type on a field of yellow. Under the photo, in letters nearly as large as the headline, was printed "REWARD: $50,000!", and then, much smaller, her name and pertinent details.

"Holy shit! Look! They doubled the reward for her."

"I wonder if that's good, or bad?" Jeff wondered aloud.

"It can't be good," said Andy. "She's been gone most of a week now. At some point, the odds of finding her go *way* down."

"Is that new?" Jeff asked the clerk.

"Yep. Just today. $4.13 is your change. Y'all have a good night."

Apparently, the clerk had no interest in starting a conversation about Jessica Hammond.

"Damn, man," Andy grumbled on the way back to his SUV.

"What?"

"$50,000. Finding her would pretty much solve all my problems."

"I'm guessing it'd be more likely to solve *her* problems?" Jeff corrected. "Besides, most of your problems, money can't solve."

"Shut up."

Andy pulled out of the parking lot and headed back up the hill. He crept along, taking one more look the Cactus Club before accelerating. Heading back toward Cornwall Street, Andy took a right two blocks down, onto Providence. For a hundred yards in front of Doc's house, the street was already lined solid with parked cars.

"Well, we waited long enough."

"No shit," Jeff agreed. "By the time we find a place to park, we could've walked here faster."

"I'll find one," Andy said, as they rolled past their destination. The party had already spilled out onto the porch of the tall, two-story white house. Clusters of people dotted the small yard, laughing, drinking, and smoking.

A hundred more feet, and Andy found a space just big enough to squeeze in the SUV, although the back of his vehicle did infringe on one of the neighbor's driveways, and it completely blocked their mailbox.

"You'll *probably* be okay there," Jeff cautioned, registering a preemptive 'I told you so', in the event Andy's fairly new car got towed or dinged.

The murmur of crowd noise and muffled music was audible as they approached the house. Between the sidewalk and the front door, they were both acknowledged several times. Jeff stopped to say hello to two girls. Andy, who was carrying both bags from the Cubby, and more interested in offloading his cargo than engaging in small talk, kept walking.

The front corridor of Doc's house was a long, narrow hallway opening to rooms on either side. Straight ahead, two rooms down, the hallway ended abruptly with a split. People filled the corridor, a few lingering on the steps that led up to the bedrooms. Andy moved through the crowd, making his way to the left of those stairs and into the kitchen. He knew he should have handed one of the monstrous bottles of malt liquor to Jeff before they'd peeled apart from each other. Left unattended, one or both of those bottles would be gone before the social butterfly ever fluttered into the kitchen. Andy had to move a few things around to make it work, but he found room for the now-open twelve-pack and tucked one of the two big bottles of Crazy Horse into the vegetable crisper. Carrying a Heineken in one hand and cradling the forty-ounce bottle like a baby along his other forearm, he made his way back toward the front door. He would take one lap around the perimeter, and if he didn't spot Jeff by then, all bets were off.

Halfway down the hall, Andy found Jeff leaning against the wall, holding court. He had his arm around another girl Andy didn't know and was telling some story to her and a couple of friends. Andy said nothing, interrupting Jeff's flow not with words, but by reaching through the huddle and jamming the huge bottle of malt liquor to within inches of his face.

"Thanks!" said Jeff.

"Yep. Drink up, homie," Andy teased. "You guys seen Doc?"

"Nicky's upstairs, I think," said the girl on Jeff's arm. She was cute, and appeared to already be drunk.

Andy looked at Jeff, entertaining two thoughts at once. The first—whether Jeff intended to pursue the wounded game already in his clutches—was answered by the slight, devilish smile his roommate gave him. The second was more of a puzzled amusement as he mouthed the word *"Nicky?"*, about to laugh out loud.

Their host for the night was Nick Haygood—known to many of them simply as "Doc", and apparently to some others as "Nicky." A year younger than Andy—the same age as Jeff— Nick was still in school. In fact, he planned to be there for a while. Nick was three-fourths of the way through his undergraduate studies, which would lead to a few more years pursuing an advanced degree and ultimately to his goal of a career as a pharmacist. His moniker was intuitive, but also duplicitous.

Nick Haygood was smart, and in all likelihood he would achieve his goal of becoming a Doctor of Pharmacy. But he was smart in a way that could be unsettling. While Andy and most of his friends may have claimed to *know* a lot about drugs, the truth was most of them had a lot of experience, but very little knowledge. Doc, on the other hand, had a deep and impressive understanding of the pharmacology of the substances they took, as well as many they'd probably never even encounter. He'd spent countless hours researching the chemical makeup of narcotics and hallucinogens in an attempt to understand their effects from a biological and academic standpoint. He could—and often would—explain to people who'd ingested various substances exactly what was happening to them chemically. Depending on the substance, its potency, and the user's level of comfort, the extra knowledge could either be fascinating, or a very scary buzzkill.

Some people distrusted Doc altogether, suggesting his passion for Pharmacy didn't really extend beyond his interest in the inventory. Others allowed themselves to believe some or all of the many salacious rumors that swirled around him. The most popular of these was that he'd set up what amounted to a mad scientist's lab in one of the house's empty bedrooms. If you subscribed to them all, Doc was churning out everything from bathtub crank to high-grade LSD, or whatever other drugs the rumor mongers believed could be manufactured in the privacy of one's own home.

"C'mon, let's go," Andy encouraged, attempting to replace his roommate's agenda with his own.

"Yeah. In a minute."

Andy took the hint and moved down the hall, leaving Jeff to finish his conversation. As he neared the base of the staircase, he was hit squarely by a compact female missile which had shot around the corner without warning. He didn't even have to see her to positively identify the projectile as Traci Nixon. At four-feet, nine-inches tall, she was probably the shortest adult he knew.

"Damn, girl. Slow it down," he said, spreading his arms and hunching forward in an attempt to dodge the spring of beer that spewed from his full can as a result of their collision.

She laughed as she steadied herself and came to a complete stop a foot to his right. Already outstretched, Andy wrapped his long arm around her, and pulled her in for a quick half-hug. She lingered there for a second, and then retreated. Andy didn't fixate on Traci physically, the way he did with too many other girls. But tonight, dressed in very tight dark blue jean shorts, cut off above the middle of her thighs, and a black spaghetti strap tank top which showcased her toned shoulders and arms, she was pretty noticeable.

"Where's Ellie?" she asked.

"Working the Green Room," said Andy. "Sort of a double for her, after helping you at The Lizard." He was surprised she didn't already know this.

"Oh shit. That sucks. She told me she had a dinner thing tonight, but not that she had to work. I shouldn't have…"

"That's Ellen for you, though. She's never gonna say no, even if it's a pain in her ass. She's just built that way."

"Now I feel bad."

"Eh. Don't worry. She'll be here later. Besides, she earned a little extra cash. Everybody likes money, right?"

"So, what? You want me to hook you up with some bonus shifts at The Lizard, too?"

"Yeah, that's not my scene," answered Andy immediately. "Besides, I'm very good at saying 'no'."

"Nice of you to join us." The voice came from behind them, but was unmistakable. Andy and Traci pivoted to greet the Good Doctor himself.

Nick's eccentricities were plentiful, and his wardrobe for the evening was no exception. His black ten-hole Doc Maartens gave way to a ridiculous pair of green, yellow, and black Scottish tartan pants, paired with red suspenders over a plain white v-neck t-shirt. Black, thick-framed glasses peeked out from the chin-length veil of brown hair that cascaded across his face. Clenched in his teeth was the black and tan, quarter-bent, squat bulldog smoking pipe he'd inherited from his grandfather. He perpetually rotated between smoking potent weed and a blend of cherry brandy tobacco from the pipe, to the extent that traces of both could always be smelled no matter which currently filled its bowl.

"Doc!" Andy was happy to see him again after almost a month's absence. They were both a little reclusive, and unless one was in the house of the other, they weren't likely to cross paths often.

"Hello, old friend." It was an odd greeting, like something a much, much older man would say to long-estranged compatriots. But Doc had taken to greeting most of the people he liked this way.

"Where's the rest of Cornwall Street?" he asked.

"Jeff's hunting wounded fawns in the kitchen," Andy accused. "And Ellen's working, but she should be here later."

"Good deal. Grab Jeff, and meet me upstairs in five minutes. I've got something to show you."

And like that, he was on his way. They watched him weave through the thickening crowd, with the agility of some deranged leprechaun. Andy scanned the scene over Traci's head in search of Jeff. He found him propped up against the kitchen sink, patiently listening to the ramblings of Eddie French. Having located his target, Andy opened the fridge and grabbed a cold Heineken.

"Beer?" he offered.

"No thanks," said Traci. "There's some crazy strong punch on the counter over there. I'm sticking with that."

"Good call," Andy agreed, sending the Heineken back to its cardboard carrier. "Doc always whips up some wicked shit."

.Approaching from behind Eddie, Andy gained Jeff's attention and mouthed the words *"come with me."* Andy cupped his hands onto Eddie's unsuspecting shoulders. Eddie flinched and nearly buckled as he turned.

"Eddie! Good to see you again."

Jeff took the opening, engaging Traci who'd kept walking slowly away toward the punch bowl.

"Hey, Shoe Boy!" Eddie chuckled, vibrating with his trademark nervous energy. "You know, most of them are still up there?"

Andy heard the whole sentence, but really only one word in particular. *'Most'?* Why did he say *'most'*? Had some of them fallen? Were they being taken down? How many is 'most'? His masterpiece had been more or less intact just the other day. And now he found himself fixating over the welfare of his latest project, as if the shoe tree was his legacy to the city itself and deserved some kind of protection from decay or dismemberment.

Andy considered asking follow-up questions, but he was trying his best to not get ensnared in a conversation.

"Yeah, man," Eddie chugged along, "that shit still looks crazy cool though."

"It does," Andy agreed, in full transition. "Crazy. Hey, I'm gonna grab some punch, and I gotta ask Jeff something. Can I catch up with you in a little bit?"

"Sure, man," Eddie said, now standing alone at the kitchen sink, smiling and looking for his next conversation.

Traci and Andy filled red plastic cups near to the brim, assuming the punch bowl would be empty by the time they returned to it. Jeff stood behind them, nursing the huge bottle of malt liquor and studying the tattoo of a half sun-half skull face on Traci's bare right shoulder.

"What's up, Traci?"

"Just workin'. I don't get out much during the week anymore. But, I still try to tear it up on the weekends." She flashed the devil horns hand sign in an attempt to give some rock-n-roll credence to her declaration, but it had the opposite effect, punctuating just how uncool it was to point out that you might still be cool.

"I hear ya. Glad you made it out."

"So, thanks for running interference on Eddie," Jeff said to Andy.

"No worries. I love that guy, too, but when he gets all wound up, you need a seat belt and a ton of patience."

"No shit. So, what's the deal?"

"I don't even know," Andy confessed. "Saw Doc a minute ago. He told us to find you and come see him upstairs."

"Ooh. You know something good's gotta be waitin' when you get summoned to the Doctor's Office."

They all laughed, Traci snorting as she struggled to swallow a mouthful of potent punch at the same time.

"Let's not keep him waiting then," Jeff suggested.

The crowd was getting denser by the minute. Their trek across the kitchen was now a labored struggled through a mass of bodies and smoke. As the three of them reached the stairs, Andy realized Doc had requested he fetch Jeff, but made no mention of Traci. He'd said it plainly in her presence, though he failed to even acknowledge her. Was Andy supposed to bring her, or not? He figured it was easier to leave it alone and let Doc dismiss her if that was really his preference.

There were a few people hanging out on the lowest couple of steps, but no one beyond that, implying the upstairs was, at least at this point, off limits. Andy was in the lead as they ascended. Jeff followed, and Traci brought up the rear. Directly across from the landing was a half bathroom. Its door sat ajar, a candle flickering on the back of the commode in the otherwise small, dark room. To the right, two doors—both closed. To the left, another, also half-open. As all of them reached the landing, Doc's voice rang from inside.

"Jeffery Aaron!" he called, as if emulating a school teacher taking roll.

Doc emerged from the master bedroom, leaving the door open behind him. The room was dimly lit, and there was music. Shaking Jeff's hand and embracing then releasing him quickly, Doc moved to Andy, and then to Traci. The joyful smile he'd been wearing flattened and was replaced by something slightly suspicious. Andy jumped to the defense.

"Nick, do you know Traci?"

It seemed he did not.

"Good friend of ours. She's totally cool," Andy asserted. Jeff nodded in the affirmative.

"Okay then," he allowed, apparently accepting their endorsement of her. "Good to meet you. Call me Doc."

"Hey, Doc," Traci offered, cordially but confused. She'd met Nick Haygood on at least two separate occasions and had probably seen him in passing countless times at gatherings around town. Granted, Doc had become increasingly reclusive, but she was still a little offended that he had no recollection of her. Even worse, he seemed wary of her for no discernible reason.

He looked her over once more and then decided to proceed. "Wait here a second."

He passed by them to the other side of the hallway. Digging into the pockets of his garish pants, he pulled out a small collection of keys. He selected one and approached the last door to their right. With the protectiveness of a hoarding squirrel, he addressed the deadbolt which had been added to the otherwise standard interior door. He unlocked and opened it only wide enough to dart inside, and closed it quickly behind him. The three of them stood in the hall, puzzled but somehow amused by his cartoonish mannerisms.

A few seconds later, he reappeared in exactly the same fashion as he had retreated. But now, he was carrying a tan colored metal lock box—the kind you would see holding the money at a charity car wash or school bake sale.

"Okay. Follow me," Doc ordered, with a bit of hushed paranoia in his tone. They were amused and intrigued, but Andy had to admit the drama didn't do much to dispel all those rumors.

As soon as the four had entered Doc's bedroom, he shut the door behind them. Doc sat on the floor, using the foot of the bed as a backrest, and ushered the rest of them to join him. He waited until they were all settled before making his next move. With enough grandeur and drama to suggest they were about to see inside the Ark of the Covenant itself, Doc inserted another small key from the chain into the lock box, and turned it. The lock sprung open. The lid rose up, but blocked their view of its contents.

Doc held aloft two sandwich-sized plastic bags filled with a spongy brown mass. "Boys and girl," he announced, "magic mushrooms."

"Are you kidding?" Jeff howled. "Thank God. I thought for sure you were gonna bust out some homemade meth or something."

"Fuck that," said Doc. "Meth is retarded all the way around. Dangerous as hell to make. Dirty as fuck to take. Chemically speaking, it's like emptying a toxic waste dump into your body. I *could* cook that shit, but I would never do it. Never. The younger kids, they're moving toward that shit, 'cause they don't know any better. They're the ones getting tweaked out on cough medicine, 'cause it's cheap and easy to get, but that's just like a little meth starter kit. All that shit is bad news.

The high is okay, but coming down is a bitch. If those idiots want to fry their brains and bodies, whatever. This is so much nicer."

Doc was rolling the plastic bags in his fingers as he spoke.

"They're fresh too," he continued. "A couple of my boys from the sticks out near Kirkwood came through on their way to the beach. They were looking for a change of speed, so I traded 'em these for some other stuff I had."

Jeff, who was sitting directly to Doc's left, had been handed one of the bags and was fully engaged, pinching the still semi-springy caps. As if by habit, he held the bag to his nose to get a whiff of its contents.

"Smells like shit," Jeff proclaimed.

"Grade-A, grass-fed cow shit, to be exact," Doc laughed. "One of those guys' dads owns a fuck-ton of land out in Kirkwood. He's got cows, so he's got 'shrooms. Probably doesn't even know what they are. Those boys are swimmin' in 'em, though. These are just the extra ones I pulled out of the sale pile. I figured I needed to try 'em out before I take anyone's money for 'em. Anyone want to go on a test drive? You never know; it could be a completely religious experience."

"Andy may have had enough of those already tonight," Jeff suggested. Doc and Traci were out of the loop, but Andy got the joke and rewarded his roommate with an ironic smile.

Andy sat quietly to Doc's right, contemplating the offer. He was about to speak, when Traci beat him to it.

"It's like acid, but not as strong, right? Do you have any acid?"

Andy and Jeff were both shocked by her ungracious presumption. They'd known Traci for years, and while she did have a reputation for being particular, she didn't usually cross the line into straight-up rudeness. Asking what else was on the menu when somebody offered you free drugs was a little bit like being mad the $20 bill you found in the gutter was dirty.

Again, Andy intervened on her behalf. "I think what Traci meant was…" He craned his head to shoot her a seriously perturbed look before circling back to complete his address to Doc. "how is this different from acid? I was wondering the same thing because I totally don't do acid."

"You've never done acid?" Doc asked with no judgment, but total surprise.

"Never have. Never will," Andy declared. "I'm not into the synthetic chemical thing. Actually, I've never done 'shrooms either, but I think I'd be more inclined to trust the natural shit."

Yeah, 'shrooms are a good bit mellower and almost always friendly," Doc said. "But not disappointing by any stretch compared to acid. And they don't last quite as long, so I prefer them. But I always tell people— don't do something you don't want to do." This last point was aimed straight at Traci, suggesting she was more than welcome to pass on his hospitable offer.

"How long does it last?" Andy asked.

"Depends. But let's just say, if you eat these, you're not driving before tomorrow morning."

Andy started doing math in his head. Their house was only a few blocks from where he sat, and Ellen was probably coming later anyway.

"That's cool," Andy said, feigning confidence. "I'm in."

"Me too," said Traci, before quickly adding "Thanks. I appreciate it." in an attempt at reconciliation.

"Ordinarily, I'd mash these up and brew it into some tea, with a little bit of peppermint to cut the taste. But, there are about a hundred people in my kitchen right now, so that ain't gonna happen. Looks like we're scarfin' 'em down the old-fashioned way."

Doc had taken four decent-sized mushroom caps, about half of one of the bags, and passed it on to Andy. Jeff, who was holding the other bag, followed his lead and then passed it along to Traci. Before Andy or Traci had even picked their caps out of the bag, Doc had already stuffed the entire handful into his mouth and was busy chewing.

Jeff did the same, without hesitation. Andy thought about taking them one at a time but decided not to prolong the process. Traci took only two, holding the others in her hand.

The four of them sat in a circle on the floor, chewing and exchanging glances. Doc reveled in what was clearly not a new experience for him. Jeff oscillated between nods of excited agreement toward Doc and anxious empathy for Andy. Traci had her head bowed, staring at the floor. Her puckered mouth chewed furiously, attempting to down the first half of her portion as quickly as possible. She gasped, as if she'd been holding her breath and then took a long gulp from her cup of potent punch.

"Blah!" she said, louder than intended. She took another drink and popped the other two caps.

It'd taken less than a minute for each of them to consume their portion, and now came the fun part. Or for Andy, the worst part of all. He'd just taken something for the first time, which he was fairly certain was going to fuck with his head in ways he couldn't even imagine. For someone prone to anxiety, the wait for the impending trip to begin could be anguishing.

Doc wasn't specifically aware of Andy's plight, but he did have exceptional drug etiquette. He'd learned just prior to takeoff that two of his passengers had never flown before, and he instinctively launched into his role as attendant for their maiden voyage.

"There's nothing to worry about." Doc's voice broke the silence. "Like I said, this should be a totally mellow trip. But the most important thing to remember is, you're the one in control. Your trip is totally influenced by your state of mind. It's really just going to take you deeper into where you already are. So, if you come into this happy, you should stay there. If you find yourself confused or tense, focus on the last comforting thought or experience you've had. And if you start to get freaked out, try to remind yourself it's like a roller coaster ride. It might get bumpy. There's gonna be some turns. You may even go upside down for a minute. But no matter what happens, you're eventually gonna come to a nice gliding stop back here at the platform. So, don't worry. Enjoy yourselves. Let go, and have fun."

"Damn, dude," Andy said, "You should write down every word of what you just said. Print that shit on business cards or something, and hand it out to people before they trip. That was like the perfect pre-game pep talk. I was a little freaked out, but that helped."

Doc laughed. He'd been where they were, and he'd been where they were going. "Just a heads-up." he said, "you've got about twenty minutes 'til the world goes a little loopy."

With that, he got up and walked out of the room, apparently in search of his own adventure elsewhere. Given the dramatic secrecy with which he'd greeted them, Andy thought it was odd that he would just move on, leaving them unattended in his own room. He shrugged it off in favor of contemplating the journey he was about to embark upon. Traci had laid down, her back flat on the carpet, her eyes closed. It was way too early for anything to be happening to her, but she seemed to be meditatively waiting for the fireworks to begin.

Andy turned to Jeff. He fidgeted through the process of lighting a smoke before speaking. Jeff could see the nervous energy building within him and a noticeable twinge of fear hiding behind his forced smile.

"Do me a favor. Stay with me. I want to do this together."

Jeff knew what he was really saying was *"Don't leave me. I don't want to be alone."*

"Don't worry. I'm not going anywhere."

"So, you've done this before, right?"

"Yeah. We've talked about this," Jeff reminded him. "I grew up out in the country; lived on farmland; had neighbors with cow fields. It's not like I've done it a million times, but yeah."

"So, what's it gonna be like?"

"Doc's right. It's different than acid—more peaceful. You might see some weird shit like tracers and bursts of color and light and stuff, but you're probably not gonna see somebody's face melt off or anything totally fucked up like that."

Traci, who was still lying motionless with her eyes closed, let out a snicker at the thought of what Jeff had described.

"So, he said like twenty minutes, right?" Andy pondered aloud. "What time is it now?" He was notorious for never wearing a watch, but always being interested in the time of day.

"It doesn't matter now," said Jeff, but pointing anyway to the green LED display on clock next to Doc's bed. Sometime in the next hour, Andy figured Ellen would arrive, just in time to see them losing their shit on hallucinogens. He made a mental note to remember this in case he found himself needing a tether to sanity later in the evening.

"If I'm about to start tripping, I think I'm gonna pee and get another drink before shit gets crazy and I forget."

"That's a good idea. You hit the head first. I'll run down stairs and grab a few cold ones. Meet you back here in five minutes."

Andy loved having a plan; it made him feel safe, like he was in control. Deep down, he knew it was bullshit, but he clung to the mirage nonetheless.

"Yeah. Do it. But seriously, hurry back." Andy knew it sounded weak.

"You need a drink, Trace?" Jeff asked, getting up and walking toward the door. She lay still on the floor, making no attempt to move or respond. "Guess not; back in a minute."

Andy continued to make mental notes as he watched his friend turn the corner and start down the steps back into the crowd. He noted the music playing on the stereo—something classical he didn't recognize but liked. He noted the layout and contents of Doc's bedroom, scanning the environment to judge its suitability for the pending adventure. The room was spacious and very clean. Then he noted that the master bedroom had its own dedicated bathroom. He hadn't seen it before, but it was of no real consequence until then. At that moment, he made a decision. At least for now, he was going to bunker down right here.

Traci still hadn't moved. He contemplated her for a second, but then moved on. He rose and walked across the room, closing the door that led out to the hallway. He figured any of the random throng downstairs who wandered up to the second story would see the closed doors as 'do not enter' signs. At least he hoped.

Having shut the door, Andy made his way to the master bathroom. It was nestled into the end of what amounted to a very short hallway of sorts, created by closets on either side of the entryway. The closet doors were mirrored, sliding panels, which created a strange 360-degree effect when you stood in between them. Andy recognized the mind-bending potential and reminded himself to avoid this zone when he returned. Before approaching the bathroom, he finally acknowledged Traci, mostly out of a growing curiosity for her sudden lack of movement or energy.

"Hey, Trace. You okay?"

Three seconds passed before the simple response came. "Yep. Just chillin'."

The fact there was any answer at all gave him the green light to revert back to his own plan.

"Cool. I'm gonna take a piss. I'll be right back."

He got no response.

Andy flipped the switch, bathing the master bathroom in pale yellow light. The floor and roughly half of the height of all four walls were plastered in shockingly white ceramic tiles. The ones on the wall were standard 4-inch squares; nothing remarkable. The floor was far more interesting. It was covered by a sea of equally white but smaller tiles, each about the diameter of a quarter. The sheer number of those tiles, along with their color, seemed to exaggerate the dimensions of the bathroom. He entered and closed the door.

Jeff Aaron was a man of the people. He possessed exceptional social skills, but an appalling concept of time. If either Andy or Traci had thought it through, they'd have known he was unfit for a time-sensitive mission through a crowd like the one downstairs. In theory, it wasn't too much to ask of Jeff to find the kitchen, grab fresh drinks, and head straight back to Doc's room. In reality though, the idea was fatally flawed.

If he concentrated solely on the task, he could probably have navigated the social minefield without getting trapped in a conversation. But this was only half of the challenge. Jeff was magnetic—the kind of person to whom others were drawn. He made it most of the way downstairs without losing his focus. There, at the bottom of the steps, stood two unfairly attractive coeds—members of a sorority for which he had recently done a photo shoot. Flanking him on both sides and sliding their arms into the crooks of his, they redirected him toward the quieter front of the house, intent on talking with him about some follow-up portraits. He never stood a chance.

Traci opened her eyes. Everything was still. The only sound was the calming procession of notes from the stereo across the room. Piano and violins weaved around each other, babbling like fluid from the speakers and washing over her. The music was pleasant, in a foreign way, and she was content to lie there, staring at the ceiling and bathing in the sound. As she contemplated the texture of the rough plaster pocks above, she became more acutely aware of a growing sense of vibration coming from the floor beneath her. It was as if the collective energy from the people on the first floor was rising with noticeable force. The longer she lay there, the more aware she became of the buzz she could now hear and feel. At the same time, she lost her connection to the soothing influence of the music. The piece Doc had been playing had come to an end, and there was no other selection coming to take its place. The combined effect was a shift in Traci's level of comfort that finally motivated her to move. Sitting up, she was surprised to find herself alone. A few minutes ago, she was part of a small group—a member of an expedition into the brave unknown. Now, she was alone, abandoned in a strange, quiet room. Replaying what Doc had told them before he'd departed reminded her she was working with a ticking clock. Traci was not where she wanted to be if things were going to get weird, and she wasn't sure how much time she had to create a better situation for herself.

She decided her first, best course of action would be to light a smoke, thinking the simple action might bring some comfort. What it actually brought was a startling confirmation of the path before her. With a cigarette hanging from her lips, Traci flipped open her silver Zippo lighter and rolled the wheel. The flame roared to life igniting the pool of fuel vapors swirling around the cap and wick. The result was a mini fireball erupting in Traci's hand. The flame was much larger than she expected, and it engulfed the lower end of the cigarette in her mouth. She made the necessary adjustment to keep from getting singed; now holding the lighter at arm's length. The flame was also remarkable for the visual effects that accompanied it. A tiny rainbow of light hovered over it in an arc. Traci felt the metal in her hand begin to warm and realized she must have been staring at it for some time. She snapped the lighter's lid shut and doused the fire.

It seemed Doc's fantastic fungi were beginning to take hold, but she wanted a second opinion. Traci took another deep pull on the cigarette and exhaled. She flipped the Zippo open, taking care to hold the lighter at a safer distance this time.

Yep. Things were about to go sideways.

The wick burst to life, again with the mini rainbow arcing and floating above the flame. But now, tiny sparkles of light joined in the dance. Then, she did what any person in that situation would. Traci started moving the lighter, slowly at first, and then quicker across her field of vision. As the fuel burned and mixed with the rush of air being added to it, the flame extended itself from the wick. But Traci saw much more than this. A full-fledged tail of light emerged from the flame, creating the same effect one gets from tracing paths in the air with a sparkler.

Traci's reaction was mixed. She was freaked out, but in a pleasant way, by the impromptu light show she was orchestrating. Then, there was the anxiety that came with the realization she was now actively tripping, a feeling compounded by the fact she was still alone in the upstairs bedroom. Snapping the lighter shut, she tucked it and her pack of smokes into her small black clutch and made a move for the door.

As soon as she opened it, it was as if she'd broken a vacuum seal, exposing herself to a rush of noise and uncertainty. She moved through the door and ventured toward the steps. Her head was filled with the buzz of garbled conversations, now supernaturally amplified in volume but not clarity. Traci's goal was singular; find a familiar, friendly face in the crowd and hang on for the ride.

49

Andy didn't see it coming either. He'd walked into the bathroom, intent on using the facilities and returning to the safety of Doc's room where he expected to be reunited with Jeff. He'd closed the door and was about to lift the closed lid of the toilet when he noticed his feet. An unassuming glance down revealed his shoe had come untied. Rather than bend down, Andy chose to spin and take a seat on the closed throne. It was a good thing he was now sitting down.

Leaning over to address his shoe, Andy's face drew closer to the small white tiles covering the bathroom floor. His hands completed the mundane task of forming and fastening the loops of his shoelace, with no help from his eyes, which were focused elsewhere.

From this closer range, Andy could see that the tiles he originally thought were squares were actually tiny hexagons, offset at a slight angle from each other. The result was a far more interesting landscape than a simple, straight grid. Still doubled over with his chest to his knees and his hands resting on the tops of his shoes, Andy contemplated the tiles. He counted the sides of a single tile twice, confirming the uniform nature of the six-sided shapes. Each was separated by a thin line of black grout.

Somewhere in the back of his mind, it occurred to him he was obsessing over the shape and layout of the tiles on a random bathroom floor. His next thought might have been to shoot upright and return to his original plan. But at that moment, his brain took a severe detour.

As Andy stared at the floor, his field of vision began to expand. He was no longer considering single tiles on a micro level, but rather viewing the entire floor through a much wider lens. It was then that his peripheral vision detected the first bit of motion just to his left. He could have sworn he saw something move on the floor, rising up dimensionally from the surface, almost jumping. He even detected the slightest noise, like a tiny click, in accompaniment. He craned his neck to the side, fully expecting to see a cricket or some other such creature, but the stark white floor had nothing at all upon it.

Still hunched over, palms now against his shins, Andy continued to stare at the floor. Out of the corner of his eye to the other side came the same sense of motion, this time partnered with a double click of sound. Andy glanced to his right, certain this time he would find something. He saw something alright, but not at all what he expected.

As he moved his gaze from left to right, across the floor, the lines of grout separating the hexagonal tiles seemed to come with him. Like the hyper-space jump scenes in *Star Wars*, the fixed points elongated with great speed and then came to an abrupt end in another place along the same line. Andy rubbed his eyes in disbelief. *Holy shit,* he thought. *Did I just see that?*

He swiped his head back toward the left. Once again, the grout lines moved with him in a blur across the floor, and then came to rest along their natural lines on the other side. Andy's instinct was to flee—to run from the bathroom screaming—hopefully into the waiting company of Jeff on the other side of the door. But his body did not comply. He closed his eyes, knowing intellectually he probably *had* just experienced what he thought he had. He channeled Doc's pre-flight words of wisdom, reminding himself this was a journey he'd chosen, and one over which he himself could exercise control, at least he hoped.

Andy sat upright. Locking his neck in place in an attempt to lose the disconcerting tracers, he opened his eyes. For now the motion was gone, but the weirdness was just beginning.

He stared straight ahead. The plain square tiles on the walls were exactly that. Nothing moved. No tracers. The world in front of his face appeared normal. This was not however the case down below. Even without looking down, he could sense bits of motion continuing on both sides of his feet. Scared, he cautiously lowered his gaze. Now, it wasn't just an inkling suspicion that something might be amiss. Clear as day,

Andy saw several of the tiles, in random placements across the floor, expanding dimensionally upward and out. The tiles were percolating—rising up for a second, separating themselves ever so slightly from their neighbors, and then falling back into place. It was weird, and it definitely freaked Andy out. But at that moment, any fear he was feeling was being overcome by sheer wonder. The visual was amazing, and though clearly a product of a break with 'reality,' there didn't seem to be anything threatening about a tiny ballet of dancing floor tiles.

Andy decided, with whatever portion of his brain he currently controlled, he was going to embrace Doc words and this experience itself. Maybe it was an instinctual understanding that he wasn't going to overpower the chemicals coursing through his brain. Or maybe he was just tired of fighting for control. In any case, in that moment, sitting on a toilet in a strange bathroom, Andy decided he was going to try to do the one thing that came hardest for him. He was going to let go—to simply exist, to *be the rushing river*, to do no work, but to allow work to be done through him. The decision was rewarded almost instantly.

Andy kept watch over the bathroom floor which seemed, in direct correlation to his choice to loosen the reins, to have elevated its activity to a whole new level. No longer was it just single tiles piping up to say hello before retreating. Now, groups of hexagonal tiles began to collaborate to form simple shapes. Inexact squares, lines, and larger mega-hexagons began to form, separating themselves by transforming the grout around them into what looked like bands of colored electric light. Remembering Jeff's assertion that his experience was likely to be tame, at least in comparison to acid, Andy confirmed his resolution to never go near LSD.

He watched with delight and horror as the shapes paraded across the floor, moving in a deliberate procession from left to right. With their glowing outlines, he thought they looked like the crude, boxy tanks from the earliest video games. Viewing them in this context led to a natural evolution of thought, and he started to recognize them for what they really were—puzzle pieces.

Again, as if by the sheer power of his will, the tiles responded to his unspoken suggestion. No longer moving from left to right, the electrified shapes began to ascend away from him, toward the door leading back out to Doc's room. Reaching the top, they slid under the border formed where the walls met the floor. A handful of these shapes made their escape into this crevice, and then suddenly everything ceased. Just when Andy had decided to go with the flow, the flow had decided to stop. Everything went still. But, before he even had a chance to worry about what might happen next, the answer came.

Andy was still glaring at the intersection of the wall and floor, scanning the baseboard for signs of activity, when it began again. Now, a single shape, in the form of a capital "L" lying on its side, came creeping out from the void under the door frame. It cascaded down toward him, taking several seconds to travel the four and a half feet between Andy and the door. A few inches before the shape reached his toes; it came to rest, but continued glowing so as to distinguish itself from the other tiles around it. He stared at it, but only for a second, as his peripheral vision detected more motion.

Scanning back up the floor, Andy saw another shape, this time a simple square, slip from underneath the door and start to inch its way toward him. He watched it proceed along the same line and come to rest in the crook of the "L" that had fallen before it. Then another shape, a longer straight line, appeared. It took him several seconds and a serving of at least three shapes, but finally the epiphany came to him. His psilocybin-soaked brain had transformed Doc's bathroom floor into a game of psychedelic Tetris. As he watched the long thin bar slowly descend toward his feet, he realized that it too was following the same line, and would come to rest stacked widely upon the other two.

Andy recognized the problem, and its solution. If only the shape would...

Holy shit! He thought to himself again. As soon as Andy had expressed the desire mentally, the shape responded. Like a dog answering the call of an unheard whistle, the long straight shape sat up vertically, and moved over two columns to the left. It came to rest perfectly aligned next to the two stacked shapes beside it.

Oh my God! Andy thought. Not only did the bathroom floor just turn into Tetris, but *I can totally control this shit with my brain?* Any fear he may have had was now completely gone. The shapes kept coming. Andy was amazed at how quickly and completely they obeyed his mental commands. He could flip, rotate, and slide them at will, and much faster than in the actual video game. There did seem to be two constraints though. The width of the bathroom's "game board" was apparently defined by the width of the door frame in front of him. He could flip or move the shapes as fast as he wanted, but no matter how hard he tried, they would not travel beyond those sidelines. He also couldn't make them stop, or even pause. Otherwise, it was exactly like he was playing the game at home—except he wasn't. He was sitting on a toilet, tripping his balls off on psychedelic mushrooms.

The shapes continued to come, faster now, as is the game had leveled-up in response to his growing comfort and understanding. Putting the pieces in their ideal places was getting more difficult, but it was still easy enough. Andy maneuvered another long thin piece into a perfect vertical hole, resulting in the completion of four lines of tiles. The completed portion of the puzzle did not simply disappear as it might have in the actual game. Instead, the tiles exploded into a bright mini-fireworks display of light, scattering dramatically across the entirety of the bathroom floor. The resulting light show was spectacular; psychedelic bonus points that provided plenty of motivation for continued success.

Andy plowed forward, directing and arranging the shapes as they fell. He had been doing fine so far, but he could tell the game was moving faster now. The task was still manageable, but the wall of shapes grew higher as the perfect piece came less and less often. Just as in the real game, the natural response to this was an uptick in anxiety. Of course,

Andy knew that normally the game simply ended when the shapes reached all the way to the top. He began to postulate what might happen if he allowed the shapes to pile all the way back up to the door frame. Clearly there was some super-natural, less-than-normal shit going on here, and he suddenly found himself hyper-stressed at the prospect of what "Game Over" might mean in this scenario. He'd been enjoying his experience so far, but hated to think that something unpleasant or even sinister might be waiting for him if he failed.

He doubled his concentration, now feeling the stress building within. The shapes had built up almost halfway from his feet to the Doorway of Possible Doom. He couldn't be sure, but he thought he noticed the outlines of the stacked shapes glowing faster and brighter the closer they got to the top. Pieces continued to fall, faster and faster. His level of anxiety rose right along with the wall. He could feel his portion of control slipping away as the blocks ascended.

I can't do this! He thought, nearing a panic.

A strange humming had been growing in his head. It got progressively louder and became more of an obstacle to his waning concentration. Andy was about to surrender.

You can.

He hadn't said it. He hadn't even thought it. But there it was. He heard it as clearly as if someone had whispered it directly into his ear. *You can.*

Auditory hallucinations were one thing, and maybe even something to be expected at this point. But what came next was completely unmanageable for Andy's mind.

He'd hunched back over, now clenched with the stress of the rising wall before him. He didn't even realize how tight his body had become. Then, in what HAD to be another hallucination, he felt the slightest weight

269

being applied to his right shoulder. It was not forceful, or aggressive in any way. It was in fact calming, like the simple, reassuring touch of a friend's hand upon his back.

You know you can.

Andy was afraid. He was hearing voices and feeling the presence of things unseen. This was deep in uncharted territory, and way more than he'd bargained for from Doc's gift.

Relax... Trust.

Andy panicked. He'd started off fine, but now the train was careening off the tracks. He had lost control, and he was out of options.

"Okay!" Andy said, very much out loud.

Again he felt the pressure on his shoulder, this time slightly different – almost a squeeze. And everything stopped.

The shapes were still there, but the 'game' had been paused. But not by him. Then, the pieces began to move differently. Each piece appeared as normal from below the door, and then hovered, flashing in the center of the open space. As if being clicked and dragged by an unseen hand controlling a mouse, each of the next ten or so pieces was placed exactly where necessary within the puzzle to clear the corresponding rows. With perfect resonance, one final long straight piece careened down the board, sliding like a dagger into the single void left for it. As it connected, completing the remaining rows in their entirety, the fireworks returned. The pieces scattered across the bathroom floor, disappearing as they reached the boundaries of all four walls.

Andy sat up straight, still afraid but also relieved. Nothing moved. Not on the walls, and not on the floor. The humming was gone too. He sat alone in the stark white, silent bathroom. A burst of emotion ran through him like the electricity that had surrounded the floor tiles a minute ago. He felt the prickly burn that preceded tears welling up in his eyes.

He sat there for a minute, breathing; waiting to see what other craziness might come for him. Nothing did. Wiping his face, he lowered his head into his hands and exhaled. He was exhausted.

Andy had forgotten why he'd gone into the bathroom in the first place, and his bladder had become uncomfortably full while he'd been playing magic-floor-Tetris. As he rose from the seat, he was startled by the burning and tightness in his quadriceps and hamstrings. Apparently he'd been there long enough for his thin legs to fall asleep; long enough to require some shaking and a few deep knee bends to restore the blood flow to his atrophied muscles. Completing his callisthenic routine, he wheeled around, lifted the lid of the commode and finally relieved himself.

As he approached the sink to wash his hands, the feelings of dread resurfaced. He was afraid to turn on the faucet, for fear that snakes or laser beams or some other ridiculous shit might come pouring out. He was afraid to look into the mirror. This he did brave though, as it was unavoidable from where he stood. What he saw staring back at him was ugly but not surprising. His face was flush—stained blotchy red from a combination of heat, pressure and tears. His hair was predictably disheveled, too.

Andy took a deep breath and gave the faucet handle a half turn. Nothing but clear, cold water sprang forth. He formed a bowl with his hands and splashed the cool liquid against his hot face several times. Andy turned off the faucet and reached for one of the three small hand towels Doc had stacked on the basin. He laughed to himself at the notion of even owning hand towels, let alone having three of them clean and on the ready in case you had company.

Feeling much closer to normal, Andy walked across the floor which had moments ago been part of an alternate reality. He was glad it didn't suddenly transform into gelatin this time or simply collapse under his weight. He reached for the door handle and broke back into Doc's bedroom. He couldn't have been happier to see what awaited him.

"Damn, dude!" Doc howled. "Have you been in there the whole time?"

"What do you mean?" Andy asked. "I just went in to take a piss."

"That was more than an hour ago!"

The fact that Ellen was now sitting next to Doc on his bed, laughing her ass off at Andy, was pretty solid corroboration. Jeff sat Indian-style on the floor, his back against the foot of the bed. His head was lowered and his hands held his cheeks as a cascade of brown hair hung halfway to his navel.

"Oh my God!" Andy gasped. "El, I'm so fucking glad to see you."

Hallucinogenic euphoria accounted for part of his enthusiasm. But an equal portion came from the recall of the mental note he'd made earlier about her. Jeff and Doc were probably just as fucked in the head as he was, but surely Ellen was sober. *She can be trusted* he thought—exactly the kind of safe harbor he needed after the storm he'd endured.

"Are you as whacked out as these two?" Ellen asked Andy, pointing at the others as she lit a fresh smoke.

"Maybe worse. Can I have one of those?"

She handed the lit cigarette to him and retrieved another for herself.

"Really?" Doc laughed. "Are you seeing crazy shit too?"

"I don't think you'd believe me, if I told you."

"Oh he might," Ellen suggested, somewhere between amused and perturbed. "I got here about ten minutes ago. I came walking up the block and found Doc on his hands and knees, crawling through the bushes like an animal."

"I might have that beat," Andy suggested.

"It's crazy, right?" Doc asked, giggling. "I don't even remember who I was talking to, but I ended up outside on the porch. From there, shit got real weird. I started to see things in those crazy shades of red and blue, like when you put on 3-D glasses. All the houses and cars looked so fucked up. I couldn't take it. I walked down the block toward the park where there's no houses. I was looking up at the trees, and they started talking to me."

"See?" said Ellen. "Bat shit crazy."

Andy was comforted in some strange way to know that he and Doc were at least in the same ball park. "What'd they tell you?" he wondered aloud.

"They just kept saying '*Come find me.*' It was some creepy little girl's voice too. You know, like in a horror movie or something."

"And so, you figured the best thing to do was to walk *toward* the noise? You know how that works out in all those movies, right?"

"I don't know, man," Doc continued, "it was hypnotic. Before I knew it, I was walking down the street. I have no idea how I ended up in the neighbor's bushes."

"Speaking of finding people..." Andy said. "Where did YOU go?" He was talking straight at Jeff now.

Jeff remained shrouded in a cloak of hair and silence. He stared straight at the floor, making no attempt to engage Andy or even move.

"He's been like that since I got here," Ellen said. "He won't talk to anyone. He's breathing, and he looked up at me when I asked him to, but he's somewhere else right now."

"He'll be fine," Doc laughed. "He's still in it, but he'll come back, just like you did."

"So, wait…" Andy asked, "is it over then?"

"Probably not. Maybe. It's hard to tell. 'Shrooms are a pretty inexact science. Sometimes you're gone for a while. Sometimes you go up and down. It's always different, and you never know. That's part of the fun."

Andy couldn't think of a worse definition of "fun." Every one of those things Doc described was the pure opposite of the predictable, comfortable consistency he required.

"You okay, dude?" Andy tried engaging Jeff once more.

Again he stayed still, but finally spoke, "I want to be alone." His voice was a shaky shadow of its usual confident tone.

"Yeah, that's not gonna happen," Ellen said. "You don't have to talk. But we're not leaving you."

"Hey, wait…" said Andy, "where the fuck is Traci?"

"Oh shit, dude!" Ellen exclaimed. "That's the even worse part. So, Nature Boy here tells me she went tripping with you guys, too."

"Yeah, she did. Why? What happened?"

"Apparently, before I even got here, shit went bad for her, too. I ran into Eddie downstairs, and I guess he had a front row seat for the freak show."

"He always does," Doc said, chuckling.

"Shut up." said Andy, suddenly showing uncharacteristic concern for Traci. He might have been the last person she'd seen before shit got weird for her, and he was trying to work out if he was responsible in some way. "What *happened*?"

"Eddie says she came walking downstairs, looking pretty glassy-eyed. He didn't think too much of it, cuz who hasn't seen that a hundred times before, right? So, he's standing there talking to someone, and he says he keeps seeing these flashes pop up. Apparently, she's playing with a lighter—you know, a Zippo. She was probably getting cool tracers off it or something. I don't know. Of course he noticed, but he didn't think anything of it. But then, Eddie said she noticed the little bits of thread hanging down off the ends of her cut-offs."

Andy was glassy-eyed too, but he was listening like an eager schoolboy at story time.

"I guess she couldn't resist the urge to see what the fray looked like when they burn. Eddie said the fringe ignited and just kept going. Before she knew it, half her damned leg was in flames!"

The boys started snickering.

"She set herself on fucking fire?"

"Yeah! And it's really not funny. It's bad enough it happened at all. Imagine that shit while you're trippin' balls. Eddie says she lost it— dropped on the floor and started rolling around, screaming like a goddamned banshee."

"So, what did Eddie do?" Andy asked.

"The fucker dumped a whole cup of beer on her." Ellen said, matter-of-factly.

The boys exploded in riotous laughter.

"Now THAT'S funny!"

"It's a damn good thing he wasn't drinking the punch. I think that shit had jet fuel in it. She'd have gone up like a dried tobacco barn."

Ellen had to admit, in hindsight, it was a spectacle she wished she had seen. Instead, she'd be one of the hundreds of people who would share the story in the future—most of whom probably weren't even at Doc's house that night, but who would claim to have been 'standing right there when it happened.'

"Oh my God," Andy said. "I had no idea. I hope she's okay."

"Yeah, lucky for her, she had some other friends here. They took her home, and I guess they're gonna hang out with her until she comes down for good," Ellen explained. "Speaking of which, I guess I get to babysit you dumb fuckers for the rest of the night now."

"Aww. Thanks, Mom," Andy teased.

"Yeah. Fuck y'all." she replied. "I think you've both had enough fun for one night. It's too late for me to start drinking now, and I gotta drive you both home. Let's go. You're both gonna pack me the biggest fuckin' bong hits ever."

"Fine with me," Andy said without pause, in full agreement that he'd reached his limit. He turned once more to his tunnel-visioned friend on the floor. "You okay to walk outta here?"

Jeff said nothing, but surprised them all by rocking forward from the bed and standing in one fluid motion. The veil of hair swept away from his face, and as he turned toward Ellen, she saw a look in his eyes like none she'd ever encountered before. His cheeks were red and swollen;

as though he'd been crying and his deep blue pupils were drowning in fear. Jeff returned his gaze to the floor and took a step toward her. She moved to meet him. Outstretching her hand, she took his and squeezed it, offering to guide him the rest of the way.

"Thanks for the fun, Doc," Ellen said, with a noticeable smack of sarcasm.

Doc offered a nervous smile but no words as Andy fell in behind his roommates and followed them out the door. They spoke to no one as they walked from the house to her car down the block.

52

"Where's the Chevette?" Andy asked, as they escaped the front yard.

"About three blocks," Ellen said, pointing up the street in the opposite direction from where Doc had reemerged from his nature expedition.

"Fuck," Andy complained, "the house isn't much further than that."

"So, walk home." she suggested.

"Fuck that," Andy said, wrestling to release the carabineer key chain from his belt loop. "Here." He tossed the keys to Ellen, who couldn't have expected the move any less. The keys bounced off her chest and fell to the ground. She just stood there.

Andy covered the three paces between them and stooped to pick up the fallen keys. He placed them gently in her hand. "Sorry. Here. You drive mine. It's right over there."

Ellen knew Andy was still under the influence of heavy psychotropic drugs, but she was still floored by his suggestion. Even before he got a nice, new vehicle, Andy had *never* let anyone drive his car. Sure, it was her, and it was only a few blocks, but it was still a shocking offer. Confused, but motivated to be home, Ellen accepted. She wasn't worried at all about leaving her own shitty car a few blocks away for the night. Nobody was gonna mess with sad little Chet.

Approaching Andy's SUV, Ellen pushed one of the buttons on the small key chain remote, unlocking all of the doors simultaneously. This was not a standard feature on the '82 Chevette. Andy took the co-pilot's seat, while Jeff piled in back.

"There's a little lever on the side of the seat to move you forward or up," Andy offered.

Ellen found it and began to toggle the switches. She still couldn't believe it wasn't fucking up Andy's world to see someone else at the controls of his car. The seat glided forward to accommodate her much shorter legs. "Ooh, fancy!" she teased, as she started to tweak the angle of the rear view mirror.

From where Andy had parked, the trip back to their driveway took roughly two minutes. It was over almost as soon as it had begun, but Ellen reveled in every second. She knew fatigue and drug-induced trepidation were behind Andy's concession, but she still viewed his surrender as a small victory—for both of them.

She guided the SUV into the driveway, pulling all the way up to the corner of the house, in the spot usually reserved for her own car.

"End of the line. Everybody out," she called, killing the engine and keeping the keys. Andy was notorious for losing them, and she figured she'd hand-deliver them inside to guarantee they didn't go missing tomorrow; something for which she'd inevitably be blamed. She waited until both passengers had opened their doors to push the lock button on the driver's side arm rest. Using Andy's same key chain, Ellen unlocked the front door and let herself in.

"Den. Bong hits. Two minutes," she commanded.

The boys hobbled up the steps, each dealing with their own unique challenges. Andy had no idea what was happening inside Jeff's head, but for his own part, every time he closed his eyes, he was still confronted by an endless procession of those hexagonal puzzle pieces. They were no longer speeding toward him in the form of a fluid challenge, but rather simply cycling through his head. The thought that they would prevent him from sleeping, or worse, invade his dreams, was horrifying to Andy. He was intent on finding something to take their place in his brain.

Jeff had stopped just inside the front door, intent on making a pit stop in his room before continuing on to the Den. "Go get you stash."

It was the first thing Jeff had said to him since before they'd both hopped on the Crazy Train. The authoritarian tone of his roommate's command bothered him, but that wasn't his primary barrier. "I don't think I can put any more shit in my head right now."

"Me neither. Trust me. But we owe her."

Andy shed his shoes and fell into the chair in front of his desk. As he reached to open the drawer where his pot was stashed, his eyes and brain began to fuck with him again.

His room was dim, lit only by the faint blue glow of a small stained glass lamp hanging from the ceiling in the corner opposite him. The details of most of the room's contents were obscured in darkness, but one object in particular was unaffected. Right in front of him lay the money clip Quenton had given him earlier that evening. The side with the full text of the Proverb faced up. Nearly all of the stitched writing was illegible in that light, but a few of the words glowed inexplicably, as if they were filled with some luminescent gel. Clear as day, the words *"the Lord, and your plans"* stared him straight in the face. It happened in a flash, the kind of thing you saw, but could probably convince yourself you hadn't really.

He looked away, training his gaze on the desk drawer and then opening it. The small plastic bag he sought was there. Andy briefly reconsidered his choice to abstain from the coming round, but given that he was still obviously tripping on mushrooms; his gut seemed to be offering sound advice.

Closing the drawer, he raised his head. He wanted to look again at the stitched money clip before departing, if only to affirm his own sanity. But fear had forced his eyes closed. He counted slowly. Reaching three, he snapped his eyes open and stared down. The money clip lay there, harmless and inanimate. By now, his eyes had adjusted to the level of light in the room and he was able to read the entirety of the inscription equally well. There was no glowing; no liquid lighted letters dancing, or distinguishing themselves from one another in any way. He breathed out deeply, relieved, and stood to join his friends in the next room.

54

Ellen had demanded they reassemble in a mere two minutes. Jeff knew that in his condition, her expectation was unrealistic. He also assumed that if Andy kept his part of the bargain and attended to her need to exit sobriety, his tardiness would be excused, if not forgotten altogether.

Jeff placed his palms flat across his face, wiping his eyes, and focused on taking a few deep breaths. Taking his wallet from his back pocket, he placed it on the wooden table beside his bed. He was about to sit and remove his shoes when he noticed the small scrap of blue paper on the nightstand. He recognized it instantly as having come from Quenton and Lula Murphy's kitchen counter. Written in Quenton's atrocious scrawl was the homework assignment he'd been given a few hours ago. *'Revelation 3:15-16'*

Fueled partly by curiosity and to a much larger extent by his own experience that evening at Doc's house, Jeff detoured across the room toward the makeshift cinder block and lumber bookshelf. The well-worn leather cover of his King James Bible was easy to locate among the other more glossy paperbacks around it. Jeff scooped up the book and returned to his bed, already flipping toward the back. It didn't take him long to locate the passage Quenton had given him.

"I know thy works, that thou art neither cold nor hot. I would thou wert cold or hot. So, then, because thou art lukewarm, and neither cold not hot; I will spue thee out of my mouth."

Even in his questionable state of mind, the words hit Jeff like a sledgehammer to the heart, penetrating in a way that tangibly constricted his chest. His eyes were presently free from the psychedelic haze and the terrible sights that had come with it. They were clear and able to see perfectly in that moment, even through the huge, warm tears that were forming.

"You made it," Ellen said from the stuffed easy chair next to the couch where Andy lay stretched out with his eyes closed. Jeff wasn't sure by how much he had missed Ellen's two-minute mandate, but he had lingered long enough for her to have shed her work clothes in favor of a pair of grey sweat pants and a bright yellow t-shirt emblazoned with a picture of the cartoon superhero Mighty Mouse.

"Uh huh," Jeff replied, swiping Andy's legs from the couch and plopping down next to him. On the table before her was Andy's stash, waiting like a tribute being laid in front of royalty.

"Excellent," she proclaimed. "Fire that shit up."

"Help yourself," Andy replied. He'd meant to suggest that she was welcome to proceed without him, but it really came across more like '*fuck you, if you want to smoke it, you pack it.*'

"I'm seeing shit I can't even explain, let alone command."

"I'm done too," agreed Jeff, lighting a Winston, and passing the pack.

"So, tell me what you saw," she asked them both before stroking the lighter again to ignite her cigarette.

Andy looked at Jeff as if to gauge whether his roommate felt like sharing. With a simple, silent gesture, Jeff declined, inviting Andy to have at it.

"I don't know," Andy began. "I don't know what's real and what's not. I went into Doc's bathroom, just to take a piss, right? The next thing I know, the floor turns into some alternate dimension game of Tetris; shapes coming out of the floor and moving around and shit."

"Really?" Ellen asked, through a billow of smoke. "That sounds kinda awesome."

"Yes and no," Andy replied. "Scary at first, then mind-blowing cool, then scary as fuck again at the end. I got to a point where I couldn't control it anymore, and I literally thought I might die if I lost the game."

"Yeah. That's fucked up," Ellen agreed. "So, how'd it end?"

"I gave up," Andy admitted. He was moving his lit cigarette at variable speeds across his field of vision, just to see if he was still hallucinating. Nothing at the moment.

"What do you mean 'gave up'?" Jeff asked, now intrigued.

"I don't know. I think I knew it was more than I could handle, and I just let go. Kind of like standing on the edge of a bridge, and finally deciding to jump. I just let go."

"So what happened?" Ellen asked.

"Something else took over. I can't explain it. All I know is one second, I thought I was master of the universe, and the next, I was real sure I wasn't. Everything got completely fucked up and panicky. But then, when I let it go, it all just sort of worked out. Like I said, scary and weird."

"Maybe you should let somebody else drive more often," Ellen suggested.

"That *is* pretty fucking weird," Jeff agreed, "but it doesn't seem all that scary."

"Oh, no?" Andy asked, more than willing to enter a pissing contest over the comparative insanity of their hallucinations. "So, what did you see?"

285

Jeff had inched back toward his more social self, but it was obvious he was still holding back.

Ellen tried to reassure him he was in a safe place. "It's okay," she said. "It sounds like everyone got screwed by that batch of 'shrooms. You can tell us. It's not like it's real anyways."

"Everything is real," Jeff replied, pondering the carpet. He was still looking down, hesitant to make eye contact as he began.

"It started out fun, like a regular party. I was surrounded by lots of people. I was in a yard, outside. There was music. It stayed like that for a while—warm, happy and upbeat."

Andy and Ellen sat listening and smoking as he talked.

"But then it all fell apart," Jeff said with noticeable heaviness. "The lights went out, and everything got pitch dark. I mean it was outside and all, so there should have at least been some light from the moon or something. But, no. It was pitch fucking dark, like I was locked in a closet."

Jeff had lifted his head and was now shifting his gaze between his roommates. His eyes were wild, wide open, and full of dread.

"Then there was a flash of blinding light, but only for a second. After that, I could see again, but it was still dark. The music stopped and was replaced by this mechanical grinding that was still rhythmic, but horrifying."

"That sounds terrible," Ellen consoled.

"That's just the beginning," he cautioned. "I realized I could see again, but only because of the fire."

That brought Andy and Ellen's attention to a whole new level.

286

"And it wasn't like a wall of fire, either. I stood there and watched as a river of lava rose from the dirt to surround me. Everything, and everyone, around me was vaporized, just like that!"

"Ho-ly shit," Andy muttered. "You win."

Jeff rolled on.

"I was the only one left, standing there alone, on a dark island, floating in a sea of flames. I heard crying, but also laughing. And the smell... the smell was awful too—like charred flesh and sulfur gas."

Now it was Andy and Ellen whose eyes were wide.

"I closed my eyes, trying to make it stop. When I opened them again, there was a path, a single path leading off that island, back toward the house. I ran. I ran as fast as I could. I got to the house and ran inside. It was empty. I ran through the house, up the stairs and into a room. I slammed the door, and when I did, everything was still. No sounds. No smells. No fire. Nothing. I sat down on the floor, afraid to move, and I hid. The next thing I knew, Ellen was shaking me, and Doc was standing over me with a big stupid Cheshire Cat grin, like he'd done me some big fucking favor or something."

"I'm never taking 'shrooms again," Andy said, as a matter of fact.

"I've eaten plenty," Jeff said, "but I've never seen anything like that. Even acid has never been scary like that before."

"What does it mean?" Ellen asked. Her brain was now wrapped in a warm blanket of philosophical fuzz.

"My shit was all about control," answered Andy.

"Isn't it always?" she said, turning her attention back to Jeff.

"I'm all alone," he muttered.

"That's bullshit," Andy rejected. "You're the least alone person I know."

"No," said Jeff. "Tonight, I was all alone. Everything else got stripped away. Destroyed. Maybe I'm supposed to get away from everything that's around me."

"Good luck with that," said Andy, finding the suggestion unrealistic. "No matter where you go, shit's the same everywhere."

"Not really," Jeff replied, now smiling for the first time since they embarked on Doc's Magical Mystery Tour. "There's still one place I have all to myself."

"You can't just lock yourself in your room," said Andy. "You'll end up like those fuckers on *Mack Riley*."

"Very funny. It's not here. It's much bigger than that."

Ellen and Andy weren't following. It was possible he was still hallucinating, imagining places unreal and speaking nonsense.

"What the fuck are you talking about?" Andy asked.

"I don't know. I've been in Bradford for a while, and I do okay here. But this isn't really me—it never *has* been. I forget sometimes where I come from."

"You come from the fuckin' sticks, man," Andy teased. "You've said it yourself a thousand times, there's nothing out there."

"That's exactly right," said Jeff. "Nothing at all. No distractions, no expectations. None of this drama or bullshit, for sure."

"No way," Ellen said. "Everyone's got drama waitin' for 'em at their parents' house."

"I'm not talking about my parents' place, either," Jeff corrected. "I've got this shitty little piece of land out in Fairview that my grandfather left me. It's like an hour from here, but it's a whole world away. It's no good for farming—or anything else really—but it's mine and it's quiet. Nothing to do out there but sit and get right with the world."

"That sounds boring as hell..." Andy started, before trailing off.

"It is..." Jeff laughed. "...in the best possible way. Back when I first got here, I used to go there all the time, even tried to fix the shack and fields up a little. But it's been a long time since I've been back. Too long, probably. Maybe that's why I saw all that shit tonight. Maybe it's just my brain trying to remind me where the center of my universe is."

"I'd like to go to the Center of the Universe," Ellen said, in a dreamy fog.

"Who are you, Eddie fuckin' French all of a sudden?" Jeff asked. "It ain't Stull, and we're not going any damned place right now."

"I didn't say right now, stupid," Ellen shot back. "But we should go. It'd be good for all of us. Right, Andy? ... Andy?"

Andy's head was slumped over on the armrest of the couch. The last remnants of his Winston burned in the ashtray in front of him on the table. He was fast asleep.

56

Ellen was not surprised to be the only one stirring in their home at 9:30 on a Saturday morning. Given her roommates' exploits the previous night, she had no expectation of seeing either of them any time soon.

The hours she spent at The Green Room last night had been neither remarkable nor taxing. Afterward, she had arrived at Doc's house to find she'd inherited the role of babysitter and designated driver to her damaged brethren. Whether or not she intended to, she had gone the entire previous day without ingesting alcohol. And even with the bong hit nightcap, she felt awake and full of energy. She replayed the evening over in her head as she swung her bare legs out of bed and sat up. A few feet away, a semi-clean pair of jeans hung over the back of a wooden chair. She grabbed the pants, slipped them on, and worked to free the portions of her t-shirt that had become unintentionally tucked.

Ellen swept long strands of hair behind both ears as she moved toward the door. Passing into the hallway, she could see Andy had vacated the Den at some point in the past few hours. She slid into the bathroom, now less concerned about making noise, and brushed her teeth. Cupping her hands, she took several swallows of cold water and then splashed a handful of it across her face. She wiped the sleep from her eyes and turned off the faucet, rising to face herself in the mirror. She hadn't showered, and her face was ruddy from the smack of cool water; her hair was mussed, and she was wearing a ridiculous t-shirt. Ellen smiled, deciding she looked plenty fabulous. She didn't need to look lovely, or even be clean, to accomplish her immediate goals.

Ellen was intent on leaving the house without waking anyone. Her small black leather tote lay in the near center of the freshly-painted wooden coffee table; her pair of blue Converse Chuck Taylors lay underneath it. She grabbed the bag off the table, thinking she had everything she needed.

Well, almost. In her hyper-efficiency, she had forgotten a key detail. Only when she stepped out onto the porch did she see Andy's shiny green SUV sitting where her Chevette normally did.

"Aww, fuck." Ellen muttered.

In a few more hours it would be ass-hot outside, but the air was still pleasantly cool. Ellen realized Chet was only a few blocks away. Ordinarily, she'd have taken the lazy way out and asked someone for a quick lift. But this morning the prospect of a short walk didn't seem unbearable. Ellen filled her lungs with oxygen and headed up the hill.

After several minutes, she'd begun to perspire in earnest. The elevation in her heart rate sent fresh stores of adrenaline through her veins.

Ellen hung a left at the corner of Pryor and Maple. Doc's house was just across the next intersection. A small fleet of parked cars lined the street. Apparently she wasn't the only one who had abandoned her vehicle last night.

Doc's front lawn was littered with souvenirs of the evening's debauchery. Empty bottles, busted cardboard beer boxes, and discarded cigarette packs were strewn about. A green plastic lawn chair lay upside down in the grass, as if someone had fallen out of it and simply left it overturned after righting themselves. By comparison, the house next door featured a well-manicured lawn and neat beds of purple and yellow flowers tucked snuggly in fresh wood chips. Doc's property would be 'presentable' by sundown, but that probably did little to lessen his neighbor's frustration. It occurred to her that on a lesser scale, the Murphys might feel roughly the same about them.

A small patch of Chet's unmistakable mustard-brown coat peeked out from behind a huge white pickup truck. As she approached, Ellen rifled through her small black bag. Keys, a small change purse wallet, a pack of Marlboros and a lighter—that was it. She knew she'd find the car unlocked. She popped open the door and climbed behind the wheel. She wasn't the heaviest smoker in their crowd, but she packed enough garbage into her lungs to make even the short walk a noticeable workout. She took one long breath and closed the door. Seconds later, she was coaxing the little Brown Beast to life. It wasn't a clunker—just old, and not unlike them most days, it took a little warming up to run right. Ellen waited for Chet's engine to level, and considered lighting a smoke. Deciding against it, she put the car in motion.

The Beast's original in-dash clock had stopped running even before she had acquired the car. The small black circular replacement sloppily Velcroed to the dashboard suggested it was 9:49. On a Saturday morning, it would take her less than 10 minutes to reach her destination.

A hundred yards away, she could see the traffic light at the intersection with Juniper was turning yellow, which justified her slow coast down the hill. It also allowed her to take a long look at the Cactus Club as she cruised past. Sometime in the past twenty four hours, the police tape had disappeared. The huge plate glass window had been replaced and re-tinted, and all of the structural repairs to the façade seemed to have been completed. Anyone who hadn't passed by the Cactus in the last week might never have even known anything had happened there. Soon, the drunkards and music lovers would flock again to the revitalized club. Few of them would remember its temporary closure, and fewer still would probably recall the details surrounding it.

The light turned green and Ellen was in transit again, piloting Chet under one of Bradford's many train trestles. Around the next bend, her destination appeared on the horizon.

57

Traci Nixon lived in a massive red brick apartment building, a few miles southeast of downtown Bradford. It was a short drive between her place and Cornwall Street, but in many ways the two homes couldn't have been further apart.

Milltown Place was rather uncreatively named in homage to the building's prior purpose. More than a century ago, the structure had been a thriving textile mill. A few recessions, some bad management and a devastating fire later, and the hulking brick shell that was left had become an eyesore to the city. It was nearly razed a few decades back. After a little inventive rezoning, the building was reborn. Smack in the middle of Bradford's industrial and commercial base, Milltown Place rose from the ashes to provide affordable housing for a couple thousand of the area's less-than-affluent residents. Ultimately, it became a glorified off-campus dorm for the university's middle and upperclassmen and their older colleagues who'd dropped out or worked jobs insufficient of funding actual home ownership. Traci fell squarely into the second category. She lived modestly, with no real responsibilities and no great prospects of future fame or fortune. And none of this bothered her in the least.

#

Ellen pulled up to the security booth at the opening in the brick wall surrounding the complex. The gate which kept the unauthorized vehicles from entering the lot appeared to be broken, cocked upward at a strange angle that rendered it useless. She drifted underneath the gate and found a space nearer to the front entrance than she expected.

The clock on Chet's dash read 9:57. Ellen puffed on her Marlboro as she cut the engine. She was in no hurry and was happy enough to lean back and continue her cigarette until she saw the flicker of movement in her rear view mirror.

Milltown Place also had magnetized security doors—the kind which required authorized key cards to open. Without one, resident or otherwise, you found yourself at the mercy of the call box, which justified from a security perspective, was mostly just a nuisance to anyone approaching the building for legitimate reasons. As soon as Ellen saw the two young men heading toward the doors, she decided it was time to move.

Chet's door opened with a creak. Taking one last drag of smoke, she tossed the butt on the ground and crushed it. She drew a bead on the two boys, locking in like a heat-seeking missile from a distance of fifty feet. She measured her approach perfectly, arriving just as they reached the landing.

"Hey," one of them said, slowing and inviting her to take the lead.

"Thanks," Ellen declined and ushered him through. "You go ahead."

Both boys ascended the steps. The leader dug his wallet out of his baggy jeans without even acknowledging her. He placed the leather square against the pad affixed to the brick wall, and a small red light switched to green. An audible click signaled the unlocking of the door, which the second boy opened and held for her.

"Thanks," she repeated, as both boys followed her inside. Again the leader disregarded her, maintaining his momentum and nearly launching himself at the flight of concrete stairs to the left of the elevators. His follower was far less energetic, but appreciably more social.

"Have a good day," he said, with a simple, friendly wave.

"You too," she replied, a thin smile on her face.

She turned to the elevators, now realizing she was a quick 2-0 against the security measures at Milltown Place. In a minute, she'd be knocking on Traci's door; and her friend, who should have had at least one warning by now, would be caught completely off-guard by her arrival.

The elevator doors opened, revealing an empty car. Ellen slid inside and pushed the button for the fourth floor. She had been operating in silence for most of the morning, and there was something quite pleasant about the muted hum of the elevator's mechanics as they churned away.

The ride was only a few seconds long, but this elevator was like a portal between two distinctly disparate worlds. The entrance of Milltown Place was well-lit and welcoming, with large windows and freshly-painted bright white walls. The buildings innards were a different story altogether. The doors banged open, ushering her into a long, dim hallway. The cold concrete floor was bathed in the uneven pall of florescent lights hung from the ceiling at 10-yard intervals. The lack of natural light created the same dreadful time-vacuum effect achieved by Las Vegas casinos. It was impossible to discern the time of day from inside those halls.

Apartment 413 was seven doors down on the left hand side. As Ellen reached it, the faint sound of music could be heard through the door. Someone was awake inside, which was only going to make things easier. She knocked four quick times and waited. Within seconds, the door opened. Traci stood there dressed in a pair of men's boxer shorts and a grey long sleeve t-shirt. A mint-green towel was draped across her shoulders. Fresh from the shower, she looked to be in a decent state of body and mind.

"Wow. Hey," Traci offered, with clear surprise. "I never heard you…"

"Yeah, I busted in. The security in this place sucks."

They stood facing each other in the open doorway; Traci backed by the hospitable light and surroundings of her home; Ellen bathed in the dim of the gloomy hall. Even at a very average 5' 5", Ellen was still a head taller than Traci.

"Come on in," she finally invited.

Ellen moved toward the light bursting through the huge window across the room. It was the television in the apartment's central room she had heard through the door.

"No roommates?"

"Nope. Krista brought me home last night, but she went to work early this morning, and Steph probably spent the night at her boyfriend's. Whatever."

"I'm just glad you got home okay," Ellen said, sitting herself at the bar that separated the small kitchen from the apartment's main living space. "I heard what happened."

"Yeah. Shit got crazy last night. Not one of my finer moments."

"So, you're alright though?" Ellen probed. "You feel okay?"

"Yeah. I feel fine. There's no hangover at all from the shrooms. In fact, I feel really peaceful this morning. I know I made an ass of myself last night, but I kinda don't care. Fuck it, right?"

"Absolutely," Ellen agreed, even though she knew Traci was more concerned about her reputation than she let on. Nobody wants to be known for evermore as 'the girl who set herself on fire'.

"Are you working today?" Ellen changed the subject quickly, moving back toward her original agenda.

"Fuck no. I did six days straight, through yesterday. I might have to do Happy Hour through close tomorrow night, but my ass is off til then. Thank God."

"Perfect. Put your non-workin' ass in some pants, and go pack a bag for overnight. I'm taking you away."

Ellen wasn't usually bossy or manipulative, but she'd learned a thing or two from her time living with Andy. Her roommate could be a colossal prick, but he was good at getting people to do what he wanted them to.

"What? Why? Where are we..."

"Less askin', more packin'." Ellen interrupted. "Go. We're leaving in ten minutes. Oh, and I need to use your phone." She walked around to the other side of the bar and helped herself to the cordless handset, further denying Traci the opportunity to challenge the request.

"I have to dry my..."

"Ten minutes," she repeated, already dialing, as Traci retreated down the hall toward her room.

58

It was barely after 10:00 when the cry of the phone blasted Andy from slumber. By the third ring, he realized neither of his roommates was going to pick it up. He rolled over and plucked the receiver from its cradle.

"Hello?"

"Good. You're home. Don't leave," urged the excitable female.

Andy was confused. He recognized the voice coming through the phone as Ellen's, but his mind discounted it as illogical. She was no doubt also asleep, no more than 40 feet away in the other room.

"El? Is that you?"

"Yeah. I need you to…"

"What the fuck? Where are you?"

"Listen," Ellen replied, now slowing her delivery. "I'm at Traci's. I'm fine. She's fine. Everything's fine. I'm coming home in a minute. I just didn't want to get there and find you guys gone."

"If you hadn't fuckin' called here, you could have come home and found me here *sleeping!*"

"Yeah. Sorry about that. Is Jeff still home?"

"I don't know!" Andy was getting more agitated by the second. "He's probably still *sleeping*, like I was, until you called."

"I know. I said I was sorry." And truly she was. "But, I need you to do me a favor."

There was no reply. Andy simply waited, eyes closed.

"Go to Jeff's room. Make sure he's still there. Then, don't leave—either of you—until I get back."

"What the fuck is happening?"

"You'll see. It'll be fun. And it'll start with breakfast."

Still, Andy said nothing. But now, at least she'd struck a chord. There was very little in the world Andy Maxwell loved more than a hearty breakfast, especially after an evening of self-abuse.

"Fine." He was about to hang up on her, but the suggestion of food had started his engine at least enough to warrant one more word. "Hurry."

59

Ellen had given Traci ten minutes. She'd only used a couple of those talking to Andy on the phone. As she watched her friend flutter around the corner from her bedroom to the bathroom at the end of the short hallway, Ellen grinned at her success in getting Traci to comply. Traci had finished running the hair dryer during Ellen's phone call. She'd also managed to pull on a pair of light blue jeans and trade the long-sleeved t-shirt for a white halter top and a short-sleeved plaid shirt.

Ellen noticed the coffee pot on the kitchen counter was one-third full and still had the warming light on. She helped herself, filling a mug half way with dark, hot liquid.

"Pack layers!" Ellen called out, casually sipping her coffee. "Something warm too, like a sweatshirt!"

A minute later, Traci entered the kitchen. She placed a blue backpack on the bar, and laid a black zip-up fleece on top of it.

"Done." she said, grabbing her own coffee mug and taking a swallow. "You want to tell me what we're doing?"

"Not yet," Ellen teased. "But I will tell you, you're probably gonna want sneakers instead of those sandals."

Traci gave her an exasperated look and kicked offed the flip-flops before retreating once more to her room.

"I'll turn off the coffee pot!" Ellen yelled.

"Anything else I need to know?" Traci replied, now re-approaching with updated footwear.

"No. You're good. Let's go."

She took one last gulp of coffee, and poured the last inch or so of it into the sink.

"Oh, by the way, can you drive?" Ellen added. "The Chevette's suckin' lately."

Traci grabbed the keys to her Jeep Wrangler and headed for the door, uttering an audible sigh as the orders piled up.

"Thanks!" said Ellen. "We just have to make one stop on the way."

60

Andy put his feet on the floor and rubbed his eyes. He sat on the edge of the bed for a moment, head down, staring at his bare knees. Fragmented memories floated through his brain, but he couldn't quite recall how the night had ended, or how he found his way into bed. This kind of next-morning confusion usually came paired with a splitting headache or other hangover symptoms. But at the moment, his mind was clear. His brain didn't hurt. He wasn't even ill-tempered. Mostly he was still asleep, and confounded by having talked to Ellen on the phone.

Her instructions came back to him and made him curious. He raised his head and breathed in deeply. Andy stood up and walked out of his room. The cheap linoleum popped, and the warped floorboards creaked as he moved across the house. From as far away as the living room, Andy could see Jeff's door was open a few inches, but no light came from the room.

Suddenly, the absurdity of his approach occurred to him. He'd been consciously trying to tread as lightly as possible toward Jeff. But really, there were only two potential outcomes. Either he would find Jeff in bed and wake him, per Ellen's request, or he'd find him absent, in which case he'd be in the house alone. Neither scenario required silence at all.

He quickened his pace and pushed the door open with less care than he would have a few seconds ago. The ambient light revealed a Jeff-shaped lump laying stomach-down, facing the wall, waves of long brown hair scattered past his bare shoulders. Andy realized he was just standing there, watching his roommate sleep. The awkwardness of it forced words from his mouth.

"Hey, dude," he uttered, with little volume or conviction.

As soon as he said it, he knew how stupid, and even creepy it sounded. There he stood in the middle of his friend's dark room, simply, meekly acknowledging both of their presence. Jeff remained motionless, undisturbed. Andy was grateful and immediately overcompensated.

"Yo! Wake the fuck up!" he demanded, now walking straight at Jeff.

That did the trick. Jeff convulsed and became more entangled in the navy blue sheet that half covered him. Locks of hair swept across his bearded face.

"What the hell?"

"Sorry," Andy apologized, now swinging back towards neutral.

"What are you doing?"

"I don't know," Andy answered honestly, still not sure exactly why he was there. "The phone rang a second ago. It was Ellen. I think she said she was at Traci's and was coming back here now. She told me to get up, make sure you were still here, and for neither of us to leave."

The mention of Traci's name brought Jeff further out of slumber. Flashes of last evening went through his head, including how that had ended for her, and for him. He sat upright in bed.

"Fuck. Is she okay?"

"Yeah. Ellen said they were both fine. Why?"

Jeff stared at Andy, wondering if he was really going to have to fill in the blanks for him.

"Oh yeah. The whole fire thing," Andy recalled. "No, she's fine. I think."

"And since when do you do *anything* someone tells you to do?" Jeff further questioned, now freeing himself of the sheets.

"Whatever," Andy said, taking a step backward as Jeff rose. It occurred to him a retaliatory punch for having been woken was a real possibility at this point. "I was confused. It didn't make sense she was calling, or that she wasn't here."

"Unbelievable."

"I'm gonna go have a smoke," said Andy, walking towards the door. "Get up."

"Shut up," Jeff replied, still pissed to even be awake.

"She's bringing us breakfast!" Andy called from the living room.

It helped, a little, but Jeff wasn't ready to be cheerful just yet.

"Are you hungry?" Ellen asked as she climbed up into Traci's ride. She pulled the door of the Jeep closed behind her, and fumbled for the seat belt as Traci loaded her bag in the back.

"I could eat," Traci admitted, thankful to have been asked a question, as opposed to the series of commands that had preceded it.

"Okay. Let's roll by Bubba's. I told the boys I'd bring them breakfast."

Traci brought the Jeep to life and reached across Ellen to open the glove compartment, retrieving her sunglasses. "I can do that," she affirmed, assuming her ownership and control of the car gave her at least a voice in the process.

Ellen had accomplished her immediate goal and was busy contemplating the next phase of her master plan. Traci seemed clear on the fact that Ellen wasn't open to questions regarding that plan and resigned herself to finding something pleasing on the radio.

A song and a half later, the Jeep rumbled through the intersection of Juniper and Townes. She'd run a yellow light to avoid sitting parked for two more minutes staring directly at their destination. She swung to the right, guiding the Jeep into the parking lot in front of Bubba's Biscuit House.

If there were an award for accuracy in branding, this establishment would win hands-down. Bubba's Biscuit House was exactly that—an old house, converted to a glorified food stand owned by a guy named Bubba, which served nothing but biscuits.

Bill "Bubba" Greer was a smart man. He knew what he was good at and what made him happy, and he'd figured out how to turn the combination of those two things into a very profitable business. What Bubba was good at was making breakfast—specifically his grandmother's famous 'cat-head' biscuits, so named for their relative size and weight. What made him happy was working less than full-time.

Bubba's Biscuit House was open Monday through Saturday, from 6:30-11:30 am, and not one minute longer. Greer busted ass, slinging biscuits 30 hours a week, and then went home with as much or more money in his pockets than some of his fraternity brothers who were working entry-level jobs at investment houses and law firms.

Exactly to Bubba's liking, people filed in, chose from a menu of less than ten items, paid him in cash, and left. But to his credit, those people came back. They almost all came back, and they brought friends with them. Because Bill Greer's mam-maw knew how to make a biscuit so good, it made you mad at your own grandma for not being able to match it. Fat, flaky and moist, Bubba would stuff those cat-heads with your choice of bacon, eggs, sausage, cheese, or country gravy. That was basically the whole menu. They cost $3 a piece, but they were priceless—perfect as a greasy sponge to cure the college kids' ranging hangovers, or as a dense carb-bomb to fuel the working class through to lunch time. And at lunch time, it was over.

At 11:16 am, Traci throttled the Jeep into park and cut the engine. They had made it on time, but they were going to wait in the near-closing time line that was beginning to back up from the counter inside. If you got there before 11:30, you weren't going to get shut out of the building. But, it was entirely possible you might get shut out of the supply. Greer estimated his output for each day and made exactly that many biscuits. When they were gone, they were gone. 'Sorry folks, we'll have more tomorrow.' Ellen had actually seen a guy pay the lady in front of him who'd scored the day's last three biscuits $30 for the $9 breakfast she'd just bought her two kids.

She reached the front door first and held it open for Traci, who scooted inside and settled in to the line that was four or five deep. At the counter stood another girl their age and a guy they assumed was her boyfriend. The girl was wearing mirrored sunglasses, so it was impossible to know for sure, but Traci sensed she was looking straight at her. The distance between the two pairs was roughly ten feet, and there were a few other people carrying on conversations in the small space, but it was still easy enough for Traci to hear the girl as she said:

"Damn. I think that's her. It is. It totally is!"

Now the boyfriend was looking at her, too. Traci pivoted and returned their stare, only to find them laughing and the girl now pointing straight at her. She heard the words 'on fire' and 'crazy' louder and more clearly than any of the rest of their garbled exchange and immediately felt the hot rush of embarrassment run through her face. Traci swung back around and lowered her gaze to the floor.

The line moved, and the gawkers began their shuffle towards the door. As they passed by, the mirror-shaded girl chuckled and addressed Traci without stopping.

"You're so hot," she teased with a condescending giggle.

Traci kept her head down and said nothing, hoping they would just keep walking, which they did.

Ellen had missed the full context. Having only heard the girl's final statement, she turned to Traci with a huge smile on her face.

"Did you just get hit on by some bi-girl, *in front of her boyfriend*, at the fuckin' Biscuit House?" Ellen said, with a little too much volume.

"Uh, no," Traci corrected. "I'm pretty sure they were at Doc's house last night." It took Ellen a second to connect the dots on the cruel pun.

"Damn. That's fucked up. Sorry. She's lucky I didn't hear her. I would have busted those stupid sunglasses in her stupid, fucking face."

Traci laughed at the unlikely prospect of Ellen making good on her threat and prodded her friend toward the counter. "We're next. Let's go."

Ellen responded like a pro. Without hesitation, she requested three Bacon-Egg Bubbas, a sausage and cheese biscuit, and one Messy Cat Head; a fat biscuit smothered in country gravy.

"And what do you want?" she asked, turning to Traci.

"Bacon, egg and cheese, please."

"$15.80" said a stoned-looking kid, who was definitely not Bubba, from the other side of the counter.

"Here," Traci offered, attempting to shove a few dollars at Ellen.

"It's on me," she replied, smiling and plunking down a twenty.

"Thanks."

Just as Ellen intended, Traci was starting to feel a good bit better about how their day was shaping up.

62

Jeff used one hand to lift and pull the other high over his head. Extending it as far as he could, he stretched the muscles in his arms and then leaned over to touch his palms to the floor. Tiny crackles raced up his spine as the tension in his back released. Raising his face to the ceiling, he let out an aggressive yawn, followed by a deep, chesty cough.

As the cobwebs began to clear, he distinctly remembered Andy saying something about food. He was ravenously hungry and glad Ellen was on her way, but he was also a little disappointed to find she'd left without brewing coffee. He filled the pot with water and tried to wait patiently for hot caffeine. Out of habit and boredom, Jeff opened the refrigerator and was instantly rewarded. Through the veil of a white grocery bag, he spotted liquid gold in the form of a single can of cold soda. He pounced on it like a gator snatching an unsuspecting fawn from the banks of a river. Jeff closed the fridge, leaving the coffee to continue brewing in the kitchen as he moved back toward the Den.

Jeff slumped down on the couch. He reached out and grabbed the golden box of Winston Lights from the center of the table. Another single cigarette rolled toward him from behind it. It was a Marlboro Red—Ellen's brand. He popped open the box of Winstons, revealing half a pack. One of the ten cigarettes inside had been flipped upside down—a signature Andy used to identify his packs. With no supply of his own, Jeff was faced with the choice of stealing from his two equally-absent roommates. Nine times out of ten, he'd have chosen to disadvantage Andy before Ellen, but the thought of the more robust smoke of the Marlboro appealed to him at the moment. He closed Andy's pack and tossed it back on the table.

"Good morning, sunshine, Are those mine or yours?" Andy asked, pointing to the box of Winston Lights.

"I don't know. This is one is mine," Jeff lied, twice, for no good reason.

He sat up, exhaled, and reached across the table as Andy took a seat next to him. Grasping the small purple bong, he spun it until the wooden bowl faced him. Jeff extended his pinkie finger and tamped at the lump of charred mass inside.

"Shit. This thing is still alive. Hit that," He passed the bong to Andy, who took it without a second thought, set a flame to the bowl, and began vacuuming smoke through the few inches of spoiled water.

It was alive indeed. A hefty helping of smoke wafted upward. He released the carburetor, shot-gunned the dose, and passed the pipe back to Jeff, who set the bowl ablaze again. Jeff held his breath and set the bong down on the table. In that second of silence, as Andy considered another helping, the home's front door opened loudly.

"Rise and shine, bitches!"

Ellen came barreling into the house under a full head of steam.

"In here!" Andy called from the home's center.

A surprising ruckus moved toward the Den, as twice as many feet than they expected trampled the floorboards. Ellen appeared, and leaned against the open door of the Den, still leaving room for Traci to fill its frame as she arrived just behind. Hungry, the boys were pleased to have her home and didn't seem to mind the extra company.

Ellen held aloft two big brown paper sacks, already stained with grease from the inside. Andy hoisted the Super Star in their direction, as if to offer a toast or salute in return.

"Breakfast?" they both asked, at exactly the same time.

63

The girls' failure to advance into the room was a sufficient declination of a narcotic appetizer to the main course. The unspoken consensus was that the Den was not a suitable place to consume food. The boys rose and followed them back out to the living room. Andy moved instinctively for the remote control.

"Uh-uh," Ellen reprimanded, "keep that shit off. I want to talk to you guys." She assumed he would comply, and started unpacking the sacks of food.

"Who wants coffee?" Jeff asked from the kitchen.

"Me," Ellen called.

"Yes, please," said Traci.

"Nope. I've got a Coke in the fridge."

Jeff stopped, trying hard not to laugh. He calmly walked back into the Den and picked up the opened soda can. He snuck one more sip from the still nearly-full, still very cold can, and returned to the living room. He handed it to Andy.

"No you don't," he said, turning again quickly, so as to hide his wide Cheshire grin.

"God dammit!" Andy fumed. The fact that he'd only been robbed of a few ounces at most was not the point.

"Sorry, man."

"But look," Ellen said, redirecting her roommate's rage. The smell of the greasy bounty had already started to fill the living room. Ellen handed a huge, warm wad of cellophane paper to Andy.

"Oh, I do love you," came the second half of his bi-polar exchange. "She brought us Bubbas!" Andy chirped at Jeff.

"Good call," he approved.

As Andy unwrapped his prize, Traci realized he was holding the bacon, egg and cheese biscuit she had ordered. There were several in the bag with just bacon and eggs, and she figured it wasn't really worth fighting an already-edgy Andy over a stupid piece of cheese. She watched as he took a big smiley bite of her biscuit and silently cursed him as he chewed.

Ellen finished laying everything out on the table and started passing around napkins to each of them. She was almost bubbling with an energy she found herself fighting to contain as she patiently waited for Jeff to rejoin them. Her attempt to bank the goodwill of her audience would probably have been completely transparent, if that audience weren't distracted by hunger. Andy continued to devour the biscuit in his hand, oblivious to both her hidden agenda and the fact that none of the rest of them had begun to eat.

"Ooh! Sausage gravy?!" Jeff said, immediately honing in on the Messy Cat Head. "Can I have it?"

"Sure," encouraged Ellen. There was plenty to go around, and she had chosen all of it. She figured she'd let the boys please themselves, and she'd still be happy with whatever was left.

Ellen and Traci took the chairs at the head and foot of the table, while Jeff and Andy were crowded together on the ratty sofa behind it. Ellen smiled. Her friends were deeply engaged in the free breakfast that had miraculously appeared before them. Hoping they were blanketed in satisfaction and appreciation, she began her presentation.

"So, nobody has to work today, do they?" Ellen asked, pretty sure she already knew their answers. She'd clarified Traci's schedule earlier, and Andy's perpetual availability was already well documented. That only left Jeff. Unbeknownst to him, he was the linchpin in her whole plan, and she tried not to look right at him while waiting for their replies.

"I'm clear 'til Monday," Traci said.

"I've got that beat," Andy boasted with sarcasm.

"Jeff?" Ellen coaxed.

He raised his index finger, punctuating the fact his face was jammed with a mixture of food and coffee.

A few seconds later, he clarified, "I've got church tomorrow morning, but nothing today. Why?"

'Oh, shit!' Ellen thought with dread fear. She'd totally forgotten to account for the obvious roadblock. She masked her panic by raising the coffee mug to her mouth, and took a long, slow sip, attempting to stall. With no Plan B in the hopper, she soldiered on.

"So..." Ellen began, more timidly than she would have liked. "... it's been crazy around here for a while now, especially this past week. Everyone's on edge. I think we could all use a little change of scenery and pace."

"Are you breaking up with us?" Andy teased. Traci giggled as Ellen's opening statement did kind of have that 'we need some space' feel to it.

"Shut up. I'm trying to be serious."

"Sorry. Continue."

Now, all three of them were intrigued. What she would say next was anyone's guess.

"I want to go camping," she blurted out.

Not in a million years would any of them have guessed *that*.

"What?" Traci and Jeff said almost in unison. Andy, who'd been swallowing a swig of Coke, nearly produced a spit take.

She had planned a much slower reveal of her master plan. But now that the cat was out of the bag, it was time to back pedal and rebuild. Ellen picked a new path and approached again.

"See, here's the thing," Ellen restarted. "I don't know if you guys even remember the conversation we had before you both passed out on me last night." She'd been talking to all of them, but now turned and looked Jeff straight in the face.

"What you were talking about, with that whole Center of the Universe shit, and getting right with the world... That really hit me. I kinda couldn't stop thinking about it. And when I woke up this morning, it was still right there."

Jeff was listening. They all were.

"I might have been joking at first when I said I wanted to go to your place out in Fairview, but the more I thought about it, the more I'm sure we should all go. I think we all could use a reset."

Jeff was giving her plea his full attention, and she could tell he was working on a reply. As usual, Andy felt compelled to assert himself. "Yeah, but camping sucks," he complained.

"Actually, it's kind of fun." Traci countered. "If you do it right."

Ellen and Jeff were holding a silent conversation of glances, as the other two finished their sidebar.

"It really is a bit of a shithole," Jeff admitted, now downplaying whatever attractiveness he may have given his meager country acreage during last night's discussion. "It's a shitty little one bedroom shack. Busted plumbing. Iffy generator. Middle of nowhere. It ain't great."

"Yeah, that sounds pretty rustic," Andy bitched.

Now Ellen was getting peeved, and she started to press.

"Damn it, Andy. I'm not talking about a week in the wilderness, I'm talking about one fucking night." Her change in tone was noticeable, and Andy stopped. He shut his mouth and let the smirk unwind from his face. But she wasn't finished.

"You know..." now there was an infusion of emotion in her voice, "...it's pretty hard to ignore the fact that things are getting ready to change around here." She was talking right at Andy now.

"I know you're not happy about the way things are going. But, in case you hadn't noticed, it doesn't make me all that happy either. I don't know about Jeff, he can speak for himself..."

Jeff had no intention of speaking or of derailing the momentum she had built.

"... but I've been trying my hardest just to sort of let you be during all of this job search bullshit. You make a lot of choices I wouldn't make, and that's fine. It's your life. But sometimes, those choices impact other people, too. I've been trying to ignore it, but it looks like you are pretty much leaving. And that makes me mad, and sad."

She wasn't crying, and she wasn't going to, but from the sound of her cracking and uneven voice, she was moving in that direction.

315

"So, last night, when Jeff started talking about clarity and getting right with the world... it hit me. If we really are coming to the end of this, whatever *this* is, wouldn't it be nice to slow down and spend some time just enjoying each other's company without some big-ass party or the constant noise of the TV and video games and all this other shit? We're damn good at having a good time, but when was the last time you sat back and appreciated what we actually have here?"

It was true, and neither Jeff nor Andy could argue the bottom line with her. And even though she'd deviated wildly from her planned presentation, she had managed to improvise a compelling enough argument.

"That's sweet," Traci said, now crumpling her empty biscuit wrapper. She'd had plenty of time to finish breakfast during the conversation that didn't really include her. She also now understood why her Jeep was sitting in the driveway with a backpack full of clothes. "But, if what you really wanted was some quality time with them, why am I even here?"

Ellen didn't hesitate for a second.

"Cuz, you've had a pretty shitty run of things lately, too," Ellen said bluntly. "I figured if sitting out in a field looking at stars was a good way to get your head straight, you could probably use some of that right about now, too."

"Besides, you think I want to go out into the middle of nowhere *alone* with these two assholes?" Ellen laughed. Her jovial turn was welcomed by all of them. She took a breath, composed herself and turned back to Jeff. "Can we go?"

"I do still have church in the morning. I've got solos. It's not like I can miss it."

"What time do you have to be there?" Ellen asked.

316

"Ten, at the very latest. Probably more like a quarter 'til."

"And you said it's like an hour away?"

Ellen was chipping away, breaking down the wall brick by brick.

"Something like that."

"So, you'd just have to leave Fairview by like 8:30, right?"

"Maybe," Jeff sort-of agreed, avoiding any commitment.

Andy had also finished breakfast and was lighting a fresh Winston as the negotiation continued. He wasn't buying it, but he also knew she'd have to sell Jeff on the idea for it to even matter. He leaned against the side of the couch and puffed away, waiting to see how things would shake out. He sat there, watching Jeff, and could pinpoint the second it happened. Even through the veil of hair that covered much of his face, Andy could see that smile start to widen as he gave Ellen's plan further consideration.

"But you guys aren't gonna want to get up that early and drive back," Jeff thought out loud.

"Probably not," Andy muttered.

"We'll take two cars. I've got the Jeep."

Andy craned his neck in disbelief to look at Traci, who'd unexpectedly stepped in to solve the problem. Apparently she too was now on board with the expedition.

Damn, he thought. *This is actually gonna happen.*

"I don't know," Jeff continued to stall. "You up for it, Andy?"

317

Jeff had given Andy a window of opportunity to express his dissent, but Ellen slammed it shut.

"C'mon," she interrupted, now addressing both of them. "I hardly ever ask you guys for anything. You guys are always making plans, and I go along with whatever, just about all the time. When's the last time you guys did something I really wanted to do?"

"What? You took us to the strip club just the other day," Andy said.

Traci aimed wide eyes and a wider grin at Ellen.

Yeah," Ellen blasted back. "Right. Cuz, that was for *me*."

She stared at Jeff, waiting for an answer like a young girl who'd just asked her father's permission to borrow the family car. Traci smiled as she gathered up the spent napkins and biscuit wrappers. Jeff studied the table top, as if looking for the answer there. He raised his head, wild intrigue stamped in his eyes.

"Why not?" he proclaimed, failing to find a respectable reason to deny her request. "Let's do it."

There was a small part of him that was excited by the chance to show his friends one of his favorite places—unimpressive as it might turn out to be. Mostly though, he just wanted her to be happy. And now she was.

"Thank you!" she burst, rising from her chair to hug him. And then, after the quickest of celebrations, she was back in planning mode.

"Awesome! You guys get cleaned up. Traci and I will gather supplies. We can probably be out of here in under an hour."

There was nothing else Andy could say. It wasn't even noon, which meant he could probably still have been asleep if the phone had never rung this morning. But his day, and at least half of tomorrow, had suddenly been planned in full for him. At that point, he knew he only had two options—be a completely selfish, astronomical prick, or go camping. Unpleasant as it was, the choice was clear.

64

Andy had also already showered, but he wasn't about to mention it. He knew if he admitted to having extra time, Ellen would gladly plug him into to one of the many jobs on the 'let's go camping' scorecard in her head. Having no interest in following her and Traci around checking shit off that list for the next hour, he rose, grabbed his near-empty can of Coke, and headed through the kitchen to his room.

"Where you going?" Jeff called.

"You grab a shower," Andy replied. "I guess I gotta pack."

"Long pants and sleeves!" Jeff called out after him. "Snakes and mosquitoes!"

"Fuck!" he grumbled, disappearing around the corner.

"Really? Snakes?" said Ellen, with some caution.

"No, not really," Jeff admitted. "Well, maybe—it's the woods. But probably not. I know he's agitated. I just wanted to fuck with him a little," he said, chuckling.

"He does sound pissed," said Traci.

"I don't care," Ellen offered, rather coldly. "He'll bitch for a while, and then he'll get over it. He just doesn't like people making decisions for him. He'll make it seem like it's about whether or not he's gonna have any fun, but it's really about him not getting to control shit. I'm about over that."

Traci had always assumed Ellen was easy-going, compliant even; but the last hour or so had shown her a side of her friend she'd never seen before. There was nothing about Ellen that scared her, but this new-found assertiveness was a little intimidating.

Jeff was half way to his bedroom when Ellen called him back.

"So, what exactly do we need?" The sheepish grin on her face betrayed the fact that at best she didn't have everything thought out or planned, and at worst, she might not have any idea what the hell she was doing. But she did know well enough to wait until Andy had departed to reveal it. Jeff had no problem rolling with the punches, and actually tended to enjoy it.

"It's one night of camping," Jeff said. "We won't need much."

"Sleeping bags. Pillows. Cooler. Beer. Water. Food. Oh, and lighter fluid, bug spray, and toilet paper."

Jeff and Ellen looked at each other in stunned silence. The list had fallen out of Traci's mouth with no hesitation, as if she'd been waiting her whole life for someone to ask her that exact question.

"What the fuck, Daniel Boone?" Ellen teased.

"What?" she replied. "My dad took us camping all the time when I was a kid."

"Damn," said Jeff. "I can see I'm not needed here. We'll have the shack to sleep in, too, but that list sounds pretty solid. We have a lot of that shit here, except food. We can stop along the way for whatever else we need. Start gathering. I'm going to take a shower."

Jeff left the girls to organize and walked back into his room.

65

Andy stood in front of his bed, stuffing random clothes into a green and black duffel bag. Taking Jeff's wardrobe consultation at face value, he gathered twice as many clothes as he could possibly need for less than 24 hours in the 'rugged wilderness' of Fairview. After adding a change of socks and underwear and donning a faded black baseball cap, he was satisfied enough with his wardrobe to advance to the next phase of packing.

Moving to his desk, Andy started to focus on the rest of what he considered his critical survival gear. At the back of the desk sat an open carton of Winston Lights cigarettes. He reached for the box and shook out two packs. He stacked the two gold boxes and placed a white Bic lighter on top. Opening the left bottom drawer of his desk, Andy pulled out an old cigar box and opened it. An aroma that was both fragrant and foul escaped, leaving no question as to the purpose of the box. Inside was what remained of his current stash of weed—at this point a few mere grams—as well as all manners of paraphernalia: rolling papers, two one-hitter pipes, and another lighter. A smattering of discarded stems and seeds lingered about the bottom of the box, along with a few sticky globs of resin that had been harvested from cashed bowls and clogged pipes. These little balls of scavenged second-hand hash were the true bottom of the barrel—the last resort when everything else was gone. Smoking that stuff was a dirty, unsatisfying high, but in a pinch, it was better than nothing.

He grabbed the larger of the two pipes and the rolling papers and placed them by the cigarettes. From the same drawer, he pulled a small purple velvet bag—the former sheath of a bottle of Crown Royal Canadian whiskey. Into it went one pack of smokes, the lighter and pipe, the rolling papers, and the small quantity of pot. Andy pulled the thin gold strings tight and placed the bag into the side pocket of his duffel. He was almost certain Jeff would be performing a similar ritual as part of his packing detail.

Andy tucked the other pack of Winstons into the breast pocket of the grey short-sleeve t-shirt he was wearing, and that was it. In less than ten minutes, he had assembled all of the personal effects he figured he would need. He heard the faint rushing of water through the pipes, indicating Jeff was still showering. He did not hear the girls' voices or any other activity in the house at the moment. He was about to return to the living room to reengage with Ellen and Traci, when one other opportunity to delay presented itself.

A cursory scan of his desktop revealed a latent reminder of yesterday's escapades. It was strange enough for his keys and wallet to be readily accessible had to search for one or both of them before leaving the house. It was even more unlikely that both items would be neatly sitting side-by-side in a place as logical as his desk. But what had caught Andy's eye was the other leather rectangle sitting right next to them. He approached the desk again and sat, contemplating. Of course he knew what it was and how it had come to be there. But still, he stared at it as though for the first time.

Andy swept aside his keys and wallet and picked up the money clip that had so recently belonged to his neighbor. It had the softness that came with being well used but was still in remarkably good condition. The leather was faded and worn in places, but the stitching was still sound. He turned it over repeatedly in his hands, considering the inscriptions on both sides. Condemning and comforting, Quenton's gift of wisdom left him as conflicted now as it had last night.

Upon further examination, Andy discovered there was more to the wallet than he previously realized. In addition to the money clip on the exterior, there was also an opening along the short top edge to accommodate cards. Wondering how his present resources would fit into this new vehicle, Andy reached over and grabbed his current wallet. Unfolding it, he came face-to-face with his driver's license. The picture was three years old, and listed him at 6'1", 195 pounds. In truth he was barely six feet tall, and now weighed closer to 220. He took the card out and placed it on the desk. Also inside was a Visa card, which thanks to constant reminders from their billing department, he was aware was delinquent and nearing its limit; and a second credit card from BP gas stations. This card, Andy's mother had given to him—or more correctly, let him borrow—when he first left home for school. Her intention was benevolent, to help him with expenses by covering his fuel and maybe even to motivate him to come home more often by removing the barrier of cost. Neither one of them had 'forgotten' he had it. He saw it every time he filled his car, and she got the bills every month. He had simply neglected to return it, and she couldn't, or wouldn't, bring herself to ask him for it back. Three years later, he was still letting them pay for his gasoline. But it was worse than that. Like every other service station, the convenience stores at BP also sold food, sodas, beer, and cigarettes. Nearly every time he got gas, he stopped the pump a few dollars short and padded the bill with incidental items.

Andy stacked the two cards next to his license and continued to forage through his wallet. Other than an auto insurance card, there was little else of actual value. He tossed aside the empty leather sheath and turned his attention to the meager contents on the desktop before him. Without even having to get up, Andy grabbed the jeans he'd worn last night from the floor beside him. He rescued a crumpled wad of bills from the left front pocket, and spread them on the desk. A twenty, a ten, a five, and three ones. $38 was no kingly sum, but it was more than the average of what he walked around with, so finding it was a pleasant surprise.

Andy organized the bills from largest to smallest, turning each one to face the same way as he built a small pile. He hadn't noticed the shower had quit running, but it was hard to ignore the loud closing of the front door and the mini-stampede that followed. The girls had returned from wherever they had been, and were moving through the house noisily. The momentary distraction served to hone his focus, as he considered what to do next. All of his monetary resources and identification lay on the desk in front of him, roughly half way between his old wallet and the Scripture-emblazed money clip.

He knew he was pushing the boundaries of how long he could stay uninvolved in the camping preparations before someone called him on it. He stood up and moved to his small closet. A quick scan of the top shelf revealed the item he was hoping to find. Under a pile of sweatpants and sweaters he hadn't considered since last winter was a huge green fleece blanket. He'd gotten it as a high school graduation present from an aunt and uncle who mistakenly believed he was going to college in the Arctic Circle and not the Deep South. The blanket was nice, but it was heavy as hell, and he had never once come close to needing the kind of heat that thing provided. Andy laughed as he hauled the green wooly monster from its perch, figuring it would at least get one good use in its lifetime.

He threw the blanket onto his bed next to the duffel bag, and moved two of his three pillows on top of it, just as Ellen peeked her head around the corner of his door frame.

"Hey. How's it coming?" she asked. Her enthusiasm was obvious.

"Good. I'm packed, and I pulled some supplies together. I was just headed out back to grab the big cooler," he lied. "I think we're in pretty good shape."

"Awesome," Ellen said, boomeranging herself back around the corner and out of sight again. "Finish up, and let's go."

Andy had managed to fake enough productivity to satisfy her, but clearly he was on the clock. Walking back to the desk, he made a quick and conscious decision. Instead of reassembling his old wallet, he chose to place his things into Quenton's old clip. He folded the meager stack of bills once, pried up the tension bar on the money clip, and slid the stack underneath it. He'd never owned a money clip before, and didn't know anyone else who had either. If he was being honest, he thought it looked kinda cool. He grabbed and straightened the small handful of cards. As he slid them neatly into the top slot, the Scripture stared up at him from his palm.

"Commit your work to the Lord, and your plans will succeed."

Well, I guess that's one way to put your life in the Word of God, he thought as he turned the now-loaded money clip over in his hands again. He jammed the money clip into his back pocket, grabbed the gear he had assembled from the bed, and headed back toward the center of the house.

66

The girls were rifling through a couple of white plastic bags in the kitchen. In further testament to Ellen's motivation, it had only taken them half an hour to get to and from the Cubby with a first wave of supplies.

Andy entered, his arms full with pillows, a blanket, and his duffel. He got a partial look at their score as he walked past—a bag of marshmallows, a pack hot dogs, and a case of Miller Lite beer.

"Nice haul."

"Where's that cooler?" Ellen called after him.

"Just a second."

Breaking onto the porch, Andy saw Jeff scrounging through the small storage area behind the bench seat of his black pickup truck. Jeff emerged hugging a large square of black canvas to his chest. Approaching the side of the truck, Andy blindly swung the duffel bag over the side rail and into the truck's bed. It was already in flight when Jeff blurted out his caution.

"Careful!"

Too late. The bag plunked down on top of two small fishing rods Jeff had already loaded. Andy's gear was light, and bounced off the rigs doing no discernible damage.

"Damn, man. Watch what you're doing. I've got rods back there."

"Sorry."

"Whatever. Help me with this," Jeff replied, unfurling and shaking out the truck's snap-on bed cover.

"We can fit everything we need back here and then cover it." Jeff explained. "I don't know what room Traci has in her Jeep, but this way, nothing will get wet, or fly out the back."

Andy cared very little about the details, but was at least glad to know Jeff was thinking ahead. He laid the blanket and pillows in the truck bed and grabbed an edge of the liner, holding it steady as Jeff fastened one row of snaps on the far side of the truck. Andy hadn't even considered the possibility of rain. Surveying for clouds, it occurred to him there was actually something that could further decrease his interest in camping. For now, the sky above was blue and calm.

"Toss it back over," Jeff called. "I'll snap it down once we load it all."

Andy gave the canvas a mighty heave and launched it back at his roommate. Deciding he was done with that task, Andy walked away, continuing past the porch, along the side of the house nearest the Murphys, on his way to the back yard. The weeds that passed for grass in their yard had grown mid-shin high. Streams of dew slid off them and onto his shoes and the bottoms of his jeans. Reaching the corner of the house, Andy expected to see the large blue and white cooler peeking out from behind the concrete steps that led back up to the house. It was not there.

"Son of a bitch,"

He took a quick look around the yard. Failing to spot the cooler, he trudged up the steps. He re-entered the house to find the girls busily packing the beer and some bottled water into the blue cooler.

"Thanks for that cooler, Andy," Ellen said dryly. "Hey though, can you take those bags of ice out back and bust 'em up?"

"Sure," Andy agreed.

"I think we're about ready," Ellen decided. "Where's Jeff?"

"Right here," he announced from behind her.

Ellen pivoted and leaned against the counter. She extended an arm toward Jeff, offering him a friendly half-hug. Jeff slid in and hoisted an arm over her shoulder. She lowered her head to his chest and gave him a solid, one-armed squeeze to the mid-section. He knew it meant 'thank you' and could tell she was probably smiling. Jeff squeezed her back, and then released.

Andy came back to the kitchen, a dripping, ten-pound bag of ice at the end of each arm. Traci lifted the cooler's lid revealing several neat rows of aluminum beer cans and far fewer plastic water bottles. Once the cans and bottles were covered in ice, Ellen came behind and started dumping assorted perishables on top. Hot dogs, a pack of cheese slices, a bag of deli-sliced lunch meat, a small jar of bread and butter pickles, a carton of six large Hershey's chocolate bars, and four bananas.

"Food's set," she announced. "Sandwiches for lunch. Hot dogs for dinner. Chips to snack on, and stuff for s'mores later on. Fruit and Pop-Tarts for breakfast. It's at least as good as you'd get if we stayed here."

"The only things we couldn't get at the Cubby were lighter fluid and bug spray. I thought they'd have both, but nope," Traci added.

"That's cool," Jeff suggested. "We can stop along the way. I've got two sleeping bags in the truck and probably two more in the cabin. Plus, there's the futon bed, with blankets."

"I brought a blanket," said Andy. It sounded roughly as lame as his actual contribution to the process had been so far.

"I think we should be good. I threw some fishing poles in, too. I know a little place we can get some worms or crickets, along with the other stuff we need."

"Awesome," cheered Traci. Her enthusiasm for live bait seemed odd to Andy, but he said nothing.

"Let's do this," Ellen urged.

"I gotta pee before we go," said Andy, for no one's particular benefit.

"Everybody go before we leave," Jeff encouraged, slipping into Dad mode. "If we just make the one stop, we can be there in about an hour and a half."

"Perfect," Ellen agreed. "Girls in the Jeep, boys in the truck." It wasn't clear whether her statement was a question or a dictate, but it didn't matter—it was obviously the best division between the two vehicles.

"Hold on," Andy called from inside the front room. They were already off the porch. Ellen stopped and waited for him as Traci and Jeff continued toward the cars.

"Can someone lock this?" he asked. "I'm not driving, so I'm not even bringing keys."

"I guess if you don't bring 'em, you can't lose 'em, right?" she replied.

"Exactly," Andy admitted.

Traci and Jeff were talking at the back of Jeff's truck. He had finished loading the cooler and other items while his friends were prepping to leave. Jeff slammed the tailgate shut and listened as Traci asked questions from behind him. He was fastening the last of the snaps over the back panel as the others approached.

"Yeah, it's simple. Hang a left on Paxton, and follow it across 19. We'll get on the highway there and head east. Once we get off, it's country roads through a couple of tiny towns, maybe the last ten miles. Just follow me. You can't get lost."

"I'm not worried. I can keep up with you," Traci said, with a smile.

"Maybe," Jeff teased back, climbing behind the wheel. It was close to 1:00 as the doors slammed shut and the engines roared to life.

67

"Hell, no!" Traci howled over the Jeep's radio. "That's just sick!"

With Bradford plenty far behind, the girls had been laughing and telling stories. Eventually, they became fully engrossed in a game they called "Would You?" Simple and crass, the game consisted of each person asking the other whether or not they would do certain things. The only rule was that you had to be 100% honest in your response, no matter the question. The clear object was to inflict maximum embarrassment on the other players. The questions always started out innocently enough; stuff about stealing and other ethical conundrums. But without fail, the questions turned quickly to topics like sex. The two girls were now taking turns grilling each other over which of the various people in their shared world they would sleep with.

Traci's loud denial was her response to Ellen inquiring about the landlord of their house on Cornwall Street, a slovenly man in his mid-50's who was prone to wearing ill-fitting carpenter pants and sweat-stained t-shirts. Ellen had no trouble believing Traci would in fact not sleep with him.

"What about the fat dude working at the Cubby today? I think his name tag said Chuck. Would you fuck fat Chuck from the Cubby?" Traci said with a heavy dose of mock sensuality.

She was already cracking herself up, but when Ellen decided to play along and answer "Oh God yes, I'd ride that big bull any day," they both broke into hysterical laughter.

They were still catching their breath when Jeff made a sudden turn, without warning or a signal. Traci caught the detour in time to turn in after him, but she still had to hit the brakes hard to keep from crashing. Placing the Jeep in park, she took a deep breath and burst into laughter again, causing Ellen to do the same.

The two cars rolled into the parking lot of the Dutch Creek Outpost. Jeff had only planned to make one stop and this must have been it.

Andy's head jerked. His body lurched forward involuntarily against the seat belt as the truck came to a stop. With no navigational duties, Andy had drifted off to sleep almost as soon as they had left Cornwall Street. Raising his head, he could feel a stream of drool run down his cheek. Jeff had left him alone in the cab of the truck and was standing on the curb in front of a roadside country store that looked like it had stood there, unaltered and unkempt, for several decades. He was waiting by the door of the shop for the girls, who were now climbing out of the Jeep. Andy began moving to meet them, but not quickly.

"See? That was easy," Jeff said to Traci.

"Easy as pie. How close are we?"

"Five or ten minutes, max. Everything we need should be in here."

Part log cabin trading post, part nostalgic convenience store, the Dutch Creek Outpost was like countless other mom-and-pop-owned shops dotting the back roads of America that catered to the needs of populations more distanced from strip malls or the ubiquitous Wal-Mart.

"C'mon," Jeff ushered the girls inside. "I hope he's here."

The door of the Outpost opened with a rusty creak. Andy was only a few paces behind the others but far enough back for the door to crash back upon its steel frame before he reached it. He pushed it again and entered the store, which was dimly lit and was almost as dirty inside as it was outside. On first glance, the store's layout was a conundrum, with no obvious rhyme or reason. Jeff had already navigated through a maze of crowded shelves and displays, and was nearing the back of the room.

"Fitz!" they heard him call out with some degree of joy.

Ellen and Traci had become distracted by a display of sunglasses. They were taking turns rotating the circular stand and plucking off a variety of gaudy eyewear that looked to be at least a generation out of style. Andy was still getting his bearings and struggling to find a focal point among the hodge-podge. Jeff's callout was enough to gain their attention, and they all turned to see their friend embracing a stocky young man wearing an orange and white mesh trucker cap.

It wasn't surprising that Jeff would know some folks in an area he'd grown up near and still visited from time to time. Hell, Jeff seemed to know someone everywhere he went. The others made their way to the back of the store, while he and his old friend continued their reunion.

"Jeff Aaron," proclaimed Fitz, now shaking his hand and smiling with great pleasure. "Look at the long-ass, girly freakin' mop on you, boy! Get a fuckin' haircut, hippie!"

The first words the others heard Fitz speak were drenched in a thick country drawl, delivered through the kind of muffle you can only get from a mouthful of chewing tobacco. Realizing they were now all gathered together, Jeff dispensed with the introductions.

"Y'all, this is Patrick Fitzpatrick. His dumb-ass, Irish-as-hell parents call him Patty, and his grandma calls him Pat-Pat, but he hates that shit. Makes all his friends call him Fitz."

Fitz's fair complexion turned a bit ruddy around the cheeks from the embarrassing explanation, but none of them noticed it, mostly because he was also flashing a gigantic smile. Two rows of snaggled teeth, stained a deep nasty yellow, took center stage in the middle of his acne-pocked face. Little tufts of his super-curly golden blond hair popped up from under the band of his hat.

"And this thing here," Fitz shot back at Jeff, "I thought this was the cutest lady I'd seen come in here in a long time... until I saw you two." He aimed the awkward compliment at Traci and Ellen, staring straight at them, still smiling. They laughed nervously, embarrassed either by or for him, and tried to avoid making eye contact.

"These are my friends from Bradford," Jeff explained. "Ellen, Traci, and that's Andy. I've known Fitz since middle school, and he's still hanging around these parts."

"Yup," Fitz confirmed. "But why the hell are y'all way out here?"

"Just gettin' out of the city for a day. They wanted to see the old farm, so we're making a quick run."

Jeff had left out any mention of camping or spending the night on the aforementioned farm.

"We needed a few supplies before heading over there."

"Hell yeah. Whatcha need?"

"Lighter fluid and charcoal," Ellen started.

"Right over there," Fitz replied instantly. "What else?"

The girls were eager to distance themselves from the Redneck Romeo. "Bug spray," Traci called out, not looking back.

"Two shelves over, on the right, at the bottom." Clearly, he'd mastered the location of every item in the store.

With the girls mobilized, Jeff added to the list "I need some bait. Crickets, or crawlers, or something. Whatcha got?"

"Both," Fitz answered, walking back behind the counter. "Fresh too." He turned around and slid the top off of what looked to be an old ice cream cooler. A quick dip inside and he returned with two plastic tubs about the size of medium soup containers from a Chinese takeout order.

"Crickets and crawlers, bro," he smiled. "What else?"

Jeff took a quick look around the store before asking his next question in a much quieter voice.

"You got any .22 shells?"

"Shit! Ain't nobody else in here today, man." Fitz laughed at what was obviously a measured precaution on Jeff's part.

"Cool," Jeff replied, relieved but still hushed.

"Lemme see what I got," he said, disappearing around the corner, and into a back room.

#

Andy was busy rummaging through a rack of cheesy t-shirts emblazoned with deer, American flags, eagles, camouflage, or some combination of the like. Amused, but unsold, he wandered back to where the girls were gathering their chosen items and placing them on the counter.

As he approached, Andy's eye drifted to the mélange of notices posted on the back wall behind the register. On the bottom right, nearest the register was a helpful reminder to whoever was manning the counter. In scraggly letters three inches tall, scrawled in heavy black magic marker, were the words, 'No Checks from these Shit Heads!' Below it were photocopies of several drivers' licenses, whose pictures were badly obscured by poor reproduction. Andy considered pointing out to Jeff's friend that 'shithead' was in fact a single word, but decided the spelling lesson would go unappreciated.

Scanning upward and left, Andy saw five state-issued flyers featuring missing persons. They included four children (two white boys, a black boy, and a black girl, each between the ages of 10-16, and one older adult female appearing to be in her early thirties). The flyers were the kind of thing most people never even noticed. But with similar posters, and even billboards, popping up all over Bradford in the last week broadcasting the disappearance of Jessica Hammond, Andy had been reconditioned to pay closer attention.

On one hand, the Dutch Creek Outpost was deep in the rural sticks. But on the other, Fairview wasn't much more than a hundred miles from downtown Bradford. He found himself wondering if the fact that Jessica's photo was not on the wall here was a matter of proximity, timing, or something else. The thought lingered only for a second, replaced by his general amusement at the assortment of crass, redneck-themed shot glasses on display at the front counter.

"I had about half a box sitting back there. Got more at home. I can spare this if you want it." Fitz said, laying a battered box of .22 caliber ammunition on counter.

Jeff slid the box open, checking the quantity. "Way more than I need. But I'll take it if you're serious."

"Serious about you buyin' it," Fitz clarified. "Twenty bucks, and it's yours."

"What?" Jeff bucked. "I can get a whole box for less than that."

"Not anywhere close. And you're already here." That same toothy, shit-eatin' grin of Fitz's that was so repulsive to his female companions was now starting to piss Jeff off as well.

He knew he was being taken. He also knew there was a good chance Fitz was gonna take that $20 and use it score some cheap meth or crank.

If he'd have thought it through, Fitz might have realized he'd have been better off just giving the shells to Jeff. State law frowned mightily on the sale of ammunition without a license. The Dutch Creek Outpost was a lot of things, but a licensed firearms or munitions dealer was not one of them. It wasn't like Jeff was going to turn him in him or anything, but if this was a racket Fitz felt compelled to continue, it was only a matter of time before he tried to fleece the wrong sheep and got what was coming to him.

"Whatever. I'll take 'em." Jeff conceded. He dug into his pocket and brought out the cash. He tossed a twenty on the counter and shoved the rest back into his pants, curling the box in his palm.

Fitz grabbed the bill and stuffed it in his own pocket as he walked back toward the front to attend to the others who were standing at the register. Jeff shadowed him along the other side of the long counter.

Andy and the girls had added to their bounty and were organizing a small pile of purchases at the register: a couple of sticks of beef jerky and a few sodas, along with the lighter fluid, charcoal, and bug spray. Fitz took stock as he began ringing up the items.

"Y'all planning to cook and camp?"

"Nah. Just a day trip. Back home again late tonight," Jeff lied.

Ellen glared at Jeff. He shook his head subtly, waving her off with a look that begged her to just let it go.

"Too bad," Fitz said. "I'm outta here around dark and coulda swung by."

"Yeah, too bad," Jeff echoed, with a tone that gave her all the information she needed.

"Can I get two packs of Marlboro Reds?" Ellen asked.

"Of course," Fitz replied, oozing a little more charm in the direction of the two girls. They had to have been much cuter and cleaner than anything he'd spoken to recently.

"$24.16," Fitz announced, jamming the items into a couple of brown paper bags.

Ellen unshouldered the small bag she was carrying and brought out her wallet. Traci stood ready with a single crisp $10 bill clutched in her hand. Andy reached into his back pocket and laid his wallet on the counter like he'd done countless times before.

No less noticeable than if it had been flashing in bright neon letters, the inscription stood there screaming silently on the countertop. 'Proverbs 16:3.'

"Uh, nice wallet," Traci mocked. "Pretty funny. Where'd you find it?" She was sure it was a joke the rest of them were already in on.

"Actually, a friend gave it to me." The seriousness with which he replied was sufficient to stifle any further commentary.

Andy ripped $10 from the money clip, matching the girls' contributions, and jammed the wallet back into his pocket. He headed for the doors, a little mad and shocked. The first public display of the gift Quenton had bestowed upon him had brought with it exactly the kind of attention and association he did NOT want. It embarrassed him and made him angry. He said nothing and kept moving toward the exit.

"Y'all have fun," said Fitz. "Good as hell to see you, man. We need to hang out a little. Let me know when you're coming back up. We'll go tear some shit up."

"Will do," said Jeff. As they gathered their bags and left the Outpost, it was obvious to all of them, except perhaps Fitz, that Jeff had no intention of doing any such thing.

Traci popped open the Jeep, and they placed the supplies in back.

"Colorful dude," Ellen said, clearly unimpressed and a little glad to be back outside. "We're still spending the night though, right?"

"Of course," Jeff reassured her, "just not with that guy. We go way back, and he's alright enough, but he's his own adventure, and this trip ain't about that at all."

She gave him a thankful grin, and they moved back toward their vehicles.

"A couple miles down the road, we'll take a left, past this big ol' burned out barn. You can't miss it. Then it's just a couple winds through the sticks. We'll be there in like ten minutes."

"Cool. We'll see you there," said Traci, saddling back up and cranking the Jeep.

68

"See? I told you. It's kind of a piece of shit."

"Eh," said Andy in apparent agreement, as the truck crept over the last few yards of the tire-worn path in the grass and came to a stop in front of a threadbare shack. His expectations had been unfairly low from the get-go, so the fact there was even a standing structure on the property was a pleasant surprise. Traci had been tailing him like a bloodhound since they'd left the Outpost, and it was mere seconds before the Jeep pulled in behind them.

She stepped out and quietly surveyed the modest parcel of land. In contrast, Ellen nearly flew from the vehicle, bounding the twenty or so feet between her and Jeff's truck. He'd hardly opened the door before she was upon him.

"This is fucking awesome!"

He smiled at her, having no idea how else to respond to her wealth of enthusiasm for his sad little kingdom. Andy scoffed, though under his breath. He was amused at her level of energy, but still unsure what all her joy was about.

With one hand cupped over her brow to shield out the bright mid-afternoon sun, Traci scanned the terrain. The house rightly occupied the highest point on the lot, with the land falling more severely off to the left. Behind the house, in what was probably a natural rain basin, a small pond had formed. Although, to call it the world's biggest mud puddle may have been more accurate. No more than a hundred and fifty feet across, its water was stained a dark reddish-brown by the southern clay beneath it, and it couldn't have been very deep at all.

There were a few trees near the small house, and a few more near a flattened structure that appeared to be an old barn or shed that had buckled and fallen sideways like a cardboard box folded at the seams.

One gnarled, but grandiose poplar rose high from the ground near the foot of the pond, but otherwise, they stood on an expansive clearing. At a distance of about a half mile, there was a tree line. Legions of loblolly pines stood tall, forming a wall of sorts around the perimeter of the property. And that was it – a shack, a mud hole, a fallen barn and a big-ass field.

"This is really nice," Traci said, now walking to join the others who were leaning against the front of Jeff's truck in silence.

"Thanks. It ain't much, but it's mine. Y'all want the nickel-tour before we unload shit?"

"Yeah. Show us around," Ellen decided for the group. Traci and Andy were both less excited, but for different reasons. Being in the outdoors was nothing new for Traci, who'd grown up on a decent-sized piece of land herself in the foothills of northeastern Tennessee. Andy, who had not, was still not even sure he wanted to be there.

Jeff exhaled a cloud of smoke and stomped the cigarette butt into the soft clay of one of the tire ruts worn into the field. With a spring in his step, he waved them on as he moved toward the small clapboard house.

He reached the rickety porch first, avoiding the single step leading up to it, as he knew it to be badly rotten and unstable. From the porch landing, he turned and offered a hand, first to Ellen and then Traci, helping them chivalrously to ascend the extra 18 inches. He offered no such help to Andy, but did make a verbal warning as he approached.

"Don't use the step. It's rotted. I need to tear it out and rebuild it, but I haven't. Just climb over it. It would suck to bust your ankle out here."

Andy grabbed the bannister and made the extra-large step over the compromised wood. Jeff propped open the rusted screen door as he worked a key into the deadbolt. Swollen from humidity, the front door stuck; but it opened easily enough with a slight nudge of Jeff's knee.

The house was dark and had a strong smell. Andy assumed it was mildew, but it was more likely just the staleness of air that comes from disuse.

"Whew! It's been a while since someone was here," Andy complained.

"Yeah," Jeff said, now propping the screen door open and joining them inside. "I'll open the windows to air it out. Shouldn't take long."

That much was true. The house was tiny. It was more of a shack, with one central area and one more room at the back, which was currently concealed behind a closed door. The main room contained a small carved wood table with two matching chairs and an old futon couch, which looked remarkably clean aside from a layer of dust. To the right, but still technically within the same room, were a small counter top, a sink, and a miniature refrigerator.

"I thought you said this place had no water or electricity," said Andy.

"It doesn't," Jeff assured him. "It used to, but that shit's been turned off for ages. No sense in paying for something that never gets used."

He had to fight to get each of the two small windows along the front of the house to rise. Eventually they both relented and began to bring a bit of fresh air into the place. Jeff moved across the room to the closed door and pushed it open.

"Tiny little bedroom right here. And one bathroom back there too, but it doesn't work either. And that's a closet." Jeff said, pointing to a second door along the wall.

With that, the tour of the house was complete. He disappeared inside the small bedroom to open that window as well. Both the girls peeked their head into the room without entering. It was barely wide enough to hold the single twin-sized bed that ran along the wall with the window. A simple two-drawer nightstand beside the bed rounded out the furnishings.

"So that's it. Pretty impressive, huh?"

"Shit. This is awesome!" Ellen maintained. "We don't even need the tents. We can all crash in here."

Andy supposed she was right, as long as they could get the smell out of the place. The prospect of not having to pitch a tent – something else with which he had no experience – was a pleasant thought though.

"It'll keep the food away from the wildlife, too," Traci added.

"That's true," Jeff said. "Let's let it air out, and I'll show you the rest of the land. Then we can bring the stuff in."

He pulled the front door open as wide as it would go and placed one of the wooden chairs against it to keep it in place. Holding the screen door open, he waited for each of them to exit and bounded off the porch.

"Let's go!" he invited, now moving down the slope towards the pond. They followed him until they'd nearly reached its bank. Closer to the water line, the clay dirt was noticeably softer. Andy could feel it give under his feet with each step he took now.

Jeff stopped and stood looking at the small body of water.

"What?" Andy asked, as he caught up.

"Just watching the surface."

"For what?"

The girls were there now too, and Andy's answer came from behind, not beside him.

"Snakes," Traci said, plainly.

"Yup. Water moccasins dip in there sometimes," Jeff explained. "I would tell y'all you could go swimmin', but I don't think you'd want to. I've gone in before, but it's not worth it. Bottom's sludgy as hell, and you just come out brown."

"Umm, yeah. Thanks for the warning," Andy griped. "I'll pass."

"There's usually some fish in there, though," Jeff offered. "Small brim and what not. I've got a couple rods in the house and grabbed some bait back at the store."

"That sounds fun," said Ellen.

"Except for the snakes," Andy reminded.

"Oh, there might not be any. But we'll shoot whatever we see," Jeff suggested.

"Shoot 'em? With what?" Andy wanted to know, having never considered the possibility of firearms. "You have a gun?"

"Relax," Jeff said, sensing the agitation in his friend's voice. "This is the country. Everybody out here has a gun. Most folks have several. A lot of people hunt; some are into the idea of protecting their land or livestock, and some just like to blow shit up for fun—but everybody out here is packing something."

"What are *you* packing?" Andy asked.

Knowing full well his roommate's feeling on the topic, there had never been any reason for Jeff to share his ownership of a firearm with Andy. Besides, it never left the farm anyway.

"I've got this shitty little .22 rifle in the closet in there. It's great for plunking squirrels or taking out a copperhead. Not much more than that, though," Jeff explained. "I'd have to shoot you with it ten times to hurt you," he laughed. That wasn't true, but he suspected Andy wouldn't know the difference, and it might make him feel better about the whole thing.

Andy said nothing, but Traci couldn't help but giggle at the whole exchange.

"Who wants a beer?" Jeff offered, successfully changing the subject and Andy's focus. Laying his arm across Andy's shoulder, he turned him around and started moving back toward the cars. The girls fell in and walked beside them.

69

Jeff lowered the tailgate on his pickup and began unfastening the snaps on the bed liner. About a third of the way up he stopped, opting to simply double the loosened portion of canvas on top of itself. It was plenty of access to retrieve the few items they'd stowed in the bed.

He grabbed Andy's duffel bag and tossed it at him, which freed his path to the object of his real desire. The large blue and white cooler slid easily out from under the cover. Packed mostly with ice and cans of beer and soda, it was heavy enough to justify him asking for help. But Jeff declined, happy to display his manly strength for the two girls as they considered what to pull from the Jeep. He lugged the hard plastic treasure chest with gusto, emitting just enough of a labored exhale to punctuate his struggle, as Traci and Ellen walked past carrying sleeping bags.

"You want help with that?" Andy half-offered from the porch.

"Naw. Just take your bag. I got this," Jeff said, letting out a short grunt.

Andy knew he was being intentionally emasculated, but he didn't care. If Jeff wanted to haul that heavy bitch all by himself, he was welcome to it, along with whatever marginal gain it earned him from the ladies.

The cooler met the rotting wood of the porch with a loud thud. Jeff stood tall, straightening his back and stretching his arms. The girls had unloaded both of their overnight bags, as well as the few sacks of non-perishable groceries they'd procured. They placed the plastic bags on the kitchen's small counter top and were lingering as Jeff returned holding a crumpled brown paper bag in one hand, and a six-pack of beer cans in the other. Andy experienced a strange sensation of déjà vu as he watched his friend once again enter a room carrying both intoxicants and a mystery.

Jeff laid the small paper bag on the coffee table, freeing his hands to distribute the cans of beer. He continued toward the small closet and pulled it open, emerging with two white and red fishing poles.

"Good." he said. "These are much better than the shitty ones I brought from home. And they're already rigged." Jeff placed them against the wall to his right and ducked back inside the closet. What he came out with next got their attention—Andy's in particular.

Clutched in his right hand was a gun—a .22 caliber Winchester model 77 rifle to be exact. Andy recoiled involuntarily at its very sight, while Ellen gazed with moderate interest as she sipped her beer. Jeff shut the closet door, walked toward the futon, and sat down. With the gun lying across his lap, its business end pointing away from the rest of them, Jeff checked first to ensure the gun's safety was engaged. He then turned the gun belly up in his lap and pulled free the 8-round magazine clip from in front of the trigger guard. Placing the rifle on the floor, with its muzzle now aimed at the back bedroom, Jeff addressed the paper bag on the table in front of him.

"Can I smoke in here?" Andy asked, now looking for an outlet for the nervous energy he felt building within.

"Cigarettes," Jeff replied. "You're gonna wanna stay sober for a few minutes."

"For what?" Andy didn't understand, already lighting the Winston.

"Winchester?" Traci asked, pre-empting Andy's quest for clarification. She had moved across the room and was now sitting on the arm of the futon, glancing down at the gun on the floor.

"Yup," Jeff confirmed. "Early '60s. It was my dad's, but he gave it to me when I was twelve." He had now revealed the contents of the paper bag to be the partial box of shells he'd gotten from Fitz at the Outpost and had dumped a small grouping of the bullets onto the table.

"Nice," Traci said. "I had an old one too growing up, but mine was a bolt."

"You what?" Andy asked with disbelief.

"Oh yeah," Traci explained. "Been shootin' since I was a wee one. We grew up in the mountains. Daddy wanted boys. He got two girls. My older sister was princess-pink from day one—not into dirt and trucks and football and guns. When I came along, and Daddy knew he wasn't getting any boys, he started training me early. Hunting, shooting, fishing, you name it. I was basically raised as a bird dog."

Andy was capable of being very perceptive, but only when properly motivated. If he had paid more attention to Traci over the years, he'd have learned more than enough about to her to be unsurprised by her current revelations. But in truth, he'd largely disregarded her. And it wasn't just her. The oversight was typical for him. Self-aware to a fault, Andy often struggled to retain even the simplest details about others.

Jeff grinned in appreciation at her account of her rural upbringing. "When's the last time you shot?" He asked, still focused on feeding the cartridge.

"It's been years now," she admitted. "I'm sure I'm rusty, but it's probably like riding a bike."

Andy and Ellen had been relegated to the outskirts of this impromptu meeting of the Fairview chapter of the NRA. She had joined him by the open front door, where the two of them stood silently, smoking and draining their beer cans. Traci held the rifle as Jeff finished loading the magazine. She handed it to him, and he jammed the clip into the breach of the gun.

"C'mon," he commanded, sweeping the bag of ammo off the table as he rose. "School's in."

Andy figured there was little or nothing Jeff had to teach Traci on the present topic and correctly assumed he was talking to Ellen and him. He had no interest at all in firing the damned thing, but he and the others followed Jeff back outside nonetheless.

Jeff's long hair flowed wildly upward as he sprung off the porch, carrying the rifle like an eager militiaman.

"Grab another six!" he called back to them. Andy had finished his first beer and gladly obliged the call for more. He reached into the cooler and dug past the hot dogs and condiments stacked between him and the alcohol below. The others were already several paces ahead, moving toward the folded barn across the field.

Andy walked slow enough to not catch up until the others had stopped. Jeff was eyeing the gun over, making sure it was properly loaded and prepped, smoke trailing from the cigarette between his lips. Andy plucked a beer from the plastic six-pack holder and passed the remainder on to Ellen. She did the same, as did Traci, until Jeff stood there in the open field with a smoke in his mouth, a rifle in one hand and three beers in the other.

"Perfect," he approved, as he started walking downwind. "These will work fine."

The others stayed put. At a distance of twenty yards, Jeff reached the first of two massive tree stumps. He placed an unopened beer can on the stump and continued to the next, which sat another 15-20 yards further down range. Placing the other can on the second stump; he began the short march back toward his troops.

"So, now you're gonna blow some shit up?" Andy asked.

"Nope," Jeff said with a wicked grin. "You are."

"No fucking way," Andy declined, immediately and emphatically.

"It's the *only* way," Jeff replied, with the calmness of someone who already knew they were going to get what they wanted. He walked straight at Andy, his rifle-toting hand extended. "This is one of the reasons I agreed to come out here in the first place."

"For what?" wondered Andy. Ellen was now intrigued as well.

"Here's my guess." Jeff began. "You've never shot any kind of gun before, have you?"

"Hell no," Andy confirmed. He had moved past agitated, straight to full-on mad.

"Right," Jeff replied, now tendering his presentation a bit. "I get that you hate guns. And of course I know why. But I thought this might be a chance for you to see things from a different perspective."

Andy felt hurt and betrayed by his roommate's apparent lack of sensitivity. He was taking the short, literal view of Jeff's proposal, failing to see the larger picture his friend was attempting to paint.

"At some point, we all have let go of the anger and fear we're holding onto. All it does is kill you slowly from the inside." Jeff had moved closer, calming his tone further and lowering his voice beyond the girls' ability to hear him. He *was* talking about the gun, but something much larger too.

"You think I can just *let go* of Tristan, and all the..." Andy's temper and voice were escalating.

"No," he said, lowering his head and placing a compassionate arm around his friend's shoulders. "Of course not. I don't have any siblings.

And I don't know the first thing about the pain of losing a brother. I can only imagine it would be like losing you."

The words were heartfelt and soothed Andy to some degree, but they also cut deep, unleashing fresh feelings within him around both past and present relationships.

"But here's the other thing I *do* know about..." Jeff continued. "You came home the other day with a potential solution to your job problem. Someone wants to pay you to write. Problem is, they want to pay you to write about guns."

Tears and angst welled within Andy, but he held his tongue.

"I know this shit makes you uncomfortable," Jeff acknowledged, "but what if you took a chance and made yourself do something completely uncomfortable. There's two ways it can go. Either you move forward or you don't. Maybe you try something heart-breakingly hard, and maybe you come out stronger on the other side. Or maybe you try it and find out you still feel exactly the same. The worst thing that could happen is you gain nothing from the experience."

"No," Andy replied, finally finding a platform from which to counterattack. "The *worst* thing that could happen is that somebody could get fucking shot and die."

Jeff took Andy's dramatic response in stride.

"Okay. That's clearly not going to happen here," Jeff said, attempting to infuse a modicum of reason. "If you can, think about it in a completely different way – a totally utilitarian way. I know it's hard, but if you put all of that other stuff aside, is it possible to think about a gun as just another tool?"

"A tool whose only job is to kill something?"

"Maybe. But, it's really just a collection of moving parts that does a job – like a lawnmower, or a chainsaw? Those things can kill people too, if the people who use them don't read the manual somebody writes."

Andy said nothing.

"I don't know. I guess I thought there was a chance you might be able to let go and actually *let* yourself do that job, instead of just throwing it away on principle? I thought it was at least worth a shot."

"I want to shoot it," Traci offered, interrupting Jeff's speech, but also affording Andy a chance to duck out on a response.

"You'll get a chance. And Ellen too, if she wants. But, Andy should go first."

"Fucking fine," Andy caved. He was still mad, and not completely convinced, but they'd reached an impasse. "I'll shoot the damned thing. Show me how."

"That-a-boy," Jeff congratulated his roommate as if he was a 7-year-old who'd finally mustered the courage to plunge off the high-board at the neighborhood swimming pool. The girls walked the short distance to the wreckage of the fallen barn and propped themselves against the last of its upright walls.

"I can't believe that worked," Traci said of Jeff's sales job.

"He played it perfectly," Ellen replied, less shocked but no less impressed. "The surest way to get Andy to do something is to let him go over the edge like that. He needs to vent and to be heard. But then you can usually reel him back in with a little guilt. It's not easy, but it almost always works if you do it right."

"Now, take the butt of the rifle and bury it here, against your shoulder," Jeff instructed. "This gun barely kicks at all, but you always want to make sure it's firm against you before you fire it. Now, this hand comes underneath, and leaves the other hand for…"

"I'm left-handed," Andy reminded him.

"That's cool. So, just switch it."

The gun was light, weighing only about six pounds. The combination of steel and wood didn't feel aesthetically terrible to Andy, but he still didn't like the sensory experience of holding the thing. He begrudgingly made the adjustments and brought the butt of the rifle to rest against his left shoulder. As his right arm extended forward to accept the barrel's length, he moved his left hand toward the trigger mechanism.

"Not yet," Jeff cautioned. "Never put your finger on the trigger until you are locked on your target and committed to firing the gun."

"Oh, I'm *not* committed," Andy grumbled, still shouldering the weapon.

"Okay. Now, the sights are a little off on this thing; shoots high if I remember. So, you're gonna wanna line your target up with this notch here, but aim a few inches low."

Andy stood tall and motionless.

"Wait," Jeff interrupted again, "forgot to take the safety off."

Andy lowered the rifle, unsure how to make the adjustment.

"Always good to have this thing on," said Jeff, reaching over to disengage the safety. "But you gotta take it off before you shoot. Now, you should be ready."

Andy brought the rifle up again. He stared down the barrel, attempting to place the sight on his target, and was surprised to see how small the beer can looked from sixty feet away. Not sure what came next, he stood there holding his form. The muscles along his right forearm began to announce themselves as he worked to hold the barrel level and still.

After nearly ten seconds of inactivity, it occurred to Jeff that Andy must be awaiting further instruction. He laughed a little to himself as he stepped once more over his roommate's shoulder.

"It's ready when you are," Jeff explained. "You can put your finger on the trigger, and when you're ready, I want you to pull it towards you with good, even pressure. Don't…"

BAM!

The .22 exploded, startling all of them for different reasons. Everyone except Andy had expected Jeff to finish the sentence he'd begun— especially since he was giving gun-safety training, and that last sentence had started with the word 'don't'. For Andy's part, it was the physicality of the experience that shocked him. He now had a better understanding of the advice Jeff had given him. The gun did kick a little, but it wasn't any great force; Jeff had punched Andy in the shoulder harder than that many times. The other thing that startled Andy, aside from the noise, was the fact that he swore he could see the bullet fly out of the gun.

"Holy shit!" Andy wailed, now swinging toward Jeff and bringing the barrel of the gun with him as he went. "That bullet flew right across my face!"

Jeff deflected the barrel as it came toward him, clasping it and pushing it down toward the ground.

"That was the shell casing. The bullet went straight out; the casings come out here," Jeff explained, now pointing to the ejector slot along the rifle's body. Most people shoot right handed, and the spent shells come out away from your body. But, because you go lefty, the shell has to travel across you. They usually go straight out, but sometimes they can come up like that. Sorry. Guess I shoulda mentioned that."

Jeff expected another assault from Andy. But none came. He was still busy processing the visceral experience of having shot a real, live gun. In fact, they were all so surprised that Andy had fired the damned thing that none of them had even bothered to look down range to see the result. Both beer cans remained undisturbed upon their stumpy perches.

"Go again," Jeff encouraged. "There's eight shots in there. No one ever gets it on their first try." That too was a lie, but why not give him a little hope, Jeff figured.

Andy hesitated, but didn't decline outright. Jeff took this as a tacit acceptance of the offer and released the rifle back to him. He stood there quietly, waiting to see what Andy would do—whether he would go through the set-up motions himself or wait to be guided through it again. Andy turned the gun slightly and peered at the safety.

"Red means ready?" he asked.

"You're good to go," Jeff said. "Aim for the closest one."

"Fuck you. I was," Andy said with a sneer, as he raised the barrel and set the butt of the gun into his shoulder.

"You'll get it this time. Remember, aim a little low, like right at the base of the can."

Andy didn't respond. He was hyper-focused, determined that if he had to do this, he was going to at least do it right and succeed. He regulated his breathing as he worked the nearest can into the sight of the gun. With the barrel now trained on his target, Andy moved his left hand up to the guard and brought his index finger to rest on the trigger. His three friends stood in silence, anticipating he might fire the weapon at any time. They were all looking down range, hoping to see a beer can explode, when it happened.

BAM!

"God dammit!" Andy howled, flailing both arms wildly upward and out. He began shaking the right one violently, as if he was being attacked by some invisible rabid dog. In the commotion, he'd hurled the gun. It arced several feet in front of him and crashed to the hard clay with a metallic thud. Thankfully, the barrel remained pointed down range and there was no subsequent discharge.

"What the fuck?" Jeff screamed, now moving toward him. The girls rushed over too.

Andy clawed at the loose-fitting flannel shirt which suddenly appeared to be glued to him. After a short struggle, full of more flailing and cursing, Andy managed to free himself of the shirt, which he flung with real anger into the dirt. He rose up, clutching the inside of his right forearm.

"What happened?" Ellen asked.

Andy removed his hand from his right forearm. A small but nasty burn mark; a dark red splotch no wider than a penny; was clearly visible about halfway up the inside of his forearm.

"Shit, man," said Jeff. "Shell must have shot right up your friggin' sleeve. That sucks."

The initial shock was over, and it wasn't like he'd been severely wounded. There would be a mark there for a while, and the burning feeling wasn't going to fade fast either, but it was his pride that got hurt the worst. Looking down range, he saw the two cans still mocking him. For him, it was confirmation that the lesson had been every bit the failure he expected it would be.

"I'm guessing I shouldn't have thrown the gun," Andy scoffed, trying his best to make light of the clusterfuck.

"Yeah," said Jeff "don't ever do that again. Next time, roll your sleeves, or just don't wear any."

"Fuck *next time*," Andy said. "I think I've had about enough of that."

"Aw, c'mon. That's just what you get for being left-handed," said Jeff. "The world ain't made for you people."

Andy was about to light a smoke when the sky ripped open with the sound of another shot going off right behind them.

By the time the boys had ducked and spun around, a second shot screamed out—this time followed by a loud popping sound. All three of them watched as Traci now took aim at the further can of beer, having just dispatched the nearer one with her second shot. A third shot rang out with no result, and finally a fourth, causing the second can of beer to explode with a magnificent thunk.

Traci lowered the rifle and switched the safety back on as she turned to face the trio behind her. At 40" long, the Winchester 77 was only about a foot and a half shorter than she was.

"Damn. Nice shootin', Annie Oakley," Jeff said.

"Thanks," she grinned. "Once a bird dog, always a bird dog. You were right. Comes off a touch high. Pretty easy adjustment though. That was fun. Who wants to go fishing?"

Like the cigarette in his hand, Andy fumed. He wasn't about to volunteer to be shown up by her again in the aquatic portion of the Redneck Olympics.

"Me! I do," Ellen piped up.

"No thanks," Andy declined.

"That's cool," Jeff said. "I've got two rods set up there on the porch. There's a tin of night crawlers and one of crickets in a bag on the floor of my truck. Looks like Chinese takeout."

"You girls go for it," he added, singularly addressing Traci. "I'm guessing you also know your way around a rod and reel?"

"Of course," she brimmed.

"It's gettin' toward late afternoon. You might get some bites. Catch and release, though. Nothing in there is worth cleanin' or cookin'."

"Will do."

"You want to keep the gun, in case there's a snake or two over there?"

"Yes," Ellen blurted, although she knew she had no intention of shooting it.

Traci hoisted the rifle and started to walk back toward the house with Ellen.

"Thanks," she said, with a flirtatious grin at Jeff as they passed.

"Sure."

"Where are y'all going?" Ellen asked.

"It'll be dark soon enough. We'll go gather firewood, and we'll see you later. Have fun."

70

A hundred yards from where they stood, the open field gave way to the first bits of dense tree line beyond. Jeff walked toward those trees, assuming Andy would follow. A little less than half way to the woods, they passed the first beer can destroyed by Traci's sharpshooting. Its frothing carcass lay inverted in the yellowed grass, still bleeding a slow trickle of beer into the ground.

"Leave it," Jeff said. "We'll grab it later."

"It's a shame two perfectly good beers had to die for that display," Andy grumbled.

Jeff laughed. "You probably wouldn't feel like that if you'd hit one of them."

"Yeah, well, we'll never know, will we? I feel pretty alright about this, though…"

Andy had decided to award himself a consolation prize in the form of a small joint he'd rolled during his packing detail. He inhaled with gusto as they kept walking. "What also feels good is not having to even think about getting busted way out here."

"Not having to think about much of anything is the best thing about being 'way out here'."

"Yeah. I don't know if I could live like this though. Seems like it might get boring pretty fast."

"It all depends on what you're looking for," Jeff said. "I don't want to be out here all the time either, but sometimes, I love just doing nothing."

"Hell. We didn't have to leave the house to do *nothing*," Andy argued.

"Yeah, but this is a different kind of nothing. You can really *think* out here. There's no distractions."

"I like distractions," said Andy. "My problem is that sometimes I can't *stop* thinking. The only way I've found to make that shit stop is to turn my brain off, or at least shift it into a different gear." He held the smoking joint aloft, as if it illustrated his point, and offered it to Jeff.

"You know, I think I'm gonna take a little break," Jeff declined. "My brain's been in some crazy fuckin' places lately."

"Whatever," Andy said. "Your loss."

"There is another way to stop thinking about shit." Jeff suggested. He stopped for a second as he reached the edge of the brush, before walking straight toward a massive poplar tree. Its trunk was easily twice the diameter of him, and as Jeff crossed behind it, he vanished from Andy's sight.

"Yeah? What's that?"

"The best way to stop *thinking* about something is to start *doing* something," Jeff said, now stretching his back against that of an old park-style bench. Tilting his head, he sent a puff of cigarette smoke straight up into the sky. He had planted himself and was inviting Andy to join him for a sit.

From there, they could see the small house across the field and the rolling hill that rose again behind it. They watched the girls walk away from the porch, each holding a fishing pole and a plastic grocery bag. As they navigated the gentle slope toward the pond, the girls began to disappear, like two tiny suns setting below the horizon. The actual sun churned westward, taking with it the clear-blue brightness, and leaving a sweep of faint pink that signaled the coming dusk.

"You're right," Jeff continued. "You *have* been thinking a lot lately. Probably too much. And it might be time to start moving toward the doing. I mean, aren't you getting to the point where you *have to* make a decision? To figure out what you're actually going to *do*?" He took a drink and waited for Andy's inevitable rebut.

"You mean like the decision *I* got to make to come out here?" Andy said sarcastically. "Or like the decision *I* got to make to shoot that stupid fucking gun? Like all those decisions *I've* been making today?"

"I'm sorry," Jeff offered sincerely. "Trust me. No one's trying to make you mad or get you hurt. By wanting to come out here in the first place, Ellen was trying to help. And so was I. In fact, we've both been going out of our way lately to help you. We know you're struggling. We've listened while you rant. We've given you advice, even when you haven't wanted it. We've tried to be patient while you worked through shit and made decisions. But now? Now you're stalled out; parked at the crossroads. We've just been trying to give you little pushes to jump-start you."

"That's the thing, though," countered Andy. "I'm tired of people trying to push me to do things I don't want to do."

"We all have to do shit we don't want to do, Andy."

"Yeah, but lately, it seems like I'm getting it from everywhere. You. Ellen. My fucking parents. That thing with the Murphys the other night. Everywhere I turn, people keep trying to tell me what to do and how to live."

Andy was getting worked up, alternately ranting, smoking, and drinking. He'd become defensive, reacting as if this was some sort of uber-rural intervention—a planned attack by those closest to him, orchestrated to isolate him and force him to make uncomfortable decisions. Like a threatened animal, his base instincts took over, causing him to strike back in self-defense, motivated by fear. Jeff was accustomed to Andy's strategies by now, but the next target of his roommate's discontent surprised even him.

"And now," Andy continued, "over this last week or so, I can't help but feel like even God has been following me around, telling me what to do. And I can promise you, I don't recall asking Him His opinion about any of this shit!"

"Wow," Jeff said in disbelief. He paused for a minute to consider what his friend had shared.

"And you think that's a *burden*?" Jeff scoffed. "That, my friend, is the very definition of a *blessing*. Whether or not you *asked* for it is irrelevant. If God is going out of His way to get involved in your life, the very last thing you should be doing is building a wall against that. There are millions of people who pray every day for that kind of guidance, who beg for God to speak to them, for Him to *tell them what to do*. If you're hearing that and thinking of that as some kind of *hassle*, you really don't know God at all, and I feel sad for you."

"Don't feel sorry for me," Andy shot back, now feeling patronized as well as chastised.

"I didn't say I felt sorry for you. I said I feel sad for you. The God I know is not some mean old dude following you around like a grumpy grandpa, riding your ass and telling you what to do all the time. God loves us, and wants us to be happy. When he sees us unhappy, he reaches out, to comfort and guide us. Sometimes, it's so subtle, you'd never even know it's Him. But sometimes, it's like he's right inside your head, telling you with painful clarity what you should do—usually when it's shit you're convinced you *don't* want to do."

They sat there, smoking and staring across the field in a thick, uncomfortable silence.

"So, what has He been telling you to do?" Jeff finally asked.

363

"I don't know," Andy admitted. "I've spent so much time being mad at Him that I'm not even really hearing it. It's like being pissed at your dad. He can yell at you all he wants, and even if he's right, it doesn't matter. It's all just noise if you're not listening. Eventually, my dad gives up and stops trying to pound sense into me for a while. I just assumed God was gonna work the same way. Besides, after He left me, I've been doing fine enough on my own."

The sadness in Jeff grew with Andy's every word. He tried to keep his own frustration with his friend's stubbornness at bay as he continued.

"See that's the thing..." Jeff said, "God *never* leaves us. You can turn your back on Him all you want, but all that means is He's behind you. But when you do that, it's on *you* to turn back around again. He's patient as hell. He'll wait as long as you want."

"I don't know..." Andy started. Jeff wasn't finished.

"And just so you know. God's not *chasing you down* either, trying to hound you into doing stuff you don't want to do. What I've seen is that God is all about giving us clues and helping us figure it out on our own. He's always trying to help, too, but you gotta be willing to listen. If you keep putting up a wall when He's trying to help, sooner or later, He's gonna put you in a situation where your only option is to recognize how much better off you'd be by embracing Him, instead of trying to convince yourself you don't want or need Him."

"Damn," grumbled Andy. "I didn't ask for a sermon."

"Yeah, you kinda did," Jeff replied, now smiling. "You're the one that brought up being mad at God. I'm really not into preaching and getting in peoples' faces about it. I try to let people be and to let them get where they're going on their own. But if you're gonna be *that* wrong about what's going on here, I owe it to you to at least get you a little closer to the Truth."

71

"You didn't bring me out here to get firewood, did you?"

"Not really," Jeff admitted. "There's probably a year or more's worth of split logs piled up on the other side of the barn over there."

"Piece of shit," Andy was folded over, forearms laid across his thighs, looking straight down at the barren earth as his roommate continued.

"Sorry, man. I know this whole day hasn't been what you wanted. But I swear, I'm really not trying to piss you off. I was just trying to help you see things differently."

"I know. And I'm sure it seems like I hate that, but I don't. What I hate is hearing stuff I don't want to hear."

"Yeah. You and everybody else."

Andy looked tired, and Jeff knew there was little left to gain on this path. "I wonder if they caught anything?" he said, changing the subject to the relief of them both.

"Traci probably emptied the pond, and shot a bear while she was at it." Andy joked.

"Ha!" Jeff laughed. "I doubt it. There's not much in there at all, but I'm sure Ellen's having fun trying anyway. Besides, I really wanted to hang with just you for a minute. I'm glad we got to talk."

"It's all good," said Andy, stopping short of reciprocating the sentiment. Stomping his feet into the ground to plant them, he stood and stretched. "Let's grab the wood and go back. I'm getting hungry."

Jeff was happy to oblige, now realizing the afternoon had come and gone with no lunch. It had been quite a while since they'd polished off the biscuits with which Ellen had bribed them.

"Okay. But we have to backtrack across the field and grab those cans Traci wasted before we forget 'em."

Cleaning Traci's kills was the last thing Andy wanted to do. He'd been trying to forget the incident altogether, but the mere mention of the cans forced it right back into his head. It also reminded him of the souvenir from his first shooting lesson that was scalded into his right arm. He looked down and rubbed the red splotch, which had ceased to burn, but still annoyed him like hell.

72

Andy's head was full, and the silent walk through the center of the field was a welcome break from the confrontations and conversations of the last hour or so. A couple beers and a few pulls from the joint had done exactly what they were supposed to, and a sensation masquerading as happiness enveloped him as he approached one of the stumps. Jeff had walked ahead, leaving Andy the closer and easier of the two retrievals.

A few paces further, Andy could see the shiny metal reflecting what was left of the afternoon sun. He reached down and grabbed the first can, thoughtfully inspecting the small, precise entry hole the .22 bullet had made. Rotating it, he found the much larger exit wound in the back side of the can, which looked more like a ferocious tear. A stream of warm beer flowed over his hand as he turned the can upside down to empty it.

He held the can, curiously inspecting the damage it had sustained. Seeing what those tiny bullets had done to pressurized aluminum, he could only imagine the kind of havoc they, or more aggressive projectiles like the .45 that had ended Tristan's life, could do to human flesh. There hadn't been much to begin with, but any possibility of him accepting the job at Firebrand Marketing was instantly eviscerated.

Andy picked up the can and turned toward the house. As he approached the vehicles, the girls were still nowhere to be found. The tailgate of Jeff's truck lie open, the bed liner still partially peeled back. Craning his head to the side as he kept walking, Andy could see that everything except Jeff's small duffel bag and a few camping chairs had already been unloaded. With some malice of forethought, he flung the decimated beer can into the back of the truck, smiling as it slid and banged its way all the way to the back.

Andy grabbed Jeff's duffel and proceeded toward the house, figuring he'd clear it to make room for the wood. Ellen and Traci were returning from the pond, carrying the two fishing poles and a couple of plastic bags but no fish. Andy couldn't hear anything they said, but he could tell they were laughing and happy.

"Do we have any trash bags?" Andy asked as his friends joined him on the porch.

"We've got the plastic bags from the Cubby Corner and that other place," Ellen suggested, having forgotten the name of the Dutch Creek Outpost.

"We might need those as we start pulling out food and piling up beer cans," Andy offered, making no mention of the one he'd just deposited in the back of Jeff's truck.

"Speaking of food," he continued, "it doesn't look like you guys pulled dinner out of the pond."

"We figured you were out bagging a deer or something," Traci returned, digging at his recent failure with the rifle.

"Damn," Andy replied. "I wasn't even saying anything..."

"Don't sweat it," Ellen interceded. "We had fun. I actually caught a fish."

"Seriously? Nice!"

"Yeah. It wasn't very big or anything, but it was a real fish."

Traci was smiling and trying not to laugh. 'Wasn't very big' was a massive understatement, as the tiny brim Ellen has wrestled from the pond's murky shallows couldn't have been more than a few inches long, tops. But she restrained herself. Ellen had indeed caught a fish, and as Traci correctly assumed, it was her first. Traci had accomplished that milestone around the age of 5, landing a much larger trout in her granddaddy's stocked pond. She herself, unlike Ellen today, had taken it off the hook and even helped clean it. But Traci figured the pride and elation was relatively the same, regardless of age or size of catch, so she was trying to stay out of the way and let Ellen have her moment of glory.

"That's cool, El. Good for you," Andy congratulated.

"So, yeah. What about food?" Jeff wanted to know, joining them with the second of Traci's cans in his hand. "What do we want to do?"

"First, I need to get the fish slime and cricket guts off my hands," Traci said. Ellen hadn't really thought about it, but she could use a good washing, too. "But you said there was no plumbing, right?"

Jeff grinned. "You're in luck. I've got what you need inside."

Returning the fishing poles and rifle to the closet, he reemerged first with a large tube of antibacterial hand wipes, and an unopened gallon jug of water. Jeff handed the items to Ellen, who immediately popped open the wipes and began to disinfect her hands.

"Damn," Andy replied. "What else you got in there?"

"Just a few basics," he smiled, walking back over to the sink and opening a drawer from which he pulled a combination corkscrew can-opener. "Most of my Boy Scout training stuck."

"Perfect," Traci concluded. "With the hot dogs and snacks, we should be more than good. Now we just need a fire."

"We'll do that, while y'all get cleaned up," Andy suggested.

"Fine by me," said Jeff. He walked to the open front door and extended his arm toward the field. "Out there, in the middle, there's a circle of stones. Come meet us when you're done."

"Cool," said Ellen, tossing the wipes to Traci and picking up the jug of water as she followed both boys outside.

"Save some of that water for drinking," Jeff reminded. He was fumbling in his pocket and surprised Andy by walking to his truck instead of past it. He opened the door and got in, without even considering the reclined tailgate or any cargo that might still have been loaded inside.

"C'mon. Get in."

Their destination couldn't have been more than two hundred yards away, but Andy was never one to choose walking when an alternative was readily available. Jeff parked along the far side of the fallen barn, with the truck's front end coming to rest in a bank of grass as tall as its hood. They both piled out, and moved toward the store of split, well-aged wood that lined the back wall of the barn.

"I'd guess about twenty pieces would get us through the night," Jeff said. "Let's just load it up once and dump it by the pit, and we'll be good to go."

"That'll work."

"We're still gonna need some kindling pieces though. Do you want to load or bust up the branches of that big-ass limb right there?"

Andy was unaccustomed to having his choice between two kinds of manual labor and was inclined to answer 'neither'. Instead, he tried as quickly as possible to work out in his head which job was the better deal.

"I'll bust branches," Andy picked.

"Okay." replied Jeff, who would have been fine with either task.

Jeff approached the stacked wood and filled his arms, taking four or five pieces at a time back to the truck. Andy approached a huge limb that

371

had obviously fallen from a tree some distance away and had been dragged to where it now lay.

"Make sure you get a handful of sticks good for cooking hot dogs or marshmallows,"

"Fuck." Andy muttered under his breath, now somehow sure he'd still ended up with the shittier of the two jobs. He surveyed the massive fallen limb, a gnarled old arm of elm that had been severed by either weather or disease. He stood there trying to identify the most skewer-worthy of its branches before finally just attacking the chore of dismantling it with is bare hands.

It took Jeff less than ten minutes to load twenty pieces of firewood into the bed of the truck. In that time, Andy had amassed a reasonable pile of kindling. With a noticeable sigh, he bent down and gathered the small hill of brush, hugging it to his chest as he moved toward the truck.

"Make room for this shit," he called to Jeff, who was leaning on the back of the tailgate.

Jeff accommodated, sliding and stacking a few of the logs to make sure Andy could dump the whole armful in the nearest corner.

"Nice job," Jeff said. "That's more than we'll need."

"Good. Let's go."

The girls had followed Jeff's lead, using the vehicles to help mule their supplies to the fire pit. As the wood-laden truck swept around the far side of the barn, the boys could see Traci's Jeep parked to the left of the camp chairs they had placed in an arc around the circle of stones. The girls stood talking in the middle of the field as the sky drew ever darker behind them.

Jeff pulled the truck up next to the white Jeep, and all four of them met at the tailgate. Working together, they emptied the truck bed in no time, creating a small square pile stacked almost within reaching distance of the fire pit. Andy once again hugged the bale of brush and transported it to the ground beside the larger logs.

"Where's the lighter fluid?" Jeff asked, knowing the girls had bought some back at the Outpost.

"Shit," Ellen said flatly. "We brought over the cooler and most of the stuff, but I think we left a bag or two back in the house."

"No worries," Jeff said. "I gotta grab a few things. I'll go. Besides, I bet all the windows are still open, aren't they?"

"I think so," said Traci.

"That's cool. I'll go move the truck back over there, and be back in a few."

"I'll come with you," Andy said. "I need my bag, too."

"I put your pack in the back of the Jeep," said Ellen.

"Well fuck it then. I'll stay here." stated Andy. Clearly his previous offer was completely self-serving.

"I'll help you," Traci offered.

Jeff was already saddling up behind the wheel of the pickup. "Thanks. Hop in."

"We'll be back," Traci announced, making a bee line for the idling truck.

Andy turned to retrieve his bag from Traci's Jeep. Ellen had taken up residence in one of the neon blue canvas camp chairs and was staring out across the field, lost in thought, enjoying a smoke.

He wanted to join her. But more so, at that particular moment, he felt he had something to prove.

73

Andy dropped his pack in the chair next to Ellen and turned toward the pile of wood. Most of the pieces were thick, dense wedges that would need the lighter fluid to catch and hold a flame. Towards the bottom of the stack, he found what he was seeking—a few logs much thinner than the rest. He pulled four of them from the stack as Ellen puffed on a Marlboro and watched him curiously. Andy stooped at the base of the fire pit, carefully laying two of the thinner wedges of wood against each other upright. Having balanced those, he grabbed the other two and repeated the process, creating a small pyramid. He turned to the heap of brush he'd collected and grabbed two handfuls of smaller branches. Ellen continued to watch in fascinated silence, never having seen Andy show either aptitude or initiative for anything remotely related to the outdoors.

Andy had packed the interior of the pyramid with the smaller twigs, but was somehow unsatisfied. He walked backed to the Jeep and retrieved a brown paper grocery bag and one of the two rolls of toilet paper they'd brought.

Ellen had changed her stance. She now sat hunched forward, forearms across her knees. She was engrossed, watching his endeavor as if some silent movie were unfolding in front of her.

Andy ripped the brown bag into shreds, and packed them inside. Still insecure about the combustibility of his structure, he proceeded to circle the pyramid, wrapping it in toilet paper as he went. Three circuits around and it looked like as if someone had mummified a miniature scarecrow.

He turned to Ellen, patting the pockets of his jeans, but coming up empty.

"Lighter," he said, with all the seriousness of a surgeon demanding a tool from a triage nurse.

The smile widened across her face as she plucked hers from the cup holder of her camp chair and tossed it at him.

"Let's light this bitch."

"Do it," she encouraged.

Andy stooped to the base of the fire pit, right next to a trail of toilet paper that seemed to lead away from the mini-mummy, like the exaggerated wick of a bomb. He lit the paper and watched as the flame crept, slowly at first along the trail, and then much quicker. He rose and walked toward the other side of the structure. The toilet paper smoldered for a second, and then sprung to life as the oxygen between its layers got consumed. The outer shell was engulfed, and it was momentarily impressive, but it would all be for naught if the kindling inside remained unlit. Andy took a long stick and wrapped its tip profusely in toilet paper, fashioning a crude torch. He lit the torch and thrust it into the heart of the pile, working to touch as many of the pieces of brown paper as possible. As the center of the pyramid began to glow and small bits of crackling signaled the smaller twigs giving up their ghosts, Andy knew he'd succeeded. The fledgling fire was generating a decent amount of smoke now and more than enough light to be noticeable in the growing dusk.

"Very impressive."

"Thanks," Andy said. "I'm not completely useless."

"Not completely. You want a beer?"

"Uh huh," Andy's attention was split between watching the growing flames and retrieving the stash from his duffel. Unzipping the side pouch, he dug in and brought forth the purple velvet bag.

Andy had been motivated to have the fire built before Jeff returned, envisioning it as a salvo in the escalating exchange his roommate had begun with the cooler stunt earlier. As Ellen returned with two cold beers,

Andy handed her the pipe loaded with a dense, bright green bud which Ellen could smell before it even began to burn.

"Thanks!"

"My pleasure."

Andy took his turn, lighting the pipe as he craned his neck back toward the house.

"Where the hell did they go?" Ellen asked.

Jeff and Traci had been gone at least ten minutes—plenty long enough to close every one of the shack's five windows and reclaim whatever gear or supplies which could possibly still be there.

"Who knows? Maybe she's in there blowing him or something."

"Nice," she said with sarcasm and a little disgust.

"It might be," Andy half joked. "although, after that display with the gun, I'm a little more afraid of Shorty."

It was mean, but not enough to keep Ellen from laughing.

"Are you having fun?"

"You know, I kind of am," Andy admitted. "I started out hating the idea of it. I really didn't want to come. But now, yeah. I'm actually starting to enjoy it a little bit."

"Good. That was mostly the point, you know?"

He said nothing but was grateful for her having articulated the thought.

The fire, now fully established, was putting out impressive light and heat. They heard the screen door slam shut, signaling the return of their friends a second or two before they could see their shapes moving toward the fire pit in the dimming light.

"Hit that pipe again," Andy urged. "Finish it."

She turned her head away from the house to mask the lighter's flame in the growing darkness and sucked in deeply. Even after two or three hits, that dense little bud still had a little love left to give. She inhaled hard and held it. Sliding the pipe into her pocket, she chased the hit with a pull from a cigarette and exhaled just as their company returned.

"Damn," Jeff exclaimed. "Nice fire, Ellen."

"*I* built that shit," Andy professed, equally proud and indignant.

"He did," she confirmed. "Every bit. By himself."

"Well done," said Traci. "Looks like it's ready for a few more big logs."

Andy couldn't decide if the remark was a criticism or an endorsement, but his default was to assume the former.

"You didn't even need this," she said, reaching down and placing a white plastic quart of lighter fluid on top of the cooler.

"Oh, we'll use it," Andy said. "Hey, Jeff, grab a couple more logs."

As Jeff worked to balance another set of wood pieces against the structure without toppling it, Andy grabbed the jug of fluid and tore away its plastic safety seal.

"Why not?" Ellen asked. "Jenga's a lot more fun when there's fire involved."

"Most things are," Andy laughed, standing up. "Back up!" It was a reasonable request with which they all complied, in particular Traci who was still understandably skittish regarding the topic of fire.

Jeff bent down and opened the cooler. "Who wants one?"

"I'm good," declined Andy.

"Me too," said Ellen, holding aloft her cold fresh can as she stepped backwards.

"Hit me, bartender," Traci sassed. Andy couldn't help but think maybe he just had, but he wasn't saying anything.

"Three... two..." Andy began counting, as Jeff was still in questionable proximity.

"So, now you're gonna count?" he teased, getting in one more barb about the rifle incident before springing up and out of the path of destruction.

"One!" Andy squawked with deranged glee as he blasted the open flame with a stream of lighter fluid. The results were predictable. A massive plume of fire erupted in the middle of the now-dark field. Jovial shouts went up around the circle.

"Where are the cooking sticks?" Traci asked.

"There's a pile of longer ones right there," Andy pointed, now realizing it would have been worth having a flash light to illustrate his directive. "We're gonna need some more light out here."

"We're gonna need some more *drugs* out here," Ellen suggested.

"Y'all go ahead," Jeff deferred. "Like I said, I think I'm taking a break."

"What does *that* mean?" Ellen asked, having missed his earlier decree.

"Nothing," Jeff suggested, trying to downplay it. "I'm just steppin' back a little. Do whatever makes you happy."

74

Jeff and Andy reclined in camp chairs on opposite sides of the stone circle, quietly sipping beers and staring at the fire as the girls each tended to separate tasks. Ellen crouched at the base of the stones, poking at the raging fire with a thick, gnarled branch, while Traci unpacked items from the cooler in preparation for cooking. The absence of conversation made it easy to notice all of the other noises around them—the crackling flames, the rustling of ice and plastic packaging, and off in the distance, a chorus of frogs and insects warming up for their nightly performance.

"You cool with the fire, or are you still a little freaked out?" Andy asked Traci. He'd meant it in a concerned sort of way, but she could have taken offense if she'd been so inclined.

"I'm fine," she replied. "It is a little weird though, ya know?"

She paused for a few seconds and then continued without looking up from her task.

"We know a lot of people who aren't exactly masters of self-control. But I don't feel like that. I've never been the kind to freak out about stuff, ya know? I'm very even tempered. Even when I get blitzed, I still somehow feel like I have things under control. Not last night though. I lost it big time."

"Oh, I know how you feel," Andy interrupted. "My trip last night was totally different from yours. But when it came down to it, I got into something I absolutely couldn't control either. At first I was really digging it, but then, when the wheels came off, I wanted out. But I couldn't make it stop. I had to ride it all the way out."

"And, the weirdest thing is," Traci said, "my trip seemed to stop almost immediately. One second, I'm seeing an evil wall of fire creeping up my legs, and the next thing I know, I'm laying on the floor soaking wet and people are gasping and laughing. But by the time Christa got me into the car, I think I was already down."

"I don't know," said Jeff. "I think I'm with Andy on this one. I've done my share of 'shrooms before, and each trip is different. Mine lasted longer than I wanted it to, and my head was still pretty fuzzy this morning. And I was *totally* out of control. It's weird. Usually, that doesn't scare me. In fact, I kinda like it—most of the time. The idea of something else pulling the strings doesn't bother me at all. It kinda gives me peace."

"So, now we're back to God again?" Andy asked.

"I told you, Andy. We're never *away* from God." Jeff replied.

Ellen had been as uninvolved in this conversation as she was in last night's hallucinogenic escapade. But to hear them tell it, she couldn't help thinking she might have gotten the better end of the deal by abstaining.

"Yeah, but when you take your hands off the wheel, that's when bad shit happens," Andy argued.

"No," Jeff countered. "Bad shit happens all the time anyway. It's gonna happen, no matter how hard you fight to hold the wheel or whether you let it go altogether."

"See, that's not cool though. After a while, if enough bad shit happens to you, you're gonna get pissed off. I mean honestly, if somebody kept disappointing you over and over again, how long would you just be okay with that before you got fed up and cut them loose?"

"I don't know," Jeff chuckled. "You and I are still friends."

Both girls, and even Andy himself, laughed.

"All I'm saying is that maybe most of the people who still trust God just haven't had enough bad shit happen to them to break that trust yet."

"I believe it works the other way around," Jeff said. "If nothing bad ever happened to you, it would probably never even occur to you that you might need more than yourself to make it in this world. The more adversity we face, the more reassurance we need that things are going to be okay. Faith in something larger than yourself gives you that."

"And some people are just more resilient than others, too," Jeff continued. "I mean, look at Graham. That dude's like fuckin' Job." He paused for a second, waiting to see if the reference brought clarity or confusion.

Sensing condescension, Andy defended his modest knowledge of the Old Testament. "I know who fuckin' Job is. What's your point?"

"If you didn't know any better, you might think Graham's got it pretty good. But he's had to go through Hell to get there. I can't really think of anyone who's had more taken away from him. And yet, somehow, he keeps soldiering on, taking it all in stride. I don't pretend to know what his relationship is with God, but if I had to guess, I'd say he knows Him for sure. And for all the hardships he's suffered, you'd have to say that guy is still living right. People love him, and through all the bullshit he still manages to be pretty fucking happy. I don't think that's an accident. I don't think you make it through all of that without a little help and a pretty big ability to let shit go. I mean, think about it. Imagine if he tried to control every little aspect of all that craziness that's happened to him. He'd lose it for sure."

"Like Cricket?" Andy asked.

Jeff paused, caught off guard by the insensitive evocation.

"Yes, Andy," he said curtly. "like Cricket."

"Who's Cricket?" Traci asked.

"You know," Andy clarified, "that cute blond hippie chick Jeff was friends with."

"What happened to her?"

"She died," Ellen said, with no hesitation. The directness of her delivery was intended to shield Jeff from having to expound.

He didn't need or want the protection.

"What really happened was she gave up," Jeff corrected. "I don't know what her demons were, but clearly, they were more than she could take. That happens all the time. I guess that's my point, Andy. Bad shit happens to everybody. Some people, like Graham, have big fat fucking shoulders, and they can carry a mountain of bullshit; but usually only with a little help. Others, like Cricket, they get buried. But the truth is, nothing is ever really over until you give up. And the only thing worse than giving up might be deciding not to try at all."

Jeff had made his points well enough, but Andy's callous reminder of Cricket had exhausted his current supply of patience.

"I'll be back in a minute," Jeff said, clearly agitated. He rose from his chair and headed toward the house without the aid of a flashlight.

"But, I was just getting ready to roll that other joint," Andy called, trying to back-peddle.

"You do that," Jeff encouraged, and kept walking.

"Damn," said Andy, turning to both girls. "I didn't mean to…"

"You *never* mean to," Ellen scolded, now also frustrated.

"Actually, sometimes I *do*, but definitely not then."

"Whatever. I'm gonna go talk to him. I'll be back."

Andy sat in silence, not even 100% sure what had just happened. He looked at Traci, who returned a shoulder-shrug that telegraphed either ignorance or apathy, or maybe both. He reached down beside his chair and started fumbling through the dark for the velvet bag in his pack.

75

"You wanna get high?" Andy asked casually, knowing her response would have no effect on his plan to stoke the fire currently roasting his brain.

"Whatcha got?" she replied, titling her head toward him with a smile.

The question surprised him. Anyone who knew Andy at all knew that he was a one-trick-pony when it came to drugs. He'd consumed several bales worth of marijuana during his few years in Bradford, but in truth, very little else. Of course everyone drank, to the point that none of them really even considered alcohol a 'drug'.

"Just weed," he replied, beginning to flatten out a double-wide rolling paper on top of a box of cookies they'd left between his chair and the cooler. "Why? What were you looking for?"

"Oh, I wasn't really *looking* for anything," Traci said matter-of-factly. "I like weed. Weed is good."

He kept his eyes on the task in his lap, sprinkling a generous portion of his remaining stash onto the paper, assuming she had finished talking.

"I've got something just as good, or better."

As Andy sealed the seam of the joint, he was startled by an unexpected noise. In her left hand, clamped between her thumb and middle finger, Traci held a standard prescription bottle. The amber plastic was nearly invisible in the faded light, but the white top shone out clearly. The sound it made when shaken was unmistakable.

"What's that?" Andy asked, expecting not to be impressed. He'd known tons of kids, all the way back to early high school, who had been prescribed any number of anti-depressants or anti-anxiety medications. Xanax and Buspar and muscle relaxers and ephedrine-based speed were all pretty commonplace, especially near campuses, where students either pilfered their parents medicine cabinets, or simply walked into the student health center and presented a combination of well-rehearsed symptoms to secure a prescription for something to take the edge off. But Andy had never developed a taste for that kind of chemical alteration. Strangely, pills, whether straight from the pharmacy or off the street, always felt somehow ominous and unreliable to him. In reality, the weed he smoked could just as likely be laced with PCP or God-knows-what, but he assumed it was trustworthy in a way pharmaceuticals seemed not to be.

"Oxycodone," she said grinning and giving the bottle a little extra shake before opening it.

"Like Codeine?" Andy asked.

"Not exactly," she clarified. "It's similar. They're both painkillers and opioids, but the chemistry is a little different."

"Now you sound like Doc."

"Nah, I don't know shit about science," Traci admitted. "But I asked the doctor the same question 'cause I'm supposed to be allergic to codeine. He told me I had nothing to worry about. All I know is, they *totally* fuck you up."

"How'd you get painkillers?" Andy wondered. His legs and lower back hurt almost constantly. His intake of weed helped for sure, and even though he'd never really considered pharmaceuticals as a solution, he was at least intrigued by the idea.

"Car crash about a year ago. I fucked up my shoulder and neck pretty bad, and started having hellacious headaches." She'd unscrewed the lid and had shaken at least one of the pills into her palm. Tossing her head back, with enough gusto for Andy to question whether she still had any lingering neck issues, she popped the pill and chased it with a long sip of cold beer.

"Are you supposed to take those with alcohol?

"No," she said bluntly. "I've been taking them for a while now though, and I've pretty much got the dosages and mixing thing figured out. My headaches got so bad, I was taking like 6-8 of these a day. The headaches are mostly gone now, but I like the way they make me feel, so I keep going back to the doctor and telling him I have the same symptoms. He keeps giving me scripts. Now, I take maybe one a day, sometimes maybe even half a pill a day. It's kind of like mood maintenance."

"That sounds 'kind of like' addiction."

"Said the pot to the kettle," she admonished. "It's no different than someone like you who smokes weed *every single day* and probably gets irritable if you don't. You know? Mood maintenance."

Andy did know. He also knew there was no point arguing with her. He was already pleasantly stoned and probably on the losing side of the logic.

"You want one?" she asked, aiming the still-open bottle at him.

"I don't think so," Andy rejected on principal.

"Go ahead," she persisted. "There's plenty more where this came from."

Addled or not, Andy's brain was always working the angles, and he quickly found one he liked. He had no intention of taking the pill, but in the economy in which they lived, drugs were drugs. Anything you had, you could probably trade or sell to someone else who wanted it more than you did.

"Sure. Why not?"

Andy held out his hand, and Traci tapped the bottle until she sensed something fall out. Andy felt two pills tumble into his hand and immediately closed his fist around them. Drawing his hand near to his chest, he emptied the pills into the breast pocket of his flannel shirt behind his pack of Winstons.

"I'm going to hold onto it for a little bit," he announced. "I've been drinking and smoking most of the day, and I'm not sure I want that piled on top right now."

"Probably a good call. I wouldn't push it. And when you do take it, break that bitch up and start with half. See how that makes you feel before you commit to the whole thing. You're not used to it, so half will probably treat you just fine, and then you'll have more left over for later, too."

"Thanks," Andy said, still certain he was never going to take them.

"You gonna light that thing or stare at it?" she teased, staring at the joint in his hand. Apparently she'd built up enough of a tolerance to not worry about stacking multiple depressants, even though she'd just applauded him for not doing the same.

"I was gonna wait on Jeff, but it sounds like he jumped on the wagon for some reason all of sudden."

"Either way, it doesn't matter. Here they come now."

Andy shifted in his chair and looked back toward the house. He couldn't distinguish their bodies amongst the shadows, but the alternating flares of light coming from two cigarettes, as they bobbed and weaved across the field, were a dead giveaway.

76

Andy grabbed the lighter, sparked the joint to life and inhaled deeply as his friends approached.

"I'm sorry," he said to Jeff, offering his hand in recompense.

Jeff, still in motion toward the fire pit, accepted. He drew Andy close, completing a quick guy-guy semi-hug before breaking apart again.

Ellen looked at Traci as if to suggest she might have somehow been responsible for or at least influenced the apology. Traci shrugged, taking none of the credit or blame.

"That was a pretty dickish thing for me to say. I shouldn't have gone there," Andy continued. "I've actually been kind of a dick most of the day. I know Ellen was trying to do something nice, and I know you didn't even have to bring us here in the first place. I didn't really want to come, but it's not because I don't want to be *here*, or because I don't want to be with you guys. The truth is, I don't have any idea what I'm gonna do without all this."

The joint made its way all the way around the circle as he spoke, with Jeff continuing to abstain.

"I'm stuck between choices I hate. I have no idea what I'm supposed to do, and it sucks!"

Jeff knew exactly what he wanted to tell his friend; that those are precisely the times when being able to turn to God was most crucial, and that if Andy would let go of that struggle, and put it in the hands of God, he would find not only comfort, but probably an answer too. But he also knew they'd covered that ground enough times that bringing it up again, especially now, would just start another argument.

"It does suck," Jeff consoled. "It sucks for you, and it sucks for us, too. None of us like seeing you pissed. But you know how we feel about it. In the end, it's on you to decide what you need to do." Jeff turned and put his hands on Andy's shoulders in a show of brotherly support.

"And I'm still gonna love your dumb ass, even if it's sittin' in your parents' basement in Atlanta. It's just gonna be harder for me to love you the way you want me to." As the last words broke from his mouth, he slipped behind Andy, hugged him tight, and ridiculously gyrated his pelvis several quick times at his roommate. As Jeff had hoped, the comic display was quite effective at breaking the tension that had built between them.

"Jackass!" Andy wailed, shooting to the other side of the fire pit to escape any further 'assault' by his friend.

"You know what?" Andy asked, now accepting the joint from Ellen. "Fuck this. I don't want to talk about that shit anymore. Let's just hang out and enjoy what we've got out here for a night."

"Best idea you've had in a long time," said Ellen. "We didn't even get to finish eating."

And so they did. The next few hours played out almost exactly as Ellen had surely imagined they would have when she'd first hatched her plan. As the fat, full moon rose high into the night sky, their spirits sailed with it. They left the talk of an uncertain future behind, choosing to relive happier days gone by retelling and embellishing stories that connected their various journeys through Bradford.

Even with as much effort as he had put into getting obliterated, Andy could still see all of this for what it was—a last hurrah. This adventure was wonderful, but no matter how hard he fought against the advancement of time, the morning would come. And after that, as little as he wanted it to, Monday would also come. Thirty hours or so from this high water mark of nostalgia and joy, the tide would inevitably roll back.

There he would be, phone in hand, making the call to Firebrand Marketing, declining their offer of employment and effectively bringing his time in Bradford to an end. There, under the surface, lay the ominous truth. This was goodbye. As he laughed at the jokes and stories of his friends and shared a few of his own, Andy couldn't help but think this gathering had all the makings of a wake—close friends gathered to honor a past, while trying hard not to acknowledge a future that would never be the same.

It was bittersweet to the core, and he kept trying to drown it. Maybe his friends felt the same, or maybe they were all just doing their best to erase sobriety from the equation. And for the most part, they were succeeding. Their voices grew louder and more slurred. Ellen was sloppily poking at the dying fire. Traci and Jeff had pulled their chairs together and were huddled together under Andy's huge green fleece blanket. Traci's head lay heavily on Jeff's shoulder, her face a tangle of drunken glee and emptiness. Jeff sat low in his camp chair, staring straight forward with a darkly distant glare burning in his eyes. Andy studied him for a moment, neither of them speaking.

He couldn't decide if his roommate was sleepy, drunk, or simply processing the shitty reality that he had to be up and driving back to Bradford in a few short hours. Noticing that Andy had been staring back at him, he clarified the matter.

"I gotta go the fuck to bed," he bellowed with regret.

"Take me with you," Traci slurred. Her request may have been amorous in nature, but it sounded more like the desperate plea of a girl who' just had her fill of getting shitfaced in the woods.

77

Jeff rose, robbing Traci of her support and causing her to slump forward. She was headed for a clumsy crash to the ground, but managed a reasonable transition to a wobbling stand. Jeff attempted to wrap the huge green blanked around himself, but it proved too big and heavy. Admitting defeat, he dumped the monstrosity across the two empty chairs.

"Fuck it. Let's go." His words were drenched with a resolve to relocate. Jeff began to move toward the cabin, and like mice behind the Pied Piper, both girls fell in line. Andy watched as the three of them retreated across the field. Their exit was sudden and seemed not to include an invitation for him to join them. But what bothered him most was that apparently none of the others were interested in the unresolved issues they were leaving behind.

Andy knew almost *nothing* about the outdoors. But even he knew leaving a live fire and half-eaten food unattended in the woods was stupid, irresponsible, and potentially dangerous. For a second, he considered not caring right along with them. Fuck it. It wasn't his land, right? But then, the images of untold creatures plodding out from the dark came rolling through his mind. He knew none of them were coming back.

Whatever buzz Andy had left seemed to be getting stripped away, layer by layer, as he started making a mental list of what needed to be done. He watched as they disappeared into the darkness toward the cabin and then tried desperately not to fixate on the mess that surrounded him. He spent a long moment considering his options before finally realizing all of this shit would still be here a few minutes from now when he brought them all back to do the right thing.

Andy took a few steps toward the house, and then for no good reason, broke into a run. He'd only covered twenty or so yards when he stopped. Andy was a sedentary creature with questionable legs who got no real exercise and who had ravaged his lungs and liver for the last half decade or so. Embarrassingly, he pulled up and slowed to a walk, now heaving for breath as he closed in on the house.

By the time he reached the porch, they were already inside. The front door was closed, as if they'd simply forgotten him.

Andy entered the house, which save for the beam of faint yellow that spread from his dying flashlight, was quite dark. The small central room was more cluttered than he remembered it in the daylight. The futon couch had been lowered to its flatbed position, and Ellen was already sprawled face down in the exact center of it. She was still wearing her jacket and shoes. Scanning the rest of the room, Andy realized Jeff and Traci were already together in the small back bedroom. Undeterred, he moved toward the closed door and banged on it aggressively.

"Dude!" he shouted, much louder than necessary in a space that small. "What the fuck? We still have to…"

"Tomorrow," came Jeff's singular reply. The unmistakable sound of Traci giggling followed, which instantly raised his ire.

"Seriously. We can't just…"

"Fuck it," Jeff reiterated, now also laughing at bit. "I'm done."

Andy didn't need the extra help of the closed door and the playful laughter of the two of them to know that 'I'm done' really meant 'Go away, I'm busy getting rewarded for coming out here in the first place.'

Now he was plain mad. With Jeff and Traci beyond talking to, Andy turned to his only other option. Wheeling around, he shone the flashlight at Ellen again. She hadn't moved an inch since his first look at her, but he figured she could still be roused.

He approached the futon and planted himself on the one corner of the surface she had managed not to cover. Quite on purpose, he allowed

394

his momentum to carry his forearm straight into the small of her back. She moved, but never stirred. Now leaning in, he tried jostling her, pressing against her hip and shoulder. She made some muffled noise but remained largely non-responsive.

"Ellen. Get up," Andy said. "Jeff and ..."

"Uhhhnnn." It was desperate groan, the sound of someone willing themselves not to be disturbed.

"Come on!" he barked at her.

The tiny house was silent. He sat there staring at her, wondering whether to hound her until she woke up or to mercifully remove her shoes and let her be. As he contemplated, the largest, most bear-like snore he'd ever heard from a female human escaped his now-slumbering roommate.

Andy huffed, assured of defeat and beginning to seethe with resentment.

"Dammit!" he growled, pushing himself up off the futon and training his beam of light toward the front door. "You people fucking suck!" he proclaimed, plenty loud enough for the couple he assumed were still wide awake in the next room to hear. They tried unsuccessfully to suppress their snickering, which only angered him further. Andy walked to the front door, opened it, and then slammed it behind him as he walked back alone into the cool dark morning.

78

Andy was pissed. Lurching across the creaky front porch, he pulled out the pack of Winston Lights and freed one from its golden box. Standing on the top step, he frisked himself in search of a lighter. As his hand ran along his chest, he felt the strange relieves of two small circles sitting at the bottom of his breast pocket. Digging in, he rediscovered the two small white pills Traci had given him earlier. He grasped one between his index finger and thumb and pulled it out. Andy sat down on the stoop and contemplated the perfect white circle in his palm. In the waning glow of his flashlight, he could still make out the inscription "Watson 933" etched into the pill's surface. Flipping it over, he noticed it was neatly scored along the center. The clinical markings on the pill suggested to Andy it was a legitimate pharmaceutical offering and not some homemade trucker speed or God-knows-what-else.

The anger he felt at being abandoned by his friends brought with it a spike in adrenaline which only heightened his false sense of sobriety. In truth, he'd been drinking most of the day, and had smoked at least his usual per diem of marijuana. But he coursed with energy, and the dangerous mix of bravado and outrage that was the forebear of countless bad decisions.

"Fuck it," he declared, to no one, and to all of his bedded-down friends in the cabin behind him. "Maxwell, party of one, your table is ready." With that, he popped the whole pill into his mouth and washed it down with a swig of beer from a mostly-full can of beer that had been left, like him, discarded on the porch.

Andy hopped up, now more resolute than ever. In the natural order of his emotional process, immediately after anger and righteous indignation came martyrdom and grudge holding. In his mind, if they were going to leave him alone to clean up, the only *logical* response was to clean so thoroughly and fervently that they'd have no choice but to recognize, and more importantly, feel shamed by his monumental effort. Yes, he'd bust his ass to make a point of picking up the mess they'd thoughtlessly left—that would show them.

He moved with determination back across the field, trailing puffs of venomous smoke as he went. It was easy to trace the straight line back to where the campfire was even though the fire was almost dead by then. He made a mental note to find a fresher flashlight as soon as he reached the camp site, as his current one was nearly useless.

Andy shuffled into camp fully steamed. In the armrest of the green camp chair next to him, he located a large orange plastic flashlight. He pushed its button and delighted in the strong bluish-white beam that sprang forth. He scanned the scene, considering it as perhaps a detective would, pouring over the scattered debris of what they'd consumed.

On second glance, the damage seemed less severe than he'd made it out to be in his mind. There were a couple of open bags of chips and a lot of empty aluminum cans, but the truth was, it wasn't going to take that long to deal with. Andy had gotten mad at the principle of the matter without doing a reality check on the problem he'd chosen to inherit. His friends probably weren't being overly delinquent in their willingness to let it all sit until tomorrow, except Jeff of course. Andy was sure that bastard was gonna sleep until the last possible second and then just jump in his truck, hightail it back to Bradford, and leave them to deal with the aftermath.

Andy pulled the last drag of smoke from the Winston and tossed it into the embers of the fire. He decided there were only three quick jobs that needed to be done—pack up the open food, put out the fire, and haul the few pieces of forsaken clothing and bedding back to the cars or house. Then he'd be satisfied. Then he could sleep.

The food issue was easy to rectify. He found a spare plastic grocery bag on the ground, stuffed all the open items into it, and tossed this in the passenger seat of Traci's Jeep. Collecting the beer cans took a few more minutes but helped accomplish the second task of killing the fire. Several of the open cans were partially full, and Andy took to liberally dumping the surplus beer onto the last remnants of smoldering timber. Hot, alcoholic steam rose from the pit as the embers got doused. It didn't finish the job, but one full bottle of water from the cooler later, and Andy was convinced he'd mitigated any real fire hazard. All that was left now was the laundry. At some point during the evening, Traci had shed at least one layer of clothing in favor of hiding under a blanket with Jeff. Her black zip fleece lay on the back of one of the chairs, already slightly damp with the coming dew. There was also a t-shirt belonging to Jeff which had been used haphazardly as a communal napkin of sorts. He gathered these items and tossed them in the Jeep, too.

He'd purposely left the two remaining objects for last. Still draped over both chairs in which Jeff and Traci had been snuggling was the massive green fleece blanket. Underneath it was a pretty decent pillow. Andy knew he'd be sleeping on the cold wooden floor of the cabin when he went back, and these two items would definitely help soften the blow.

He rolled the green monster several times in an attempt to make its mammoth girth easier to carry. Even compacted, it still required two hands, forcing Andy to awkwardly bear hug it and the pillow with one arm while holding the flashlight with his other as he plodded back toward the house. The fleece was hot against his face, which he now noticed was awash with fresh sweat. He was surprised by the profuse perspiration. He also began to feel dizzy in a very foreign and uncomfortable way. He'd drunk away his equilibrium countless times before and the dizziness of alcohol was a feeling he knew well – a spiraling right between his temples, around and behind his eyes. But this was something altogether different.

Close to the house now, Andy began to struggle in a way that made him wonder if he was even going to make it. There was tangible warmth rising up from the base of his neck. It ran flush across his face and seethed from the top of his head. A disconcerting pulse rose in his brain, as if his skull were filled with fluid and someone dropped a pebble, causing endless waves to ripple outward. He began to swoon, floating along a decidedly non-linear path.

Andy reached the truck, which was parked just to the right of the front porch. Its lowered tailgate was the first resting place to which he came, and he embraced it. Mostly falling, Andy allowed himself to land hard on the tailgate, and used the pillow and blanket to soften his impact. He let go of the cargo and instantly popped up, as if loaded by a spring, and reset his focus on the small flight of stairs. He staggered up them using the handrail to steady himself. Nearly launching himself across the porch, he came to rest with a thud against the screen door. Its metal grating was cool to the touch, but the screen was abrasive as his face slid along it. All he had to do now was open the front door, and fall onto the futon next to, or even on top of Ellen. He was going to make it.

Locked! The fucking front door was locked. Maybe he'd done it himself as he slammed it. Maybe it was one of the others, before or after he'd come and gone the first time. Maybe it was an accident, or a coincidence. In a different frame of mind, the hows and whys would have mattered much more to Andy. But now he was incapable of focusing on the specific cause of his misfortune. The door was locked. This was all he was able to process, and the only thing that really mattered. He stood, or more accurately leaned, for a moment, trapped and partially supported between the screen and wooden doors of the cabin. It never even occurred to him to bang on them in hopes of rousing his friends.

The alcohol and weed his body was so used to processing were now clearly collaborating with the pharmaceutical accelerant Andy had thrown carelessly into the mix. His eyes became heavier as the pulses of warmth spread further down his neck and shoulders. With waning coherence and strength, Andy pushed himself off of the door frame and wheeled back around toward the steps. He knew things were headed south quickly, and he could think of only one other solution for surviving the night.

The sound of sparrows in the early morning can be less than pleasant; grating even, with their high pitch and relentless delivery. Joined by a bevy of wrens, it becomes more symphonic, but considerably louder. Rural Fairview had far more of these birds than the mini-metropolis of Bradford, and certainly far fewer competing sounds. In fact, the avian cacophony surrounding the cabin was the only sign of life, inside or out. But it was sufficient to rattle Jeff from a tenuous sleep.

His eyes shot open, but immediately shut again in reflex to the light of day. The first thing he felt was a dry burning under his eyelids, then the coarse itchiness of the bedding against his bare chest.

Jeff had no desire to move. But the incessant bird calls and an aching bladder were beginning to force the issue. The quarter turn from lying on his right side to flat on his back brought with it another revelation. He was not alone in the tiny twin-sized bed. As his arm came to rest on the soft, unconscious lump that was Traci, Jeff achieved a whole new level of awareness and wakefulness.

Memories of the previous day and night flooded in. He fast-forwarded, skipping through the general merriment of the evening and replayed the last chapter. Traci had stumbled back to the cabin, clearly damaged but willingly amorous. He recalled the determination with which she had pursued him, a strangely aggressive passion aimed in the general direction of the target she held in her blurry sights. He recalled his shock at finding her nearly nude, lying in wait for him, before he had even discarded his shirt and shoes. And then he recalled the most shocking detail of all—that he had spurned her advance altogether.

In his years in Bradford, Jeff had rightfully earned a reputation as a Lothario, amassing a body count many of his friends would surely envy. He was known for many things, but saying no to the ladies wasn't one of them. And it wasn't that Traci was unattractive. In fact, she was just one of a slowly shrinking number of girls in town with whom he simply had not yet gotten around to bedding. Even just a few days ago, Jeff would have scoffed at the notion of declining such an opportunity. But this had been no average week. The escalating turmoil with Andy, and in particular their adventures at Quenton and Doc's homes, had seeped through his subconscious. His unlikely abstinence from chemicals yesterday had also furthered his clarity, allowing him to see how fruitless and unfair a conquest Traci would have been under those circumstances. For once, guilt had actually prevented him from doing the *wrong* thing, and in retrospect, he couldn't honestly say he minded the outcome.

Jeff swung his legs off the bed, placed his bare feet on the floor, and stood up. A wave of atypical modesty washed over him. With impressive quickness and quiet, he lunged and stooped for his jeans a few steps away. He stepped into and zipped the jeans before turning on his heels to face the bed again.

He expected to see Traci there staring back or laughing at him. She was not. She was curled on her side, facing the wall which was only inches away from the edge of the bed. Her head was buried in a pillow, and from his perspective, her face was fully obscured by her hair. She lay motionless. His exit from the bed had left the covers peeled back enough to reveal the entirety of Traci's short bare back. He stood there silently, allowing his eyes to survey the succinct landscape of flesh. At the end of the trail, just before the coverage of the blankets resumed, he noticed a swatch of pink and purple fabric contrasting against the stark white sheets. She had managed to retain a pair of shiny satin panties featuring a wild paisley pattern. He considered peeling the blankets further back to steal an extra glance at her sleepily susceptible body, but he refrained. He chose instead to find the rest of his clothes.

As his focus intensified, the real priorities of his morning reasserted themselves. He had to piss like a fire hose, and he had to find out what time it was. From the light beaming through the thin gauzy curtains, he knew it was well past dawn, but just how mad of a dash he was in for was not yet clear. He pulled a clean t-shirt from his bag on the floor and slipped his bare feet into pair of beat up Converse sneakers. He knew he had socks and church shoes in his bag, but he could slip those on at the last minute, back in Bradford.

Jeff hastily crammed a few items into his pack, and without zipping it, made for the bedroom door. It creaked slightly, but not enough to wake Traci. He peered in mild horror at the black plastic clock on the wall near the cabin's front door. 8:28 am.

"Motherfucker!" he said, plenty loud enough to have woken both of the women who were sleeping within ten feet of him.

Ellen didn't move. She lay almost exactly as she had fallen last night, still completely dressed, but without shoes, and snoring lowly. Traci did finally stir, shocked into partial awakening by the blunt, expletive alarm.

"Huh?' she mumbled, beginning to turn over.

Shit. Thought Jeff, wanting to get out of there as fast as possible. *I don't have time for this.*

"It's okay," he reassured her, turning around. "Go back to sleep."

Traci was still caught somewhere between passed out bliss and a rude awakening. She rolled toward Jeff's voice, and in the process further disturbed the bedding that had been partially covering her. She instinctively reached to adjust them, but not before treating Jeff to an inadvertent look at her, wearing nothing but that small swatch of psychedelic satin.

"You're fine," Jeff reiterated, softer and now smiling. She was still responding only to sounds, and hadn't yet opened her eyes.

"What time is it?" she asked, rolling and tucking herself deeper under the cover of the blankets.

"Early," he said. "Keep sleeping." He thought about leaving it at that and was about to turn and walk out when decency reared its ugly, interrupting head.

He stepped closer to her and whispered, "Do you know where you are?"

"Uh huh," she replied sleepily after a second of pause.

"Can you get home from here?"

"Uh huh," she repeated, as though it were the only thing she was capable of saying.

Jeff, who was now under extreme pressure from both his bladder and the ticking clock, took the semi-lucid girl at her word. He closed the bedroom door and kept walking, past an unconscious Ellen. Creeping out the door, he took care to keep the screen from banging behind him. He turned and made a bee-line to the edge of the porch, where he unzipped his pants and relieved himself onto the dry grass and red dirt below. The most pressing of his needs now managed, Jeff walked back towards the steps, fumbling in his open pack for his keys. He stopped short of the steps and opened the bright blue cooler. Bobbing in still-cold water were several beers and sodas. He said a small prayer of thanks for the bounty, grabbed a can of Coca-Cola, and bounced off the porch.

Jeff's black pickup truck was parked less than fifteen feet away and already pointed toward the exit. He walked quickly to the truck. Tossing in his pack, Jeff closed the passenger door and moved toward the back of the vehicle. Only the last snap on each side of the bed liner was unfastened, which he deemed acceptable given his hurry. He turned the corner of the truck, slamming its tailgate shut and sling-shotting toward the driver's seat in one sweeping move.

Jeff hopped in and revved the truck to life. The clock on his radio showed 8:33 am. He was going to have to cover close to a hundred miles

404

of road, change shoes, slip on his choir robe, and be in line for the processional in less than 90 minutes. Thankfully he had plenty of fuel, as there would be no time for stops on this express trip to God's house. In fact, in the absence of a visible police presence, STOP signs and traffic lights would probably have to be relegated from mandates to mere suggestions, too.

Traci laid there for several minutes, eyes still closed, trying as hard as she could to not think. She had the vague echo of Jeff's whispered directives to go back to sleep in her head, but she knew that was impossible. Her body was content to remain still, but her mind had been activated.

Gradually she became aware of her skin and body temperature. She felt a sudden chill run through her—not like a wave of horror; but more like an electrical impulse adjusting her internal thermostat. She knew without sight she lay in a foreign bed, nearly naked, but she was neither alarmed nor mortified by the discovery. She slept fully nude most nights at home, so the sensation of the cool, course sheets against her bare skin was nothing shocking. With growing clarity, she recalled the events that had landed her here. She had harbored an interest in Jeff for some time. And she had not only semi-subtly pursued him during their brief stay on the farm, but had also been perfectly willing to be bedded by him, under a thin guise of mutual inebriation. It was at this juncture though that her train, driven by assumptions and a lack of awareness to Jeff's relative sobriety, had jumped the tracks and wrecked.

She knew eventually she would have to emerge from the room, where she would no doubt encounter the others. In her original plan, the discovery of them together by Andy or Ellen was something she relished, an opportunity for her to bask in the triumph of *her* conquest of Jeff. But now, as she sat alone in the bed, a sense of sick dread rose in her. She hadn't considered the possibility of finding herself alone upon awakening, and now the tables were cruelly turned. Now, it was entirely possible she'd be perceived by the others not as the conqueror, but as the plundered treasure. And worse still, she'd be condemned as guilty for committing a sin she hadn't even been afforded the benefit of enjoying.

Traci sat up in, leaving the quilt tucked under both her armpits. She reached a few inches to her right and peeled back the drape. The morning sun cut a sharp diagonal line into the field beside the house, dividing its sunned and shaded portions into clearly discernible shades of greyish green. Aside from the birds twittering in the berry bushes, there were no signs of life. She relaxed her arms and then raised them slowly, stretching them to their limit to relieve the tightness that had come from a night of scrunching to share a too-small bed. The covers fell limp into her lap, exposing her bare torso to nothing more than the aforementioned birds, and a patch of pleasantly warming sun. Rolling onto her side, she lodged herself against the wall under the window and looked down. Lying on the floor in the two-inch crevice between the bed and the wall was the object she sought. She shot her arm into the chasm to retrieve it and rolled back to the center of the bed. Sitting up, she strapped her cold-hardened chest into the garment and threw on the colorful flannel.

Traci grabbed her shoes and tiptoed toward the bedroom door. It opened easily, with less noise than she expected. She stopped and peered through the crack. Her worst case scenario was coming face-to-face with a wide-awake congregation of Andy and Ellen, smugly waiting for her to perform some unspoken walk of shame. Instead, she saw no one. The front door was closed and, from her vantage point, the room outside appeared to be empty.

Sneaking into the front room, she only needed to travel four or five steps before she could see the ends of Ellen's legs hanging over the edge of the futon. She was fully dressed, and had apparently slept the entire night on top of a blanket instead of under it. Andy was not there.

Smiling at her relative good fortune, she slipped past Ellen like a cat burglar. Traci reached for the knob and turned it. The front door required a bit of a nudge to pull toward her, eliciting a decent pop which still did not wake Ellen.

Damn. Traci thought. *That bitch can SLEEP! Good for her.*

She moved through the screen door, leaving its wooden mate ajar behind her.

Jeff's truck was gone. She wasn't wholly surprised by this, given the foggy exchange they'd shared before he left. And of course he'd made the disclaimer before they had even come here. They all knew he had somewhere to be this morning. But like everything else so far today, she sort of figured it would have played out differently. Standing in the farm's vast front yard, she felt a real sense of awkward loneliness, knowing he'd actually left the three of them and driven back to Bradford solo.

82

Traci walked toward her Jeep, motivated to make a few hygiene and clothing adjustments. She knew this was where she would find Andy, likely smoking and or sulking next to an extinguished or possibly rekindled fire. Now that she was outside the cabin, or to be more precise, Jeff's room, she had no real qualms about encountering him.

She reached the Jeep and opened the driver's side door, tossing her shoes and socks across to the opposite floorboard. Slipping her muddy bare feet into a pair of sandals, she noticed her fleece from last night and what appeared to be bag of half-eaten food, piled randomly in the passenger seat.

It did seem odd, but not grossly out of order. Retreating from the cab, she left the door open and headed toward the back of the vehicle. Everything there was as she remembered leaving it.

From behind the Jeep, Traci could see the fire pit. Looking up from her luggage, she realized it too was deserted, as the whole farm seemed now to be. Even the birds had ceased their chattering. No birds. No squirrels. No crackling fire. No Andy. Everything was silent, and the area where they had partied last night was surprisingly tidy—her first real clue that something was out of sorts.

Traci rummaged through her pack and brought out a small makeup bag. Devoid of any actual cosmetics, which she used sparingly anyway, the case carried a few more practical items—a toothbrush and paste, a hairbrush, some deodorant, and the amber prescription bottle, half full of Percocet tablets. She had spent many a day and night in the woods of Tennessee, and was unfazed by the absence of working plumbing. But she was also cosmopolitan enough to want to knock the stink off her breath and armpits if given the chance. She shouldered her pack and moved back to the Jeep. She grabbed a mostly-full bottle of water from the driver's side cup holder and headed toward the outskirts of the field. At the tree line, she kept going until she was ten feet into the underbrush.

From here, she could still see the camp site and the front porch of the house, but she was concealed from both.

Traci dropped her pack, and unbuttoned her flannel. She stooped casually, laying the shirt at her feet as she dug out and used the deodorant and changed into a fresh long-sleeved grey t-shirt. She brushed her teeth, leaving a froth of spat foam on the pine needles to her left, and placed the toiletries back in their case. Before closing it, she pulled out the pill bottle, unscrewed the lid and emptied a white circle into her hand. She tossed it into her mouth and washed it down with a long drink of the water. It was barely 9:00 in the morning, but she could already tell she would probably benefit from a little 'mood maintenance'.

She stuffed everything back into her pack and stood up. The slight crunch of dew-moistened leaves under her sandals was the only sound. Traci scanned the horizon again. Satisfied she was still alone in the woods, she unfastened her jeans. She quickly dropped her pants and underwear and squatted. She was amused to see a fat, fuzzy caterpillar making his way across a leaf by her feet. She smirked, watching him wriggle along as she relieved herself.

Traci popped up and zipped her pants. She was 'camping clean', with an empty bladder and what would soon be a head full of painkillers—in perfect condition, she figured, to face whatever came next.

83

What came next was Ellen, emerging from the cabin. The screen door banged behind her and echoed loudly in the crisp morning air. So did her strained voice when she tried to speak for the first time since waking.

"Hello?"

Her grumbled, woozy call was followed by the unmistakable bark of a smoker's hack. She was more than 50 yards from where Traci stood concealed in the bushes, but the sound really carried. Traci appeared from the edge of the field, carrying her backpack and meandering toward the front porch, eyes to the ground. But Ellen didn't see her until seconds later, as she was preoccupied with lighting the day's first cigarette. The influx of nicotine was giving Ellen a jolt; but the rest of the chemicals, combined with the remnants of last night's intake, were having the opposite effect. She was jittery, yet lethargic and not quite ready to welcome the day.

"Good morning," Traci offered gingerly, sensing the damage. "You okay?"

"Mmmm."

"You slept hard as hell last night."

"Yeah. No shit. I fell out like a ton of bricks. How are you?"

"I feel pretty fucking great," Traci said with a level of cheer that was almost assuredly annoying to Ellen. She had no real hangover and the dose of narcotics she'd taken was beginning to make its presence felt in the form of a warm wave of euphoria.

"Good for you," Ellen mocked.

"Hell, at least you beat Andy. Looks like he's still passed out."

"Where?" asked Ellen. "He's not in there."

"What do you mean? Are you sure?"

"Positive. I checked the back room and bathroom before I came out here. It's not like there's anywhere to fucking hide in there."

"Well shit," Traci replied frankly. "I just went out to my car to get clean clothes, and he's not over there or by the fire either."

The mention of cars triggered Ellen's brain to another level of awakening.

"Jeff's gone," she realized.

"Yep. Left in a hurry, maybe thirty or forty minutes ago. I think he was running late for church."

"He'll make it. He always does."

"So, where the fuck is Andy?" Traci asked.

"Maybe he's passed out in a ditch in the woods somewhere."

"Or maybe he got up early and went to church with Jeff."

Ellen scoffed, choking on the last drag of her cigarette. "Seriously? Which of those two scenarios do you think is more likely?"

Traci turned to scan the horizon, now questioning her choice to load up on painkillers first thing in the morning.

"Fuck," she proclaimed with a sigh. "Put your shoes on. We gotta go find him."

Jeff was making exceptional time. He had long ago left the country roads of Fairview behind and was humming along the highway at more than eighty miles an hour. Traffic was light, and as he'd hoped, he hadn't seen a single cop. The small digital clock on the truck's dashboard told him it was 9:17 am. In fifteen minutes or so, he'd reach the exit that would take him back into Bradford. Another ten minutes on city streets, and he'd be pulling into the parking lot of St. Timothy's Episcopal Church.

Far too often recently, Jeff made the trek to church through a dense mental fog—fighting feelings of regret for the transgressions of Saturday evenings, and a sense of obligation to arrive joyfully and serviceable. This morning couldn't be more different. His commute was much more difficult, but he wasn't bothered in the least. For the first time in a long time, he felt a sense of genuine excitement, a joy that *compelled* him to be there.

The last time he was alone on the open road, just a few days ago, it had been in return from Overton. That had been a devastating ride, full of anger, sadness and attempts to numb himself to the pain and confusion of Cricket's inexplicable decision. This stretch of highway was far kinder. With nothing but desolate blacktop and time ahead of him, Jeff achieved greater clarity with every passing mile. His head was unburdened by chemicals. His chest was light, yet full of anticipation. The revelations of the past week had crystalized in his heart and mind; he was headed home. And with any luck, he was going to make it right on time.

"When's the last time you saw him?" Ellen asked, pushing herself up from the porch.

"Same as you. Last night. We all gave up at the same time, didn't we?"

"I don't remember a whole lot about how last night ended. To be honest, I'm not even sure how I got back to the house."

"I thought we all walked back together," Traci said. "But then Jeff and I pretty much went straight to his room, and..." She stopped in mid-sentence; partly because she was trying to remember if she'd ever seen Andy in the house last night, but mostly because she realized she'd just incriminated herself.

Ellen looked down at her from the porch stoop, a combination of mild surprise and wry amusement on her face. She wasn't being judged, but Traci went on the defensive anyway.

"What?" she asked, trying but failing not to smile.

"Nothing," Ellen replied. Her dismissive tone confirmed they were both dancing around the same subject. "Again, good for you."

Traci saw the opportunity before her, and seized it by the simplest of means—saying nothing at all. If Ellen wanted to think she and Jeff had crossed a threshold last night and was going to let it go without further comment, she was willing to play along.

In truth, Ellen couldn't care less about who Jeff slept with or Traci's place in that fairly large universe. All of that was drama for another time. Right now, they needed to concentrate their thoughts and efforts elsewhere.

"Anyway," Traci said, "I don't know for sure if I saw Andy or not."

"Well, there are only two possibilities," Ellen surmised, slipping on her shoes. "Either he's here—out in the woods somewhere—or he's not. Let's walk the perimeter and see if we can find him. If we don't, I say we grab our bags and bust ass back to Bradford."

"What about all the rest of the stuff?" Traci asked.

Most of what they had brought with them had come in Jeff's truck, which was now also gone. The camp chairs, the cooler, and the few other things that remained might all fit in the Jeep if they tried, but it would be tight as hell.

"If we pack it all," Ellen countered, "there won't be any room for Andy when we find him. We can leave most of this shit here. We'll come back for it or make Jeff deal with it later, since he's the one that left us without talking to anybody."

Traci endorsed the plan, and the notion of repaying Jeff for having rejected her last night and for deserting her this morning was just fine with her too.

Ellen bent down and deposited the spent cigarette butt into an empty can next to the cooler. On the way back up, she lifted the cooler's white lid. She was pleased to find several non-alcoholic beverages floating alongside a few leftover beers.

"You want one?" she asked, as she popped open the soda.

"I'm good. Let's start out by the pond and get the worst-case scenario out of the way."

If Ellen were still struggling to wake up, this suggestion by Traci brought her all the way back, and fast. For the few seconds she'd spent thinking about it so far, their search for Andy was little more than an inconvenient game of hide-and-seek. She fully expected to find him propped up against the back of the house, or under a tree somewhere in the shade. But Traci was implying something far more ominous.

Holy shit, she thought. *What if he's fucking dead?*

That thought, and then the next, that of discovering the lifeless body of one of her best friends floating in a pond or lying in a desolate field, scared the crap out of her.

"How can you even fucking say that?"

"What?" I was just... never mind. He's fine. C'mon."

They cleared the edge of the house and moved toward the sludgy pond. Ellen's imagination had kicked into overdrive, and she now somehow *expected* to see Andy's dead body floating face down in the shallow mud hole. A few feet further down the slope they gained full line of sight on the small body of water. The sun had finished burning off the last wisps of mist that had hung just above the surface earlier this morning. There was nothing in the pond.

"See?" Traci reassured. "I guess we should walk along the tree line? Make a lap around the field and see if we spot anything?"

"I'm following you," said Ellen, knowing full well that hunting and tracking were much more in Traci's wheelhouse than hers.

Fifteen minutes later they'd walked the entire perimeter of the field, checking behind clusters of trees and peering into the deeper brush. At intervals, each of them would call his name, hoping for a response. None came. Circling back toward the house, they walked by and around the collapsed barn building. They peered inside and once again called out to Andy. Again, there was no response.

Both girls were considerably more worried than they had been a few minutes ago. Both had assumed they would find him, and neither had a solid plan now that they hadn't.

"Let's go," Traci urged. "We have to go. We can be back in Bradford by noon."

"We can't just leave him out here." Ellen demanded, now becoming more frantic and agitated.

"He's not *out here*," Traci answered. "We looked. You wanna look some more?" She thought about waiting for Ellen to respond, but they both knew the question was rhetorical.

"Besides," she continued, "when we get back, he's either gonna be with Jeff; or if he's not, Jeff will know what to do—who to call, where else to look; something."

Ellen didn't want to admit that she didn't have a better plan than that. And it wasn't going to help anything to stand around staring at each other in an empty field.

"Fine. We'll go. Fuck!" Ellen cursed loudly, creating a vulgar echo that would have been comical under just about any other circumstance.

"My stuff's in the Jeep already," Traci said. "Go get your shit out of the house." In stark contrast to yesterday morning, Traci was taking her turn giving the orders.

The girls started walking in opposite directions. Then Ellen broke into a run. Her mind was racing, filling fast with anxiety, helplessness and real fear.

417

St. Timothy's looked more like a Spanish fort than an Episcopal church; unlike any of the buildings in its proximity, or any other in Bradford for that matter. The cathedral's exterior walls were grandiose slabs of terra cotta-tinged marble, asserting themselves a hundred feet into the sky.

The church loomed at the corner of Gault and 11th Streets. In the late mornings, the shadow of the squared-off spire towers blocked the sunlight, creating a veil of shadow that enveloped the intersection of the two roads.

Jeff made the final left turn onto Gault, and eased the truck into the parking lot. The spots nearest the side doors, where the ministers, deacons and choir entered, were already occupied. He was not the first of the cast to arrive, but he might still have a chance at not being the last. He aimed for the first empty space he saw, at the exact spot where the building ended and the chest-high, red brick wall surrounding the church's cemetery began.

9:49 am. With or without him, the morning's processional would begin in precisely eleven minutes. Most of the parishioners would never even notice if he didn't make it, but there were several people likely sweating the fact that Jeff Aaron had yet to appear.

Already free of his seat belt, Jeff put the vehicle in park and reached across the cabin for the choir robe draped over the passenger seat. In one fluid motion, he came back with both the robe and the black leather slip-on shoes he'd placed in the seat. Both hands now full, he bound from the truck. He shut the driver's side door with an awkward thrust of his bony ass, and ran for the doors, his long, unclean hair flapping behind him.

For the first several minutes of the journey, the Jeep had crept slowly up and down the dusty, unpaved road along which Jeff's farm sat. They had traveled the half mile on either side of the property three times, attentively scanning the alternating swatches of dense tree line and open fields for any sign of their missing friend. Finding nothing, they'd resigned themselves to leaving without him.

Traci clutched the steering wheel, fighting the slight spin the Percocet had created in her head. Her eyes were a little glassy, and she probably should have abdicated the driver's seat. But as they decided to stop searching for Andy and start heading back toward Bradford, she saw an even more debilitating look in her passenger.

Ellen's eyes were distant empty orbs filled with fear and sadness. Traci may have been inebriated, but Ellen was in no condition to safely operate a vehicle either. Traci gripped the wheel and forced herself to concentrate, deciding for better or worse, that she would be piloting the ship.

Those first few moments of the drive, during which they'd clung to some desperate hope of finding Andy near the farm, had been wrought with nervous energy. Now, they were flying down the highway, no less tense, but completely drained. The radio was low and all but drowned out by the wind whirling through the Jeep's open windows. Ellen sat despondent, looking out the window and chain smoking. They'd left a good portion of the excess gear back at the farm, and she couldn't help fixating on the empty space behind her where Andy was supposed to be sitting, but wasn't.

Neither of the girls had spoken for a while, when Traci abruptly broke the silence.

"Fuck!" she blurted, slamming both her hands against the steering wheel for punctuation. Ellen sat up, sufficiently startled.

"We're not gonna make it." she said. "Goddamned gas light just came on."

"Seriously? What the fuck?"

"I'm sorry." Apologizing was the first and only thing she could think to do. "I had no idea we'd be in such a hurry to get back. How was I supposed to know?"

"How far out are we?" Ellen asked.

"I don't know. Fifty miles maybe. We're right in the fuckin' middle."

"Right in the middle of fuckin' nowhere is more like it," said Ellen. "Is there even anywhere to pull off?"

At that moment, the answer was no. There weren't even any signs suggesting what 'the middle of nowhere' was called. The Jeep plowed on, the amber colored fuel light on its dashboard serving only to torque their anxiety a few notches higher. Finally a billboard appeared on the horizon. They saw it before they could read it, keeping their eyes trained on the huge white canvas with plain black lettering as it approached.

'Traveler's Truck Stop', it read, 'Exit 58, Purvis, 2 miles.'

"That'll work." Traci said optimistically, grateful for any solution to the problem.

"Traveler's?" Ellen asked, randomly. "Just one traveler?"

"What?"

"Their sign. It's wrong. The apostrophe is in the wrong place. It should be 'Travelers', with the apostrophe *after* the s, not before it."

Traci gave her a ridiculous look, failing to understand the functioning or priorities of her friend's brain.

"What?" Ellen replied. "It's something I picked up from Andy. He's forever pointing out misspellings and fucked up punctuation on signs. Sometimes it's annoying, but a lot of the time it's pretty funny. Once you start noticing the mistakes, you see them everywhere. Andy used to say he could get rich just fixing other peoples' incorrect billboards."

"Well, he *does* still need a job, doesn't he?" Traci joked, purposely moving the language back to present tense.

"Yeah. He does."

"I don't care what it's called, as long as they have gas."

"And a bathroom," groaned Ellen. "I've been waiting all morning to take a dump."

Traci wrinkled her nose in disgust as she pulled the Jeep into the exit lane.

A thin black woman wearing screaming yellow Capri pants and a white, neatly-tailored blazer held the door for Jeff. His arms were full as he scooted into the church's side entrance at full speed.

The choir, along with the other players in the weekly production that was Sunday mass at St. Timothy's, had already assembled. There were just a few minutes before the curtain went up, and the sanctuary was filling fast.

The first snap unfastened inconspicuously, as if by simple accident or happenstance. A second later, a full quarter of the black vinyl tarp covering the bed of Jeff's truck was violently displaced by some great, quite intentional force. That force was Andy's fist. Two more punches, and a kick for good measure, from underneath, and he'd dislodged it entirely from the truck.

Andy sat up. The tarp lay in his lap, covering him like a blanket in the bed of the truck. He tossed it aside, and inhaled almost to the point of exaggeration, as if he'd been holding his breath the entire time he'd been trapped in the lightless box. His eyes were blurry from the prolonged ride in the dark, and he rubbed them vigorously with his palms as he rested his head against the truck's back window. An older, smartly-dressed couple who were rightly startled by his unlikely appearance went out of their way to put extra distance between him and their path to the doors of St. Timothy's.

He didn't move; partly because he physically couldn't. He was exhausted. The big fleece blanket and the pillow had helped, but even so, the back of a Toyota pickup truck is not the most comfortable place to spend an evening. Throw in being tumbled like clothes in a dryer, mercilessly absorbing every bump and pothole in the road for an hour, and it was no wonder his body was sore in more places than he could even process.

Even in his disoriented state, Andy still knew exactly where he was. This was the other reason he found it nearly impossible to move. There he sat, propped up against the back wall of a muddy black pickup truck, shoeless and disheveled, no doubt stinking to Hell of cigarettes, spilled beer, and the general earthiness of camping. He sat motionless, desperately wishing for invisibility, as a flock of Bradford's civilized faithful marched past. Not all of them noticed him. Many did and tried their best to ignore him, keeping their eyes forward and down as they shuffled toward the doors.

Andy was equally uncomfortable. Given a choice, as he had been so many times in the past, he would not have been there at all. He could sense the unspoken disdain of the passing church-goers. He waited, trying so hard to stay quiet that he was almost holding his breath. For a moment he was alone in the parking lot. But he knew it wouldn't last. Now was his chance to escape, or at least make less of a spectacle of himself.

He pushed aside the tarp and kicked away the part of the green fleece blanket still covering his legs. Andy scanned the bed of the truck and quickly located one of his shoes; the other was still hiding. Spreading his hands wide, he rummaged around more feeling than looking for the missing mate. Among several empty beer cans, a fishing tackle box and some assorted clothing, Andy found his target buried in the folds of the blanket. He unearthed it, determined to shoe himself before encountering more passersby. He failed.

Andy's feet dangled over the edge of the truck's tailgate. He had worked one foot into a muddy shoe when he sensed someone approaching from his left. The woman walked brisk and confidently, and seemed to be coming right at him. Andy bent one knee, and focused on tying his shoes as she came near. He wanted very much to ignore her, but basic human instinct took over, causing him to lift his head in anticipation of her arrival. What he saw was a thoroughly average looking older woman, in an anything-but-average fuchsia pant suit, progressing steadily toward him. Unlike the others, she did not look not away, but instead, directly at him. At a distance of six feet, Andy made eye contact with her. A pleasant smile unfolded across her face, which carried no trepidation about him at all. Taking note of her silvery-white hair, he figured she must have been in her late fifties or early sixties. Her smile surprised him. He again fell prey to human nature, as the involuntary instinct to speak over-rid his desire not to.

"Good morning," he uttered with a thick smoker's rasp.

"Oh, it's a *blessed* morning," she cheerfully corrected him. The lady smiled even wider, and gently patted the leather bound Bible she was cradling like a baby.

She never stopped, or even waited for a reply. She simply continued on her way, moving toward her morning infusion of Glory. Less adamant now, but still motivated, Andy tied the second shoe and hopped off the tailgate. He hadn't really considered until that exact moment that he had no idea what he was going to do next.

He began by patting himself down. Running his hands along his shirt and pants, he confirmed that even through the travails of last night and this morning, he had managed to hold onto Quenton's former money clip and a pack of crushed and slightly damp cigarettes. Not surprisingly, he'd lost his lighter. Deciding the smokes were unsalvageable, he tossed the damaged box into the bed of the truck and closed the tailgate. He limped to the driver's side door and found it unlocked.

Jeff had taken the keys, which sealed Andy's fate for the next hour or so. It was at least a two mile walk from St. Timothy's to their house on Cornwall Street. Even in his best condition, Andy would never really have considered it. He sat down in the driver's seat, placed his head against the padded headrest, closed his eyes and exhaled deeply. What now?

His next thought was for food. A quick audit of the area surrounding St. Timothy's produced no real options within walking distance. There

424

was a gas station a couple blocks up, which would at least have cold drinks and a bounty of nutritionally-bankrupt snacks. It was a possibility.

Scanning the cab of the truck, Andy noticed Jeff had not left him completely without rations. A pack of Marlboro Lights sat on the passenger seat and there was an open can of Coke in the cup holder under the dashboard stereo. He grabbed first for the cigarettes. They weren't his brand, but given the state of his own supply, he was willing to overlook his usual disdain for what he considered the less satisfying flavor of the Marlboros. Andy opened the flip-top white box, pleased to discover a handful of smokes still inside. He tucked one behind his left ear and scooped up a small blue lighter from the passenger seat.

Next he reached for the soda. To his surprise, there was at least of third of a can left. Ordinarily, he'd have been much less eager to share whatever ick Jeff had left in the backwash, but he was parched. Dehydration trumped germ phobia, and he took a hefty swig. It was lukewarm, but it was wet and sugary which were both big plusses in his current condition.

Andy could have sat in Jeff's truck for the next hour, windows rolled down, smoking those cigarettes. He also briefly considered getting high, right there in the parking lot of St. Timothy's. It might not have even been the most sacrilegious thing he'd ever done, but somehow it didn't feel right. He knew he wasn't about to walk all the way back to Cornwall Street, but he did need to stretch his legs a bit, and a change of scenery couldn't hurt either.

89

The smell of diesel fuel hung thick in the air as the Jeep limped to the top of the off-ramp and turned right. A few hundred feet down sat The Traveler's Truck Stop. It was gnarly, dilapidated, and massive, and it appeared to have Exit 58 all to itself. There were no other buildings for as far as the girls could see.

At nearly ten o'clock on a Sunday morning, the huge parking lot was surprisingly full. Rows of eighteen-wheel big rigs stretched on for at least a quarter of a mile. A few were being refueled at stations along the perimeter, but the vast majority sat resting where they'd been put down the night before.

"Jesus," said Traci, "that's a lot of fuckin' trucks."

"Do they even sell regular gas—you know—for regular cars, here?" Ellen asked.

"Of course," Traci guessed confidently. "They have to."

"Why? Is there a law or something?"

"Oh. No," Traci corrected. "I meant they *have* to have gas for us, 'cause we're coasting on fumes, and we're not getting back on the highway. It's this place, or we're fucked."

"They also *have* to have a bathroom I can use," Ellen reminded. "I'm about to 'splode over here."

"Good luck with that."

Traci swung left, away from the rows of trucks. Now closer, she could see a couple of gas pumps near the front doors of the main building. She pulled the Jeep in; relieved to see she had the option to purchase good old 87-octane regular unleaded gasoline. "Thank God," she sighed, killing the engine.

"Amen!" replied Ellen as she tore off her seat belt and thrust open the door. She shot from the car and slammed the door. "I gotta go."

"I know. You said. Just go, already," Traci insisted, watching with amusement as her friend walk awkwardly toward the building. Ellen stopped at the double front doors.

"Dammit!" Ellen groused, plenty loud.

"What?"

"The fucking diner's closed."

There was a sign that read 'bathrooms' with an arrow pointing around the corner. Traci chuckled, trying to conceal her amusement from her suffering friend.

"Great. An outside shitter at a dank-ass truck stop in the middle of fuckin' nowhere," she complained, as she headed toward the corner of the building. "It better have paper in there."

"You better hope that fucker's not locked, too."

"Shut up. I'll be back."

"Take your time." Traci laughed as Ellen disappeared around the corner.

90

Andy passed through the gap in the brick wall surrounding the cemetery behind St. Timothy's Cathedral. Roughly five feet tall, the wall obscured all but the most grandiose of grave markers beyond it. Several massive live oak trees formed a canopy that kept most of the mid-morning sun at bay. They blanketed the plots in a cool, dark shadow Andy found instantly pleasing.

The beginning of the service was only moments away, and there were no doors that led directly from the cemetery into the church. Andy felt himself relax a touch and allowed a small smile to form on his face as he realized he was unlikely to be disturbed, or even noticed, at least until the congregation was released again.

He slowed his pace, now wandering the time-beaten brick sidewalk that wound through the bone yard. The cemetery itself was small, confined by real estate limitations to less than an acre. But it was densely packed, almost absurdly so. The spaces between rows of grave markers were uneven and sparse, and from certain angles it appeared as if the headstones might even be stacked on top of each another. The combination of low light and the actual age of the stones made some of them impossible to read; but others were easy enough to make out. None of them were particularly modern. In fact, Andy remembered Jeff telling them that the most recent internment there had been more than fifty years ago, and there would be no more; there simply wasn't room.

Andy stepped from the path into the yard itself, a patchwork of soft red clay and shoddy grass interwoven amongst the headstones. He moved gingerly, trying not to disturb the souls that slept beneath his feet. Winding through the narrow paths, he stopped near the center of the plot. There, he found a crude bench chiseled from aged, unpolished marble. He glanced from side to side to confirm he was in fact alone, and sat.

The marker directly in front of the bench was among the largest and most prominent in the whole cemetery. Carved upon it was the name T.

Bullit Dancy. Just below, and smaller, were notations identifying Dancy as a lieutenant colonel whose proud service to the Confederate States of America apparently ended with his death on September 20, 1863. Scanning left, he encountered a small cluster of sun-bleached stones, each no bigger than a loaf of bread. The inscriptions, which were faded but still legible, signaled the loss of three small children – siblings within the Bartow family. There were two sisters and a brother, all of whom lived and died in the brief span between 1881 and 1887. Andy felt a sudden and deep sense of sadness. Thoughts of Tristan and their parents invaded, reminders of the unspeakable pain of parents who lose children. Then he considered the compound misery of having to endure that same tragedy thrice, and in such a short span of time.

Andy forced himself to look elsewhere, anywhere but at those three stone loaves. As he turned his head to the right, in search of less morbid scenery, the cigarette tucked behind his left ear grazed the side of his neck. Instinct, boredom, and the need for new stimuli converged. He placed the Marlboro Light between his lips and lit it. He filled his lungs with smoke, looked up at the thick oak branches above, and exhaled.

He sat in cemetery silence for several minutes. As he exhaled another lungful of smoke, the undeniable bombast of a pipe organ came roaring through the huge wall of stained glass behind him. The opening processional was beginning. *'Good'*, he thought. *'The sooner it starts, the sooner it's over.'*

Andy stayed there in the shadow of Colonel Dancy's grave, smoking his cigarette and fixating on the grand tone of the organ. He closed his eyes and focused on the boisterous sound pouring through the walls of the cathedral. It was a joyful noise, deliberately calling the faithful to worship. The sound itself wasn't calling Andy to do anything in particular. But then it stopped, abruptly, as if the organist had died. The sound ceasing startled him almost as much as its appearance had, and the accompanying silence brought to him an instant and unwelcome realization.

Jeff had invited Andy to visit the church, if only to hear him sing, on numerous occasions. Each time, Andy found a reason – an excuse, really – not to go. But here he sat, in the back yard of that very church. Whether by divine ordinance or some grand irony, he had been delivered straight to God's house.

The curtain was rising. The show was about to start. And here he was, sitting in a graveyard smoking a cigarette he honestly didn't even want anymore. The more he thought about it, and regardless of how badly he wanted something else to be the truth, the clearer it became. Not only was he supposed to be here, he was supposed to be inside. His stomach clenched at the thought. His brain screamed at him to stay put, or even better, to just start walking home. But a smaller, stronger part of him was calling the shots. By the time he realized he was no longer sitting on the bench, he had already stood up and taken several steps back toward the break in the wall. For better or worse, he was now headed straight for the huge Episcopalian fortress. For better or worse, Andy Maxwell was going to church.

91

As far as Traci knew, her late-80's model Jeep Wrangler was supposed to get 14-15 miles per gallon, though she suspected it averaged less. The gas light had come on ten miles before they stopped in Purvis. As she watched the outdated rotary dials on the gas pump roll ever onward, a sense of relief came over her. She knew just how close they'd come to running bone dry and ending up stranded on the side of the highway.

She finished topping off the tank and wrestled the fuel nozzle back into its bent, beaten holster. It had taken her only a couple minutes to fuel up, and there was still no sign of Ellen. Traci assumed her absence meant she'd successfully gained access to the bathrooms around the corner.

She walked toward the complex, aiming for the set of doors to the left of the ones her friend had found shuttered. Ellen had been correct. Lickety's Diner was in fact closed for renovations – and by the looks of it, had been for some time. The tiny convenience store beside it was open for business, though.

She entered and began casually browsing the store's two aisles, garnering little or no interest from the middle-aged, overweight Hispanic woman reading a tabloid magazine behind the counter.

Traci opened the fridge case and pulled out a chilled Cheerwine soda. Wheeling around, she saw two big boxes of Hostess Fruit Pies, one apple and one cherry, sitting there just begging to be plundered. The mere sight of them was enough to make her forget whatever assorted breakfast items might have been hiding in the back of the Jeep. She scooped up one of each, almost able to taste them by touch alone.

With the minimal charm of the convenience store wearing thin, Traci advanced toward the cashier. She had hoped her friend would reappear in time to help cover the thirty dollars of fuel she'd put in the Jeep, but Ellen was still nowhere to be found.

The Hispanic woman behind the counter said nothing, barely looking up from her Hollywood gossip rag as she rang up the drinks and snacks.

"I've got gas out there for the Jeep, too," Traci divulged, thinking it entirely possible the attendant hadn't noticed.

The woman remained mute, and chose instead to repay Traci's honesty with a snide look that suggested Traci thought she was stupid.

"Thirty-four, sixty-five," she said, addressing the cash register, instead of her customer.

Traci pulled her last forty dollars from the pocket of her jeans and slid it into the tray under the pane of glass that separated them. The cashier took the money, quickly made the change, and went back to reading her magazine. No 'thank you', no 'have a nice day', no nothing.

Traci was surprised to find the Jeep still unoccupied upon her return. Apparently Ellen was in worse shape than even her bemoaning had implied. She considered moving the vehicle, but there was no one waiting to use the pump.

Suddenly, Traci became hyper-aware of how alone she was in the massive expanse of the Traveler's Truck Stop. For her size, she was a tough girl who could mostly take care of herself when push came to shove. But she was more than ready to find Ellen and move on.

Rounding the corner of the complex, Traci encountered three non-descript cream colored metal doors. The first said 'Men'. The second had a small sign reading 'Authorized Personnel Only', and a giant padlock the other two doors lacked. The third door, the one farthest back, read 'Women'. *Typical*, Traci thought of its less-than-thoughtful placement.

The door to the women's bathroom was closed. Traci approached, expecting it to also be locked. She considered busting in, but instantly thought better of it. What if there were no stalls? The last thing she really wanted to see was Ellen glued to some disgusting truck stop toilet in the midst of severe gastrointestinal distress.

What she was about to see was far more disturbing.

92

The front doors of St. Timothy's Episcopal Church were impractically huge and heavy. Fashioned from dense, dark wood and accented with steel banding and rivets, the medieval-looking portals stood over ten feet tall. When shuttered, they presented anything but a welcoming façade.

On Sundays and Wednesdays, or any time the faithful were expected en masse, the doors were left wide open, which is exactly how Andy found them. He stopped briefly at the bottom of the small flight of stairs that led up to the entrance. Compared to the bright sun beating down on Gault Street, the foyer beyond the boundary of those doors was as dark as a cave and just as foreboding. Andy stood there, still not certain he was going inside. He had extinguished the Marlboro but was now suddenly aware that he must smell awful. Another reason to turn and walk away, but he didn't.

He took a deep breath, let it go, and advanced with trepidation up the steps. His first thought was that something terrible and tangible might happen when he crossed the threshold – a buzzer, or alarm, or some other loud and definitive, scrutinizing exclamation of his arrival. Of course there was nothing.

Just inside the front doors was a highly decorative portico – a transitional space no larger than five by eight feet. On either side, ornate tables sat under gilded frames holding paintings of Saints which Andy could not identify. Straight ahead, another smaller set of doors which were closed tight; to the right stood a baptismal fount. Andy recognized this from the painful trips to weekday masses with his Catholic grandmother during childhood. His brain flashed back to the portion of holy water Jeff had 'borrowed' from the church a few days earlier. Stationed to the left of the doors, an old grey lady in a hideous green floral patterned dress sat motionless – until she noticed Andy.

The moment he took one more step toward those inner doors, the geriatric sentry sprung to life with a speed and agility that surprised him.

The pipes of the organ had been silenced, and no other sounds escaped the chamber which she guarded. He could have easily heard anything she would have chosen to say to him, yet she operated silently. Standing firm between Andy and the doors, not menacing, but still authoritative, The Grey Lady raised a bony index finger to her lips. Simultaneously, she extended her opposite hand, offering him a small white leaflet. Andy took it, trying not to look her in the eye. Once her hand was free, The Grey Lady swept it across her body, pointing dismissively toward a flight of steps to her left. In one simple, silent gesture, she'd ushered, shushed, and shepherded him. Andy wasn't sure if he was being denied access to the main sanctuary based on the time or his appearance. It didn't matter – he wasn't getting past her. He turned and headed toward the stairs that clearly led to the cheap seats.

Andy slipped through a small doorway and looked up. The stairway was more narrow and steep than seemed practical, and he somehow couldn't imagine The Grey Lady or many of her elderly compatriots navigating them. A heavy wrought iron railing ran along the right hand wall going up the steps, with nothing on the left. He pulled himself up the steps, legs still tight and aching from the horrific night's sleep and even worse transport in the back of Jeff's truck. As he neared the top, a volley of voices rumbled in unison, accompanied by more of the organ's bombast.

Holy shit, Andy thought, quickening his pace up the stairs. *I'm missing Jeff's thing.* In truth, it was only the opening hymn.

Andy reached the top of the flight and found himself at the precipice of another small doorway, this one leading out into the Cathedral's ample balcony. The contrast between the plain claustrophobic chute he'd just ascended and the spacious cavern of opulence into which he'd arrived was immediate and dramatic. Inspired by the openness around him, he took in a huge breath and exhaled.

The cathedral chamber of St. Timothy's sprawled before him. The floor of the church sat twenty feet below and held rows upon rows of

435

pews hewn from dark, rich wood, most of which were full of parishioners – easily numbering several hundred. The ceiling vaulted another forty feet over his head, and was supported by a series of enormous wooden arches of a similar finish. Viewed as a whole, the supports resembled the inverted hull of a giant ark bolted to the ceiling. Along both sides of the cavernous room, alabaster columns rose from the floor creating a series of arches that echoed the shape of a bishop's miter all the way down the center aisle. Each of the sanctuary's two stories featured rows of similarly curved stained glass windows, with more behind the altar. In total there were over fifty panes of colored glass, each beaming brightly with the backlight of the sun shining through.

Andy had never been inside the building, and he found the room breathtaking – especially from this elevated perspective. A moment later, he realized he'd been lingering there in the doorway, taking in the glorious scenery in a bit of a daze. He snapped back to awareness, suddenly dreading the prospect that a balcony full of people might be staring at him. To his relief, it was almost completely empty. The only other person in the entire balcony was a young woman who looked to be in her mid-twenties. She stood six or seven rows from the front railing of the balcony, in the dead center. Cradled in her arms was a white and blue blanket, which Andy assumed held a baby he could not see. She smiled at him, seeming to notice he appeared lost – or at least out of his element – and then shifted her gaze back to the center of altar. Andy returned an embarrassed grin and shuffled forward, moving to the front row of the balcony. He remained standing, following the rest of the congregation, and began scanning the rows of choir robes assembled behind the rectory table for a familiar face.

Almost as soon as he'd turned his attention their way, the choir fell silent, as the last gasps of the organ echoed up and out toward the cathedral's ceiling. Andy was still looking for Jeff when the next voice came.

"Blessed be God: Father, Son and Holy Spirit."

The voice was a bit high-pitched, but still solemn. Andy shifted his gaze again, now looking for its owner. Before he could find it, another surprise.

"And blessed be his kingdom, now and forever. Amen."

Several hundred voices responded in unison. Andy was startled. Looking for some sort of cue, he turned again toward the young mother behind him. She smiled once more and raised her non-baby-holding hand to show him the small white pamphlet – the same one the Grey Lady had given him. Apparently it contained the order of the service, and would prove useful if he had any chance of understanding what was happening around him. He quickly opened it and scanned the first few lines. Assuming that they'd just completed the Processional Hymn and Opening Acclamation, he correctly surmised that the next item on the docket was something called the Collect For Purity.

"Almighty God," the nasal voice continued, "to You, all hearts are open, all desires known, and from You, no secrets are hidden. Cleanse the thoughts of our hearts, by the inspiration of Your Holy Spirit, that we may perfectly love You, and worthily magnify Your Holy Name; through Christ our Lord. Amen."

"Amen," the congregation affirmed.

Andy focused on the man making his way slowly to the front of the altar. The priest was dressed in a flowing black robe with gold piping from shoulders to hem. Dual crosses were emblazoned across his chest in the same gold thread.

Andy took once again to the bulletin in his hand. If the program was accurate, he was staring at The Very Reverend Dr. Jarvis Frost. Frost wore glasses with thick black frames which looked absurd enough on their own. But the full effect of the spectacles was further magnified by the man's noticeably bulbous head. Frost's disproportionate cranium was bald, save for an unfortunate ring of black tuft that ran along the back of his skull from below his ears, to the middle of his neck. Andy couldn't help thinking the man looked like a cartoon character come to life.

"A reading from the Word of the Lord," Reverend Frost announced.

"Thanks be to God," came the congregational response. Andy had no compulsion to participate in the dialog, but he did find it at least intriguing to follow along. He suspected it might be like this for the remainder of the service.

"From the Old Testament, the Book of Joshua, chapter 1, verse 9," said Frost, 'Have I not commanded you? Be strong and courageous. Do not be frightened, and do not be dismayed, for the Lord your God is with you wherever you go.'"

"And Psalm 27:1," Frost continued. "The Lord is my light and my salvation; whom shall I fear?"

"Praise be to God for the Word of the Lord. Amen."

"Praise be to God," the faithful repeated in unison.

"You may be seated."

The flock complied with Frost's invitation, folding themselves back into the pews. Andy did likewise, and began again to peruse the program in his hand. He was genuinely looking forward to seeing Jeff showcase his brilliance, but he also wanted to know what else he had to sit through to witness it.

93

Traci pushed down on the door handle and was surprised to find it moved easily. It didn't appear to be locked, but the door was stuck a bit in its frame, causing her to jiggle the handle. She had just begun to exert full pressure on it when a voice barked from inside.

"Occupied!" she heard Ellen scream with a strange urgency.

At the same moment, the extra force Traci had applied accomplished its goal, sending her headlong into the women's bathroom. She felt a rush of humidity across the bare skin of her face and arms. The air inside the truck stop bathroom was far warmer and wetter than that of the convenience store she had just left.

"Get out!" yelled Ellen, from inside the larger of the two sea-foam-green stalls.

"It's me!" Traci blurted back. She'd instinctively averted her eyes toward the ceiling which was badly stained by water damage, cigarette smoke and who knows what else.

"Traci?"

"Yeah," she affirmed, the clear distress in her friend's voice now drawing her attention downward.

The second stall extended beyond the door of the first and had a wide entrance to accommodate handicapped access. Without stooping, Traci could see the empty floor of the nearest stall underneath its paneled wall, but not all the way to the one behind it. Scanning to the left, she saw something she couldn't even process on first view. She stopped breathing and stared.

Jutting out from behind the cross-piece between the two stalls was a single limp bare foot. From its angle and position, Traci assumed the rest of the body was lying on the disgusting bathroom floor. The slender bare foot was cocked right at her, offering a perfect view of the chipped coat of glossy pink polish on the toes. Just above the ankle was the tattered cuff of a pair of black denim jeans.

"Traci!" Ellen demanded, as she swung open the door to the stall and shot out, "Go get the fucking car! Now!"

94

"These words come to us from the Old Testament," Dr. Frost asserted, launching into his sermon. The mild, tinny timber of his voice matched his rail-thin stature, but Andy was struggling to reconcile both against his notions of what a priest should look and sound like. He considered closing his eyes to see if losing the visual reference made a difference in how he perceived the speaker, but he decided it didn't matter. Really, he was only interested in seeing Jeff at this point. The sermon he supposed was superfluous.

"But they're part of a larger message," the Reverend continued. "One as old as time, and at the very heart of our relationship with our God, and our Savior."

Oh Hell, Andy thought. *Here comes all the righteous bullshit that makes me hate the thought of even being here.*

"In fact, it's probably the one thing Jesus wanted us to know above all else."

Let me guess, Andy mocked silently. *It's gonna be something about love.* There was a sad irony in the guess, as it came from a heart that had been hardened and conditioned over recent years to reject just such a message.

"It's an idea whose seeds are sown deep throughout the Old Testament, words sent straight from the mouth of God to the ears of the prophets. But it's really in the in New Testament – in the life and teachings of Jesus – that the message I share with you today springs to life."

Andy had used the first minute or so of Frost's sermon to determine that Jeff would likely be singing his solo during the Offertory and Holy Communion, which would directly follow the sermon. It was the only choral presentation on the program that did not seem to involve congregational participation, and was a hymn entitled *Sicut Cervus*. Andy figured the title was in Latin – of which he knew none – but he couldn't help but laugh a bit at its phonetic similarity to 'secret service'. He wasn't even paying attention to what the Reverend was saying, until Frost got to the next line of the sermon.

"It's the most repeated command in all the New Testament – by a lot. And it's as crucial today as it was two thousand years ago. It might just be the simple wisdom we need to live in perfect peace in this difficult world. That command, my friends, is 'do not fear'."

It didn't strike an immediate, deep chord within Andy, but it did at least register – primarily because it was not at all the path he expected the priest to take. He allowed himself to invest a small portion of attention, to see where Dr. Frost was headed.

"Ask yourself..." the Reverend invited the audience, "how often are you afraid?"

Andy's first thought was *not all that often*.

"And I don't mean like 'scared of monsters' afraid," the Reverend clarified. "Real fear comes in many forms. Anxiety. Uncertainty. Concern. Desperation. And so forth."

Well, shit. Andy thought. *In that case, I guess the answer is more like 'all the time'.*

"But the Word of God tells us to reject that fear, and offers us peace instead. Jesus wanted us to know that despite our worldly troubles, there is truly nothing for us to fear—that with Him in our hearts, there is nothing that could overtake us; because there is nothing He could not handle for us."

Andy's skepticism flared. The Reverend's assertion was a concept he struggled with mightily – the idea that belief in God, or Jesus, or a higher

442

power of any kind or name, had any real power to soothe our souls, let alone lessen our actual burdens in daily life.

"But that is not to say there will not be hardship—tragedy even. To think as much would be unrealistic," Frost continued. "There are no guarantees that life will be carefree or that things will happen just as we want. Of course not. God wants us to live our lives to the fullest. And to be honest, that requires some degree of risk on our part – a willingness to accept there are things beyond our control. Indeed, it requires faith."

Now, Andy was finding himself even more irritated, but for different reasons. Now, it wasn't just that the slim, bald priest with the squeaky voice was telling him things counter to his desired beliefs. Now, it was as if the other two hundred people in the room weren't even there; as if Frost had colluded with Jeff to craft a sermon aimed directly at him, designed specifically to conflict and convict him. The message seemed to pick up right where Jeff had left off yesterday, and it was hitting Andy uncomfortably close to home.

"But rejoice," Frost carried on, "God did not create us to carry fear in our hearts. He created us in His image, to live in His glory. In 1 John 4:18, it says 'Perfect love casts out all fear.' God *is* that perfect love. He is literally inviting us to hand over our burdens, our worries, our fears to him, so that we can live in the peace of His perfect love."

"So, how then does this comfort come to us?" Frost asked.

That's what I'm saying! Andy thought, still doubtful the answer was coming.

"Listen to the Apostle Paul. In Philippians 4:6-7, Paul writes: 'Do not be anxious about anything, but in everything, by prayer and petition, with thanksgiving, present your requests to God. And the peace of God, which transcends all understanding, will guard your hearts and minds."

"And Paul goes on. In Romans 8:26-28. He writes: 'We do not know what we ought to pray for, but the Spirit himself intercedes for us, with groans that words cannot express. And he who searches our hearts knows the mind of the Spirit, because the Spirit intercedes for the Saints, in accordance with God's will. And we know that in all things God works for the good of those who love him, those who have been called according to his purpose."

"There are many among us today who hear that calling, loudly, daily; those who know the love of the Lord deeply and truly in their hearts. And for you, God is abundantly happy. But He yearns to share His love with all of us. He wants us all to be happy. And it was for this happiness that He sent his Son, our Savior, Jesus Christ to be with us. Because the true miracle is this – through Jesus, through a real relationship with Jesus — there are no barriers between us and God. That happiness is here for all of us."

The well of conflict grew deeper within Andy. Here was a man, a meek, bony man whom Andy had never even met, and who had no stake whatsoever in his personal happiness, serving up to him on a silver platter answers to questions that had plagued him for as long as he could remember. Why? And even more curiously, why could Andy not bring himself to believe; to accept that gift of happiness?

He began to process the many possibilities. The reasons had shifted and snowballed over the years, to the point that it was not a single obstacle that stood between him and God. Like every other person at one time or another, he'd been let down, disappointed by prayers that seemed to fall on deaf ears. But unlike others, he'd held on to each and every one of them, stacking them up until they created a giant wall of grudge. Atop that foundation of frustration, he piled his recent impressions of so many people he encountered who proclaimed to be Christians – shouting the mantle of God's love with their tongues, but showing nothing but intolerance, hatred and judgment with their deeds. Not only could he not reconcile the hypocrisy, it had made proclaiming that same allegiance the very last thing he wanted to do. And speaking of judgment, how could he live as he had for so long, surrounded by law-bending degenerates, and walk with God at the same time? It was the same hypocrisy he'd charged Jeff with; and if his supposed God-loving roommate couldn't pass that test, what hope was there for Andy himself?

It seemed a Catch-22 of judgment – a choice between his current lifestyle and friends, and embracing a relationship with God. In his mind, the winner would celebrate his decision to be counted amongst them, while the loser would surely spurn and condemn him. His desire for acceptance among the people with whom he'd chosen to associate, even in light of their obvious flaws, had driven the wedge even deeper.

"Rest assured. God wants that happiness for you," the Reverend rolled on. "In Luke 12:32, we're reminded once again: 'Fear not! For it is your Father's good pleasure to give you the Kingdom."

"And here's the best part."

Dr. Jarvis Frost had spent most of the sermon standing placidly near the lectern, moving little and speaking with an even, straightforward tone. But now there was a tangible excitement growing inside him. He moved toward the front of the altar, closer to the congregation and spoke with enthusiasm. He began to project a sense of joy, an abundant joy that might at any second exceed the physical limitations of his slight frame.

"All we have to do is ask him. Ask him to share His love, His comfort, His Spirit, and His Glory with us. To do what Paul urged of the Philippians – 'to present our requests to God, with thanksgiving'."

Andy had been playing mental chess with the good Dr. almost from the second he'd begun speaking – each point met, blocked even, by a defensive counter. He'd deflected each parry thus far, dismissing what he perceived to be threats to his very identity and being. But now, as the Reverend was winding up into another gear, and winding down his sermon, his 'opponent' suddenly found himself disarmed. Andy, ever the expert at grinding out a debate, the one always ready with an argument

445

or snarky response, had gone to the well of discontent, a fount which historically overflowed, and suddenly found it empty.

"When we come to Him and thank Him for the many blessings He has already bestowed upon us, and we ask Him to fulfill our hearts' desire – He can, and will. All we have to do is ask because He wants for us what *we* want for us: happiness, and the absence of fear."

Caught in the current of Frost's suggestion, Andy got carried further downstream. He actually allowed himself to consider the possibility of acting on that suggestion. What if he allowed himself to ask God for what he wanted? What could happen? If the Reverend was wrong, he'd get nothing – which he figured was probably the same thing that would happen if he did nothing at all.

"Let us take the advice that David gave to his son Solomon. As 1 Chronicles 28:20 tells us: 'Be strong and courageous, and do it! Do not be afraid, and do not be dismayed, for the Lord God is with you. He will not leave or forsake you, until all the work for the service of the house of the Lord is finished."

And that was the final truth. Andy *was* afraid. Afraid to change. Afraid to believe. Afraid to ask. Afraid to be let down. Afraid to be wrong. Even more afraid somehow of being right. But now, he was also afraid to stay put. Afraid to be alone, especially if there was the possibility of something else.

"And when we do – when we ask God to grant us the desires of our heart – we know we can expect blessings in return. Just as God told Abram, 'Fear not! I am your shield. Your reward shall be very great'."

"So, let us go now to the Lord in prayer. Let us lift up our desires to Him, knowing that through Him, all things are possible and all needs are met; secure in the reality that with Him, we need fear nothing and no one; secure in the knowledge that when we commit our work to the Lord, our plans will succeed."

You gotta be fucking kidding me. Andy thought, so incredulously he almost said it out loud.

Any doubt that Dr. Jarvis Frost had been speaking to him and him alone that morning was shattered. He supposed it was possible he heard him incorrectly, or that perhaps that last line just sounded familiar. But in his heart, he knew it wasn't the case. He knew exactly what he'd heard, and he knew that when he pulled that small leather rectangle out of his back pocket it would echo the Reverend's parting words almost verbatim. He started to reach for the money clip, but stopped. He already knew, and nothing would be gained by visual confirmation. In fact, the weathered inscription was all he could see in his mind as he closed his eyes.

"Let us pray."

95

"Oh my God! What the hell happened?"

"I know. It's bad. Did you get the fucking car? Is the car here?"

"It's right outside! It's running!"

"Good. We gotta get the fuck outta here!"

"Can she even move? Hey! Can you move?"

The young woman piled limply on the floor of the truck stop bathroom lifted her head enough for Traci to see the collage of cuts and bruises covering what was surely an otherwise beautiful face. Tears streamed from the one bloodshot eye of hers that was not swollen shut. It was all she could do to nod slightly in the affirmative, fighting back the sobs.

"Fuck it! We'll carry her. Let's just go!"

96

Reverend Frost led the congregation in a moment of silent contemplation, reiterating the invitation for the faithful, and perhaps even the not-so-faithful to lay their burdens at the feet of God. Andy knew the priest was speaking, but again had lost a connection to the actual words. There was only a low mumble humming through his ears as he sat in the balcony pew stunned, like a prize fighter stung by a nose-breaking sucker punch. He was aware of a mild tightness in his chest and a slight warm tingling at the back of his skull. He knew all too well what panic attacks felt like. This was not that – not exactly – although his body was definitely having an involuntary response to the stimuli around him. He wasn't high or drunk, nor had he been sober for long enough to be going through any sort of withdrawal symptoms. But still, there were real chemical reactions happening within him.

Frost concluded the prayer and began the transition to the Offertory. Ordinarily, the plate-passing hymn would not warrant additional commentary, but the Reverend felt compelled to connect the last of the dots this morning. The minister's words were still not reaching Andy's ears with clarity, and he missed Frost's added context:

"... from Psalm 42:1, in the original Latin, *Sicut cervus desiderat ad fontes aquarum, ita desiderat anima mea ad te, Deus.* As the deer longs for running water, so longs my soul for you, O God."

"Fear not. Let your soul long for the love of God, and may He bless you."

Andy dropped his neck, bringing his forehead to rest on his hands folded atop his knees. He kept his eyes closed, thinking it might help calm the barrage of sensations building in his brain. In reality, this only caused a more severe corollary to what happened next.

A single voice cut through the silence – not speaking or even singing in any manner Andy recognized. It was more of a chant, a rich tenor

449

bellow that at first seemed small and far away in the huge, open cathedral. It played alone for just a moment and then was joined by others, a volley of sopranos soaring high over the top and a deep baritone rounding out the exquisite sound. It came as if from nothing, leaping forward to fill Andy's mind and ears. It startled him, causing him to open his eyes. But his head was still bolstered by his hands and his field of vision was filled only by his forearms straight ahead and the dark wood of the pews to either side. He kept his eyes open but did not move his head or arms. Eventually he would be compelled to see exactly what was making that glorious sound, but for a moment he wanted to just *hear* it without the distraction of added visual input.

The chorus continued to grow as more and more voices entered the fray. It swirled to the very top of the cathedral, bouncing back off the ceiling and filling the room with a tone that could be felt as much as heard. There was no musical accompaniment, no domineering organ blasting away in the background, nothing to diminish the pure quality of those voices weaving together in a call to God that was somehow both lachrymose and joyful.

Andy closed his eyes once more, allowing the sound to fill his head. His breathing had become shallow, but now, as he inhaled, the tone seemed to pour into his chest. He held that breath, clinging to it, almost relishing it. He released it and opened his eyes.

He was grateful again to have been seated in the balcony. As he peered over the railing, he realized that nearly every one of the two hundred plus parishioners on the floor below had risen to their feet. Another wave of heat passed through him, one he recognized as embarrassment. Thankfully he was almost completely alone up there. Andy turned slowly around to find the young woman behind him standing, blanket-obscured babe in arms, and swaying subtly to the hypnotic chorus that filled the room. She smiled at him, seeming to appreciate the depth of his distraction.

Andy froze, locking gazes with her, unsure what his next move should be. He didn't understand why they were all standing and didn't know what it would mean if he did or didn't. It occurred to him that only the girl behind him, and possibly her infant child, would ever notice what he did at that moment. He remained seated and slowly turned back to face the altar. At least thirty seconds had passed since the hymn began, and he realized with some degree of horror he was missing the one thing he'd been intent to witness in this entire production. He widened his eyes and rattled his head back and forth in an effort to reset his attention and then focused it entirely on the altar.

Just to the left of the lectern, at center stage, stood Jeff. He was partially obscured behind a knee-high white pillared barrier, but still very much a focal point. He stood alone. A small cluster of his choir mates – three women and two men – were gathered on the opposite side of the lectern. Behind them stood the rest of the choir of St. Timothy's Episcopal Church, perhaps fifty voices in all. Andy trained his eye on Jeff, excited to watch his friend shine in the spotlight at last.

Jeff was at least 150 feet away from Andy, but he was impossible to miss. Andy stared intently at his roommate, noticing that he seemed to be looking directly back at him. He knew Jeff would have no reason to believe Andy was even there and doubted that from this distance, in this lighting, that he could spot him. Watching his friend like this was surreal for Andy. He had seen Jeff perform plays on stage, and songs in bars, but never anything like this.

For a moment, Andy had become disconnected from the pure beauty of the sound these artists were creating, distracted by finding his friend. He tried to do both and it proved difficult, but if he focused solely on Jeff, he could make everything else slide into the background.

The ebb and flow of the music was visceral and otherworldly, a literal epiphany for Andy. The voices rose and fell with dramatic effect, but Jeff stood nearly motionless, head tilted high, singing straight into the balcony. Andy couldn't see detailed expressions from that far away, but he could only assume there was a quiet, confident joy plastered on his friend's face.

What Andy couldn't have seen was the struggle in which his roommate was currently engaged. It wasn't wholly unlike his own experience – a battle for composure against a tide of emotions – but one borne of different circumstances entirely. The forces Andy may have labeled as invaders, attacking the thick-walled fortress of his heart, Jeff saw clearly as liberators of his own. A true showman, Jeff soldiered on, beating back the waves of joy and adrenaline that threatened to compromise his performance. To an ignorant ear, their effects on him were imperceptible. But he struggled nonetheless. Dr. Frost's message hadn't been lost on him either, and the invitation to let go of his own fears – to revel once again in the practice of praise – was one he relished. And then, the immediate opportunity to reciprocate, to offer his own gifts back to God in the form of melodic worship, filled his heart near to the point of bursting.

At the same time, a similar rise began to well within Andy, although his felt unfamiliar, foreign almost to the point of discomfort. Andy's breathing shortened and a rash of heat ran across his face. A thin bead of sweat formed across his forehead. The tightness under his ribcage returned, this time more severe. His pulse raced along with the voices, climbing ever-higher until he could feel the beating of his heart in both his chest and his temples. He tried to breathe deeply but struggled. A tangible ache announced itself at the center of his sternum. His throat felt tight and dry and the skin above his sinuses began to burn.

Andy was so busy trying to control the sensory overload in his gut and head; he didn't even realize his brain had been sending signals to his extremities, without his awareness or consent. Before he knew how or why, Andy found himself stretching his aching legs to stand – the last of the congregation to rise and acknowledge the celebration that was happening around him.

Aware now that he had somehow forfeited control and become a mere passenger in the vessel of his own body, Andy grabbed the railing of the balcony to steady himself. Struggling to catch his breath, he clenched the hard polished wood. The choir below, led by his dear friend, was reaching a crescendo that only exacerbated his physical struggle. In an act of near desperation, Andy lifted his head, extending his neck fully to try and open his parched and constricted throat. He found himself staring at the ceiling – the dark underbelly of that massive inverted ark, illuminated on all sides by sunlight bursting through the stained glass windows of the cathedral.

And then, he could hold on no longer. In one final gasp, one gloriously deep exhale, the dam burst. As Jeff and the choir climaxed, Andy closed his eyes, sending a flood of tears rolling down his face. His chest heaved, pushing him over another physiological cliff. Alternating waves of joy and shame converged. They washed over him, wrapping him in an electric heat unlike anything he'd ever felt. Under the swelling pressure of an uninvited yet undeniable Spirit, his heart was summarily crushed. It wasn't so much shattered as melted, as if a piece of cold, bloated steel was being cauterized, causing an intense internal pressure to be relieved.

Andy felt helpless, completely devastated, hollowed out but somehow lighter for it. He was unable to move, but he didn't really want to, either.

There were no words. In fact, there was no sound at all. The last gorgeous notes of *Sicut Cervus* had wafted to the rafters a few seconds ago, leaving Andy standing in the balcony, beautifully broken as tears of confusion rained from his eyes.

The hymn had ended and the priest, clearly unaware of Andy's ongoing struggle, had begun to lead the congregation through the ritual of the Nicene Creed, affirming his and their shared belief in the sanctity of the Holy Church and the divinity of their Savior Jesus Christ. At its conclusion, as if by sheer reflex, the entire congregation knelt in unison partaking in a final prayer of confession.

Not knowing what else to do, Andy joined them. He bent, not quite kneeling, but lowering himself against the balcony rail in front of him and bowed his head. He was aware of the Reverend's words, but was more clearly led by the ones attempting to form in his own mind.

God? Andy offered silently, as much questioning as addressing him directly; *I don't know what I'm supposed to do here. I do know I've been mad – at You, at everyone, at myself – just mad, for a really long time. I wanted away from You, and was sure You felt the same. I felt You leave me. I don't know why You came back, and I have no idea what you're saying, but I can't deny I hear You trying. I'm scared. I'm scared to try again.*

I'm scared... but I will; I'll try, Andy confessed. *I'll try.*

When he was done, so were the tears. He lifted his head, and looked out again over the railing. The congregation had been released, but they were still milling around on the floor below. The faithful were greeting one another, shaking the hands of those around them as they waited their turn to file out of the sanctuary.

Andy was watching the proceedings with strange fascination when he felt the lightest of touches across his left shoulder. He turned slowly, figuring an usher would be there to ask him to vacate the premises. Instead, he was met by the young mother who'd been sitting behind him during the service. Now standing only inches away, he could see the very pink face of the bundle of joy she'd been cradling. Her tiny infant son was sleeping peacefully, a slight smile curled on his lips. She too was smiling as she extended her thin arm, inviting him to shake her hand.

"May God be with you," she said.

"And with you." Andy replied. He wondered if this was the appropriate response, or if there even was one, because it sounded incredibly awkward to him as he said it.

She shook his hand firmly, smiled again, and walked away.

Andy turned once more toward the altar, now looking to see if he could spot Jeff in the thinning crowd. He saw several robed choir members milling about, but his roommate did not appear to be among them. It took a couple of seconds before the panic really set in.

"Dammit!" he said, with at least enough restraint to do so quietly. It wouldn't have mattered, as he was now completely alone in the balcony. Knowing he might only have a few minutes to catch his ride home, Andy wiped his still-damp cheeks with the sleeve of his disgusting shirt and made a break for the stairs.

97

The girl sat huddled in the passenger seat of the Jeep, curled almost in a ball, knees pulled tight to her chest. It was hard to tell if she was rocking gently or just shaking. Ellen had climbed into the back seat and was cupping her shoulder gently from behind as Traci manned the wheel. She'd let the two of them carry her from the bathroom to the car without so much as a word, waiting until she was safely inside to speak for the first time.

"Get me out of here!" she pleaded. Her voice was raspy and hoarse as though she'd been coughing, crying, or screaming a lot recently. She made the demand several times, growing more adamant with each refrain. It was all she could say until the Jeep had broken the boundary of the truck stop's parking lot and moved down the interstate on-ramp. Neither Ellen nor Traci pressed her, and it took another minute or so before she spoke again.

"I want to go home," she cried, still balled up and sobbing into the palms of her hands.

"Where's home?" Ellen asked.

"I don't know," she bawled with a stunning, matter-of-fact blankness that threw both of them for a loop.

"I'm Traci. That's Ellen. What's your name?"

"I don't know!" she repeated, the sobs growing more hysterical with each exchange.

Traci craned her neck to look back at Ellen. Their faces were mirror images of disbelief and confusion.

"Who did this to you?" Traci followed up, as delicately as possible.

The girl hesitated, her tongue held in lockdown by shock and shame.

"A man," she stammered. "A man in a truck."

"Is that how you got here?"

"Yes..." she started, but then reconsidered. "I don't know."

Sensing for the first time that she might now be safe, the girl took a series of deep, labored breaths and attempted to calm herself.

The girl stared blankly at the Jeep's floor for nearly a minute before she continued. Traci and Ellen waited with patience and nervous energy, allowing their passenger to unravel at her own pace.

"We've been driving for days. He had me blindfolded and tied up in the back of his cab. I don't know where we've been, or where we are. I don't know."

"How'd you get in the bathroom?"

"He had me tied up the whole time. Kept me gagged with a blanket over me when he'd stop. The only time he'd untie me is when he..."

She didn't want to say the next words, and neither of them wanted her to either.

"So, how...?" Ellen attempted to fast-forward.

"He untied me. He wanted me to use my hands..." She was still tearful, but now the fear in her voice was giving way to rage. "He held a knife on me 'til he got off, then he'd tie me back up. Last night or this morning, he came at me again. Untied me. Did his thing. But I guess he tired himself out. Tied the knots for shit."

Her words came faster now, loaded with anger and adrenaline.

457

"Afterward, he'd smoke weed. Then he'd just sit there and babble about shit. But he must have scored something stronger. The last time, when got done, he went back to the pipe. He got crazy high, like freaky manic. He was all jacked up for a few minutes and then he just passed out. I waited, pretending to be asleep, seeing if he was gonna move. He didn't. It was easy to slip those shitty knots. I crawled out of the truck as quiet as I could; left the door cracked. It was already light outside. The parking lot was full of trucks. I'm sure somebody must have seen me get out. And I'm sure they saw me run into the bathroom. But I didn't know where else to go. I wasn't gonna hitchhike. Probably get picked up by another fucking psycho just as bad, or worse, than that other piece of shit." Now she was seething.

"I don't even know how long I was in there when you came along, but it seemed like forever. I just knew he was gonna come in there and find me. And then, he would have killed me."

"We gotta get you to a hospital," Traci urged, now destroying the speed limit in the hopes of actually getting pulled over by a cop.

"I wanna go home!" she repeated.

"Do you know where there's a hospital between here and Bradford?" Ellen asked.

"No," Traci admitted. "But I'm sure as shit looking for one."

"Fuck." Ellen blurted.

"What?"

"We still gotta find Andy. One of us has to get back to Jeff and tell him we don't have Andy. We can't just leave him. We have to go home."

98

Andy had flown down the stairs and out of the church, desperate to make it back to the truck before Jeff. After all this, the idea of walking home was unimaginable.

He rounded the corner in a near sprint and slowed only once the muddy black truck came into view. It looked as though he had in fact won the race. Andy walked the rest of the way, lungs burning from the burst of impromptu exercise. He casually lowered the truck's tailgate and plopped down heavily in the center. The bed of the truck was a mess. The vinyl cover hung loose, partially covering an assortment of random items. Andy considered tidying it, but thought instead Jeff would have a greater appreciation for his experience if he found it more like this.

Andy exhaled, feeling strangely relaxed. A stream of churchgoers filed past him, but their reaction seemed different than that of the few he'd encountered on the way in. Maybe they'd already turned their focus elsewhere, to brunches or family visits or yard work or who knows what else. For some reason, the tangible magnetic repulsion he'd felt from a few of the faithful just over an hour ago seemed to be gone now. He reclined against the side panel of the truck watching people mill through the parking lot, unsure how long he'd have to wait.

Andy had been looking at the corner of the building which led back to the front doors of the church, thinking Jeff might appear from there, when the side doors suddenly opened. A small horde of people emerged, a few of them with choral robes slung across their forearms. The choir had been released. Surprisingly, Jeff was not the first person he recognized in that crowd.

The first familiar thing Andy saw in the pack headed toward him was that unmistakable fuchsia pantsuit. He smiled and then laughed. As the hot pink lady with the sleek silver hair approached, he saw she was walking right next to his roommate.

Andy's first instinct was to hide, to crouch down in the truck and surprise the living shit out of Jeff. But he didn't. He just sat there, watching as the small group came nearer. Jeff was engaged in conversation with Mrs. Fuchsia and wasn't even looking at him. They got almost all the way to the front of truck before he even looked up.

"Andy? Why the...? How...?" Jeff was astounded to see his roommate propped on the tailgate of the truck. He quickened his pace, leaving Mrs. Fuchsia a half-step behind as he approached.

Jeff walked right up to Andy and gave him a hug; but not a sweet or gentle one. It was more like a stern squeezing that said *Hey; this is my place of work. Why the Hell are you here, especially looking like that?*

"How the fuck did you get here?" he whispered, low enough that the ladies behind him couldn't hear the swear.

"Oh, that's a pretty funny story," Andy scoffed, throwing his thumb over his shoulder and pointing at the disheveled truck bed.

Mrs. Fuchsia had caught up and was now standing next to Jeff. The awkward moment when two strangers were waiting to be introduced by their common acquaintance had arrived. Jeff flummoxed, clearly uncomfortable.

"Umm... Andy..." he stammered, extending one hand at him, and the other toward the older black lady, "this is Dr. Valerie Cobb. She sings with us in the choir." Dr. Valerie smiled a big beautiful, friendly smile at him, recognizing him instantly.

"Dr. Val, this is my friend, Andy Maxwell." Andy noticed he'd chosen the title 'friend', instead of 'roommate' and wondered how intentional the extra distance was on Jeff's part.

"Believe it or not, we've met," Mrs. Cobb said, cheerfully shaking Andy's hand.

"You what?" said Jeff.

"I passed by Andy on the way in this morning," she grinned; now speaking more directly to him than to Jeff. "You didn't look so good earlier. You look much better now. I *told* you it was a blessed day."

"It's nice to meet you," Andy offered, unsure what else he could possibly say.

"Well, I'll let y'all get to the rest of your day," Valerie said, giving Jeff a quick hug. "You did good today, boy," she praised. "Will you be here Wednesday?"

"Of course."

"Well good. I'll see you then. Bye, y'all!" And she was off.

Jeff turned back to Andy, who was standing there with a strange smile on his face unlike Jeff had seen before.

"I don't even know what to say. I don't understand how you're here."

"I was supposed to be here," Andy said with a grin his friend didn't understand. "I'd have preferred a smoother ride, but I guess we don't always get to choose the path, right?"

Jeff was even more confused. If he understood correctly, Andy had ridden nearly a hundred miles in the back of a covered pickup truck. If he knew his roommate at all, that's the kind of thing that earned a nuclear explosion kind of reaction. And yet, Andy was calm, cheerful even, in a way Jeff couldn't fathom.

"I don't understand," he repeated.

"I'll tell you all about it," Andy suggested, stepping toward his friend and pulling him in for a hug. His was a genuine embrace, warm, hearty, and relaxed. It might have been the only reaction that could have further befuddled Jeff.

"Thank you," Andy said kindly, giving him another tight squeeze before releasing him.

"For what? Rolling your ass around in the truck for an hour?"

"No," laughed Andy. "That part sucked balls. Thank you for this," Andy spread his arms outward, encompassing the entirety of the massive church.

"You gave me something I didn't even know I wanted."

Jeff had no response, but he somehow understood. Andy wasn't the only one who had received at gift at St. Timothy's that morning.

"C'mon," Andy summoned, closing the tailgate of the truck heading for the passenger side. "I'll tell you all about it."

"Andy?" Jeff asked. "Where are the girls?"

"I'm not sure," he replied plainly, having not thought once about them yet today. "But I'm hungry. Let's go home."

Andy was right. St. Timothy's was more than two miles from their house, but not much more. It only took them a few short minutes to make the trek. It was enough time for both of them to finish the cigarettes they'd lit as they rolled out of the parking lot, but not nearly long enough for Andy to share the entirety of his journey.

The truck chugged up the hill on Cornwall Street. Ellen's Chevette and Andy's SUV both sat just where they'd been left the day before, and there was no way to tell from the outside whether the girls had come back yet or not.

Andy hopped from the truck and headed for the front door. More than anything, he wanted to pee, wash his face, and get a cold drink of water. Jeff was content to linger. He sat propped against the porch considering another smoke when the Jeep came flying down the hill.

Traci angled aggressively into the driveway and came to a stop behind his truck. Jeff watched with curiosity as she bounced out and released Ellen from the back seat. The huge oak tree in their front yard was casting a shadow over the windshield, darkening it past Jeff's ability to see that someone else was riding shotgun.

Ellen broke into a run, covering the twenty-five feet between the car and the porch in just a few seconds.

"Jeff!" she shouted. "Andy's gone. He's lost!"

His cavalier smile was the last thing she expected.

"Actually," he said calmly, "I think he's been found. He's inside. He's been with me this morning."

"What?" she gasped, glad and mad at the same time.

"Yeah. And the most unbelievable thing happened."

"Whatever it is," Ellen replied, "we've got it beat," sounding quite sure of herself.

"Is Traci coming in?"

"No. We have to go!" she panted, already turning back toward the Jeep.

The front door opened, and Andy walked back outside.

"Hey, El!" he shouted.

Ellen wheeled back around and stood there, ecstatic to see him safely on their front porch. Traci blasted the Jeep's horn, disturbing Ellen's moment of relief, along with the general tranquility of the neighborhood.

"Geez! Relax!" said Andy, walking toward the front yard. Ellen met him halfway and hugged him hard.

"You scared me, you fucker," she chastised, giving him a small kiss on the cheek. "We'll talk later. Right now, we gotta go!"

"Go? Where?" Andy wanted to know.

"C'mere," she replied, ushering both he and Jeff toward the waiting Jeep.

Jeff, Andy, and Ellen walked together toward the driver's side of the vehicle. Traci was leaning out the open window when they got there.

"Hey," she said to Andy, "look who it is." She was clearly less concerned for his safety than Ellen had been, and obviously in the middle of something she deemed more important.

Jeff and Andy leaned toward the window and saw the lump of a girl in the passenger seat. Her shoulder length sandy blonde hair was still long enough to obscure her face, which was turned mostly away. Her black jeans were caked in red clay dust, her t-shirt badly ripped at the neck.

"Where are you going?" Jeff asked Traci.

Just as he asked the question, the girl turned her bruised and swollen face to look at them. The cab of the Jeep was not well lit under the shade of the huge oak, but they'd seen her enough times in the last week to know exactly who she was.

"Jessica?" Andy said in disbelief.

The girl's rescue *was* cause for rejoicing, but as Ellen looked upon her roommates, she found both boys beaming, in a way that somehow transcended that singular event.

"I don't know what you guys have been into this morning," she said, climbing back in behind Traci. "And we've gotta go. But when we get home, can I get some of what you've got?"

"Sure." Andy smiled. "You can get it any time. You just have to know where to look."

THE END

###

Your talent is God's gift to you. What you do with it is your gift back to God. – Leo Buscaglia

About the Author

Steven Crane is a freelance writer and twenty-plus-year veteran of the advertising industry – a career which is both to thank and blame for parts of this story.

Having edited manuscripts from fellow authors in various genres, and penned a yet-to-be-published children's book, *Staring at the Ceiling* marks Crane's debut novel.

Steven graduated from the University of South Carolina with a degree in Journalism, and now lives in Atlanta, GA with his wife Carie and their two sons. Here, when not writing, he devotes considerable time and energy to his quest to create the perfect pancake.

More from Steven Crane at: www.brainsofsteel.com